EMANCERIAN CHRONICLES

Signs of the First Emancer

This book is dedicated to all those who follow through on their dreams never giving up on the hope that they can achieve anything!

EMANCERIAN CHRONICLES

Signs of the First Emancer

M Y A E L   C H R I S T O P H E R

S I M P K I N S

ISBN: 1499369395
ISBN 13: 9781499369397
Library of Congress Control Number: 2015902501
Createspace Independent Publishing Platform
North Charleston, South Carolina

CONTENTS

The secret of change is to focus all your energy not on fighting the old but on building the new...

Excerpt from:
Way of the Peaceful Warrior by Dan Millman

Signs of the First Emancer

Chapter I
AWAITING THE TRIAL

It was a day that would linger in the minds of many for years to come. For weeks, a multitude of publications had plastered updates on the upcoming trial. On this particular morning, a Wednesday, the sky had a purple streak of color stretched across the horizon line, making it look like an oil-painted canvas. Centered in the far distance, an orange sun had just begun to peek its way out through the clouds. It was beautiful to admire.

Despite its diminutive size and the bars blocking the view, the window that Michael J. Magnus looked out from was large enough to give the illusion of a perfect world. Staring out from across the room, Magnus wondered what scientific principal could be attributed to the wondrous flaunt. He yearned to be on the other side and did not care that this desire was unrealistic. The hours of his imprisonment had turned to days, and days seemed like weeks—it felt like twenty-five weeks had gone by, but actually he was nearing the end of his first month.

Every morning when he woke up, Magnus had a ritualistic pattern of looking around his cell and then at himself. He positioned himself against the concrete wall, surveying his dismal surroundings. Everything was gray—the walls, the granite floor, the sink and toilet, even his bed sheets. To put it plainly, it was monotonous. Approaching the mirror above the sink, he noticed a few strands of gray hair stemming from just above his forehead. He also noticed that his oak-colored hair had grown a little wild since the last time he looked at himself. His face seemed thinner, pale, and a bit dry. It concerned him briefly, but he simply continued his self-evaluation. Directing his attention toward his midsection, he noticed that the extra weight that used to be there had nearly vanished.

Even without shoes, Magnus stood roughly six feet tall. *A grand height*, he thought, trying to distract himself from larger issues. Next, he assessed his clothing. He wore a cotton white T-shirt and black pants that, if nothing else, were at least comfortable. Remembering the sensation of being tattooed, Magnus rolled up his left sleeve and examined a partially faded Yin/Yang symbol. Placed on his arm just beneath his shoulder, it had always symbolized great opposing powers. Observing it made him smirk; he wondered if he would ever be that balanced.

Lifting his right pant leg, Magnus exposed a bruise that had formed on his shin. The day before, a cruel guard had kicked him without provocation. The bruise was sore, but not as sore as his pride. He had wanted to strike back but knew that taking action would only lead to more trouble.

Magnus often dealt with abuse. Usually it was just verbal, but on occasion, he was a victim of one of the more aggressive security guards. The violence was becoming a problem, but instead of focusing on it, he forced himself to think about his upcoming trial. As the sunlight streamed its way down the wall, an outline seemed to form around his body. The warmth was peaceful and calmed his anger.

Magnus tried to think of something positive. He remembered a joke one of the nicer guards had made. He had told him to think of his cell as a luxurious hotel suite and the guards as butlers. At the time, Magnus had brushed the remark away, but in his solitude he grinned. The guards, unfortunately, were the only company around. In truth, the guard who had made the comment was fairly decent to Magnus. He had even offered to bring him a glass of clean water occasionally when he could. Magnus accepted the gesture, even though he was unsure if he could really trust anyone at the detention center. Although, He was grateful for any decent company.

The moment passed. Temperance gave way to anger at himself for having a passive moment. Magnus crossed the room and aggressively clenched the bars on the window. Although the room itself was a moderate temperature, the bars were cold. Magnus leaned his body backward, as if he were trying to pull the bars off. Then he hung his head and groaned again. The trial would begin in just a few hours—a trial that to him was ridiculous! He blurted out, "Damn it! If I only had more time, I could find a way out of this situation!" The concept pierced his mind. Magnus pondered escape, but he had no way of getting past the steel-reinforced door at the end of the hall.

His cell, unit A38, was the eighth of twelve that resided in the A section of the third floor. There were about thirty sections in the DEDC (Delinquent Entrapment Detention Center) building in total. The DEDC itself was built on a gated, six-acre property surrounded by a twenty-foot-tall fence. Just south of the premises lay fifteen wooded acres, and to the north was a roadway, which bridged the site to the rest of the city.

During his time at the DEDC, Magnus had made many attempts to remember the events that led to his imprisonment. His memory was damaged. When he tried to concentrate, the only thing that popped into his head was her—the last face he saw before he was imprisoned. Her name was Arie. He wondered, would anyone aside from him remember her? A single tear rolled down his cheek as he tried to shake the terrible feeling he had.

Magnus let go of the bars and closed his hands tightly into fists, as if that would help him control the emotion he felt. He wanted out *so badly*. Beyond his control, her face appeared in his mind again. Her intensely beautiful green eyes penetrated his very soul. He could still remember how soft her skin felt when she embraced him...the warmth she personified. He couldn't believe that he had nearly forgotten the tenderness of her very presence. All of it now seemed out of his reach. Was she dead? He could remember only that something terrible had happened.

Settling on his stiff mattress, he closed his eyes. A slight breeze grazed his face, causing him to relax. Soon, he drifted off into a subconscious state and began to dream. At first all he saw in his mind a pinkish color, but then shapes began to form—gray shapes, to be precise. Then a distorted face appeared. It looked like him, but it wasn't quite a reflection. The face started to laugh at him. He yelled in the dream for it to stop, but it seemed to take pleasure in his annoyance. Eventually, he migrated away from it only to discover a river made of molasses. Perhaps if this hadn't been a dream he would have escaped falling in, but instead something knocked him into it. As he sank, he began to jerk his body back and forth on the bed.

Next there was an unexpected flash, and instead of being stuck in molasses he was floating in outer space. The dream, at that point, seemed less threatening. Magnus often dreamed of floating through space, and it was usually with a purpose, such as trying to find something in its vastness, but this time he was drifting aimlessly. That is, until he lost control and started spiraling toward a star. This fate seemed even worse than drowning in molasses. Incineration wasn't the most pleasant thought to him. As he got closer to the star, his feet started itching and then burning. Rapidly, the heat spread to up his legs until his whole metaphysical body felt inflamed. Magnus tried to swim away, struggling to make a difference, but the gravitational force kept pulling him back toward the gigantic ball of flame. Then luckily, yet somewhat painfully, his elbow smacked into the concrete wall, waking him with a start.

Relief from the vividness of his dream left Magnus breathing heavily. He had temporarily lost his senses and forgotten where he was. He thought, for just an instant, that he was in his bed at home. For Magnus, home was in New York State. He was neither from the fancy suburbia nor the industrialized metropolitan area of New York City, but rather a small town known as Duanesburg.

A rustic little community, Duanesburg was one of those places that had decided to remain historically perfect to the nineteenth century. Magnus grew up on a farm riding his bike, fishing on the edge of a pond, and sleeping under the stars. When he was about thirteen, he met the love of his life. Arianna Elizabeth Shoomer, Arie for short, had moved there from a neighboring town at age twelve. Magnus instantly became infatuated with her and somehow stumbled into being her friend. As one might expect, the friendship blossomed into quite a romance once they were old enough to appreciate their unique bond. Things were great between them until Arie was accepted at a college in Missouri. The distance was great, and it had torn them apart. Magnus regretted having said some hurtful words to her back then.

The sun had risen higher now, and the light reached his carvings on the wall. Picking up a piece of chalk, Magnus carved a line on his makeshift calendar. Day twenty-five—had it really been nearly a month since he tasted the freedom of the outside world? In his mind, he vividly recalled what it was like to live an ordinary life free of what real stress was. He truly missed the simplicity that was no longer available to him. Stewing on that idea, he once again tried to remember how he had ended up imprisoned. Although Magnus seemed OK physically, his memory lapse wasn't getting any better. In fact, he still had no concept as to why he was at the DEDC. There was just a big blank. He assumed it had something to do with Arie, but he wasn't sure of anything. In the quiet solitude, Magnus would concentrate endlessly and try to remember, but after a month he was beginning to give up hope.

The silence was interrupted. He heard a faint squeak coming from somewhere. Then Magnus heard the door open down the hall, followed by footsteps. It was Julius, a heavyset balding gentleman who walked with a bit of swagger. In his hand, he held a glass of water. Once he arrived, Julius stretched it through the bars to Magnus. Neither uttered a word. Magnus respected Julius. Thus, he merely nodded at him after handing back the glass. After that, Julius turned and started on his way to the next sect. Magnus was the only occupant in this sect, and Julius had obligations elsewhere.

Julius was mild-tempered for a security guard. The others thought his lack of aggression made him a bit odd. He stood out, and it was not surprising that he and Magnus became friends. When Julius looked at unit A38, he didn't see a criminal. He saw a man, just like him, who was misunderstood. That morning, he too was concerned about the trial. As Julius exited, Magnus raised his head and said, "Thank you, friend." Julius paused and responded, "It's the least I could do; good luck today."

Julius exited the room but didn't lock the door. It was cracked open, which seemed odd to Magnus. Always in the past, he would hear the snaps and crackles of bolts. The quiet was interrupted again. Coming from the other side of the door, Magnus could hear a conversation between Julius and one of the other guards. He heard someone with a loud and insufferable voice teasing Julius for being so kind to Magnus, whom he referred to as the freak. He snickered and said things like, "Why don't you and your best friend go to a movie together?" and "What are you, his fucking servant?" They went on for quite some time, and Magnus began to regret taking the water. It wasn't the first time Julius had taken slack for his kindness toward him. Magnus looked over at the mildew-ridden sink and nearly vomited. Julius had been nice enough to bring him some clean water, but he let out a sigh and felt guilty for asking.

After a few more minutes, the conversation seemed to have quieted down. The door was promptly shut and triple locked. The clock on the wall sounded; the time was now eight. Magnus knew what this meant: five hours to go. His trial was scheduled for four o'clock in the afternoon, which gave him plenty of time to dwell on what to say. The guards were not allowed to discuss any details with him, making him anxious about the unknown.

Magnus's first few days at the DEDC had been the hardest. He would just scream over and over, "Let me out, I've done nothing wrong!" Some of the guards would just laugh and bang on the bars to quiet him down. He eventually realized the futility of his groaning and anger.

That week, every morning as he awoke to being imprisoned, all he could do was cry for Arie. Her face called to him. She was in danger; he could sense it. But after a month, he now believed he had lost her. Denton, one the largest of the guards, had made a crack that he had probably killed her and was simply pretending not to know. This was a terrifying thought. All Magnus was holding onto was the love he had for her. If she was gone and he was the cause, then he didn't want to be alive either.

Julius had told him that Denton was just trying to get a rise out of him, but that didn't shake the fears he felt. Magnus was furious at Denton from that day on, and Denton knew it. On one occasion, Magnus had spoken out to him, and that was the first time he had ended up with bruises. Antagonizing Denton had brought the brute's wrath upon Magnus.

In everyone's childhood, there is always a schoolyard bully, the kind of kid who bothers the smaller kids and picks on them—the instigator or badass who starts fights in order to display dominance and control over everyone. Well, Denton was a prime example of that kid…all grown up. Denton was a six-foot-four-inch behemoth of a man who carried a large nightstick along with a chip on his shoulder. His head was shaved, and the veins on his neck looked like they might pop at any moment, but the truly scary and intense thing about him was his eyes. When Magnus looked Denton in the eyes, there was no kindness behind them at all—just pure hatred. *A formidable enemy,* he thought to himself. And he knew quite well he was not in a position to do anything about it. Challenging his foe was not an option.

A bad feeling came over him. Magnus could tell he had jinxed himself. Whenever you think too hard about something you don't want to happen or someone you don't want to see, that's precisely when that person shows up or when that something occurs. Just then, the door slammed open with a bang. "Hey, freak!" The voice was immediately familiar to Magnus. "Did you miss me, freako?" Magnus found himself face to face with the worst enemy he had in the DEDC...possibly in his entire life.

A wicked smile, similar to that of the Grinch, formed on Denton's face. He received such twisted pleasure whenever he got the chance to bother a prisoner. It had been a while since anyone had been in section A, so he relished every moment of torturing Magnus as much as he could. Magnus, however, did not wish to deal with bad treatment. And so, he decided not to get off the bed or to even respond. "Aww, is the freak sleeping?" Denton harped. "Let me help." Before Magnus could react, Denton took the cup of water he was holding and splashed it onto him. A loud shriek and much laughter followed. "Next time I talk to you, freak, you get the fuck up! You hear? And by the way, that's the only way you'll be getting water from now on! What do you think this is a fucking hotel?" He snarled, "Don't expect any more damn room service!"

Denton loved using profanity. Not only did he think it was the best way to get his point across, but he just thought it made him sound tougher. As one might guess, Denton wasn't exactly a charmer, but still, he fancied himself a lady's man. He often bragged to the other security guards about his conquests, clamoring on about how his brutish charm always seemed to get him attention in the local bar. His philosophy was, "The bigger asshole you are, the faster they come running." Unfortunately, in most of the places he frequented, this was true, which only added to Denton's cockiness. In any case, that morning he was extremely ticked off for a number of reasons. For one, he was hung over, and two, he knew that it was the day of Magnus's trial. He was annoyed at the prospect that he might not be able to pick on his favorite pawn.

There was an awkward period of silence. Denton and Magnus locked eyes. Denton's breathing was so heavy that even with the door closed anyone nearby on the other side of it would have heard him. Magnus didn't want to back down. He didn't want to show fear. This was nothing new. He knew Denton was demented.

Denton broke the silence. "Don't think that you'll be getting away from me, freak. Just because your little hearing is happening later today doesn't mean we won't be playing anymore. We'll have plenty of good times to come. I'll be seeing you real soon." Magnus stared intently at his antagonist. He thought to himself that Denton was the real freak and that he should be the one in a cage. Denton gave him a twisted smirk and walked away, but not before banging his nightstick excessively hard on the bars, causing Magnus to jump back. An enormous cackle could be heard as Denton made his exit.

Magnus's face contorted as his adversary departed. The last thing he needed that day was to deal with some psychopathic schmuck. He thought to himself, *if the rest of this day is going to be like this, I should just crawl under the bed and stay there.* Unknown to him, however, across town something else was brewing that was going change his life forever. The eyes of danger were opening to start a new day, and they were focused on him.

Chapter 2
TROUBLE IN PARADISE

The forest-green clock hanging near the roof of the local plaza sounded loudly as its hands struck nine o'clock. Officer Charles Rivera sat quietly in his squad car outside the donut shop, sipping his morning coffee. Each morning, he ordered a medium, light and sweet, to start off his daily routine. As he sat there enjoying the start of a new day, a few familiar pedestrians waved at him as they walked by. He smiled casually and nodded. Charles was known for being a friendly policeman. He had been on the force for more than five years, and at age thirty-five he was the typical officer with two kids and a wife at home. Most of his friends referred to him as Chuck.

Chuck gave his wife a quick call to check on the kids and tell her he loved her. She went on about the chores she had for the day. Apparently, there was an abundance of laundry and one of the children was late for school, so she had to drive him. Earlier that morning, there had been a major trash issue. Chuck had forgotten to take it out the night before, and of course it had to be done before he left for work that morning.

Suddenly, something bumped into the car, causing Chuck to spill his coffee all over his left pant leg. He let out a shriek as it burned him. Quickly, he told his wife he had to go and that he would call her later. "Goddamn it!" he cursed. He hopped out of the car and saw a young man dusting himself off. "Hey, what's going on out here?" Chuck looked over at the ground and saw a twisted and scratched up bicycle lying on the sidewalk. "You gotta be kidding me, guy, this is a new freaking car!"

The young man, who appeared to be in his late twenties, remained silent as the officer leaned over and examined his bumper. There were definitely some scratches on the side of the car and a little dent where the tire must have impacted. Also, he could definitely see some dirt marks. Still pining over the damage, Chuck said, "I'm going to write you a ticket for this, kid. Reckless riding is an offense." Chuck paused and then continued griping. "Were you drinking or something? Sheesh!"

Chuck stood up and turned around; the young man was gone. He looked down; so was the bike. Puzzled, he continued to search nearby for a minute or two but found nothing. It was peculiar; he had only bent over for a minute, and there was no way someone could have ridden out of sight that quickly. Certainly he would have at least heard it. Plus, the bike had been badly damaged. "Where the heck did he go?" Officer Rivera said out loud, as if someone would respond. He peered in an upward direction, thinking the crazy idea that maybe the guy had gone up, but saw nothing.

Chuckling at the idea of the guy going upward, Chuck reached into his car and sipped a bit of what was left of his coffee. Then he walked into the coffee shop, grabbed a few napkins, and started wiping down his pant leg. He asked the cashier if she had seen the man on the bike. To his annoyance, the teenager hadn't even witnessed the event. "Thanks," he said smugly. Chuck returned outside and got a huge shock. On the driver's side back window, it looked as if someone had etched an emblem into the glass. Chuck's mouth dropped wide open. Flabbergasted, he hurried over to the car and then scanned the area very angrily. He peered under the car and even up at a nearby tree. The lot was deserted, aside from an elderly woman hobbling her way into the coffee shop. For a moment, he thought about asking her if she had seen anything, but he figured he would probably have the same luck he did with the cashier.

It seemed likely that the guy with the bike had somehow done this, but why? He looked closer at the symbol; it wasn't any kind of symbol he had seen before. It looked like two number fives placed back to back with an oval in the middle, and a vertical line extended upward from the top of the oval. The insane part about the etching was the extreme detail, which would make the job seem impossible in such a small span of time. The fives in the symbol were more deeply engraved than the oval. Chuck ran his fingers over the etching. It wasn't warm. *OK,* he thought to himself, *if this was burned, then why isn't it hot?* Chuck ran his finger through the etching another time. There was no chemical residue. *This whole morning is getting weird, he thought to himself. First that guy hits my car and disappeared, and then now he somehow engraved this symbol on the window.*

Chuck decided right then and there that no one was going to make an ass out of him. He climbed into the squad car and started driving around, look-ing for the mysterious bike rider. After circling a few blocks with no success, he picked up his CB and started to call in the incident. As he drove, he felt someone grab the back of his neck, which made him frantically swerve the car and look in his rearview mirror. To his horror, there were demonic red eyes staring back at him. Chuck slammed on the breaks in an effort to throw off his assailant. Instead, because he wasn't wearing his seatbelt, he was thrown head-first into the steering wheel. The impact left Chuck dazed, but could hear the breathing of whatever it was behind him in the back seat. He tried to move, but felt paralyzed. Fear was the last emotion he felt, as his body was hurled through the windshield. The jagged glass cut through his face and midsec-tion, causing tremendous pain. Halfway sprawled out across the hood, Chuck permanently lost consciousness. No one was seen exiting the car, but had any nearby witnesses looked down the road, they would have seen a hooded bicy-clist riding away from the scene.

Chapter 3

INSIDIOUS PATH

Officer Rivera was not the only person to fall in the path of the unknown male rider. An unsuspecting woman was walking with her baby when she bumped into a tall male whose face seemed plain yet distinguishable. He wore dark clothing, and his ominous red eyes were filled with contempt. The man was pushing his dented bike through the busy streets because there was no room to ride. After she bumped him, he grabbed her arm and locked eyes with her. She screamed, and a wave of fear caused her to foolishly rush out into the street where she was by on-coming traffic. The taxi that struck her could not stop quickly enough to avoid horribly mangling her body. The baby's stroller started rolling out of control causing a number of collisions. A fiendish smile crept its way across the face of the dark figure. Pleasure could not have come from a more heinous sight. The stroller continued rolling barely making it through traffic before slamming into a parked vehicle. Unnoticed, the assailant proceeded on his way as people began to swarm around the body.

A large crowd formed around the woman on the ground. People's expressions varied from disgust to total horror. One woman was crying, and so was the victim's baby, as a female officer tried to calm it down. The paramedics and police arrived on the scene and quickly carried the victim into an ambulance. The detective on the scene, Joseph Warren, had pulled up several minutes earlier. He interviewed a few pedestrians before examining the body briefly. According to witnesses, she had just gone crazy and ran out into the street. *It never gets easy*, he thought to himself.

A small boy ran into what was now a blocked-off area. Detective Warren felt a tug on his pant leg. The boy started asking him the typical questions a child would ask about death. "Hey, Mister Policeman sir, how come that lady had to be carried away?" Even someone who deals with such situations on a regular basis can once in a while get choked up. Joseph bent down and focused on the child. His throat was a little dry, and his heart kind of slowed. He spoke softly. "Son, where's your mom or dad?"

Just then, a woman screamed from the crowd, "Jonathon Douglas, you get back over here right now!"

"OK, Mommy," the boy responded. As the boy ran back to his mother, Joe's focus returned to his task.

The female officer, whose last name happened to be Baker, walked up to Joe and started discussing the incident. "Detective, the victim's ID was still intact. You are not going to believe this. Apparently, this woman was Charles Rivera's sister." The detective was silent for a moment and then he asked about the baby.

She responded, "Fortunately, the baby seems fine. We plan to take the child to the hospital. Joe nodded and said, "All right, I'll leave it in your hands." Joe thought about having to break the bad news to Chuck, but while they were standing there, he received the call about Officer Rivera's death. Officer Baker's face remained calm as she heard it over radio, but inside she was ready to burst. Silence and a shake of her head was all she could respond. She had known Officer Rivera since he had joined the force, and so the shock of both him and his sister was unnerving to say the least.

After hearing the report, Joe went to his car and drove about twenty minutes away. When he arrived on the scene, he had to honk his way through a second crowd. Speaking out loud, Joe uttered, "What a day...can it get any worse?" Little did Detective Warren know, but his day was about to get much worse. As he exited the vehicle, he noticed the glistening shards of glass on the ground. Like a path, they led up to the scene of the accident. Sprawled across the hood was a man who for the last fifteen years he had called friend. He was the one who had convinced Chuck to become a police officer. Back in college, they had even shared a dorm room.

Seeing Chuck in that moment was too much for Joe to handle. He had dealt with a friend passing before, but this time his initial response kicked in. He turned his head and covered his mouth from the smell of blood and death. A fellow officer placed his hand on Joe's shoulder. Joe was annoyed at the gesture but didn't shake it off. He spoke with slight tremble in his voice: "I'm fine." He then moved forward, getting closer to the body. A plastic bag was draped over Chuck, exposing only the marred hands.

The wind was still, and yet a chill came across Joe's body. He scanned the back windshield with his eyes and then asked if anyone had gotten a picture of the symbol etched into the glass. Joe was just about to lose his temper from the lack of efficiency when he remembered that there were pedestrians present. He contained his now angry feelings and told a few men to try to disperse the crowd. After that, he borrowed the camera from the crime scene photographer and snapped a few photos of the etching. Then Joe instructed the forensics people to get the body down to the lab for examination.

Joe decided it was time to head back to home base. Inside, he still couldn't cope with what had happened, and then a thought occurred to him. He would have to call Chuck's wife. He couldn't imagine what her reaction would be. Silently, as he drove away from the scene, he prayed that there wouldn't be another incident.

Chapter 4

THE PRECIPICE

The twenty five-minute drive back to the station was for the most part un-eventful. Joe snapped on the radio and tuned to a soft music station. It was a feeble attempt to calm his nerves. During the drive, he wondered about the chances of two siblings dying in separate incidents on the exact same day. Then he thought about the cryptic symbol again, it wasn't like anything he had seen before. The evidence specialists had removed the window to take back for testing. Joe hoped that they would find something to give him a lead.

The announcer on the radio interrupted a popular song to deliver a daily news report. He started off reporting about the traffic patterns, but eventually he mentioned the accident that involved a baby carriage. Even though there were no names mentioned, Joe knew exactly what accident the radio personal-ity was describing. As it turned out, a number of people had been mildly in-jured as well. Joe continued to listen. The announcer also mentioned the death of a police officer at the smaller traffic accident. He stated that the poor victim was thrown clear through the windshield. Following that, he urged his listen-ers to wear their seatbelts, and to be more aware of pedestrians he finished the report and played a Coldplay song. The song titled "Clocks" made Joe look at the time. It was twenty passed ten. He pulled into the back parking lot of a large brick structure with black letters above the door that read Chicago Police Department Precinct 7. Grabbing his bag, the troubled detective walked up the outer staircase, through the glass doors, and into the lobby. Once inside, Joe had to walk through a security door that required a badge to unlock. He heard the air pressure of the door releasing, and he proceeded forward. He walked across the room and a few people noticed him. Contrary to his normal practice, Joe walked right past them. He fixed his view on the clock, which read ten thirty; entered the elevator; and took it to the eighth floor.

The door to his office was slightly ajar. Walking in, Joe noticed that some items on his desk were in disarray. Some papers were on the floor, the pens and pencils were scattered, and his laptop was on. Joe threw his bag down in frustration, wondering who had been in his office. Then he started organizing items on his desk. As he did, Officer Baker walked in and said, "Hey, Joe, you know the chief wants to talk to you ASAP."

"Sharon...has someone been in here? It's a wreck." She looked at him with a smile and said, "Just you. Don't you remember running out of here yesterday afternoon to meet up with some of your buddies? You ran out so fast, you were a blur. So, how was the guys' night out?" she asked. Secretly, Sharon wished that Detective Warren had asked her out instead. For a while now, Sharon had been trying to get Joe to notice her, but he was always consumed with work. So much so, in fact, that he never realized how interested she always seemed to be in what was going on in his life.

Joe answered briefly, "Oh, yeah, I forgot all that. There's a lot on my mind. It was OK. A couple of my friends came over and watched the game, and we had a few beers."

Sharon pressed for more. "Sounds like a big party. How come women weren't allowed to attend?" she asked.

He smirked and said, "Sorry, Sharon, I've got way too much to do today, and I can't lose focus now. We'll have to talk later."

Sharon answered, "Can't blame a girl for trying to take your mind off things." Then she mumbled to herself, "Even if it was just for a minute."

He called out, "Thanks," grabbed his paperwork, and started walking toward the main office down the hall.

Robert Oliver Frank. If the fact that he had three first names wasn't enough, he lived up to his last name unquestionably. Very frankly, he yelled at Joe, "Joe, get in here!" The detective shuffled into the room and noticed that the chief was staring at the door. Joe was quick enough to realize he should have closed it. So he stood up and did so. The room was fairly large and had a few nice windows that offered a great view of the city.

The chief's office was covered wall-to-wall with hunting and fishing paraphernalia. There were antlers, fish, and even a bear claw resting his desk. The chief felt that his office gave him character, and the men who worked under him feared that he might hunt them down if they got out of line. "Joe," the chief said very curtly, "Why do I have a man down? What is this crap about a car accident and some shit carved into Chuck's window? Do you have anything yet? Joe waited for his turn to speak. "Well, answer me!" the chief yelled. Joe started to respond, but before he could the chief started up again. "And what about Chuck's poor sister, having an accident within the same hour? Joe! I smell something here. You better check into it." Joe opened his mouth and a sound came out, but before a full word could be formed, Chief Frank interrupted yet again. "Joe! I don't want to hear that this is some mob shit or that Chuck was a dirty cop. That would be total BS and you know it! Now get out of here; I've got things to do. I'm keeping an eye on you, Warren. Don't mess this up!"

Joe managed to squeeze out a "Yes, sir," and then he scurried out as fast as he had come in.

Walking back toward his office, Joe heard the chief call out to him. "Warren, I want you to drive out to the Rivera place and break this to them. They deserve more than a call!" Joe hung his head; he knew it was coming but knowing it had to come now was even worse. Sharon noticed that Joe was upset. She promptly ran over to him and offered to accompany him. Sharon also asked if he could accompany her to the hospital. The baby's father was on his way there and she needed to return. Joe sighed and agreed. Together they took the elevator to the ground floor. Taking her squad car, they headed for the hospital.

The drive was silent. Neither of them spoke a word until they pulled up at the entrance. They walked in to find an attendant sitting at the front desk. She advised them that the father had phoned and would be arriving shortly. Sharon asked her what the father's name was again. "His name is Teague,

Daniel Teague. The mother, God rest her soul, was Nathalie." Joe coughed for a moment, unhappy at this predicament.

The conversation continued until the door opened and a broad man about five-feet-nine in height approached the desk. In a very monotone voice, he said, "Excuse me my name is Daniel Teague." He addressed his statement to the attractive blond officer who was approximately the same height as him.

Sharon looked him square in the eye and said, "I'm so sorry for your loss, Mr. Teague. The events of today are truly horrible."

He looked at her and said, "Events? You mean something else happened in addition to my wife being massacred?" His tone changed and his face went red.

Joe stepped in and spoke in a defensive manner. "Mr. Teague, Charles Rivera also died this morning. He was found at the scene of a car accident that he didn't survive. Hearing this news, Daniel said, "Where's my child?" The attendant responded that the baby was resting in the back room and as far as they could tell had not experienced any trauma after being bumped by the oncoming vehicle.

"Are you the doctor?" he replied in a nastier tone. She shook her head. "Well, then, I'd like to hear that from him; please take me to see my baby now!"

No one blamed him for being upset, but the attendant was almost in tears. She walked toward the nursery and subtly motioned for him to follow. Daniel followed, leaving Sharon and Joe behind. Joe turned for a moment and said, "Mr. Teague, are you going to be here for a while? I need to ask you some questions." Teague didn't respond, so Joe kept talking. "If you prefer, I can wait until tomorrow, but I will need to speak with you."

Daniel Teague turned around, his face red and flustered. Then he roared as loud as he could, "For crying out loud! Leave me the fuck alone! Can't you people just get out of my fucking face?"

Teague turned the turner and was out of sight. Joe walked across the hall and sat in a waiting chair. After a moment, Sharon joined him. "Ouch!" she uttered. "I guess we'll take that answer as a later this week.

Joe placed his face in his hands and grabbed his hair, pulling it. "Sharon, I tell you, on some days I wish I never got out of bed."

Sharon was about to respond when Joe got a call on his cell phone; it was a dispatch person. "Detective Warren?"

"Yes," he replied.

"Sir there has been an incident at Lincoln Memorial Elementary School. Two children were taken from the school during recess. Please get down there as soon as possible." Joe wondered why he would be reassigned before having a chance to speak with Chuck's wife, but orders were so he turned towards Sharon.

Sharon overheard the conversation. She stood up immediately and said, "Let's roll." Joe jumped up and they both ran out of the building. The car was close by. They jumped in and drove off right away, sirens blaring.

Chapter 5

SCHOOL YARD MAYHEM

Joe and Sharon skated through a few red lights and arrived very quickly at the school. The scene from the outside was quiet. However, as they walked into the building they could hear someone somewhere crying hysterically. Quickly, they approached one of the administrative offices. Inside was a petite, red-haired woman with a pale complexion. As they entered, she looked up and began making a whining sound that was barely tolerable to the human ear.

Both Joe and Sharon knew her well. Sarah Rivera had come to the school after receiving the news about the day's events via a phone call from a friend. She had intended to pick up her children and tell them the awful news about their father, but they were nowhere to be found. Not ten minutes before she arrived, teachers had been frantically searching for the children, neither of whom had returned from recess.

Sharon immediately ran over to Sarah and gave her a hug. On the verge of a nervous breakdown, Sarah managed to cry out, "Where are they?"

Sharon replied, "We're going to find out, Sarah, I promise we're going to find out." Joe felt like he was going to break down himself. He asked an administrator for the respective location of each child prior to recess. One of the women responded that Roberto was in the third grade, room 301, and Jorge was in the fifth grade, room 503. Detective Warren left the room while Sharon remained behind to console Sarah. He wanted some answers and he wanted them now. Someone must have seen something.

Joe made his way to room 301 and knocked on the door. The teacher quickly opened it, telling the children to behave while she stepped out into the hall. "Excuse me, ma'am, I'm Detective Warren, Chicago police, and I understand Roberto Rivera is one of the students in your class." His tone was serious but polite.

She responded, "Yes I'm his teacher, Miss Grimes—Lora Grimes."

"Miss Grimes"—Joe paused after saying her name and then continued— "were you with the children during the recess period?" Joe questioned.

"No, she answered, "Today was not my day to watch them."

He continued to probe, "I see; so do you know whose day it was?"

"I believe it was Mrs. Stevens's and Mrs. Keller's rotation today." Joe then asked if any of the children had seen anything. She looked at him and said, "Sometimes it's hard to tell."

Joe asked Miss Grimes to announce him as a detective so that the children might be truthful with him. He entered the class and she asked the twenty-five children to pay close attention. She explained that Detective Warren was there because he had some very important questions for them. He asked if they understood why he was there. Simultaneously they all answered yes. Joe continued, "Now, were any of you playing with Roberto during recess? If you were, please raise your hands." Two small boys by the names of Oliver and Theodore lifted their arms. Joe then asked Miss Grimes if she would accompany him and the two children out into the hallway. Outside, Joe asked what had happened during recess.

Oliver spoke first, "Wow! Are you a real policeman?" he inquired. Joe nodded. Theodore started crying.

Joe leaned down and said, "Don't worry, son, you can tell me whatever you saw." Theodore looked like he was going to say something but then puked on Joe's pant leg. Miss Grimes ran Teddy to the bathroom. Oliver spoke quietly and cautiously once they were alone. He told Joe that they had all been playing tag and that Roberto got mad at them for tagging to hard and knocking him to the ground. He then elaborated by saying that Roberto ran to tell his brother, who was across the yard. He also told Joe that after that he went to hide because he didn't want to get beat up by Jorge. The detective thanked Oliver for being brave enough to tell him. Joe just had one more question. He asked if there were any unfamiliar adults around during recess. Oliver was pensive but finally answered, "Yes, there was a scary-looking man riding a bike." That man, Oliver said, had stopped at the fence and stared at us right before we tagged Roberto."

"What did he look like?" The words came naturally out of Joe's mouth. Oliver said that the man was very scary. That he was tall, but not too tall. He was dressed in dark clothing and had a hood over his head. He also said that he saw the man bend down on one knee and touch the ground. "Then the man just disappeared," the boy continued. "After that, I ran to hide from Jorge and I didn't see him anymore." Joe jotted everything down and then instructed Oliver to return to his seat in the classroom.

When Miss Grimes and Teddy returned, she found the detective sitting on her desk watching the children. He told her that he needed to go to Jorge's classroom but he would return later for her statement. While he was walking, Joe started to review his notes. Teddy's sickness had given him time to question the other children. One little boy said he saw a monster dressed like a man. Another little girl said it was a handsome man who was tall and dark. A third child said it was a druid. And one little boy said it was the devil himself come to take them all away. Joe smiled at the imagination of children.

Joe proceeded upstairs and without much difficulty found room 503. Before stopping there, he had found his way to the men's room and cleaned his shoe and pant leg. The teacher for this class was Mrs. Stevens. She stepped outside, and he asked her a few questions. First, he inquired if she had seen the suspicious character the children had described. She hadn't. Mrs. Stevens responded that she was reprimanding some children who had gotten into a fist fight, and so her attention had been focused on them. He then questioned the children in her classroom. A few of them had seen Jorge go off with his brother toward where the younger kids played.

Joe spent some time getting more details from the fifth graders, and when he felt he had gathered enough information he decided it would be best to look over the playground. He returned to room 301 and asked Miss Grimes if he could once again borrow Oliver. She agreed, and Oliver accompanied the detective outside. Together they walked out to the parking lot where the children played during recess. Oliver showed him where he and the other two boys had been playing tag. Sharon noticed them exiting and followed.

Oliver turned a little red as she approached them and said hello to him. Joe introduced the young boy as Oliver, Roberto's friend. She said, "Hello, Oliver, Roberto's friend." Oliver giggled a little and said, "Wow, a hot officer lady." This made Sharon blush a bit; she fluffed the little boy's hair. She smiled and then said to Joe very professionally, "Have you found out anything, Joe?" He quickly briefed her on the young male character who had been described to him. Then he turned to Oliver and said, "Do you remember, you told me you saw the man touch the ground? Can you show me where?" Oliver was a little scared but agreed.

As they walked over toward the fence, all of their faces changed. As they looked down, they saw a circle splattered on the sidewalk and inside of it was the exact same symbol that had been etched into the window of Charles Rivera's squad car. Joe bent down and touched it. This time the symbol wasn't carved in. When Joe touched it, something came off on his fingers. He looked over to Sharon in horror. Without a word she already knew what Joe was thinking. She didn't want to say in front of Oliver, so she whispered in his ear, "Its blood…" The wind tore through them, sending chills up their spines. Joe got the feeling they weren't alone. He quickly instructed Sharon to take Oliver back into the school, and then he ran to his car to radio for backup. One thing was evident: this was now a crime scene. There was clear evidence of malice. Chuck's death and his children's disappearance were linked, and it was possible he was tracking a serial killer.

Chapter 6

CLOSE ENCOUNTERS

A squad of Chicago's finest had arrived at Lincoln Memorial Elementary School. Detective Warren was feeling a little less on edge because he finally had some backup. When the men arrived, he ordered some of them to guard the building and a few others to patrol the surrounding area, including the school grounds. Then he returned to oversee the forensics team that was taking samples. Sharon had left, taking Sarah Rivera with her to the precinct. Joe had told her not to mention the blood they had found.

Joe watched carefully as blood samples were taken; the blood was still fresh, and that worried him. He wondered what the motivation behind these attacks could be. It seemed to him that the assailant was targeting persons related to Chuck Rivera. Furthermore, the apparent male had a knack for getting away and leaving no evidence other than his intentional call sign. Which led to another question: was there a connection to Nathalie Teague's death? No one had mentioned the presence of a suspect at that accident. Was it just a coincidence that she was Chuck's sister? It seemed highly unlikely that Chuck died in a car crash, his sister was hit by a car, and now his two children had gone missing without there being some connection.

Joe continued his deductive reasoning, asking himself, *why would the assailant travel by bike? And how could he have transported the children that way?* A horrid feeling suddenly came over Joe. A light had gone off in his head. The assailant had no intention of taking the children anywhere. He had no way of transporting them. Joe looked toward the school and signaled a few men to follow him.

Once inside the building, Joe made his way to the principal's office. There he addressed the principal, Mr. Flannigan, about the school's layout. Specifically, he asked if there were any sections that were cut off from student usage. Mr. Flannigan pulled out a schematic of the building. He pointed out a few rooms downstairs that surrounded the gymnasium. Joe immediately rushed there, trailed by some men. They walked across the gym and saw a gray door labeled Boiler Room. There was a sound from the inside. Joe's heart started to race. He signaled the men to be ready. Slowly, he placed his hand on the doorknob and then yanked the door open, yelling "FREEZE!"

Holding out his gun, Joe was steady. Inside the room was a small man who had dropped a broom when he was startled. "Who are you?" Joe asked intently.

"Pedro Martinez. I'm the janitor." Joe was still suspicious, but he lowered his firearm.

"Mr. Martinez, please come with me." The two of them walked up the stairs back to the principal's office. As they approached Mr. Flannigan, Joe asked, "Mr. Flannigan, this man right here, do you know him?"

Mr. Flannigan looked concerned and replied, "Yes, this is Pedro, the custodial worker."

"Can you account for his whereabouts throughout the day?" Joe asked.

Mr. Flannigan responded, "Yes, Pedro clocked in this morning at eight thirty and has been in and out all day. I saw him cleaning the halls and offices."

Joe had to be extra thorough. "So there was no time period where you weren't aware of his whereabouts?" Flannigan was slightly annoyed at being asked the same question in a different way. He thought for a moment, and then he answered, "During recess, Pedro was sitting at the table across from us eating lunch. There's no possible way he could have been outside at all."

Joe asked, "What about after recess?"

Flannigan spoke very clearly now. "Detective, this man is innocent. After recess, I asked him to look at the boiler because the heat was cutting in and out."

Joe thought for a moment. He no longer suspected the custodian. He still had a feeling he was missing something. He returned downstairs and proceeded to check out all the other rooms. There was the theater room behind the stage, and the band room, which had a storage closet. Each room was empty.

Before heading back upstairs, he returned to the boiler room and checked it out thoroughly. There was nothing. He again went back to the principal's office. This time he sat down for a few minutes trying to organize his thoughts. Flannigan and Martinez were sitting also.

An awkward silence lasted for about five minutes. Then Joe said to both of them, "This is a pretty big building. How come there is only one small boiler? How could that possibly heat this entire place? The principal just shrugged his shoulders, but Pedro said, "Well, sir, that isn't the only boiler."

Joe focused his attention on Pedro immediately and asked, "Where's the other one? I didn't see it downstairs."

Pedro responded, "That's because there's two more upstairs above the classes. I hadn't checked those out yet."

Joe jumped up and said, "Pedro, are the doors to those boiler rooms locked? Pedro nodded his head affirmatively, and Joe asked Pedro to bring the keys and show them the way there.

At the other side of the main school corridor, there was a staircase that led to the mysterious third floor. The students were always curious about it given the fact that they were not permitted to go up there. Pedro went up the stairs to open the third floor door. He paused, slightly unnerved, and then he gasped, "S-s-sir, its open." The tension in the air was so thick it couldn't be cut by a chainsaw. Joe silently signaled Pedro to get behind them and then he motioned for the men to follow his lead. He slowly inched the door open and peered down the poorly lit hallway. There didn't seem to be anyone there. They all piled through, Pedro taking up the rear. Then they came upon two doors across the hallway from each other. They split into two groups of three and simultaneously opened the doors.

Pedro turned completely green in the face. Horrifically, inside of each door was one of the bodies of the boys. Roberto was in the left boiler room and Jorge was on the right, both dead and tied to chairs. The cause of death was uncertain. Each of them had his right arm terribly gashed near the elbow, causing the blood to puddle on the floor. Aside from the victims, the rooms were both empty. The killer seemed to have gotten away yet again. Joe surmised that the cuts had been made to get the blood the symbol outside was drawn with. He advised the men to barricade off the crime scene. Sickened, he left the room and placed the ambulance call. How was he going to tell Sarah about this?

The ambulance came, and he told the forensics people to examine the bodies for fingerprints or anything they could use to identify the psycho. Joe was developing a migraine; the stress from this situation seemed to be getting worse. Leaving the building for a moment, Joe went back out to his squad car. He rolled his windows down, leaned his seat back, and turned on the radio. Some soft music was playing. Some of the men were coming back to report to him there was still no sign of the killer. Joe advised them to keep looking.

Joe closed his eyes to try to get a handle on the situation when he heard a voice, "I suggest you back down, Detective. Oh, and I also suggest you keep your eyes facing forward and don't move." Joe remained still, but his heart began pounding in his chest. The voice coming from the back of the car continued, "There are just a few things I want to say to you. First of all, your efforts are pathetic!" A slight chuckle. "Listen, why don't you just give up, Joseph? I'm almost done for today. I would have finished earlier, but there was a slight complication. Either way, by the time you figure it out you'll will be far too late again. It's almost fun to watch you squirm, so, baffled by my movements. So I've decided to give you a little help. The voice from the backseat chuckled again. Well, I guess I'll give you a hint. You see one of my targets survived earlier today, so I've decided to go back and finish the job. Good luck. The voice let out an insidious laugh that made the detective shiver, and then there was just silence.

Joe had been slowly inching his hand toward his gun. As his finger unsnapped the holster and grasped the trigger, he took a deep breath. He knew he would only get one chance to take this man out. Then he remembered Chuck, Chuck's sister, and the children. He snapped his arm back and squeezed the trigger knowing that he might miss and give the killer a chance to retaliate.

A single gunshot echoed throughout the entire school parking lot, and in the building the children started screaming and piling under their desks. The teachers tried to calm them down and then carefully peeked out into the hallway. The principal made an announcement that everyone should lock their classroom doors and wait for further instructions. .

In seconds, Joe's car was surrounded. Inside, they could see Joe's arm stretched out with his gun in hand. From what they could tell, he wasn't moving. One of them yelled into the car. "Detective, are you OK?" Everything was still, and then there was the slightest movement; Joe opened his right eye. The same officer spoke. "Sir, I repeat. Are you OK?" Joe sat up quickly, turning his body to look in the back passenger seat where he had fired. There was a hole in his seat that went straight through to the outside. He got out of the car.

"I don't believe this shit," he said abruptly. "Yeah, I'm fine." He looked around and saw that no one was in the back of the car.

He told one of his men to go report to the principal that everything was OK. Then he opened the rear driver's side door. On the floor was a tape recorder. He covered his mouth and started cursing under his breath. Then Joe remembered what the tape had said. He started to order a withdrawal to the hospital, but just then he heard a sound from the passenger side of the car. He walked around and saw that the bullet had punctured the gas tank and gas was leaking inside the car. Just then, the tape recorder started to smoke. It had been rigged to explode. Joe barely had time to signal his men to run from the scene after determining what was going to happen. The car exploded, which sent the students into a panic for the second time.

A few men that were inside the building ran outside, saw the exploded vehicle, and then ran up to Joe. "Sir, are you OK?" Joe was getting tired of answering that question and grudgingly acknowledged that he was fine. Gritting his teeth together and dusting himself off, he looked around for the nearest police car. He got in, advising the others to follow him except for one team, who he commanded to call for the fire truck.

"Damn it!" he yelled as he switched on the sirens and headed back toward the hospital. There was a rookie cop sitting in the seat next to him fearing for his life a bit at the frantic way the detective was driving. They arrived at the hospital in seven minutes flat. Joe jumped out the car and started running toward the building. He got to the attendant and asked her where he could find Michael Teague. She informed him that Michael Teague had left not ten minutes earlier with the baby. Joe let out a gasp, then asked, "Do you know where he was going?"

She was about to answer when a worker entered the room and said, "I need a police officer." Joe turned toward him. The man was a little shaky. He said some people in the parking garage were screaming so he ran over here to get help. Joe followed the man as they ran toward the parking garage. When they arrived, there were five people standing around a car in horror. Inside was Michael Teague, slumped over the steering wheel. Unfortunately, he wasn't what everyone was looking at. On the hood lay probably the most disturbing image that Joe had seen in his life. Literally nailed by its hands and feet was the infant who had escaped death earlier.

The people crowded around were frozen in horror. Some were crying. Joe looked for a moment, but he then turned his face away because he noticed that carved on the forehead of the baby was the symbol. Plain as day there it was— the third symbol. Now there was no doubt the three attacks were linked. Never in ten years of service had he seen such a vile act committed on an infant. Joe walked away from the crowd and pulled out his cell phone.

The chief picked up the phone on his desk. Joe began to speak. "Sir, I'm not sure I can handle this case anymore, maybe you ought to take me off it." A tear rolled down his face. "The baby of Nathalie and Daniel Teague was just found crucified on the hood of their car! Literally crucified sir!" Joe paused and continued. "Sir, that symbol, whatever it means, was carved by knife into the child's forehead. I think he did it while the baby was still alive." The chief didn't have any words for once. Joe spoke again, "Chief we better get a team down here a.s.a.p., this is a bad scene. The chief agree and then disconnected. Once the team had arrived Joe took a moment and walked off to contemplate.

Across town, a bus was traveling from a DEDC facility to the courthouse. On board were a few guards and one prisoner. One of the guards was being particularly loud and obnoxious. The time was 3:45 p.m., and they were running a little late transporting their prisoner. Making its way through traffic, the bus stopped at a red light. A hooded bicyclist crossed its path and then rode down the street in the opposite direction from the bus. Magnus peered out his window and saw the bicyclist wave at him with a smile. His face was puzzled as the bus pulled away. The bicyclist stopped and watched the bus as it continued on its way. He smiled before he rode off and then he blurted, "What a glorious day."

Chapter 7

THE HOUR OF RECKONING

It just had to be a gray bus. Magnus smirked at the thought, as it continued on its way to his pending doom. He was glad for the moment, because Denton had fallen asleep. With a few minutes of peace, Magnus was finally able to truly enjoy the scenery as they passed though the small city. Julius was reading a book—something about witches and wizards being trained at a school called Pig Warts. The drive itself was about an hour or so. Magnus let out a yawn and leaned back in the somewhat comfortable seat. He thought to himself that at last he was going to get some answers. Julius had informed him that he would finally get a chance to speak with a lawyer. He was supposed to have met with a lawyer two weeks earlier, but it never happened.

It felt good to be on the move and out of his cell. Magnus wasn't claustrophobic, but being cooped up for so many days had started to get to him. Magnus hadn't thought of anything to say once he was at the trial, except the traditional *I didn't do it.* All he could do was deny the allegations, tell the truth, and pray that the judicial system worked. Folding his hands, he thought about Arie again and prayed for her safety. He thought to himself that he would rather be imprisoned and know she was all right then be free but discover she was dead. Whispering her name, he finished his little payer. Then he felt the bus slow down. They pulled into the back of the parking lot. The courthouse was attached to the seventh precinct. Julius walked over, cuffed Magnus, and escorted him off the bus.

Denton followed them with the other two guards. As they proceeded up the stairs, Magnus noticed an attractive blond officer leaving the building in a rush. They locked eyes, and for a moment he smiled a soft smile at her. She reminded him a bit of Arie. She paused also giving him a somewhat bewildered look, but then continued on her way to a squad car and drove off. Without warning, a large group of reporters ran up and surrounded Magnus and Julius. Cameras were flashing, and the reporters started to bombard Magnus with questions.

"Mr. Magnus, are the allegations true?" The question came from a squeaky-voiced brunette woman with glasses.

"What allegations," he responded. The guards attempted to intercede, but she got louder.

"Oh come on, gentlemen, this is our first chance to interview the Chicago Bomber!" she yelled as they moved passed him. Magnus's jaw dropped in astonishment at her statement.

"Chicago Bomber?" he uttered. *She was talking about me,* he thought. As far as he remembered, he had never seen a bomb in his life, let alone set one off.

The five men entered the building. Denton and Julius were in front and the other two guards, Derrick Frost and Thomas Rutger, flanked Magnus. Even though Magnus was cuffed, they had added the extra security detail to be extra cautious. They entered the elevator and went to the sixth floor, two levels below Detective Warren's office. They moved into a holding area, where Magnus requested the removal of his cuffs. Julius was about to do it when Denton abrasively said, "Fuck that." Denton looked Magnus right in the eyes as if he were hoping Magnus would try to escape.

Magnus just stood his ground. Eventually Denton took out his key and removed the shackles. As he did, he said, "You just try something, freak. You're lucky these have to come off in this courtroom. Don't get comfortable, though, cause they're going right back on after the hearing." Magnus scowled at Denton but then began to listen to the judge in the next room, who was handling some ticket infractions. She didn't sound like she was in a good mood.

Magnus overheard the judge impose a three-hundred-dollar fine on a minor for driving twenty miles over the speed limit. Denton just started laughing.

He smiled and turned to Magnus, saying they don't call her the terminator judge for nothing. There was a knock on the chamber door. Frost answered it. "Sir, this is a restricted area," he said to the man in the cheap-looking business suit.

The man replied, "Yes, I know; I've been appointed to be the attorney of our friend over here." The name's Kenneth M. Lockhart, but you can call me KM—everyone does. I've been advised that now is the time for me to confer with Mr. Magnus.

The man sat down at the table and gestured for Magnus to sit as well. He spoke with a southern accent, "Now, son, I don't know anything about you, but I gotta tell you, things don't look good here. First off, you have two hard noses you're up against. Number one is the district attorney prosecuting you today. His name is William G. Haight III, and let me tell you, he lives up to his last name. He's a hater if I ever met one. The second and more important problem you have is Kathryn L. Schmitz. She's no pushover. You can sit there and look as innocent as a baby and she'd throw the book at ya. Lucky for you, I've dealt with them both before, so maybe if we plead guilty I can get you lighter sentence."

Magnus starred at the man like he was crazy. He addressed him for the first time. "Mr. Lockhart, is it? I'm sorry, but up until today, when I was standing on the steps of this building, I had no idea what this trial was even about. In fact, I'm still not even sure. I heard a reporter call me the Chicago Bomber." The man across the table looked at Magnus intently for a moment, trying to read his expression.

"Son, you had better not be feeding me some horse shit! 'Cause let me tell you, I don't really care to listen to garbage. A lot of folks died that day." Magnus looked at him and shrugged. KM Lockhart reached into his briefcase and pulled out a newspaper from precisely twenty-five days earlier. Magnus read the headline and story.

Is Chicago Under Siege?

Last Night at precisely 9:00 p.m. on the west side of the city, a tremendous explosion quaked this city! The explosion took place at Johnson's Warehouse, but it was an explosion of such great strength that a large portion of the block was caught in the blast. The Chicago Police and city officials scrambled to piece together what happened. There were 53 dead and 203 injured. At the warehouse, police found a survivor of the blast and have identified him as the likely assailant. Michael J. Magnus was taken to the closest hospital, St. Louisa and is currently under heavy guard there until he regains consciousness. Police say that they found him in possession of detonators and other materials that point to his apparent guilt. It seems likely he didn't give himself enough time to escape.

The article continued on; Magnus scanned for any details about Arie, but there was no mention of her or any possible reason behind the bombing.

KM took the paper back and said, "So you see, son. Nobody else survived except you, and that don't look so good." Magnus sat thinking for a moment. The gravity of his situation fell on him like a ton of bricks. Denton, who should have left the room for client/attorney confidentiality, just smiled and said, "See, freako, blowing shit up wasn't a good idea. Especially for your health, since once they sentence you we'll be spending lots of time together." Denton went on to say, "They only care about you *before* the trial, not after."

Magnus shook his head in disbelief. "Mr. Lockhart, I didn't do this. I don't even know how I got to Chicago."

"Well, Mr. Magnus, if we plead not guilty and you are convicted, you will face a heavier sentence," KM responded. "Like, say, the *death sentence* instead of just life imprisonment."

Denton spoke up from the corner, saying, "Yeah-h-h-h-h, Magnus, why don't you plead guilty? Doesn't life with me sound fun?" Denton let out his horrific laugh and then exited the room. He wasn't sure what would be more fun, pulling the switch or regular beatings. But either way, he was sure he would enjoy himself.

The other officers left the room after KM motioned for them to follow Denton. When they were all gone, he said "Son, in all honesty, I'm a pretty good attorney, but I'd be lying to you if I told you I could get you off of this one."

Magnus replied, "The evidence is circumstantial. According to this article, they just found things on me that could have easily been planted."

KM retorted, "What about the fact that you were almost on top of the blast area and yet you survived? Besides," he continued, "Do you have any way to account for you being there? As you said, you're not even from around here. So what were you doing here in this fair city?"

Magnus shook his head. Then he said, "I don't know. I can't remember anything leading up to my incarceration."

"Well, isn't that convenient!" KM snapped sarcastically. The attorney looked annoyed, as if he felt he was being toyed with.

Magnus protested, "Look, you're my lawyer! Help me! I didn't do this! It's not a game, and it's not BS. I think I would remember deciding to blow up half of Chicago."

KM took a moment to write down Magnus's statement in his journal. Then he said, "Are you sure you want to go down this road? Pleading not guilty is gonna drag things out. And you know that pisses people off, especially judges…if you get my drift."

Magnus looked him dead in the eyes and hit the table, yelling, "If they send me away, they are punishing the wrong guy!"

KM mumbled, "Well, sometimes the people need a scapegoat."

Magnus screamed, "Your job isn't to appease the people; your job is to represent me, and if you don't want to do that I'll protest you as my attorney."

Lockhart was surprised by Magnus's outburst. He replied, "OK, OK. I get the picture. You're serious about going not guilty on the plea. Welp, I had to be sure." Lockhart stood up and stretched out his hand, saying, "Alright then, Mr. Magnus, you've got yourself an attorney. Magnus grudgingly accepted the peace offering. KM sat back down and decided it was time to get down to business. His first question was about any details his client might remember. Magnus told KM about Arie and how he remembered he was on his way to see her in Missouri where she went to school. He paused and then mentioned feeling that she was in danger somehow.

Somewhat enthusiastic about the challenge, KM said, "Well son, that's a start. I reckon I have to work with that. If you were traveling from New York to Missouri, then there should be a record of your flight. You were probably stopping through Chicago to transfer. The question is, why didn't you continue all the way?"

Lockhart continued with his reasoning. "The second thing I want to look into is your possessions. Where is your suitcase? You most likely had one of those. And if you changed your flight plans, it's possible ya made reservations at a hotel. At this point, pleading not guilty today will at least buy me time to do some research. Hopefully, we'll get some answers."

Magnus felt somewhat relieved. KM told him it was time to speak with the district attorney. Before he left, he looked back at Magnus and with his hearty Texan voice accent said, "I took one look at ya son, and knew you were innocent!"

Chapter 8

THE TRIAL POSTPONEMENT

A gavel resounded in the distance. "*The People versus Michael J. Magnus* is now in session," a bailiff shouted. Julius and Denton escorted Magnus through the courtroom. The people in attendance stared as the three made their way toward the front. Magnus decided it was best not to make eye contact with any of them.

As he sat down beside Lockhart, the bailiff shouted that all should rise. The judge had taken a recess and was now returning. A small, gray-haired woman of about sixty made her way behind the podium. Kathryn L. Schmitz sat, and as she did, the rest of the room followed. Her tone was strong as she asked the prosecutor to approach the bench. "Mr. Haight, are you prepared to make your opening statement?"

A stubby man in his early forties placed his glasses over his eyes, lifted up some paperwork, and looked up at the judge. His voice was nasally. "I believe Mr. Lockhart is going to request an extension because his client wishes to plead not guilty. However, Your Honor, I also believe that no matter how much time he gets, the evidence will show the defendant's guilt." Haight leered over at Lockhart, who now was standing.

"Your honor," KM said out of turn, "every man deserves a chance to be defended fairly. Isn't that why I'm standing here? Furthermore, I wasn't aware a man was guilty before proven innocent."

The judge looked over at Magnus, now sitting very still. She was pensive and seemed to expect a reaction from the defendant. Magnus made eye contact and thought he'd better not back down from this staring contest. "Michael J. Magnus, it is the opinion of this court that every man deserves a fair defense. However, it is also the opinion of this court that the travesty at the heart of this case needs a speedy resolution, so I will allow for no more than two weeks to pass before this trial begins working toward one."

KM took that as a small victory and spoke again to the judge, seriously, "Your Honor, my client has spent the last month in a prison with not so much as a day to stretch his legs in the outside world aside from coming here. Since there has yet to be anything determined, couldn't you possibly set bail for this man?"

Mr. Haight nearly choked at the request. "Your Honor, this request is outrageous!"

Judge Schmitz also took offense at this remark. "Mr. Lockhart, I have already granted you time to defend him. I will not allow him to not be in custody."

"Your Honor," KM replied, "may he at least have visitation rights?" Magnus was surprised at this statement; he had never even thought about that. Maybe Arie was OK and she was here to visit him. He looked up at KM.

The judge asked the very question on Magnus's mind: "Who wishes to visit this man?"

KM looked turned toward Magnus and smiled. Then he turned back and replied, "This morning, it was brought to my attention that a family member has been trying to reach Mr. Magnus for some time now."

Astonished by this, Magnus's face twisted in confusion. As far as he knew, no one in his family even knew he was there. An entire month had gone by and he hadn't heard a thing from his parents. He had actually given up hope on them finding him.

The judge grudgingly allowed for family and close friend visitation under heavy guard. Then she addressed both lawyers and asked if there was any further business to discuss. The prosecutor stood up and approached the bench. "Your Honor, the state is requesting capital punishment for this crime. If the defendant is found guilty, I want the people to know he will receive the full force of the law!"

The judge spoke directly to Magnus. "Let it be known that if at the end of this hearing you enter in a plea of not guilty, then the full extent of the law can be brought down on you. This court is not without mercy if you enter a plea of guilty right now; I will bestow an imprisonment sentence instead of the death penalty."

Judge Schmitz paused and then spoke again. "Michael J. Magnus, please stand." Magnus rose to attention and faced the judge. "How do you plead?" she asked him.

Magnus didn't hesitate, "Your Honor, I plead not guilty." The spectators began to mumble among themselves.

"Order!" she exclaimed. "This court will reconvene in fourteen days."

The crowd began to file out. Denton came up behind Magnus and firmly grabbed his arm. "OK, freak." He spoke in a lower tone than normal so none of the nearby people would hear him. "Time to head back to your luxury suite. We have two more weeks of fun and games ahead of us."

KM walked beside Magnus and said, "Well, this was the first step. Hopefully, we will conquer all the rest as easily. The judge didn't say it, but I'm allowed as many consultations as I see fit. So I will be in to see ya in a day or two, once I pull together some more info. Meanwhile, I hope the visit from your brother goes well." KM walked away before Magnus could respond.

He thought to himself, *I don't have a brother.*

Julius walked up and took hold of Magnus's other arm. Magnus asked him if he knew anything about the visitor. Julius hadn't spoken in a while, but he looked at his friend and said, "That guy gave me creeps; hard to believe he's your brother personality-wise, but he looks just like you."

Magnus's face contorted. He mumbled, "He looks like me?"

Julius replied, "He's your spitting image—like your twin brother. You never told me you had a twin."

Magnus was confused. Had he forgotten his own brother? He searched his memories but came up blank. He thought about telling Julius he didn't have a brother, but then he thought maybe this guy could answer some questions for him. Maybe he knew something and was pretending to be his brother to pass on information. He contemplated the possibilities as they exited the building.

The reporters were so numerous they formed a sea of people in front of the bus back to the prison. Video cameras and microphones were everywhere. "Mr. Magnus," one male reporter yelled, "do you really think you'll get off?"

This time Magnus was ready. He retorted, "If there's any justice in the system, yes!" The reporters were all quiet for a moment as they wrote that down.

"Mr. Magnus," another women yelled, "what were you doing at the crime scene if you are, as you imply, wrongly accused?"

Magnus was about to answer when Julius stepped in front of him and said, "You people are impeding the law from passing through. Now part before we arrest you!"

The ocean of people parted, and Magnus was ushered aboard the bus. The four security guards also boarded and found their original seats. The time was now 3:00 p.m., and they had a long drive ahead of them.

The bus driver pulled out and they started back. Frost asked if they could stop at a Fast Burger to pick up some snacks for later. Denton looked at him funny, but then his stomach rumbled.

"Sounds like a good idea," he said. Then he looked at Magnus. "Don't even ask, freak—you get to suffer while we scarf Fasty Bs." He laughed out loud and then told the bus driver to stop at the nearest burger joint.

Magnus closed his eyes and started to drift as they drove. The ride was fairly smooth so it was easy to sleep. There was a mirror at the end of large hallway. Magnus approached it. The room was a little distorted, but on the walls were portraits of people. He walked up to the mirror and saw no reflection. He touched it and his hand fell through, and then he was pulled all the way in. He heard laughter, the same laughter from his last dream. Yelling at the voice, he clamored, "Where are you?"

The voice responded, "Closer than you think," and then started to laugh some more. Then the words *closer than you think* echoed over and over. Magnus tried to follow the voice but was lost in a world of emptiness. He tried to hold still to control the dream, but everything started spiraling around him. Dizziness overtook him. The bus came to a halt and he woke up to find Denton staring at him.

Denton looked at him maliciously and said, "What you looking at, freak?" Denton shoved a burger in his mouth and started chewing loudly. "You're not getting any, Mister Magnus! It's the prison slop for you." He sneered and took another bite and with his mouth full, he said, "And right before they gas you, don't be asking for any good last meals, cause you still getting prison slop, freak."

Magnus turned and looked out the window. Then he thought, *what a shithead*. Denton's face was awful. For a man in his mid-thirties, his acne was as bad as a teenager's and the scar on his left cheek didn't help matters.

Denton crumpled the food bag that contained his garbage. Then he tossed it as hard as he could at Magnus's head. "Two points!" he yelled as it bounced off the side of Magnus's ear. It was only paper, but to Magnus it was infuriating.

Julius looked up from the book he was engrossed in. "Hey, Denton, lay off the poor guy. He's going back to the lockup. Give him a break!" he yelled toward the midsection of the bus.

Denton leered down at Julius, feeling his authority was now challenged. "What are you going to do about it, tough guy?" This was the first time Magnus had witnessed the full extent of Denton's wrath toward Julius. He picked up the bag and tossed it at Julius, hitting the book. Julius stood up, as did Frost and Rutger.

Rutger said, "Just take it easy, McKay! Spencer is right; sometimes you go too far picking at Magnus." Rutger used everyone's last name when he talked.

Denton punched the seat near him. "I'm not taking any shit from you guys! I'll do what I please, damn it!" Rutger held his night stick tightly, fearing Denton might strike.

Frost was the smart one. He knew how Denton thought. He yelled out, "Wow, look at the body on that chick!" There really wasn't a girl, but he knew Denton would look. When he looked, Frost said, "Aww, man, you missed her! She was hot as hell; I bet she was hotter than that chick you scored with the other night."

Denton smiled and sat down, "No way, man, you're talking to the man; and even if she was, I could get her too." Denton settled into his seat and started to brag about his conquests. Frost pretended to idolize him a bit and then winked at Julius.

Magnus tried not to think about Denton or the fact that this freedom was only temporary. He thought about events yet to come. He wondered, could he really trust KM Lockhart? He also pondered if he had a chance in hell at acquittal. He sighed over the possibility of never knowing Arie's fate, but then his thoughts were interrupted.

"Denton must have used too much energy," Rutger laughed and called out. "Look at him, he passed out that quickly."

Julius smiled and said, "Good work, Frost."

"Yup," Frost replied with a smirk. Julius stood up and handed Magnus a bag. Magnus took one whiff and smiled.

"Sweet," he said as he took a bite of the cheeseburger inside.

The rest of the ride was fairly uneventful. Once they returned to the detention center, they checked Magnus back into his "suite" and returned to their duties. Before Julius left, Magnus asked him when he would get to see his brother. Julius said that they would notify him tomorrow. Julius asked if Magnus was anxious to be reunited with him. Magnus replied that he was anxious to get some answers. Julius was a bit puzzled but didn't continue the conversation. He had some work to do. Magnus thanked him for the burger and then retired to his familiar gray-sheeted bed.

Chapter 9
THE MEETING OF IDEAS

The next morning was cloudy. If the sun was up, there was no way of telling. From the corner of his bedroom, Joseph Warren sat peering out his window. He hadn't slept much during the night. His back was stiff and his eyes were dry; in short he was a mess. The alarm clock had sounded at seven, but two hours later it was still ringing. Joe hadn't budged an inch even to turn it off.

A strange growling noise emanated from his stomach; hunger had finally caught up with him. He wanted to move, but his body was slow to respond. He started with his arms and then eventually slid his body toward the bed, where he grabbed his blanket and pulled himself to his feet. As he dragged himself toward the bathroom, his doorbell rang.

Joe stopped and headed toward the front door. As he approached, he heard knocking. "Who is it?" he called out. There was no response. He got to the door and looked through the peephole. The image was blurry. As his eyes focused, Joe noticed a middle finger sticking up at him. Slightly stunned, he took a second look and saw the smile of a familiar face: Sharon. He cracked the door, leaving the chain on. "Can I help you, madam?" He said jokingly.

She replied, "Yes. Can I come in?" Joe thought for a moment and then closed the door, removing the chain.

"Well, thank you, sir," she jokingly retorted.

Sharon entered the third-floor apartment somewhat cautiously. This was her first time visiting. She surveyed the room and quickly learned that her coworker was a slob. She stared at a half-full pizza box sitting on his coffee table. Then she noticed a pile of laundry tucked under the couch. There were posters on his walls and various guy magazines thrown around the room, not to mention a pile of dishes in the kitchen sink that seemed to be alive with dirt. Sharon also noticed that somewhere under the mess was a hardwood floor. *Well,* she thought to herself, *this place isn't a complete disaster.*

After opening the door, Joe had made his way to the bathroom. There, he started to clean up a bit, realizing that he must have looked like crap. Sharon, still slightly apprehensive, continued through the apartment. She got a peek at his bedroom and turned away, slightly blushing. *Those were definitely unmentionables,* she thought to herself. She kind of smirked at the animal patterns on his boxer briefs.

"Joe," she called out, "are you hungry?" With his mouth full of toothpaste he called out yes. "Let's go to a diner then," she said.

Joe had started to shave and hadn't heard her say that. He opened the door and stuck his head out, saying, "Why don't we go to a diner?"

She looked up and said, "Great idea."

Joe tucked his head back in the bathroom, and then Sharon heard him start the shower. She decided to use this time for a more thorough investigation. Curiosity was calling her; she couldn't ignore it. She walked up to the shelf and saw a few trophies for soccer and baseball that looked decades old. She also noticed some pictures of Joe standing next to friends and people she assumed to be family members. She noticed some bills sitting on his kitchen table. She peeked at those and thought to herself that at least he had cable. She turned on the kitchen sink to wash her hands and heard a scream come from the bathroom. Then she heard Joe call out, "Don't mess with the water while I'm showering!"

She felt bad but then did it again quickly and called out, "Oh, sorry!"

Continuing with her survey, Sharon made her way to a closet and decided to snoop. Luckily, she hadn't opened it all the way. An avalanche had almost toppled down on her. The amount of junk was ridiculous, she thought. Then she called out, "Joe, I think you need a maid." Under her breath she mumbled, "Or a wife." She smiled and decided she had had enough sleuthing for the moment. She found a clean spot on the couch and sat there awaiting his return. She heard the shower turn off and then the toilet flush. Then she listened to his gargling. Finally, a very wet detective emerged and scurried into his bedroom, closing the door. Sharon blushed after getting a glimpse of his bare, muscular chest.

Joe yelled that he would just be a minute. He started to search for some pants that were clean, but the best he could do was a wrinkled pair of stone-washed blue jeans. Putting them on, he grabbed a dusty brown collared shirt and squeezed his head through the top. He then scrambled for his belt, wallet, cell phone, and keys. Then, jetting to the mirror, he fluffed his hair and finally joined his company in the living room. Seeing that Sharon was patiently waiting, he asked smugly, "Was it worth the wait?"

She twisted her face and replied, "Due to the fact that I wouldn't have been seen in public with you before, yes." She stood up and started moving toward the exit. Joe looked back to see if he had forgotten anything. Sharon paused and said, "If you forgot something, you won't find it in this mess!"

"Ha, ha," Joe said sarcastically.

Together, they left the apartment and started on their way to the elevator. Sharon's car was parked outside the front steps of the building. He told her it was a nice looking ride. It was a red, two-door coupe with white leather interior. Joe sat on the passenger side and was pleased. The seat felt plushy and comfortable. Sharon snapped on the radio, and Joe asked her what her favorite kind of music was. She replied, "Punk," and then he told her that she was a punk. Joe then shared that he was an easy listening and jazz man. He asked if he could change to one of his favorite stations. Since she was pretty happy with the overall situation, Sharon allowed him to tune to what she considered to be dull music.

They drove for about fifteen minutes before she turned into the local diner. Interestingly, the diner was called Culinary Providence. Sharon giggled but didn't share why. The diner's named amused her. She thought that perhaps she could use a little divine intervention to get Joe to favor her.

They parked and walked into the quant establishment, which was designed to look like an old sixties-style restaurant. When they entered the front door, a woman with dark curly hair asked if it was just the two of them. They nodded and proceeded to the booth where she led them. Both started perusing the menu. Joe had lifted his menu and was hidden behind it. Sharon got annoyed. "Do you know what you're going to order?" she asked him.

"Yeah," he replied and then peeked over his menu.

Sharon looked him right in the eyes and asked the question that had been plaguing her all morning. "Do you really want to be off this case?"

Joe was silent. He had purposely been avoiding the topic. His eyes became glazed. Then in a trembling voice, Joe asked, "Sharon, can we just eat? I was up all night thinking about this and I need to just put it out of my head for a bit."

She looked at him and said, "Joe you can't ignore the situation. The chief is going to reassign this case to somebody else. I think Chuck would have wanted you to do this for him."

The waitress came to the table with drinks. Joe took a sip of the tea that was now in front of him. He closed his eyes and started to speak in a very low tone. "I just don't know if I have the objectivity required for this; this guy knew every move we were going to make before we made it. Not only was he able to commit the crimes, but he had time to fuck with my head too. The squad car exploded and five people are dead, Sharon. Maybe if I had been on the ball, it would have only been two. We should have seen this guy's pattern. He practically wiped out Chuck's whole family!"

Sharon interrupted. "Joe you're best qualified person for this; everyone knows it." She paused then continued. "Listen, we are all with you. I talked to the chief. He said if you called him today he would keep you on the case conditionally." Sharon told Joe that the condition was that he would have to have her as a partner.

Joe looked at her like she was crazy. "Haven't you heard what I've been saying?"

Sharon placed her hand on his, looked at him in a way that only a person who truly loved another person would, and said, "Joe, I believe in you."

In that moment, Joe completely forgot everything and realized that Sharon really felt something for him. He smiled at her, and then the waitress came back again and the moment was over. Sharon let go of his hand.

Joe sighed and said, "Let me call the chief." But then he said, "On second thought, let me eat first. I'm starving over here." Sharon giggled at his cheesy humor. Joe thought to himself that his life was crazy. He couldn't think straight anymore. Here he was sitting across from this beautiful woman who obviously had feelings for him. For the moment, at least, she made him forget that he was probably facing the most stressful and difficult case of his life.

Joe took a bite of one of his sausage patties and started to wolf down the eggs he ordered. Sharon watched him, wondering what his next move would be. After a few moments, he placed his credit card on the table and smiled at her. Sharon quietly sipped her coffee, trying not to blush. The two of them didn't need to speak; it was understood that despite the circumstances they were both happy in the moment.

Joe stood up, stepped outside, and dialed the chief on his cell. It rang a few times, and the chief's voicemail came on. Joe didn't want to leave a message, so he decided to try again in a few minutes. Sharon watched as he stood outside the diner. She thought to herself that the aggressive move she made had finally caught Joe's attention. Her feelings had been lying in wait for a long time. She couldn't help but smile like a teenager on a first date thinking about it.

Joe returned from outside. Sharon stood up and asked what had happened. He told her he didn't like voicemail. She smiled and grabbed her coat. The two them finished paying and left the diner.

Driving down to the station was uneventful. When they parked outside the precinct, Sharon looked over at Joe from the driver's seat and said, "Listen, I know this is hard on you—it's hard on us all—but I think we owe this to Chuck."

Joe looked back at her said, "I know; I just needed to be reminded of that." Courageously, he took her hand and thanked her.

The two walked through the lobby to the elevator. As soon as they got to the eighth floor, Chief Frank yelled for Joe to get in his office. Joe pulled open the door. "OK, hot shot," the chief blurted out, "What are you, a fucking rookie? I don't even know where to start. You blew up a fucking squad car! With evidence in it, no less! You scared the living shit out of those kids! Not to mention we have more murders on our hands—lots and lots of related murders!

What the hell is going on with you?" Joe started to speak but as always the chief interrupted. "Then I get this call that my main detective is fucking flaking out on me! You can't flake out on me now, Joe. You've got to keep a straight head. I've been thinking that maybe you're right. Maybe you should be off this one. Never thought I'd say it, but you're starting to crack under the stress."

Joe stood straight up and said, "Look, chief! I changed my mind. I'm going to do this for Chuck. I'm not going to let it get to me anymore. I'm going to get that bastard and bring him in!" Robert Frank sat in his chair, spun around, and thought quietly for a moment. This was the first time someone had spoken up to him, and it annoyed him. The phone rang and interrupted the silence. He picked it up. "Yeah, this is Chief Frank. Yeah, well, hurry up! We don't have all fucking week. OK, fine, *get it done!*" The chief slammed the phone down on the base so hard that Joe jumped a bit.

Chief Frank was no fool. He had a lot of confidence in Joe's ability. He turned around and said, "Look, Joe, I'm going to give you one more shot at this one. I don't want to hear about any more cars exploding. From the report that was logged, it seems this guy is gone for now. Let's hope he's not smart enough to skip town. I want you to figure out the motive behind these attacks. Maybe then we can pin down this fucking culprit."

The chief paused and then continued, "By the way, Sarah Rivera is here. I want you and Officer Baker to question her. See if you can get any clues. Then I need you to take her to a safe house. I want a protection unit around her for the next ninety-six hours. Every other member of her family has been hunted down, so we need to keep her safe.

Joe said, "Thank you, sir," and began to walk out.

The chief let him walk five steps, giving him the false impression that the lecture was over. Then he blurted out, "I'm not done you yet, hot shot! If you think you can get off that easy, you're crazy. I'm sending you to see the local cop shrink, just to be sure you're OK, and I'm assigning you a partner."

Joe said, "What?!" Then, more calmly, he said, "Sir, I have never needed a partner before. When I need backup, I call for it."

"Shut up, Warren; it's just for this case. Besides, you're lucky—I'm giving you one of the cutest girls on the force as your partner. You should be thanking me. The way I see it, she is already knee deep in this case. So maybe with her help you can keep things from *blowing the fuck up!*"

Joe started to respond, but the chief said, "Not another word! Now get fuck out of my office! Dr. McPherson is waiting for you on the third floor in room 324. Don't BS her either; if she tells me you are unfit your ass is off this case!" The chief stood up, lightly shoved Joe out of the office, and slammed the door. He grabbed a Cuban cigar and starting smoking it. Then he let out a relaxing sigh. He was impressed with himself and the power he commanded.

Joe walked down the hall and glanced over at Sharon, who was busy on the phone. He frowned and continued to his office. The idea of talking to a shrink was not very appealing. Sharing his feelings wasn't exactly his idea of a good time. Joe sat down in his chair and started to drift off, looking around his office. It was pretty empty, he thought, compared to the chief's. And it was smaller. Joe looked at the picture of him, Sharon, and Chuck from last year's company barbeque. It depressed him as he was reminded of how Chuck looked sprawled across the hood of the squad car.

There was a knock at his door. He looked through the window and saw a feminine outline. "Sharon?" he called out. "I need a few minutes here." The door opened and a sleek, sexy, brunette wearing glasses walked in the room. Joe's mouth hung open for a second. She spoke curtly, "Detective Warren, you were ordered to come to my office. Why didn't you obey?"

Joe was still reacting to her appearance. "Excuse me—who are you?" he barely uttered.

She was still annoyed when she replied, "I'm Doctor Sonya McPherson, and I don't like to be kept waiting, and so if you'll accompany me back down to my office, please, I would appreciate it."

Joe sprang up and started to walk toward the door. They caught the room's attention as they made their way to the elevator. It especially did not escape the attention one Officer Sharon Baker. In fact, she almost jumped up before gaining control over her emotions. Other men around the office were following the doctor's movements with their eyes. Sharon noticed this as well.

The two of them stepped into the elevator. When they arrived on the third floor, Joe looked around a bit, trying not to stare at the doctor's tight skirt. Joe had never been to the third floor before. It was more like a typical office layout then the rest of the precinct. Sonya said, "My office is right down here." Joe didn't respond; he just continued to walk behind her down the hall toward a glass door that said Dr. McPherson. She pulled out a key and opened the door. The phone was ringing. She skirted over and picked it up, speaking much more gently now. "Yes, hello? Yes, Robert, he's here. You were right; I ended up going there to get him. Yes, I'll send you my report as soon as we are finished here."

She sat down at her desk and stared at Joe. Then she said, "Listen, I understand that you don't want to be here, but this is a routine thing." Joe's face contorted. "Shall we get started?" He nodded.

"Well, Detective, I have some formal questions for you. To begin with, how did you sleep last night? You look pretty tired." Joe was hesitant to respond. She said, with a smile, "Are you trying to make my job harder? Think about it from my point of view. I have to go through this with tons of employees, and none of them like it."

Joe thought of a wiseass response but didn't say it. Instead, Joe decided to respond, "I didn't sleep so well last night, but what do you expect? There's a psycho out there killing people."

Sonya nodded and then asked, "Do you feel you can handle this case with your personal involvement with the first victim?"

Joe said, "You know what? Chuck was a good cop and a good man. He deserves to rest in peace. That's not happening until that lunatic is behind bars."

"Detective, that doesn't answer my question," she retorted.

Joe wanted to leave right then, but he knew he had to go through this inquiry. "Honestly, I'm not sure. Every step of the way yesterday that guy was ahead of us."

Sonya took an advocate point of view and said, "Well, it's natural to feel that the situation is out of your control. You are one step behind because you are trying to follow the clues left by the assailant. This may sound cliché, Joe, but you are not facing this one alone. There are many people behind you on this. Robert doesn't want to take you off this case. He just wants you to do the best you can. How do you feel about him assigning Officer Baker to be your partner?"

Joe was open about this question. "I didn't like the idea of a partner, nothing against Sharon."

Sonya continued to probe. "Do you think you'll be able to work with her effectively?"

Joe replied, "I'm sure it will be just fine. Damn, you do have a lot of questions."

She answered that with, "There's no need to act like a child, Detective. We'll get through this in no time." Then she thought quietly for a moment and said, "Well, would you feel better if you could ask me some questions too? That way this doesn't feel like a grilling."

Joe smiled at this idea and said, "OK, what's the real purpose behind all these questions? The chief knows I can handle this."

She responded that psychiatric evaluations were going to be mandatory from now on. Not just for him but for all field officers monthly.

"Christ!" Joe clamored. "You've got to be fucking kidding me."

She looked at him and asked, "You really don't like me that much, do you?" She made a little pout face and Joe smirked.

He thought to himself, *is she flirting with me? Wow!* He responded, "Well, you do come across a little bossy."

Sonya stood up and walked to the edge of her desk in front of him. Her stocking-covered legs were right in front of him. "Well, mister, you didn't show up at the appointed time. How would you like it if you were stood up?" Joe smiled again. Then she said, "Well, I guess I can be a little pushy." Sonya considered moving from the edge of her desk and jumping into his lap, but she thought it would be somewhat unprofessional. Instead, she looked him seductively in the eyes and smiled. "What do you think about this idea, Joe? You help me get through this evaluation, and I'll let you take me out for dinner tonight? Joe pondered a moment, but then agreed. Sonya leaned in and pressed her lips seductively on his lips. After that, the evaluation proceeded without any further difficulties.

Before he left, she handed him her card and wrote on the back that she would be done at 4:30 that afternoon. She circled her cell phone number and gave him the kind of smile he wouldn't be forgetting any time soon. Joe left her office still a little hot and bothered. One thing was for sure, he would never see psychological evaluations the same way again.

Chapter 10

TAKING THE BULL BY THE HORNS

"Woo Hee!" The exclamation echoed loudly from room 519 at the Radcliff Hotel. Inside the room, the Texan representing the infamous Michael J. Magnus was sitting on the edge of his bed watching television. There was no one else in the room, but that didn't stop Kenneth Michael Lockhart from hooting and raving. The stock channel was reporting a growth in the market, and KM was fired up due to the fact that his stock had gone up quite a bit. He yelled, "Woo, it's climbing!"

There was a knock at the door. KM got up and opened it, with the chain still attached. Peering out, he said, "Yup?"

The young boy on the other side responded, "Good morning, sir, I have your room service order."

KM got a big smile on his face. "Why didn't you say so, boy? I'm starving over here! Yessiree Bob, Ima hankering for some chow." KM tipped the bellhop—not too frivolously—and started to munch down his eggs and pancake assortment. Again, he spoke aloud as if someone was there. "Mm mm, this is some great chow."

KM started channel flipping and finally stopped on a news story that was recapping the bomb incident because of the trail. They were showing pictures and discussing the police theory of how the bomb spread down the entire block. According to the story, fragments of wiring and triggering devices were found on Magnus. The reporter then said that they had a special treat for the audience. In their studio today was the prosecuting attorney William G. Haight. KM ran up over to the television and turned the volume up. The newscaster began to question the now semi famous district attorney. "Mr. Haight, Do you believe that this is going to be an easy win for the state?"

The DA paused and responded carefully. "Well, Brad," he started, "no case is easy. They take diligence and preparation, not to mention a keen grasp of the law." Brad invited viewers to call in with questions on a toll-free line. One guy called in and said Magnus should fry. Another person called and said that they had lost someone and justice should be served.

Brad interrupted the calls and said that he wanted Mr. Haight's personal opinion of his opponent in the trial, KM Lockhart. Haight paused again to carefully consider his answer to the question. "Well, Brad," he began. "Mr. Lockhart is highly respected in the legal community, although maybe not in the high society community. I must say that I don't see why he would bother dragging this case out. The evidence is quite strong. Had I been the defense attorney, I would have taken the judge's plea bargain and had my client plead guilty."

Haight continued, "At the very least it would have spared his client's life. In our profession, we must take into consideration what is best for the client even if he or she disagrees. It's our job to interpret the law for our clients."

KM nearly jumped out of his skin when he heard the DA's statement. "Why that bastard," he yelled. He darted to the phone and dialed the television station. An operator picked up and answered. He yelled at her, "Little Lady, this is KM Lockhart, and you had better get me on the air right now! I will not have that bloated porpoise talk down about me like that."

The girl on the other end said, "Yes, sir." She knew that this was exactly what Brad and the executives had hoped for to boost their ratings.

The young woman waved to Brad and pointed to the phone. He knew what this signal meant, and he smirked and looked into the camera. "Ladies and gentleman, it seems we have Mr. Lockhart on the phone right now. He has some rebuttal statements for Mr. Haight." A picture of KM was flashed on the screen, and then Brad addressed him. "Mr. Lockhart, you are on the air now." There was a quick pause and then the sound of a southern accent raising hell.

"You fat cocky jackass, Haight! What is your deal? I see you kissing the media's ass." The television bleeped out the cursing, but the DA heard them. He decided he would respond with class and style to Lockhart's ranting.

"Well, Mr. Lockhart, if you handle your case like your manners, I'm sure this will be a short trial."

Lockhart didn't even wait before responding. "If you bring that horse manure attitude into the courtroom, there will be twice the amount of shit, one load of in your pants and the other from your mouth!" The audience started to laugh uncontrollably. KM took it as a personal victory. Mr. Haight just huffed on the air and folded his arms.

KM decided to attack Brad next. "And you, Brad the vulture, turning a man's life into a media circus in order to get your pitiful broadcast some ratings. At least Haight over there just *makes* the horse shit, that's better than *being* the horse shit!" The audience exclaimed, "Ooh!" Lockhart then said he couldn't stand the smell of shit and hung up.

Brad looked over at his assistant in the back and just smiled. "Can you believe that, ladies and gentlemen?" He stood up from his chair and approached the camera. "Guess we upset our Texan friend. And Mr. Haight over here was no stranger to that abuse. This trial is going to be the event of the century! Everyone should tune into WLIB. We'll keep you up to date with everything that's going on. Mr. Haight, any final words before we close today's session?"

Haight picked up his book and said, "If you want to learn about what being a *real* lawyer is like, read my book. It's called *When the Law Is Your Calling.*"

Brad took the book and said, "Thank you, Mr. Haight. The first ten people to call in right now will get a free copy of this book, along with everyone in our studio audience." There was applause and cheering. KM picked up the remote and snapped off the television. He decided it was time to get the hell out of bed and do something with his day. He walked across the nicely furnished room. The walls were covered with copies of famous paintings. There was a Van Gogh and a Rockwell, and a few others. KM had just started the shower when he got a call. It was his wife back in Texas. She yelled at him for being such a loud mouth. She was quite embarrassed by his outburst on the television.

"Ken, why don't you do a professional interview so those people will take you seriously?" He didn't want to discuss it.

"Look here, Madeline, I just don't like these folks always sticking their noses where they don't belong."

She raised her voice, "Kenneth Michael Lockhart, you do what your wife tells you and make a good name for yourself! I'm tired of being embarrassed by your big mouth!"

He was now frustrated. "Dear Lord, woman! I'm trying to get in the shower here; can you give me some freaking peace?"

Annoyed, she hung up the phone, expecting him to call her back. KM just took this as a sign to go about his business, and that's exactly what he did.

After performing the three S maneuver (shit, shower, and shave), KM got dressed and exited his room. He looked at his cell phone: ten missed calls. He just smiled and thought, *Guess she wanted to finish that conversation.* Lockhart got in the elevator and pushed the button for the lobby when a call came in from an associate of his. Apparently, they had put together some information about the bombing that he needed to see. KM exited the hotel and was picked up by a black Lincoln town car. He asked the driver to head toward the seventh precinct.

On the basement floor of the seventh precinct was a section where evidence was taken. The people who worked there catalogued and watched over materials from various cases. There were two men standing at the gated entrance—George the security guard and Bill Meyers, a local law assistant who had been assigned to Lockhart while he was here in Chicago. George had pulled out some evidence that was taken from the scene of the explosion.

Sealed in some plastic containers were some wiring and fuses. The detective who had brought the evidence in and found Magnus at the crime scene walked up to them. "Hey, George," he said with a fairly happy attitude.

"Joe," George responded, "how you doing?"

The detective shrugged his shoulders and then turned toward the other man he didn't recognize. The man stretched out his hand and said, "I'm

Bill—Bill Meyers." Joe reluctantly shook the man's hand, introducing himself as Detective Warren.

"So, Mr. Meyers, where is the famous lawyer I'm down here to speak with?" Meyers appeared a little intimidated by Warren.

"Mr. Lockhart should be here any minute. We do appreciate you taking the time to speak with us. I've been watching the news, and that serial killer guy is a menace."

Joe looked the small man of about five-foot-five in the face and said with a frown, "He's more than a menace. He's a fucking animal who will be caught." Joe was annoyed at Meyers for taking up his time. He had other things to do.

A buzzing sound could be heard coming from down the hall at the floor's entrance. KM, along with an armed escort, approached the three men. "Good day to you, sirs," Lockhart blurted out.

Bill walked up to him, shook his hand gleefully, and said, "Good morning, sir." Meyers was quite young, in his early twenties. He was short and skinny and was one of those guys who looked like they might just blow away if a big enough gust of wind came along.

Meyers shuffled back over to the other two men. "Gentlemen, let me introduce you to the famous KM Lockhart." KM wasn't very fond of the people he had to work with, but he always got a laugh from Bill's idolatry.

KM laughed and said, "Well, it's more like infamy then fame." He let out a big laugh and stretched his hand to Joe, whose mood had remained destroyed thanks to the mention of the serial killer.

Joe made a wisecrack as he grasped Lockhart's hand, "I'm not sure if I should shake hands with a lawyer. I may not get it back."

"There's a critic in every crowd," KM retorted. Then he said, "I'm not a lawyer, I'm an attorney." KM laughed out loud again while greeting George with a firm Texan handshake. No one else really got Lockhart's joke, but they all sort of smirked. "Well," KM said, "Let's get down to business, shall we? As you gentlemen know, I am representing Michael Magnus in the upcoming trial. I need to get some testimonies and see the evidence against him. So, Joe, can I call you Joe? You were there. In your own words, tell me what you saw." KM signaled to Bill to pull out the tape recorder. Joe was a little annoyed that they were recording the conversation but figured he should participate.

"Well, I was home that night. That is, until I got a call to get down to the warehouse district. There had been an anonymous tip that something was going down out there. So the chief ordered me to meet up with a few of the men and check it out. When I was on my way down there, the whole sky lit up and a big puff of smoke rose above the city. As I continued to head toward the warehouse, fire trucks and ambulances started to race behind and alongside of me."

In his mind, Joe pictured that night. The other men were all silent and attentive. There were some stools sitting inside the security post. Joe paused and sat down on one. Then they all followed suit. His voice was mesmerizing when he started to speak again. "When I got there, people were running around and children were screaming. Some people were actually rolling around, trying to put themselves out. Some of the warehouses had collapsed. We all spread out, trying to help as many people as possible. It was a mess, total chaos.

"We made our way to the warehouse, and inside there was debris everywhere. On the ground, we found the remains of a bomb. Later we discovered it was mostly composed of C4, and then as we exited someone noticed a body. It looked like it had been thrown quite a distance. At first we thought the person was dead, but upon closer inspection we found he was still breathing, and hanging out of his pockets were components for the bomb and a detonator—"

KM interrupted. "And over here on the counter—these are the articles you found?" Joe looked over and confirmed it. "Were they dusted for fingerprints?" Joe looked over to George, who pulled out the record. He read from the sheet and said there were two additional unidentified fingerprints. KM noted this and then asked Joe if he could tell him the names of the other officers at the scene that night. His reasoning was that maybe another officer might have seen someone else at the scene. He then told Joe that he would most likely be asked to testify to what he had seen that day. Joe had already assumed that would be the case and simply nodded.

KM thanked George for his assistance and then asked Joe if he would escort them up to the eighth floor so he could question some others. They rode the elevator, and when they arrived they were greeted by the chief. "Mr. Lockhart, I wanted to come over and meet you personally. I'm Chief Robert Frank."

KM stuck out his hand and with the biggest Texas smile said, "It's a pleasure, Chief. I want to thank you for allowing me to speak with a few of your men. I don't have to tell you, I'm in a hard position here and I'm trying to get my facts straight."

Bill just kind of shrank behind KM during their exchange. The chief hadn't even acknowledged him.

Pausing from the conversation, Chief Frank learned forward and gave Joe a stern look. The look implied the question, "What are you doing just standing around here?" Then he escorted KM and Bill to a room where it would be easier for them to conduct their interviews. KM also requested copies of the reports taken that day. He explained to the chief how helpful those would be. The chief acknowledged and advised Lockhart that he would get someone on it.

KM and Bill started their interviews. After a few hours, they had gathered a large amount of intelligence. They had just started to review them when KM blurted out, "Damn it! It's lunch time. I need me something good to eat." He asked Bill to get all the paperwork together. Then Lockhart walked down to the chief's office, entered the room, and looked around for a minute before speaking. "Mr. Frank, I like your style. You have a mighty fine office here." Chief Frank thanked him and then looked at him as if waiting for the next request. KM spoke again, "Well, sir, you see. Ah heck, I'm starving! If I don't get me something to eat 'round here I'm gonna blow."

Chief Frank started laughing. Outside of the chief's office, nearby officers were astonished—they never heard the chief laugh at work. KM then sat down in the guest chair in front of the chief's desk and threw his boots on top of the desk. Then he said, "Where does a chief go to eat around here?" The chief let out another laugh and then stood up.

"Let's go," he said.

"Now you're talking!" KM responded.

Bill was left behind with the paperwork. KM instructed him to organize the stuff by date before he got back. Bill was annoyed, but at least Lockhart had agreed to bring him something back to eat. While he was organizing, Bill came across something in a report. A bicycle was reported as missing. For some reason, it stuck in Bill's mind, and then he remembered why. In the newspaper, he had read that the only lead the police had on the serial killer they were chasing was that he was a bike rider.

Bill jumped up and went to tell Detective Warren about this possible correlation. He knocked on Joe's office door, but there was no response. Sharon looked up and advised him that Detective Warren had stepped out. She offered to relay a message. Bill was immediately attracted to her. He walked over to her and said, "I found something in the reports from the bombing." She took the paper from him and read it.

"Holy shit!" she exclaimed. Bill tried to introduce himself, but her jacket was already on. He asked her where she was going. She responded that she was going to see the people who had reported the stolen bicycle. According to the report, they had actually witnessed the theft. Sharon bolted out of the building right past KM and the chief on their way back in.

When they reached the eighth floor, KM tossed a bag of tacos at Bill and said, "See, son, I didn't forget ya. Bill set the food on the table and started to explain what he had found.

The chief walked over and introduced himself. "The name's Chief Frank. Good work, kid. I'm glad you told Sharon about this. Now, if you gentlemen will excuse me, I need to radio her and tell her to report her findings ASAP."

KM and Bill worked for a bit longer. They made copies and took various notes about the case. Then KM looked at his watch. It was four thirty, and he said, "Son, I'm done for today; that's that. I'm heading back to my hotel to relax and rest awhile. I expect you to be ready bright and early tomorrow morning to work on this with me some more."

Bill nodded, and together they gathered up the reports and went down the elevator to the car. KM pulled out a cigar the chief had given him earlier. He took a puff and boarded the vehicle. "Well, kid, stay out of trouble." With that he was driven off.

A few hours later, back at the Riley Hotel, a man with a strong Texas accent could be heard ranting from his room. He was asking for some bold steak sauce to go along with his huge Texas-style steak. On the other side of the table was an attractive younger lady he had picked up at the bar. "Hello, darlin'," he had said to her with a wink, followed by a prompt invitation for her to join him for dinner. She must have liked the frankness of his approach, because she agreed to let him buy her a meal. Once they sat down, she asked him if he was that lawyer on the television.

Lockhart smiled, acknowledging his greatness. "My dear," he said, "You are looking at one of the world foremost lawyers. Why, I could have gotten Nixon off if I'd been around during his presidency. Just like that Whitewater thing with Clinton. Hell, had they asked me to represent him that man would still be in good standing.

The seemingly impressionable young lady smiled at him and asked, "Hey, do you think that guy Magnus did it?" KM changed his expression. He put down his fork and looked the woman straight in the eyes. She got a bit nervous.

"Young lady, I expect you'll join me in my room for a nightcap with a question like that."

She giggled a bit but agreed. After dinner, she accompanied him back to his room. As they rode the elevator, he slapped her butt numerous times, telling her that he was the cowboy and she was the steer. They flirted around, kissing and tickling each other, until they exited at the fifth floor. When they entered room 519, he told her that he wanted to see what she had to offer. The young woman was not the shy type. She started by removing her shirt, exposing a frilly red bra, and then she dropped her pants and exposed the matching thong panties. She noticed that her playmate was aroused by her actions. KM, feeling a bit cocky, unbuttoned his shirt, revealing his body and its mixture of gray and brown hair on his chest. The woman was aroused by his older masculine physique.

Like a fine wine, KM felt that with age he had only gotten better looking, although had had to admit that he wasn't as trim and tight as a man closer to her age would be. Next, he told her that he wanted to see her run her hands up and down her body seductively. She complied, and the act increased her sexual appetite. KM kept the ten gallon hat on as he watched her. Then he began to do some self-exploration of his own. The woman moved toward him, and as she unzipped his pants he let out a Texas yell. A lot more noise followed. To any listener in the adjacent room, their stamina must have seemed enormous. As they exchanged control and various positions, the bed creaked boisterously and the walls thudded.

After their ferocious thundering, KM pulled out his cigar, feeling thoroughly satisfied. He puffed a few drags and thought about how he might ask her to leave. She was quiet also, feeling satisfied. KM turned over, his back to her, and said, "Boy, you reporters sure will do anything for a story."

She responded, "Well, how about it then?"

Lockhart laughed and said, "I think you've got all the information you'll ever need!" She stood up, cursed at him, and started to get dressed. Then she left the room with a slam of the door. KM remained in the bed. He smiled, thinking things were starting to go his way. Putting out the cigar, KM snapped on the television. There was some paperwork he needed to go through, but he was too tired complete it. He decided that in the morning he would plan for his visit to see Michael Magnus. With that thought, he fell asleep a very happy attorney.

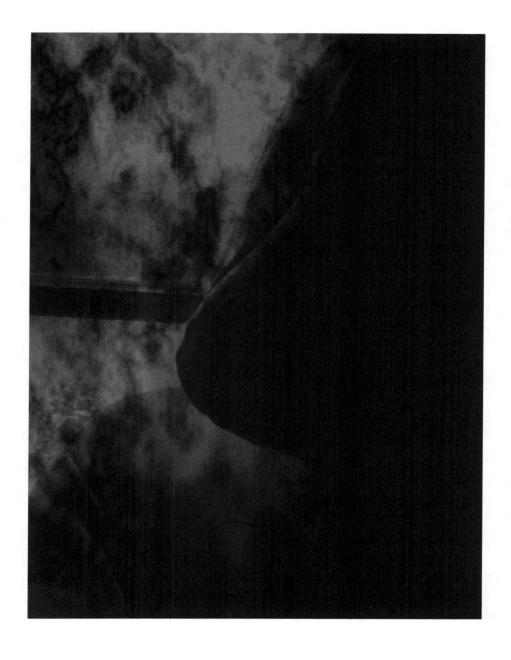

Chapter II
MORE GOOD NEWS

Flash back to 3:30! *After* reading the report about the missing bicycle, Sharon got into her car. She couldn't believe that it never crossed their minds that the attacker's bike might have been stolen. She left the station and began driving through the busy streets of Chicago. It was a good twenty-five-minute drive down to the warehouse district.

Sharon turned on some punk music and then realized she wasn't completely sure where the house was or if anyone would even be home to talk to. She radioed into dispatch. They contacted the residence for her and discovered that one member of the family was home. They also provided her with an address to plot into her GPS.

When Sharon arrived, she pulled up to a white mobile home with black shutters. It looked as though it had been years since it was painted. She thought to herself it was quaint, although it gave her a weird feeling. The home was surrounded by a small fence, and there was a driveway with a car parked in it. Directly in front of the car was a garage.

Sharon parked on the street. As she walked up to the house, she noticed some other houses down the road that had damage from the bombing. She shook her head and rang the doorbell. Without warning, a large pit bull came running at her. The dog stopped in front of her and snarled aggressively. Sharon pulled out her night stick in defense, but luckily the owner called for it to calm down from inside the house.

The front door opened, and a small man wearing glasses stood in the doorway. The pit bull quieted down and ran toward the man. Sharon watched the dog's movements and slowly approached them. "I'm sorry for my dog," the man said. "He's my brother's and is still getting used to being here." Sharon had a particular dislike of dogs, so she simply nodded at the apology while continuing to carefully watch the dog.

She spoke to the man, "Excuse me, sir, are you Alexander Blunt?"

"Yes, I am. You must be the officer they told me was coming. They didn't tell me you were so pretty though."

Sharon finally broke the stern look on her face and smiled. Alex spoke again, "He's really a pushover; his bark is truly worse than his bite. Not to worry though, I'll leave him outside. Would you like to come in for some coffee?"

Sharon agreed and entered the domicile. They sat at small table in the kitchen. She looked around and noticed a roach crawling on the floor. Her face twisted. Alex spoke again, leading the conversation as he began to pour some coffee. "So, I assume you have some news about the bicycle that was stolen from me."

Sharon responded, "Well, yes, we believe that the culprit may be using it as his main source of transportation. The reason I'm here is to get another description of the criminal. The thief might be linked to another crime we are investigating. It's a long shot, but we were hoping you could come down to the station and identify him from pictures."

Alex handed her a cup of coffee and then took a sip of his own. "Well, officer. It wasn't me that saw him; it was my daughter. In fact, it was her bike that he stole."

Sharon looked at the report, puzzled. "The paperwork doesn't mention that."

The man looked at Sharon and said, "Well, ma'am, my daughter was so scared she didn't want to leave the room. You see, he looked right at her, and she hasn't been the same since."

Sharon took a hard gulp, and with a very raspy voice she asked, "How is she not the same?"

Alex stood up and motioned for Sharon to follow him. They walked together toward the back room. He cracked the door and whispered, "Susie, are you awake?"

A little girl of about twelve put her eye right to the crack and said, "What do *you* think?" With that she slammed the door as hard as she could and locked it.

He spoke again. "Honey, we need to talk to you for a minute. There's a nice police lady who's here to get your bicycle back." There was silence. The two of them stood there waiting for a response.

"Go the fuck away!" she screamed. "Leave me alone!" Sharon was stunned at the language the child was using. Alex shrugged his shoulders and told Sharon that she had been like this for the past few weeks. Sharon asked if the bike was a small child's bike. Alex explained that it was an adult bike the two of them had shared.

Sharon was determined to get the testimony from the preteen. This whole situation was starting to seem strange to her. She motioned for Alex to approach her and whispered, "Mr. Blunt, I think something is wrong here. Are there any windows connected to that room?"

Alex began to feel a heightened concern. He nodded, and then Sharon whispered, "Keep her distracted." She then spoke aloud. "Well, Mr. Blunt. If your daughter refuses to come out, I cannot sit here and wait for her to change her mind." She winked at him and then walked heavily away.

Alex began to speak through the door. "Susie, the lady is leaving. Can you come out of there? I'm not going to ask again. The front door closed and then he continued. "See, the lady from the police station is gone."

Susie emerged from the room. As she did, she started crying and ran over to hug her father. He bent down and placed his arms around her. Suddenly, he felt something on his hand and said, "Oh, no." As he looked down, he saw blood. He was about to scream when he felt something smack his head. The last thing he saw before passing out was a dark figure walking toward the front door.

Sharon began her approach toward the back window of the house. She passed by the first window and saw the kitchen. Peering in, she saw nothing, so she continued on her way. The second window was the bathroom. There was also nothing in the room as she peered in. Finally, she came to the girl's bedroom window. As she approached, she noticed something reflective coming from inside the room. She looked a bit closer—it was the bicycle. The hairs on Sharon's neck stood on end and she immediately pulled out her gun. She approached the window, jumping in front of it and yelling, "Freeze!"

There was no movement. Then suddenly she felt a strong tingle on the back on her neck. She felt behind her. She knew that someone or something was directly right behind her. A bead of sweat dripped down her brow. Sharon spun as quickly as possible. The gun was knocked from her hand as she looked into the eyes of the hooded killer. She was paralyzed by fear; her legs gave way. She fell to the ground and passed out. In her half-conscious state, she felt something move along her back, at which point she passed out completely. The sun shone on Sharon's pale face, and a cool breeze brushed against her cheek.

Chapter 12

THE TIES THAT BOND

"Ah, this is perfect! I'll just take this squad car and ditch it when I no longer need it." Speaking the words out loud, the hooded bicyclist was now a driver. During his brief encounter with Sharon, the keys had come into his possession. He had also borrowed some of Alex Blunt's clothing. They were a little big on him, but anything was better than that smelly hoodie he had been wearing for quite some time. The attacker snapped on the CB and started listening to the police band. There was a robbery in progress somewhere downtown. Laughter overtook him. *What fun,* he thought as he stopped down the road from a tuxedo shop.

Grabbing the gun he now possessed, the man walked casually into the store and started to look around. He surveyed the place in a nonchalant manner, noticing that there were quite a few people around and taking note of where the cameras were. He dropped some clothing on the floor as if by accident and then bent down to pick it up. As he did, in a movement far too quick to catch visually, he slipped the gun under the clothing. Then he pulled the trigger through a shirt and, with pinpoint accuracy, hit a nearby customer's lower leg. The man screamed and all the shoppers scrambled in chaos. With the distraction created, the thief quickly kicked the gun and pretended to be afraid and terrified. Then he pulled out a plastic bag he had on him already and stuffed some clothes in it. As quickly as he had caused the distraction he concealed the bag and pretended to be panicked. Then he darted out of the store.

Once he was safe he decided not to head back to the squad car. Instead, he started walking down the road. There was a taxi approaching. He signaled for it, and it pulled up to the curb. The man told the cabby to drive down toward a hotel on the other side of town. The driver acknowledged and began to head in that direction.

As they made their way down the road, they witnessed police vehicles with sirens blazing heading in the opposite direction. The cabby tried to make casual conversation. He jovially said, "I always wonder where they're heading." Then he looked into the back of the car and noticed his passenger was looking out the window. "Sir?" the cabby questioned.

The passenger responded, "Keep driving and shut up!" The cabby was a little offended but continued.

They were approaching a hotel when the passenger sat up and addressed the cabby again. "Just stop here." The cabby looked in his rearview mirror. The man looked different somehow from when he had first gotten in. Then he realized that the passenger was now wearing a business suit and glasses. They pulled over to the curb, and the man reached into his wallet to give the cabby a five. The cabby was annoyed since the fair was $4.75. He said, "What, no tip?" In an instant, the pleasant face of his passenger changed and the look of death was in it. The cabby went wide-eyed and yelled, "Never mind!" The man exited the cab and the cabby screeched away from the curb. In a blink, the cab was flying down the road. That is until, the cabby smacked into a pole about two blocks down.

The businessman entered the hotel. It was a nice building and had decent accommodations. A sign on the wall, in big red letters, said Riley Hotel. The head clerk addressed the very professional-looking man headed toward the counter. "Can I help you, sir?"

The man leaned on the counter and said, "Yes, I need a room just for the night. Do you have anything available?"

The clerk punched up some data on his screen and said, "Yes, room 521 is available. We have a special today—two nights for the price of one." The man agreed and provided his name and credit card.

The clerk addressed him as he handed him the key. "Well, Mr. Blunt, I hope you enjoy your stay here."

Without responding, the man assuming the identity of Alexander Blunt rolled a suitcase that he had picked up outside to the elevator and pressed the up arrow. As he entered the elevator, a man in a ten-gallon hat and a woman also entered. The man talked loudly, with a heavy Texas accent. He grabbed the woman's bottom and yelled, "Woo-ee!"

She let out a little squeal and said, "Mr. Lockhart, you're terrible." He responded that he was just getting started. They continued to act as if they were alone in the elevator; neither of them had really noticed the annoyed-looking businessman standing on the other side.

The elevator stopped and made a ding sound. The doors opened, and KM smacked the woman's butt again, letting out another Texas yell. She went running down the hall, playing along with his roundup game. Before he gave chase he said, without looking at the man, "You see, son, that's the way to treat 'em." He then began his hooting and hollering and caught the woman outside of his room. They went in and finally the hallway was quiet again.

The Alex Blunt impostor walked to his door, which happened to be adjacent to theirs, and heard the consorting in the next room. Still annoyed, he sat on his bed and snapped on the news. This made him smile. There was a story on the recent murders. They were interviewing Chief Robert Frank about it. He told the reporter that they were following some new leads and were hoping to get a lead on the hooded killer once the detectives returned. He laughed out loud, knowing very well that they would find nothing.

Lockhart's room finally quieted down after some time, and then he heard the door slam and the footsteps of the woman walking away. A twisted thought curdled in his mind. He exited the room and quickly caught up to her. She turned and asked, "Where did you come from?"

Instead of answering the question, he said to her, "I would like you to come with me back to my room." The tone he took with her was very authoritative. She didn't like it and was about to say no when he took her neck and squeezed in a way that caused her to pass out.

He carried her quickly back to his room. Once inside, he threw her body on the bed and ripped her clothes off. She awoke as he began to force himself on her. With his glasses removed, he looked her dead in the eyes and she was paralyzed with fear. She felt a pain on the front of her neck, and then nothing. Tossing her body in the closet, he went to sleep.

The next morning, he showered and left the room very early. Checking out of the hotel, he ditched the stolen wallet, the glasses, and all of the clothing except the suit in a nearby Dumpster. The businessman then began walking. He walked for at least an hour before he knew he was getting close to his newest objective. He continued walking down a side road, unnoticed by pedestrians, until he came to a gate in front of a building. Inside was a security guard. "Excuse me, sir," he said in a pleasant tone, "I have an appointment today to see my brother."

Derrick Frost approached the man and said, "Can I have some identification, sir?" Reaching into his pocket, he handed Frost an ID card. Frost thanked him and stepped away from the gate. He looked over the ID and then radioed inside the maximum security structure. "Hey, Rutger, I've got a Mr. Darius K. Magnus down here. Is he scheduled for a visit today?"

There was a momentary pause and then Rutger radioed back, "Umm, yeah. That's an affirmative." A loud buzzer sounded, and the gate cracked open. Frost approached the man and said, "Sorry, Mr. Magnus—routine search."

"Just call me Dar," he responded as Frost began to check him for any concealed weaponry. Frost ran a metal detector around him and didn't detect anything.

Then he spoke to Dar. "OK. Please wait right here to be escorted in." Frost returned to his post but kept a close eye on Dar's movements.

After about five minutes, Julius Spencer walked across the parking lot and nodded over to Frost. Then he asked Dar to accompany him. They walked until they came up to the building. Dar peered around, noticing everything... the distance between each window, the fact that some windows had bars and some didn't. He also kept track of the number of guards.

They entered, and Julius swiped his badge, which opened a large steel door. As they continued, Julius had to badge through a few more metal doors. Some of them had windows. Finally, they stopped at room 170, and Julius asked Dar to go in and sit down. Dar complied and began to survey the room he was in. First, he looked out the window—it was not covered with bars—and figured its approximate location based on their entry point. He also spotted the hidden cameras in the room.

He walked toward the center of the room, where there was a wall set up for visitors to communicate with the prisoners on the other side. There was a telephone attached to each side of a glass window. Dar knew how it would work. He was annoyed but then decided to sit down and wait. There was a clock on the wall, and the time seemed to pass very slowly. Dar started to tap his fingers on the counter connected to the station.

Eventually, Dar heard a bang and then footsteps. A very large officer walked in the room on the other side of the glass window. He scowled at Dar and said, "So you're the freak's brother." Normally visitors couldn't hear anyone on the prisoners' side of the glass unless they used the phones, but Denton suddenly felt that Dar had heard him; he stood up and gave Denton a look that nearly made him shit his pants.

Just then, as Dar began to sit back down, he got a sixth sense. It wasn't the first time it had happened. However, it was the first time that Magnus had felt it. He entered the room on Denton's side and looked for the first time into the face of someone he had been curious about for a while now.

A smile came to Dar's face, but not the sort of smile one would expect from a person's brother. Magnus didn't return it. Dar picked up his phone and looked at Magnus. Magnus reached for his and then got a strange pain in his head. He picked it up, but found that oddly enough he was hearing things without it. Dar started to speak out loud, saying things that were completely unimportant. He hadn't known it before now, but when he'd sensed Magnus's approach he knew that telepathy was possible. It was a funny sensation for both of them. Dar had a more focused mind, so he was able to send stronger images.

A telepathic conversation is not quite the same as a verbal one. One would imagine that it would be words of a commonly expressed language, but in this case it was the language of the mind—pure imagery. Magnus was bombarded with images from Dar's mind; they were almost maddening. He witnessed the murders one by one. Each one made him more and more sick until finally he heard a bang on the glass. Whack! Magnus looked in front of him and saw a demonic image. It was like his eyes were playing tricks on him. Dar's face was green and he had reptilian eyes. Magnus felt surrounded, and his instinct was to yell, but he felt short of breath.

"Hey, Magnus, hurry up your little gay reunion." Denton's voice brought him back to reality. On the other side of the glass, sitting calmly with a smile, was the man who claimed to be his brother. It was like looking into a mirror. Magnus felt confused and disoriented. Everything that Dar had said verbally hadn't even registered in his mind, and the images he had seen were terrifying.

Dar decided to speak without imagery. "Well, dear brother, it was great to see you. I'm sure I'll be seeing you again," he pause and then finished, "real soon." By the way, don't worry about Mom and Dad. They are doing just fine." In that instant, Magnus saw a final image of his own parents strung up and hung by their necks in the kitchen he had eaten in as a child. Dar smiled and then nodded at Julius, who was at the door. As he left, Magnus began to breathe easier.

Denton grabbed him by the arm and said, "You didn't talk so much in there, freak. What's the matter, rat got your tongue?" Denton laughed, thinking it was clever of him to substitute cat with rat, being that they were in a prison.

Magnus mustered out the word *bathroom.* Denton took one look at his face and rushed him to the bathroom, shoving him through the door. Once inside, Magnus puked his brains out. He remained in the bathroom for about five minutes, trying to clean himself up as best he could. He still felt sick. Worst of all, he had no answers. In fact, he now had more questions than ever. *What the fuck was that,* he thought to himself. *Whatever that thing was, it wasn't my brother. How did it put those images in my mind? Were those images real? If so, were they past, present, or future?* Once again, Magnus felt completely out of control of the situation.

Denton was thoroughly grossed out that Magnus had puked. He walked him back to the cell and pushed the staggering Magnus in. "You better not get me sick, freako." He walked away quickly, locking the door behind him. Magnus walked over to his window. Looking out, he saw Dar exiting. Suddenly, he was thrown back into a battle of the minds. The room started spinning. Magnus was again bombarded with images of murder and chaos. He didn't know it, but he was seeing Chuck Rivera and his children being hunted down, all the way up to the murder of Susie Blunt. It was just too much to take. His feet gave way. Magnus collapsed. There he lay on the gray floor, and in that gray moment there was silence.

Chapter 13
WHERE THE LINES BLUR

Sharon awoke and found herself in unfamiliar surroundings. There was a large window to her right—the shades were drawn and the sunlight was pouring into the room. In the distance she noticed a bird flying back and forth. She looked up and noticed the ceiling. Then she heard noticed a beeping sound and turned left. There was a heart monitor connected to her. Suspecting that she was in the hospital, she looked down at her arm and noticed an IV tube in it. She tried to sit up but felt too weak. Then her eyes moved forward and she noticed a familiar person sleeping in the corner. A smile came over her face.

In the metal chair was perched the vigilant Detective Joseph Warren. He had spent the past two nights watching over her. Sharon didn't want to wake him, but then she decided that she needed to find out what was going on. "Joe," she said, and then she felt a wave of pain in her head. Surprised, she raised her right arm and felt some bandages around her head. *Oh God,* she thought to herself, *what has happened to me?* She said, more panicked this time, "Joe! Wake up."

The detective made a snorting sound but then drifted back to sleep. Sharon looked around and spotted a piece of candy on the table next to her. She picked it up and threw it at him, pegging him right on the forehead. "What? What!" Joe woke with alarm. His neck was stiff and his back ached a bit. He looked over at the conscious Sharon and forgot about his pain. Joe stood up and walked over to her. "Hey there, partner." He had an endearing tone in his voice that worried Sharon a bit. She looked at him and asked what had happened. Joe asked her if she wanted to really get into all of it right then.

She responded, "Hell, yes! Right after I go to the bathroom. Joe smirked.

He got up and started to walk toward the door. "I'll go get a nurse to help you."

A few moments later, a very pleasant woman walked into the room. "Hello," she said. "My name is Elisha Bennett. I'm the nurse assigned to assist you." Nurse Bennett rearranged the wiring so Sharon could walk with the solution bag attached to her arm. When she stood up, Sharon felt another pain in her head and flinched, closing her left eye from the pain. She walked over to the bathroom and felt very cold. There was a draft and the socks she was wearing were very thin. Realizing that she was in one of those hospital gowns, she asked the nurse if she would tie it in the back for her. Nurse Bennett complied, and Sharon entered the bathroom.

Once she was alone, Sharon walked up to the mirror and looked at herself in horror. Her hair was a mess and she had a bandage wrapped around part of her head. She splashed some water on her face, cleaned up a bit, used the restroom, and returned to the room. As she did, she asked Nurse Bennett what was wrong with her head. The nurse replied that Sharon had suffered a mild concussion and had a small knot on her head. Sharon felt her head and flinched again when she touched a raised, sensitive spot. Annoyed, she walked back over to the bed and covered herself with the blanket. She asked the nurse how soon the bandage could come off. She responded that in a little bit they would give her some ointment and she would be able to remove it. She also added that Sharon would be allowed to leave the hospital today.

Nurse Bennett smiled and jokingly said, "You were out cold during most of your visit here with us." Sharon looked at the woman and asked how long had she been there. "Two nights," the nurse replied. Sharon was stunned to learn that she had lost a day and a half of consciousness. She wanted more answers, so she asked the nurse to call in the detective and get her a blanket.

Joe reentered the room and pulled a chair up next to the bed. Sharon was now sitting up against the headboard. The nurse brought in some extra blankets as Sharon had requested and left the room. "So," Sharon began. "What happened over the last day and a half? I mean I can't believe I was out for that long."

Joe looked at her deeply and said, "Well, from what we have gathered, the Faceless Killer—as they are calling him now—was using the Blunt residence as a hideout. That symbol was carved into the wall of the back bedroom. Suzanne Blunt, the child whose bike was supposedly stolen, was stabbed and killed moments before you were attacked."

Sharon covered her mouth, appalled. Joe continued, "The father is here at the hospital; he suffered a mild concussion as well. Unfortunately, he hasn't woken up yet. After attacking you, the culprit stole your squad car and proceeded to drive it to a local shopping strip. There he caused a disturbance, shooting a local resident in the foot with a gun."

Sharon's eyes widened. "Did they catch him on film at least?" Joe sighed. The problem is the cameras didn't catch his *face* on film. We are just guessing that it's the guy because he bent down just as the gunshot thing happened. It could have been a reaction, but it seemed too quick. Plus he was the only patron missing after it happened. He was not seen shooting or anything. It seems impossible, but it's true. They did, however, find the gun on the grounds. It was your gun. Obviously, he took it from you."

Sharon's eyes began to swell. "Did they get fingerprints from the gun?" she asked in a low voice.

Joe shook his head again. "No, they found some scratches on it, but that was about it. Apparently, the guy kicked the gun away after firing it. Based on the probable trajectory of the bullet, that guy must have kicked that gun super hard. It was nowhere near where the camera saw him looking at clothing. We believe he created the diversion in order to steal some clothes and make his escape."

Joe paused, noticing that Sharon was crying. "Do you want me to go on?"

Sharon spoke in a whimpering voice. She said that she felt responsible because she let the Faceless Killer get the drop on her. Joe realized that Sharon had been through a lot, so he stood up, moved to the bed, and gave her a hug. She rested her head on his shoulder. There they sat for endless minutes in silence.

Joe's mind began to wander. Sharon didn't want to let go. Her mind was filled with all sorts of emotions. She felt vulnerable and not strong enough to carry on alone. She began to pull back; as she did, her check rubbed against his and before she could stop herself she pressed her lips to Joe's. It was a silent, soft kind of kiss that takes a person's breath away.

After a moment, they paused. Joe put his hand on her check and then leaned in, kissing her a second time. The experience was intense for both of them, like a high from a drug for those few moments. They were numb to the world and all the problems they faced. Sharon had been waiting for this moment for a long time. She almost laughed thinking to herself that it had to happen here in the hospital. Joe's mind again wandered. Two nights ago, he had gone out with Sonya. They'd had a fairly nice dinner that ended up with him going back to her apartment for coffee. He was sure that something was going to happen between the two of them, but abruptly he had received the call about Sharon's incident. When she failed to check in after three hours officers were dispatched to check her status. Joe immediately told Sonya he had an emergency. As he got up to leave, Sonya had walked him to her door and given him a seductive kiss.

Joe compared it to what he had just felt with Sharon. It was meaningless. In fact, he began to feel bad for ever going to dinner with Sonya in the first place. Sharon sensed him drifting, so she ended the second kiss. She looked at him and said, "What is it?"

Joe looked her deep in the eyes and said, "I don't want you in danger anymore." Sharon just smiled and hugged him again.

She whispered. "That's part of this job, Joe."

Joe thought to himself that he would tell Sonya he couldn't see her again. He figured it was the right thing to do, because he actually had feelings for Sharon. Joe reasoned it out with himself, thinking about how he had spent the last two nights by Sharon's side. He hadn't even called Sonya. He belonged here; he was sure of it. Coincidently, Sharon was thinking that too. She was so happy to have woken up knowing he was there to protect her. The nightmares that had haunted her were terrifying. She saw the victims walking, each of them dead and on fire. She couldn't put them out in the dream, and course the terrible eyes. All she kept seeing were the terrible eyes of the killer.

"Joe…" She started to speak. "I didn't get a good look at him. In fact, all I saw were the most terrifying eyes I've ever seen in my life."

Joe reassured her. "We'll get him. He'll slip up and we'll get him. When he does, I'll be waiting for him." Sharon took comfort in his words. She always believed in Joe. She smiled and thought of a future where she and Joe would be content together.

Abruptly, Nurse Bennett returned to the room in a frantic state. Joe and Sharon's embrace finally ended. "Excuse me, Detective," she said, "but one of the officers down the hall asked me to come get you. A school teacher was just brought in. Her name is Eileen Keller. They thought you would want to speak with her. Joe was curious and stood up immediately.

As he walked down the hall, he noticed some of his men standing outside of a room. He walked in and on a table was a thin, red-haired woman of about thirty years in age. She looked completely pale in the face. He walked over to her, and only her eyes moved as he approached. "Are you the detective?" she asked. Joe nodded. The woman said in a ghostly voice, "I saw his face, I saw his face."

"Who are you?" Joe asked. She responded that she was the second teacher on watch the day the Rivera boys had disappeared. Joe suddenly remembered that he had never spoken to the second teacher. The obvious question came out of his mouth: "What did he look like, ma'am?"

Eileen's eyes traveled around the room, finally resting again on Joe's. She said in a stern voice, "Have the rest of these people leave." Joe made a motion with his hand and the men departed the room one by one, closing the door. Once they were gone, she sat up and touched his hand. "He has been in my mind for days now, ever since I saw him. Before now, I was too afraid to tell anyone, but since I'm here and probably will fade anyway, I need to tell you, because he knows who you are."

Joe went to pull out a pad and pencil so that he could write down the description. She stopped him and said, "You won't need that." Joe was puzzled until Eileen stretched out her hand. He couldn't believe it. On her palm was the symbol. Like a scar, it was burned into her palm. As he held her arm, Joe felt temporarily paralyzed. Finally, he pressed the hand with the mark against his forehead, and there was an immediate rush to Joe's mind. He experienced disorientation and then, almost naturally, his eyes closed.

There was motion. At first it was blurry, but then it began clarify. There were buildings that seemed to be moving by at an alarmingly fast pace. Crowds of people were walking, and then everything was still. In the vision, everything suddenly focused on one person. It was a woman, and around her body was a strange, whitish-blue light. As he got closer, the woman's face became clearer; it was the teacher. The light around her body began to slowly pull him in. Then there was a brilliant flash, and the woman turned to face him. Her face was horrified, and in her eyes was a face that caused Joe's heart to beat thunderously. The light faded, and her body fell to the ground. He saw a hand touch her neck and the symbol formed on her.

The scene went dark, and Joe's eyes opened. Before him on the hospital table, Eileen Keller lay motionless. He tried to shake her and then checked her pulse. Joe called for help. The doctors and nurses rushed in, but there nothing any of them could do. It was recorded that she died at 2:00 p.m. Cause of death was a massive heart attack. The detective walked out into the hallway and then down back toward Sharon's room. He walked in and sat on the bed next to her. His eyes were blank, almost as if he was asleep. She sat up, shook his arm, and called his name. "Joe?" She called again a bit louder. "Joe!"

His head turned, and the numbness of his body caused him to just fall on her shoulders. There she held him in the cold hospital room, and there he told her that for the first time in his life he was truly afraid. The man who had once stood tall was terrified to move. Sharon held him close to her and looked out the window at the skyline. She asked him what he was afraid of, and all he could say was that he didn't know, except it wasn't human. "Not a man Sharon—it's not man at all."

Chapter 14

SINS OF A PAST LIFE

The sky was bright, but it was so foggy that visibility was almost nonexistent. The dew on the ground was still fresh and settled on the grass outside of the law firm of Shuster & Haight. The time was a quarter past one, and all morning long William G. Haight III had been reviewing reports for his pending case. The case would be coming up in just over a week. Haight, on this particular afternoon, was feeling annoyed with KM Lockhart for so rudely embarrassing him during his television appearance. *That fucking bastard!* He thought to himself. *I'll make him suffer for that.*

The best way to describe Haight's personality was a pompous upstart who always got his way by any means. He believed that he was always right, and he snidely let everyone know it. In his career, Haight had never lost a case, and that fact only added to his smugness. This public trial was not going to be an exception. Haight intended to win by any means.

As he read through his files, Haight came across photos of the incident. There were pictures of the burning buildings and of bodies lying on the ground. There was also a report detailing the explosion. He reread the account. The forensics report listed the specific items found on Magnus. These items were the sort that one might use for a crude but effective explosive. Discovered on the items were the defendant's fingerprints along with a few others that could not be identified. Haight considered the argument that most likely Magnus's accomplices had escaped undetected. He also believed that Magnus was faking his amnesia. And if he pressed hard enough he figured he could get the defendant to reveal his coconspirators.

As Haight continued to brainstorm possible ways to trip Magnus up, he was interrupted by his secretary, Patricia Zellman. She was a tall woman of about five foot eleven, and she fancied herself very attractive, especially since she was one of very few women in the office. As she walked into the room, she strutted with a confident gait. Strutting right up to Haight's desk, she leaned forward slightly, showing off her cleavage.

Haight looked up and from behind his glasses completely ignored her obvious display. "Ms. Zellman, what is it?" he said curtly. "I'm very busy today."

She returned to a more professional stance, slightly annoyed. "Well, Mr. Haight, you asked me to remind you when it was about one thirty so that you would remember to get ready for your meeting with the defense attorney." Haight looked back at his paperwork and didn't bother to respond.

Patricia stood there for a moment before stomping out of the room. "What an ass," she said in a low tone. He simply smiled and relished how he was able to get people's goats.

Thinking about how inferior the rest of humanity was to his brilliance, William G. Haight sat up in his chair and organized his desk. Then after a moment he pressed a button on the intercom, saying, "Patricia could you please let me know when Mr. Lockhart is here?"

She was stilled annoyed but responded, "No problem, sir." Haight smirked again and then stood up and walked over to his window. He peered out into the dense fog. Then he heard his buzzer. The voice of his secretary echoed through the office: "Mr. Lockhart is here to see you, sir." Haight's expression changed to disdain. He groaned and asked her to let his adversary into the room.

A familiar Texan smile came strolling in on the face of KM Lockhart. "What are you so smiley about, Lockhart? If I were you, I would be hiding and hoping that someone doesn't change their mind and arrest me for fooling around with that girl."

"Hey," KM retorted, "there's nothing wrong with a little fun as long as both parties are willing."

"Yes, Mr. Lockhart," Haight responded, "except when you're married!"

KM started to respond but changed his mind and said, "Look, chubby, I didn't come here to talk about me. You called me here to discuss the upcoming trial again, although I don't see why."

Making his way to his chair, the older of the two men, Haight, squeezed into his chair and then gestured for KM to sit across from him. "Let's try to be gentlemen here, Lockhart."

KM sat down and let out a big breath. "Fine, Haight. So why am I here?"

"Well, some rather interesting information has come to my attention that I thought you would be interested in." Haight responded with a bit of a smirk. KM raised his eyebrows as if to as the obvious question.

Haight lit a cigar and started to puff it without offering one to KM. Then very slowly he said, "Well this kind of information isn't free, Lockhart. It comes with a price."

KM started to get annoyed, but then he thought to himself that whatever Haight knew must be important. So very carefully, KM responded and said, "How do I know your information isn't a load of horse shit, Haight?"

Haight puffed a long drag of the cigar and then released it toward the ceiling and said, "What if I told you that there was another survivor of that explosion?"

KM twisted his lips and said, "We already suspect that the Faceless Killer was there."

"What if I'm not talking about him?" Haight smirked, looking KM right in the eyes.

"OK, Haight! Spill your guts before I spill 'em for you."

Haight responded strongly, saying, "First, you need to tell me what Magnus has told you. The way things are looking, he wasn't alone in this bombing. It seems he had accomplices."

KM's face twisted again. Then he said, "Looky here, Haight—I wasn't born yesterday. I can see when the dog is being led by the neck. You can try your manipulation games on somebody else. Cause this horse shit stinks, and I ain't the horse, if you get my drift."

Haight stood up and walked toward the window. "I guess I should give you more credit, Lockhart. You aren't as foolish as most people believe. I can see there's no fooling you. Why don't you just throw in the towel, though? You know that you can't win with all that evidence against him. If you want to, we can ask the judge back down from the death sentence. I'm sure she'll listen to me. Kathryn can be reasonable, especially when she believes her time is being wasted." Haight turned around and noticed Lockhart was getting up to leave.

KM said, "Haight, the only person whose time is being wasted here is me. You bring me all the way down here just to try to get me to back down. No way, chump! This trial is going all the way, and there's nothing you can do to stop me."

Infuriated, Haight slammed his hand down on the windowsill. "Goddamn it! Why can't you see that this is a good offer, Lockhart?!"

KM just laughed and said, "Man, you must be really scared, eh? What's the matter: starting to see how circumstantial your evidence is?"

Before he could respond, Haight's eyes widened, causing KM to look behind him. They were no longer alone. The room had filled with five very intimidating men dressed in black, each armed with a pistol.

One of them spoke, pointing his gun at Haight. "Sit down." Haight complied and then one of them backed KM up and shoved him into a chair.

KM wasn't as intimidated as Haight. "What do you gentlemen want from us?" he said confidently.

The leader of the group stepped forward and smacked KM across the face. "Shut up! I'm doing the talking here, Lockhart. We've already spoken to fat boy over there, but obviously he isn't convincing you."

KM looked over at Haight, and it suddenly dawned on him that these people wanted Magnus to be blamed for the crime. KM spoke again, "You boys got a lot of guts threatening two well-known lawyers like us. If we disappear, there'll be more heat on you than wood on a fire!"

The leader walked up to smack KM again; then suddenly he stopped and said, "Listen to me. You guys are going to do exactly what we say. You may be untouchable, but your wives and children aren't. Yes, we know who, what, and where on them, and we can get to them real quick." The leader took his gun, struck KM's brow, and said, "You had better watch your mouth, you wiseass Texan. My patience is very low. For now, you can go ahead and make it look like you're defending him, but when the trial comes we expect you make a few mistakes and for poor little Magnus to get the blame." We'll be in touch—room 519, is it? We've been watching you, and we'll continue to watch you."

With that final statement, the men left the room. Zellman came running in and apologized to Haight for letting them in, not that she had any choice. Then she asked if she should call the police. After a minute of heavy breathing, Haight shook his head no. "We need to think about how to handle this. He looked over to KM, who had pulled out a cigar and was lighting it.

He spoke between puffs, "What kind of corrupt shit are we dealing with, Haight?"

Haight didn't respond to the question; he simply said, "I can't risk my family, Lockhart...can you?" KM thought about his nagging wife and was about to make a joke when he remembered his eldest son and his new grandchild.

"Fuck!" he yelled out loud. "We're in a big heap of shit. I'm out of here for now, Haight. I've got to go see my client. What the hell am I going to tell him? I know for sure he's innocent now."

Chapter 15

BROKEN PERCEPTION

Lunch today was far too brief, Julius thought to himself as he returned to the prison encampment after only a thirty-minute break. He walked past a few officers and began to head up the stairs when his keen sense of trouble started to go off. The men at each of the guard doors seemed to be too complacent. As the old expression goes, things were just too quiet. After passing a bathroom that was closed off for cleaning, he approached Denton, who was starting to nod off.

"Hey, McKay, what's going on around here?" Denton looked up with an annoyed look.

"Eh," he responded.

Julius spoke again, more sternly this time. "What's going on around here?"

Denton yawned and replied, "Nothing, can't you see that?"

"What about that cleaning crew—why is the bathroom sealed off?" Julius said. He was still trying to justify his bad feeling, and he was going nowhere fast. Denton put his feet up on the desk and bellowed that Magnus had puked his brains out earlier.

Since he had gone home after escorting Darius off the premises, he didn't know that Magnus had gotten sick two days before. He pulled out his keys and decided to go check on his friend. "You going to go babysit the freak and nurse him back to health? How sweet of you, Spencer. You're a real pal, aren't ya? Maybe you could spoon feed him while you're at it."

Denton started to chortle really loud. Julius ignored him and entered the holding area.

As he walked up to the cell, Julius smelled something awful. He looked in the cell and found Magnus lying face-down in a pile of his own vomit. Julius was disgusted but immediately ran to the intercom and signaled a code blue medical emergency. In a matter of minutes, the onsite medical crew was buzzing in the main doors. While he waited, Julius opened the cage and lifted Magnus onto his bed. He smacked his face a few times, trying to get him to awaken, but to no avail. Julius checked his pulse and breathing. Thankfully, he seemed to be stable.

The paramedics came barreling in. After verifying the vitals, they lifted Magnus onto a stretcher and rolled him down to the infirmary. Julius accompanied them and waited while they examined him. The medical staff couldn't find anything wrong. The patient was hooked up to monitoring equipment.

Magnus, deep in a subconscious state, began to experience REM sleep. His eyes began to convulse back and forth at an extremely fast pace. The medical personnel didn't notice.

At first, the imagery was blank; there was only motion. He was moving through space. The stars were flying by, and he didn't know where he was or what he was heading toward. Suddenly, there was a door right in the middle of space. With slight hesitation, Magnus reached out and opened it. Behind the door was a room with a bed. And on the bed was a peculiar sight: it was him. He looked around the room and noticed that it was some kind of medical room. There were things connected to his body and strange people moving around him. He moved closer and then felt a pull. Before he knew it, he was pulled into his own body, and then he woke up. *What an odd dream,* he thought as he regained consciousness, until he opened his eyes and saw that the room he was in was the same as his dream. For a moment he paused and was a bit frightened.

The medical staff noticed that he had regained consciousness. One of them asked how he was feeling. Magnus couldn't bring himself to respond to the question. He was still dazed. Taking a deep breath, he got a whiff of the smell of vomit and started coughing. He coughed again and thought that a wet cloth would be useful. One of the attendants walked up to him and handed him a cloth. *How convenient,* he thought as he proceeded to wipe his face. When he was done cleaning himself, Magnus thought about how thirsty he was. A nurse handed him some water.

She spoke very pleasantly to him. "Hello there, are we feeling better?"

Magnus smiled. He started to speak but then she interrupted, saying, "I'm Nurse Wood." Nurse Wood was a very attractive African American woman. She wore glasses and had long black hair and beautiful brown eyes. Aside from that, she had an extremely pleasant way about her. Magnus hadn't spoken to a woman in quite some time, and it surprised him how nice this one was being to him. After all, the entire city was calling him the Chicago Bomber. It seemed odd. She stretched out her hand, and when he returned the gesture she grasped both of his hands and said, "Don't worry—everything is going to be OK." In that instant, Magnus's mind was flooded with the memory of his encounter with Dar. He sat there stunned until a single tear rolled down his face. Soon more followed.

It was the first time he was able to react to the sight and knowledge of his parents' demise. As an only child, Magnus was very close to them. He spent much of his time helping them the best he could. Sometime earlier, it had occurred to him that something must have been wrong, because after a month they hadn't come to visit him. Their death seemed so real. It was a terror.

As if she knew his pain, Nurse Wood gave him a hug and sat with him for a while. Once he finally gained control over his emotions, she stood up and left.

Magnus lay there for some time before Julius came and told him that had a visitor. Never before had Julius seen the face Magnus made. Julius couldn't help but laugh at his friend's reaction. "Shit! I thought *I* hated lawyers." Magnus's expression changed to confusion. Then he remembered that KM Lockhart was due to show up and discuss the case. Julius asked Magnus if he could walk. Still feeling odd, Magnus looked down at the floor and turned, placing his feet on the floor. He stepped extra hard a few times and then jumped up and down before responding that yes, he could walk.

Julius started to laugh again and said, "Well, let's go then; that crazy man is going to start talking to me if you don't get in there fast." Magnus chuckled, forgetting his predicament briefly. They walked down the hall into another room.

As they approached, they could hear the loud voice of KM on the phone: "Yes, the girl is just fine. No I don't know how she got into that closet. Yes, I'm willing to come down and testify to that. Shit! You people drive me nuts." KM remained on the phone for a few more minutes while the two men entered the room.

Julius told Magnus he would be back in a while. Magnus sat down at the table and sipped a cup of water that was waiting for him. Eventually, his mind began to wander. He thought maybe he was going crazy. First, he lost his memory and wound up in prison. Then after a month, he learned that he was accused of blowing up a big chunk of Chicago. Not that he really knew why he was in Chicago. And now, here was this psycho claiming to be his brother, and he had some kind of attack. It was all very confusing. He felt like reality was slipping from his grasp.

"Son, Mr. Magnus, is anyone home over there?" KM had completed his phone conversation and noticed that Magnus was drifting. Magnus turned and looked at KM, annoyed. He had seen a copy of the newspaper.

"Mr. Lockhart, are you doing anything to work on my case? I read that article in the newspaper. It seems to me you are partially responsible for that woman being attacked. What kind of man are you?"

KM leaned back and put his feet on the table. "Son, who are you to be telling me anything? You are sitting in here on trial for blowing up half of this God-damned city. You let me worry about my business, ya hear me? And as for your trial, if you don't like the way I'm handling it, you can try to find yourself another lawyer."

Magnus was still annoyed, but he knew that finding someone even willing to listen to him would be next to impossible. KM leaned in and said, "Look, son, shit happens to everybody. You were in the wrong place at the wrong time, and maybe so was I."

Magnus sighed and sat back in his chair. "I just want out of this place. I'm beginning to forget what it's like on the outside." KM paused a moment and thought back to what had happened in Haight's office.

Both parties were holding back information. Magnus was unsure if he should share the experience he'd had with Dar, and KM did not want to let on that there was a possibility that he might not want to represent Magnus anymore. He thought to himself that when it came to his son and grandchild, nothing else mattered.

Magnus interrupted Lockhart's thinking. "What makes you so sure I didn't do it?"

KM looked up and said, "Well, it's the way the prosecution is sweating. They are itchy to blame you and forget the whole matter, which says to me that there's a cover-up going on."

Magnus looked up and said, "A cover-up?"

"Yes," KM responded. "I don't know if you know, but I gather since you read about me you must have read about that serial killer out there. It seems as though that same man was there during the explosion." Magnus's face lit up. KM continued, "Well, son, an officer stumbled on his hiding place a few days ago after tracking a bicycle theft that happened the night of the explosion. She was injured but survived the encounter. Either way, this killer was at one point traveling by that very same bike. It's speculated that he stole it on the night of the bombing to get away."

After KM filled him in about the incident, Magnus asked about the killer. Pulling out a fresh cigar, the lawyer sat back and said, "Well, if they knew more about that lunatic they would have caught him by now. They call him the Faceless Killer because no one has seen his face and lived to talk about it. It's either that or the police around here are just incompetent. Back in Texas, that boy would have been tarred and feathered by now…if ya get my drift."

Magnus gave KM a strange look, because he had actually pictured in his mind someone getting covered with tar and having feathers dropped over them. "Lockhart, this is all well and good, but how's does it help me?"

KM just shook his head. "You see, it's the first step to unraveling this mystery."

Magnus responded with a sigh and said, "Do you think you'll have a strong enough case by the end of next week?"

KM smiled and said, "You're in good hands, Mr. Magnus. I'll make sure this is an airtight defense. That's a hell of a lot more than I can say about the prosecution's case. Their case is as holey as the Bible." KM let out a big laugh. He knew his joke was a little corny, but nevertheless he was going to enjoy it.

Magnus simply shook his head. KM stood up and stretched out his hand. "This has been a very productive first meeting," he said. "I'll be back in at least two more times before the trial day, and don't worry, I'll definitely keep you posted."

Magnus stood up and shook hands with KM, looked him right in the eyes, and then knocked on the door. Julius came into the room to escort Magnus back to his cell. As they were walking, Magnus could feel his faith in KM wavering. He decided he was going to have to take matters into his own hands.

Julius had been silent for most of their walk but finally decided to speak his mind. "Magnus, what the hell happened with that visit?" Looking up at the only friend he seemed to have, Magnus just shrugged his shoulders. There was a pause again before Julius spoke again. "There was something really strange about your brother, Dar. I think he even irked Denton, which is saying a lot." Magnus was about to answer when he considered what Julius would think.

They would lock me up forever, he thought.

Julius continued, "Listen, you know you can tell me what's going on and I won't tell the others. I just got a bad feeling about all this." Magnus looked over at the man, who seemed genuinely concerned.

"Julius, I don't think that man was my brother."

Julius stopped walking. "What do you mean? He was your spitting image—"

"I know, but when I was talking to him I got this sick feeling inside, and that's what made me puke. I know this is going to sound crazy, but I think he's killed a lot of people, including my parents," Magnus said.

Julius's face became more concerned. "How do you know all this, Magnus? We recorded your conversation, and there was nothing on it. Except him going on about some girl he was looking for."

Magnus's stomach dropped. He realized that he had no recollection of the actual words that had come out of Dar's mouth during the whole telepathic event. They took a detour and the two of them entered a room Magnus had never seen before. A small man with square spectacles and an old-fashioned uniform was sitting on a stool. "Hey, Butler," Julius called out. "Can you play that conversation for me and Magnus from when his brother was here? I know this is breaking the rules, but this is just between the three of us. I need Magnus here to see and hear this."

Butler was a squirrelly little guy, so when he responded it was out of fear. "If-f-f-f I do you-u-u-u won't tell-l-l-l Denton, right?" Julius winked at him. Butler rotated on his stool and pressed play. They looked at the video monitor, which showed the visiting room. At first the double-sided room was empty, and then Dar entered his side. It was odd—for some reason, Dar's face was blurry on the video. Magnus saw how Dar paced the floor a few times before sitting down. Then he saw Denton open the other side, and he almost laughed at Denton's reaction to Dar's stare down. As soon he saw himself enter the room, Magnus saw something that made his stomach turn.

The others were apparently unable to see it, but there was a strange bright cloud of light coming from his body and a much larger dark cloud from Dar's body. The two clouds nearly filled the room. Magnus saw the auras collide as he sat down in the video. Then he witnessed the result—himself becoming stunned. Magnus looked over to Julius and Butler. Neither of them had any reaction to the strange things Magnus could see. He returned his focus back to the video.

Dar became to speak, and his words sent a chill down Magnus's spine… the kind that paralyzes a person entirely. "I am searching for her too; I'm very concerned about Arie, and you know exactly what I'll do when I find her— don't you, dear brother? Since you care so much about her, I feel like it's my obligation to find her for you." Dar went on a bit longer before saying, "Well, I guess you have nothing to say; I suspected as much, and don't worry about Mom and Dad."

Magnus's breathing had become heavy. He needed to sit down. He panted as he spoke to Julius. "Julius, he's going to kill her; we've got to stop him. We've got to stop that…that thing from killing her." Butler looked at Magnus like he was crazy. Julius thanked him and reminded him to keep this between them.

He then walked Magnus back to his cell. Julius spoke in a tone Magnus had never heard from him before. "Listen, a friend of mine is a detective. I'm going to have him check out your parents' place. As for Arie, I'll do some checking and see if there's a missing person's report on her. If there isn't one, I'll make sure to file one. I know that this isn't much, but it's the best I can do to help you for now. Most importantly, you've got to keep quiet. If you start spouting stuff about murders they are liable to think you did them, and you already have enough shit on your plate you didn't do."

Magnus agreed, thanking him for all his help. Then Julius walked away. Magnus walked across the cell and looked in the mirror. He sighed and splashed some water on his face from the recently cleaned sink. He felt an odd itch on his arm. He scratched it and then continued to look in the mirror. Unexpectedly, that same spot started to burn. Lifting up the sleeve of his shirt, he revealed his tattoo. It was slightly red from the scratching, but more importantly, it looked different. The darker side was taking up two thirds of the circle, which had once been in balance. Magnus knew he was losing it—light was becoming dark, order was becoming chaos, and now clarity had become insanity.

Chapter 16

A DARK MOURNING

The next morning was very cloudy. It looked like it was going to rain, but the sky was still holding it back. Joe was in the shower, and his mind was cluttered. The time was about seven thirty, and he had to get down to the station early. Later that day, he had some unpleasant business to deal with. He snapped on the bathroom stereo, trying to lose himself in the music.

The night before, Joe hadn't slept very well. After dropping Sharon off at her apartment, he had gone home to sleep, but nightmares had plagued him. Keller's death had freaked him out. The symbol, the vision…what did it all mean? He felt that the answers were out of reach. Joe finished showering and walked across the hall into the bedroom, where he looked in his closet to pick out some clothing. He found a black collared shirt and black slacks. He hated to wear all black, but he knew today called for it.

Getting dressed only took Joe a few minutes. After he was done, he entered his kitchen and started to make a cup of tea. He looked over at his phone and saw five messages waiting on his answering machine. He pressed play and the first message began to play. "Joey, its Mom. I just wanted to let you know that if you need to talk after the funeral tomorrow, I'm here for you. Give me a call when you get this, OK?" Joe skipped to the next message; it was Sonya. "Hey there, cutie, it's Sonya. I had a really good time the other night. I know you've been busy, but how long are you going to keep a girl waiting for a callback?" Joe just placed his hand on his forehead and thought about how he was going to handle that situation.

He sipped his tea as the messages continued. "Hey, Joe, this is Chief Frank. I think it would be best if you came down to the station in the morning. We are all going to drive over together. OK, see you tomorrow." The chief's tone was not his normal harsh, scolding voice; he suspected that even the chief had a heart. The fourth message began to play. "Joe, this is Julius Spencer over at the District East Detention Center. I need to speak to you directly. If you could call me back at the DEDC, that would be great. I'll be here until eight o'clock tonight, and I'll be here starting at seven tomorrow morning. Thanks." Joe stopped the messages.

He picked up his receiver and called the DEDC. "Yes, this is Detective Joseph Warren. I'm looking for Officer Spencer, please." The attendant on the other end asked him to hold, and with a click Joe was listening to some annoying hold music. Eventually, the phone went silent, and then he heard some people talking on the other end.

Finally, he heard a familiar voice. "Officer Spencer here."

"Hey, Julius, this is Joe Warren returning your call. How you been?"

"For the most part, same old shit. Some information came my way, though, and I think it might tie into the homicides you've been investigating."

Joe sighed. He had hoped to avoid the topic this morning, but of course it was impossible. "OK, Julius. Fill me in." Julius began to explain that his current assignment was guarding Michael J. Magnus. Joe was obviously familiar with him. Then Julius told him how a guy visited who looked like Magnus's twin but had a very disturbing manner. He explained how Magnus got a sick feeling from being around this guy and that they couldn't verify was his brother. Joe was still confused until Julius told him that Magnus believed his parents were murdered by this guy.

Joe started to piece it together. If the MO was the same on the parents' murder, then that would confirm that this guy Dar was most likely the Faceless Killer. Joe knew all too well that if it was the same killer, the strange symbol would be present somewhere at the crime scene. Either way, it was a possible lead. Julius also told Joe about a girl both men were looking for and how she might be another victim or lead. Joe took note of everything and then thanked Julius for the tip. He also asked Julius if he could schedule a time to come down and speak with Magnus the next day. Before replying, Julius explained to Joe that he believed Magnus was not guilty of the bombing. His profile just didn't fit the bomber type. But his supposed brother's sure did.

Joe understood and told Julius he would get back with him soon. They disconnected, and Joe grabbed his jacket and started toward the door. Then he remembered that there was one more message left on the machine. He decided he would listen to it later. Exiting his apartment, he passed by a few people, and one of them gave him a weird look. Joe paid them no attention and got into his car. Typically, Joe would turn on the jazz station and strum along with the beat, but this morning was different. He drove in silence.

Looking ahead, he thought about how long it would be before the rain stopped falling. There were people scurrying through the weather. Joe noticed them as he sat at a red light. He rolled down his window and took a deep breath. There was a slight jingle noise. Joe looked over and saw a bicyclist riding by. He jumped in his seat, but then he looked harder and realized it was a kid riding. The light turned green and he proceeded on.

The seventh precinct parking lot was fairly empty. It was the weekend after all. Joe parked in front and climbed the stairs to the entrance. Taking the elevator to the eighth floor, he was greeted by the rest of the team. Some of them were dressed in black; others were full uniforms. Sharon was at her desk working on some things. Joe smiled at her and she reciprocated. Then he continued to his office. The door was locked this time. Fishing for his keys, he saw someone approach him out of the corner of his eye.

"Hey, Joe, after you get settled in I want you to come down to my office, OK?" Robert Frank was still talking in a subdued voice. Joe agreed and entered his office. It was, of course, a mess. He hadn't spent much time cleaning it since the case had begun. Joe picked up a newspaper, flipped through it, and continued to straighten up. There was a tap at the door. Joe looked up and was not surprised to see Sharon. He acknowledged her and she entered the room and closed the door behind her.

Joe felt slightly funny because of their relationship and the fact that they were now in the workplace. Sharon said, "Look, I just wanted to talk to you because I know things are different now. I want us to remain professional here."

Joe agreed and said, "I know; it will take a little adjustment though." He smiled when he said it, and she was about say something else when there was another knock at the door. Joe didn't have to look to know who it was; the hair on the back of his neck stood all end and he just knew it was Sonya.

The door opened, and Sonya walked in. Joe's reaction wasn't quite what she expected. Sharon looked at Sonya and then back at Joe. Very quickly, Joe said, "Sonya, could you please give me a minute? We are in a meeting here."

Sonya was no fool. She knew instantly that Joe was trying to brush her off, so in the most spiteful manner possible she replied, "Oh, sorry—I just wanted to tell you how wonderful you were the other night. I suppose that can wait until later though." She walked out of the room, strutting the whole way.

Joe had a sinking feeling as he turned back to Sharon, who was so angry and hurt that she started bawling her eyes out. He got up and shut the door as quickly as possible. Then he knelt down in front of her, searching his mind for the best way to explain.

"Sharon," he began, but before he could continue, she got up and left the room, slamming the door behind her. Joe was about to give chase when he stopped and thought maybe she needed to blow off some steam first. He sat on the floor and leaned against his desk. Placing his head in his hands, he thought to himself, *Could this day get any worse?*

The next knock on his door was no better than the last. "Joe, I've been waiting for you in my office, but I guess we can talk here. Why are you on the floor? Get up! We didn't give you that chair for nothing."

Joe stood up and sat in his chair. The chief asked if he was comfortable. Joe responded, "I guess so."

"Good; now get up and come down to my office. I don't like yours." The chief exited the room and Joe got up and followed. On his way out, he saw that Sharon had returned to her desk. Some of the other female officers gave Joe a dirty look. Joe just shook his head. He reached the chief's office and entered, closing the door behind him.

"Look, Joe," the chief started right away. We have a few things to discuss. Joe was about to respond when the chief continued. "Number one, I'm not going to yell today because it's Chuck's funeral. So in reverence I'm trying to keep myself calm. But listen, Joe, why don't we have the guy who did this yet? There have been all sorts of leads and people have been attacked, including my people, and I'm getting fed up." Joe waited; he had given up trying to respond in the chief's office. "Joe, I expect some result next week. I want this guy locked up. He's still around; we know that much. Get on it."

Joe managed to squeeze in a "Yes, sir."

"OK then, number two: if you think as a chief I don't notice things, you're wrong. I see what's happening in your little triangle. Fix it!" The chief's tone rose a bit, but then he quieted back down. "I don't need love turmoil floating through my office that doesn't belong in the workplace. You get me?"

Joe squeezed in another "Yes, sir."

The chief got up and grabbed onto the horns of one of his trophies. "Lastly, when this case is done, you are on a leave. I mean, you were just sitting on the floor of your office. I know you're under stress but chairs, man, chairs!"

Joe's face lightened as he acknowledges the chief's attempt at humor. He stood up and said, "Thank you, sir." Joe knew exactly what his next move would be. He left the room, walked right up to Sharon, and kissed her in front of everyone. Openly, he then said, "I want everyone to know I love this woman."

Sharon smiled slightly, but then she said, very angrily, "What about that bitch?"

Joe said in the most truthful voice he could muster that he had only had dinner with her and that was it. He also said he had no interest in doing so ever again.

Sharon didn't care. She covered his mouth and said, "You better not, or you'll have a lot more to worry about than that faceless guy." The reaction of all the workers was a very loud "Oh!"

Joe sighed and closed his eyes for a moment. Then he felt Sharon hug him. The chief stuck his head out the window and yelled, "Get back to work, people! Just because you have the afternoon off doesn't mean you can slack off now!" The funeral was an hour away, so everyone returned to business as normal until then.

Chapter 17

SPLENDOR GAITS OF FANCY

The skyline was blocked by gray clouds. They sort of looked like ice cream scoops rolling through the air. The wind bustled as it blew by the face of Darius Magnus. A smirk crawled its way across his face as he stepped up to the edge of the roof of a very tall building. He looked down at all the people walking about. They were like an ant colony moving in various directions, unaware that he was watching them from above. Dar took a deep breath and filled his lungs with air. He felt stronger. In fact, every day he was getting stronger, and he loved it. The carnage simply delighted him.

With every new experience, he was overcome with feelings that no physical pleasure could compare too. Life and death were playthings to him. He felt no remorse and no regret. He simply acted. This morning, he was deeply immersed in his own ability. Things had changed for Dar ever since he had visited Magnus. He felt a new awareness. Before he could manipulate people as long as he was in close proximity to them, but now he just had to picture them and concentrate.

He had relished invading the mind of Eileen Keller. "How delicious," he said out loud. When she died, her death was different from the others. Somehow, it touched him in a new way. Looking around, Dar double-checked to be sure that there were no people near him. This location was perfect for hiding out. Dar walked along the edge with precise balance. Never did the idea of falling even cross his mind. He leaned over the edge at a forty-five-degree angle and spit downward, hoping to hit someone.

After a moment, he leaned back in, disappointed. He continued to walk along the edge. The truth was, he was bored. He wanted to do something new and exciting. *A game,* he thought suddenly. *I need a new game.* The roof was not very accommodating, but he sat down anyway and began to think about the people he had already interacted with. Then he got distracted. New clothing was necessary. The suit was becoming very dirty and smelly. Actually, he realized he needed a cleaning himself.

The excitement of something to do filled his cranium. Dar crawled over to the edge of the roof that faced another building. Looking down, he noticed an aura similar to that of Magnus, but not as bright. A vicious smile ensued as pushed his body off the edge and began to fall. The freefall motion was exhilarating. Complete freedom felt amazing. After a few seconds, he stuck his hand out and caught a ledge, which was attached to the window where he'd seen the aura. He hung for a moment before thrusting his body through the window. Inside was an elderly man.

One look from Dar, and the man had a heart attack. Like a demon, Dar hovered over the body and drained the remaining life force from it. When he was done, he checked out the man's apartment. There were no other people inside. *Perfect,* he thought to himself as he checked out his new hideout. He walked over to the window he had come through, covered it with the shades, and proceeded into the living room. There was a prehistoric television running with a game show on it. Dar couldn't help but laugh at the ridiculousness of the people. There were people on the screen running through money with glue on their bodies. After kicking the power switch, he decided to clean himself up.

Dar took a solid hour to wash completely. The human side of Dar shone through as he dried himself. He went into the bedroom and rummaged through the old man's closet to find something to wear. Most of it smelled like mothballs. But he found some normal clothes in the dresser. After getting dressed, he needed to do something with the body of the old prune. He thought about chucking it down the garbage chute, but then he figured someone would find it.

Despite the mothball smell, Dar actually liked the apartment. However, he worried that if he got too comfortable he might have to deal with a full confrontation. Despite his strength, Dar was not quite ready for that. He needed more time to work on it. He picked up the old man and threw him in the closet, figuring it was as good a place as any. Then he walked into the kitchen and opened the refrigerator. It was time to eat something. After one look in the fridge he shut it, saying, "Crap!"

Dar decided to go to the grocery store. He found some money in the old man's wallet. Since he had time to eat, he was going to do it right. He grabbed the keys and locked the door behind him. This was so much fun—he was playing house. There was a small supermarket down the road. Upon entering, he smiled at the cashier and freaked her out. Then he picked up a large pot, two lobsters, and a big tub of butter. He was on his way back to the apartment when he saw three police vehicles screaming down the road. They stopped right in front of the building. "There goes the neighborhood," he muttered.

Dar jumped in a cab and was once again on his way to find a new adventure.

Chapter 18

THE DREAM OF FREEDOM

"Look at the time. Actually, where am I?" The room was a dull color, and people were moving through it like the crowded streets of New York City. Looking around, Magnus felt lost and in despair, and then there was clarity. In the back corner was a light, and sitting in the center was someone who looked almost heavenly. She looked up and said, "Michael." His heart dropped. It was Arie. She was there, right in front of him, beautiful as ever.

He started to approach her. Almost nervous, he opened his arms and they embraced. In that moment, nothing in the universe mattered to him. For what felt like an eternity, he looked into her eyes. Then he remembered how long it had been and said, "I've been worried about you." Her expression was vacant. He shook her and yelled, "Arie!"

She looked at him and said, "I don't know where I am. How did I get here? Help me. Help me, Michael, I'm scared."

He looked her right in the eyes and said, "No matter what, I'll save you. I love you, Arie." He closed his eyes, and when he reopened them she was drifting away. He gave chase only to encounter bars. He pulled like mad at them until finally one broke.

Magnus opened his eyes and found one of the metal bars from the window in his hands. His eyes widened as he realized that the dream wasn't all imaginary. *How the heck did I pull a bar out of a concrete wall?* He thought. He stood there stunned for a minute before he decided to put this ability to the test. Placing both hands on another bar, he pulled. It didn't budge an inch. "Shit!" he said, "I *know* I did this." He got angry and kicked the nearby toilet. The pain in his foot focused his mind on the task. He pulled again, and the bar bent. Magnus smiled, and then with fantastic energy he pulled the bar completely out. With two bars gone he could actually squeeze his way through.

Magnus slid his bed over and stuck his head out the window to look down. He was three stories up. Pulling himself up, he noticed a window directly down and to the left. Thinking that he needed to act fast, he grabbed his sheets and secured them tightly to the remaining bars. Taking a leap of faith, he jumped and squeezed through head first. The sheet held, and he swung over to the lower window. He grabbed the ledge and realized he had a ten-foot drop the rest of the way. Had a camera caught him, whoever was watching would have laughed at his tumble down to the ground.

Security, at that moment, was minimal, and he lucked out that the rain and fog had left the cameras practically useless. He ran along the building away from the front gate until he came to a corner. The coast was clear. There was a fence about twenty feet high. At the top was barbed wire. Magnus sighed. He was getting soaked by the rain. He had to think quickly, so he ran up to electrified fence and threw a tree branch at it. The branch caught fire and spread very fast. He ran toward the back of the gate. Then he heard the gate being shut down. With everything he had, he ran up to it and literally ripped it open. Without a second thought, he ran out into the wild.

Thunder and lightning crackled boisterously. Magnus stopped under a tree and took a breath. Never had he run with such fear before. He thought of Julius and Denton. "Damn you, Denton!" He said out loud. "That fucker will hunt me down. I've got to keep moving." Magnus continued on until he found a road. He knew he had to stay out of sight; his face was everywhere. "Shit!" He said aloud. Magnus followed the road west, staying incognito to oncoming drivers.

After walking for a bit, he saw an abandoned car at the edge of the woods and decided to approach it. Fortune was really smiling on him—the doors were open. He got in and felt better being out of the violent storm. Temptation dared him to rest for a bit, but he knew better. He knew that they would soon be on him. Luckily, the rain would help deter them from using dogs to track his scent.

As he sat there, he decided to briefly search the car. He found an old, ratty blanket. It smelled horrid, but it was better than nothing. Throwing it over his shoulders, Magnus lowered the backseat and felt around in the trunk. His hands touched something that felt slimy but solid. He pulled back in surprise. The street light was shining down into the car just enough for him to make out that it was a hand…a woman's hand. Magnus's heart began to pound. He had to know. He just had to know.

Pulling the switch, he got out and approached the now open trunk. In one fell swoop, he grabbed the corpse's shirt and pulled it toward him. Lightning flashed and he got a good look at the face. It wasn't Arie. "Thank God," he said, letting out a sigh. He quickly realized that he needed to get the fuck out of there before someone pinned another crime on him. *Shit!* He thought. He had touched everything on the car, and now his prints were all over this whole crime scene. He was about to leave when he saw something shiny on the ground. At first he thought it was money, but on closer inspection he realized it was a key. He picked it up and went back to the car.

After looking at the fuel gauge, he reasoned that the car would be enough to get him a good distance away, assuming it would start. Once again, fortune smiled on him—the engine started right up. He didn't want to drive with the body, so he wrapped it up with the blanket and laid it on the ground against a tree. Feeling bad, he apologized to whoever it was and got in the car. In a matter seconds, he was gone.

Not five minutes later, a group of men with dogs were hovering over the body, which was identified as Patricia Zellman. Almost immediately, a call was placed to put a high alert for the fugitive Michael Magnus. It was recorded that he was traveling in a stolen vehicle and had murdered Zellman. Julius shook his head as Denton made and the call and smiled. "Well, Spencer, looks like the hunt is on. This is my favorite part, you know. I can't wait to put the laser target between his eyes, watch him squirm, and then bang! No more Magnus. I know you'll be real happy then, won't you, Spencer? You can't protect that freak anymore. He's all mine now." Denton let out a sinister laugh and they started back to the DEDC. Unknown to them, their actions were being watched from afar by five dark figures.

Chapter 19
SILENCE AND SOLACE

Earlier that day at the police station, Chief Robert Frank was looking at his watch. The funeral was about to start. "OK, people, it's time to go!" The voice echoed with power from the chief's office, and all the faces in the precinct went from being mildly jovial to being as emotionless as the face of a stone. Everyone knew what this meant. People began to lock up their cabinets and drawers. Joe observed this from his office. It definitely wasn't a typical sight. Normally, everyone was in and out at different times, but today it was more like a calm evacuation.

Things had really quieted down since Joe's outburst in the morning. For a while, the office had been gossiping about his love triangle, but now obviously more important matters were at hand. Sharon had returned to her desk and was reading through information about the murder of Stanley Kuchinsky. The male, seventy-eight years old, had been found stuffed into his closet. There were no witnesses to the crime, but there were impressions on his neck, not to mention the Faceless Killer's trademark carved into his forehead. The body was found by his nurse aid. She had lucked out and had not encountered the culprit.

When Joe had arrived on the scene, he instantly knew that it was the Faceless Killer again. They were closer this time. He was certain of it. Joe had deduced that the killer planned to return to the crime scene. The refrigerator door was left open. Which had led Joe to believe the assailant was hungry.

However, if the killer intended to return, it was too late to hide the police vehicles from sight. They dusted the apartment for fingerprints, but there were none, of course. The nurse reported that Kuchinsky did have a weak heart. She had been crying a lot, because she had deeply cared for the man. After talking to her, the police scouted the area, but no one had seen anything out of the ordinary.

As Sharon flipped through the pictures, she saw the trashed apartment and the body of the victim. Feeling kind of off kilter, she stood up and took a swig of coffee, which was when she noticed that the rest of the room was emptying out. She reached for her jacket and noticed it wasn't there. Joe was standing behind her holding it out for her. He smiled at her, and she thanked him for the gesture. Together they walked toward the elevator. Their faces, along with the others, became vacant.

There were three people in the car on the drive to the funeral—the chief, Sharon, and Joe. The chief decided he would sit in the back. His mind was filled with a combination of grief, concern for his men, and stopping the killing. For the most part, the drive was silent, but the tension could speak volumes. The chief rambled on about how it was important that coworkers get along, which annoyed everyone else in the car, because no one wanted to discuss the topic. Joe snapped on the radio. Sharon sat gazing out the window. Her head was hurting. She opened her purse and popped two aspirins.

Joe reached over to hold Sharon's hand, but Sharon didn't want to be comforted. She had a headache from all of the day's drama. Chuck had been a close friend to her when she needed advice and she truly missed him. He was there for her as she struggled to find her place in the department. The chief had noticed, but he was too busy thinking about what he should say at the funeral. Chuck had been under his care, so as chief he felt partly responsible for what had happened. He sighed and looked out the window. The rain was forming river-like patterns on the windshield.

Eventually, Sharon decided that she was going to start a conversation. "Chief, are you going to speak today? I think you should."

Robert looked up and said, "Yes, I'm going to speak, but I'm not sure exactly what I'm going to say."

Joe suggested, "Just say whatever comes naturally. No one expects an award-winning speech." The chief nodded.

They arrived at St. James Cathedral on the south side of town. They all filed out with umbrellas. The sky had opened up; it was almost as if it too was crying. There was a large crowd of people lining up to enter the building. Included among them were some of the students from Lincoln Memorial Elementary School. A few of the little boys waved at Joe, remembering him from the day he was there. Joe just sighed and took Sharon's hand. Together, they walked in and sat on the nonfamily side of the church.

As funerals go, this one was fairly typical. The chief took his turn to speak, as expected. He spoke gently—even though it was not in his nature—and his words rang true. "When a person, man or woman, makes a choice in life, they hope that it will lead them in a certain direction. Sometimes that decision comes easily, and at other times it is something we stumble into. For Charles, and let me use his formal name for just a moment, for Charles, it was a privilege. Every day that he came into work, there was no gripe. He simply did what was necessary to serve and protect. He loved the people of this city, and he certainly loved his family." The chief paused a moment to regain his composure. "I stand up here before all of you today to say that I also feel privileged, yes in my job, but today I stand here privileged to have known Chuck. Yes, we called him Chuck because we knew him, because we loved him for who he was. We may not have been family by blood, but we were family just the same." He paused one more time as his eyes began to cloud.

After wiping his eyes he began again. "There are so many things I'd like to say up here. This travesty is appalling. Not only are we mourning my close friend today, but his children and sister as well. I did not know them, but I knew of them. Chuck often spoke of how proud he was to be a husband and father."

Sara Rivera looked terrible. She looked like the living dead from the pain she was enduring. The chief looked down at her and said. "Sara, no one here can possibly know the full extent of what this loss has put you through. I want you to know that we are here for you. You may have lost a lot, but please remember, you can lean on us if you need anything.

The chief stepped down and joined the others in the pews. The service ended and the mourners proceeded to the cemetery. The storm had worsened; lightning and thunder blazed as they all stood on wet ground paying their final respects. The priest said, "Ashes to ashes and dust to..." Before he could finish, the priest started to choke. He fell to his knees and started to speak very strangely. A barrage of foul words poured from his mouth, and he cursed Chuck by saying he deserved it. The people were all dumbfounded by his behavior.

The chief and Joe started walking toward him, but he suddenly jumped back and started to address them. "Well, Joey, taking the day off, I see. Well, I guess you didn't get my message. Since you ignored me, I'll have to make an example now." The priest laughed. "You people are so small and insignificant, and yet you all stand here wasting time mourning that idiot who tried to capture me. He was just as big a fool as you, Joseph."

Then he looked over at Daniel Teague and smiled. "I see you're here too. How nice and quaint." His eyes then turned to Sharon and he said, "The whole gang is here, what fun." The priest wasn't standing quite still. He was swaying back and forth.

Someone called out, "Father Bartholomew! What's wrong?" The priest stretched out his hands and placed them upon his own neck. After a moment he collapsed to the ground. They quickly ran to his side. He had no pulse; his heart had stopped. On his hand was the symbol, the symbol they had all come to know meant death.

The chief took out his phone and called for an ambulance. Sharon ran up and said, "I don't believe this is happening." Just then Joe's cell vibrated. He looked and saw that it was the precinct. He sensed it was trouble. He opened it, and the voice on the other end said, "Sir, there has been a jail break at the DEDC. Michael Magnus has escaped." Joe closed his phone and threw it to the ground, fed up. He yelled out loud, "Enough of this shit! I can't just stand around. It's time for some action!"

Chapter 20

TRACKING BREADCRUMBS

The ground was covered in puddles, and getting across town was nearly an impossible task due to all the traffic. Horns were honking and people were yelling because they weren't making any progress. Inside a Lincoln town car was a very irate Texan. "Bill Meyers, you lied to me, son! You said you were a banging good driver and that you could handle it when that lazy good-for-nothing chauffer of mine called out today. But you're not doing shit up there. We aren't even moving, boy! I saw a cripple passing us on the sidewalk. Shit!"

"I'm sorry, Mr. Lockhart. I'm trying my best, but I can't go through the cars in front of me," Bill replied somewhat timidly.

"Dang it, boy, you could at least honk the Goddamn horn and act tough. Everyone out there is thinking there's a bunch of pansies in this car."

Bill Meyers gently tapped the horn, and KM threw a plastic cup toward the front of the car at him. Bill flinched, even though it didn't hit him. "Don't the people around here know how to move out of a man's way? Have a little gumption, son! You need to slam on that horn!" For the second time, a very mousey honk of the horn sounded. Meyers smiled, looking quite proud of himself. KM, on the other hand, just shook his head in disbelief.

Lockhart had begun searching for something else to throw when his cell phone rang. He answered and was quickly distracted. "Haight, what do you want, you bloated buffoon?" He had Haight on speaker, so Meyers heard quite loudly the sound of William Haight coughing. KM quickly deactivated the speaker, deciding to keep Meyers out of it.

Haight responded, "I received a call this morning from those crazy people. They said that if Magnus contacts you they want you to tell me immediately. They also said that if you didn't, you know the consequences for both our families."

After punching the chair with his fist, KM responded, saying he would comply. He hung up the phone and thought about how to handle the situation. KM hated being manipulated, but even more so he hated being told what to do. He was a man of action. Being stuck with no control over where he was going really pissed him off. For a moment, he thought about Magnus and wondered where he had escaped to. Part of him was relieved, because he knew the chances of a fair trial were slim for him anyway.

Traffic finally started progressing. KM was slightly appeased. The delays had made him late to his first appointment of the day. The first stop was the DEDC. Denton had requested a meeting with him to ask a few questions about the time he spent with Magnus before his escape. Then Lockhart needed to see Judge Schmitz at the courthouse. He knew she didn't particularly like him, so he wasn't exactly looking forward to the meeting.

After driving for another forty minutes, they pulled up to a familiar gate. Rutger walked up to their car, peered in quickly, greeted them, and allowed them to pass. Once through the parking lot, they pulled up to a smaller building around the back of the main structure. Both men exited the car. There were no bars or security doors on this building. It resembled a normal office arrangement. Once inside, they both sat in a waiting room until KM was called.

Inside, the office was very large and there were many objects that demonstrated expensive taste. On the desk was a nameplate that read Peter S. Cahill. Warden Cahill and Officer Denton were already seated. Cahill addressed him with an authoritative tone. "Mr. Lockhart, we have reason to believe that you may have had something to do with this escape. McKay here has informed me that you were one of the last people to see the prisoner before he broke out. Let me tell you that no one has ever gotten free from here, and we find it highly unlikely he accomplished it on his own."

KM recognized the authority of the man seated in front of him. "Sir, I'm a man of the law. The only way I help a man accused of a crime is by defending him with that law. So with all due respect, I don't appreciate your accusation."

Denton puffed up his chest and gave KM a nasty look. "Are you hiding that freak?" Denton bellowed, letting out a large amount of air as he spoke. The warden looked at him sternly, and Denton clearly understood that he had spoken out of turn.

Warden Cahill stood up, walked to his window, and peered out. After a minute, he scratched his beard. The warden was a short man in stature, but he looked as though he carried a heavy burden. He wore a business suit and glasses, and his breathing was labored. He let out a rough, smoker's cough. "Lockhart. Damn it! If you're hiding something, you better tell us now."

For the first time, KM Lockhart felt overwhelmed by his situation and decided to spill his guts. "Sir, there are five men threatening me. Before Magnus escaped, they wanted me to throw the trial and get him locked up. They are threatening my family, but I swear to you I had nothing to do with Magnus getting out. I didn't tell anyone else about this. They are also threatening the prosecuting attorney. Normally, I'd whoop the tar out of those chumps, but I can't because they're watching my every move, possibly even now."

Cahill looked at KM. He turned to Denton and asked him to leave the room. When Denton left, he pulled out his night stick to intimidate Meyer as he walked by. He loved intimidating people smaller than him. Meyers took a big gulp and was relieved when Denton left the building. Cahill had sat back down. "Listen to me, Mr. Lockhart. I want you to carry this with you. If you are being followed, obviously it's someone on the inside." Lockhart took what looked like a pin and attached it to the lapel of his suit jacket. Cahill explained to him that if he tapped the pin twice a homing signal would be sent out. "There's a bigger picture here, Lockhart, I'm sure you can see that. I need to know I can trust people. That's why I had McKay leave. For a while now, I've suspected him of not always being on the level."

KM smiled and said, "Mr. Cahill, I like your style."

Cahill looked extremely stern before he spoke again. "I've been watching that Magnus character. He's not the typical kind of fellow who comes into this place. He was calm and passive despite obvious agitation. Although I am not happy about his escape, I don't think he will cause any further destruction. One thing is for sure, however: we need to find him. If you come across him, let me know. I'm going to look into crime syndicates and see what I can find out about these mysterious five people. Can you tell me any more about them?"

KM described them to the best of his memory. When he finished, Cahill thanked him and told him that he would let him know if he found anything.

Cahill was done talking, and KM knew it was time for him to leave. He stood up and thanked Cahill for his help. As he was leaving, he stopped in front of Meyers, who had fallen asleep in his chair. He kicked Meyers on the ankle, awaking him. Bill let out a yell, and KM laughed at his pain. They left and began to travel toward the courthouse. KM looked down at his pin. He sighed and hoped that he would soon be free of these problems. He liked his customary free-wheeling lifestyle. This case was bringing him nothing but misery.

Peering out his window, KM's nose lit up with the smell of good eats. "Meyers. Stop the car! My stomach has a hankering. Oh, yes! Ultimate Taco here I come."

Bill sighed—he already knew the pain of what refried beans did to KM, but he had no choice. There were times Bill hated being an assistant. After going through the drive-thru, they proceeded to the seventh precinct. They parked and made their way up the stairs. KM got a glimpse of Sonya McPherson as she was heading out to lunch. Like a lost puppy, he started trailing her.

When she noticed, she stopped and turned around. "You had better have a good reason for following me, mister. I don't take kindly to leering."

KM smiled the biggest smile ever and said, "Darling, with looks like yours you better get used to it. The name is Lockhart, KM Lockhart, and I was wondering if I could discuss some important matters with you. That is, Miss...?"

KM paused, awaiting her response, which came quickly and rather harshly: "its doctor! Dr. Sonya McPherson. And what sort of matters would you possibly need to discuss with me?"

"Why, darling," he continued with confidence, "We need to discuss what we should have for breakfast after we have dinner tonight."

She looked at him and said, "You're a lawyer, aren't you?"

KM simply smiled and awaited her response.

Sonya thought to herself that there was no way she was going to sleep with the jerk. However, a free dinner didn't sound so bad, since she was still upset about Joe. She agreed and gave him her phone number. KM let out a Texas yell. "Yee haw! I'll call you at five, sugar!" With that, off he went toward the building. Before entering, he paused, expelling some flatulence with a smile. Then he thought to himself that the day wasn't going to be as bad as he had thought after all.

Chapter 21
RETURNING HOME

"Shit! I'm nearly out of gas." Looking down at the gauge, Magnus knew the first leg of his daring escape was coming to an end. During the night, he found a full parking lot and slept for a few hours. He expected the police to search the open roads but not a supercenter parking lot. The next morning, Magnus debated what his next step ought to be. He figured if he laid low until midafternoon he would have a better chance of getting out of the city. The other thought in his mind was that he wanted to go back home to Duanesburg. He needed to get some answers, but everywhere he wanted to go posed the risk of being discovered.

Magnus looked around the car, hoping to find some money. In order to continue his journey, he needed gas. He discovered seventy-three cents in the cup holder, but that wouldn't get him far. The car was quiet, so Magnus started to talk aloud to himself: "What do I do now?" The sun peeked out of the clouds and shined down on him, helping him relax. In all the commotion, he hadn't had the time to enjoy his newfound freedom. Then his mind began to wander. Soon, once more, he entered a dream state.

"Hello?" he asked, but there was no answer. "Is anyone here with me?" The dream was empty. No colors...no stars. Magnus began to float. Then he saw that he was approaching something. It looked like a stone wall. Floating up to it, he began to run his fingers along the grooves. Part of it was damp. Reaching through the less dense section, he felt something. He tried to pull at it until he heard a loud sound that diverted his attention. There was another wall approaching him. He turned left, then right, and spun around, realizing he was about to be boxed in. He hurried to make it around a corner but felt his leg get snagged.

The walls closed, interlocking with each other and forming a square prison. Magnus looked down and saw that a hand was holding his leg. He yanked with all his might and pulled free. Then a body emerged from the blackness that was the ground. The eyes of evil opened and focused on him. The body took shape and formed itself as Dar. "So, you're free, are you? This will make the hunt more fun." He scowled.

Magnus shouted, "What do you want from me, Dar? Why are you doing all this? Who are you really?" It echoed throughout that infinite place that exists between thought reality and physical reality.

There was silence—the kind of silence that could drive a person mad if they couldn't be still internally. Dar had vanished. Magnus sat down. He needed to calm himself; he closed his eyes in a meditative state. Dar reappeared behind him. "You cannot fathom my reasoning. You don't even understand yourself. You sit there as if you can control this place, when in actuality it controls you! Obviously you are undeserving, so I intend to take your *vunaze* like I did with all the others."

Magnus's face twisted; he didn't understand.

Dar became more annoyed and yelled, "You simpleton! You don't even know what that is, do you?" Dar laughed sinisterly. "It's the very energy that fuels your life and everything around you. And it will soon be mine. You cannot hide it from me…" Dar paused and laughed again, "…Brother!"

The silence returned, and Magnus felt that Dar had departed. Normally at this point he would have awoken from the dreamlike state, but this time he remained, floating through what seemed to be another world all together. He came across a statue. There were words written at the base of the visage. *For those who search eternity questioning existence, know now that the answers can be found only within oneself.* He reread the words aloud. "…within oneself?"

A wind blew across Magnus's face, and he awoke in the car. The parking lot had emptied a bit. Some parts of his vision remained in his mind. *How could he look inside himself?* Well, in any case, he needed to do something. The vision had changed his mind. Now he realized that he needed to avoid both the police and Dar. But where could he find a place to lay low for a while? There was a gurgling noise from his stomach. Hunger started to bother him, and he was beginning to feel sick.

Just as he was about to drive away, he noticed a homeless man. Quickly he got out of the car and asked the man if he had a coat or some food. The man smelled terrible, but he smiled a toothless smile. He reached into his shopping cart and handed Magnus a beat-up coat. "If you want food, follow me. I'm heading to the shelter. There's a bed there and a hot meal."

"Thank you, sir," Magnus replied, I will not forget your kindness."

"What's your name, young man?" The man asked.

"Michael. And yours, sir?"

"Just call me Rubins."

Magnus placed the car keys in his pocket and followed Rubins down the road. After walking fifty minutes, stopping periodically to pick up cans, they finally came to the shelter. It looked worse than Rubins did, but the aroma of a hot meal was coming from the inside.

Magnus noticed a small sign above the staircase that read Riley's Shelter for the Less Fortunate. As they entered, he spied a bathroom and made a break for it. Magnus hadn't gone in six hours and was well overdue. Once in the bathroom, he noticed his face in the mirror. Fearing that he might be recognized or stand out, he rubbed his hands on the dirty coat and wiped the dirt on his face. Then he left the bathroom and walked up to a woman who was taking peoples' names. She addressed him, "What is your name, sir?"

Without thinking, he responded, "Michael."

"And your last name, sir?"

He paused and fretted for a second before responding, "Um…Lockhart." She looked at him for a moment—perhaps she wondered if he had made it up, but she probably didn't really care.

She stretched her hand out and said, "Mr. Michael Lockhart, here's your name tag. You can have two helpings, but that's it. Don't get greedy. There are a lot of mouths to feed here. Just one more question: Are you intending to stay the night?"

"Yes, I will stay for the night, thank you." He muttered out the words, a little surprised at how a place like this was run.

The burly woman looked him right in the eyes and said, "I'm Josephine Walters. You stay out of trouble you hear? This is place for people in need of help. As long as you remember that you'll be fine, but if you get out of line you can take that shit and leave!" Magnus smiled and nodded before heading to the end of the line to get some food. He wasn't sure how long he could stay at this place, but one thing was clear, he needed time to figure out what to do next, and this was as good a place as any to start.

Chapter 22

DANGEROUS GAME

Far above the city, Darius Magnus sat on a rooftop reading a newspaper. His method for getting it was far from conventional. In fact, he had throttled an unsuspecting man and taken it. Regardless of how he had come about getting the *Chicago Tribune,* Dar relished reading about his newly acquired fame. The Faceless Killer, they called him—he delighted in the title. However, today he scowled when he looked at the front page, which featured a story that was not about him. "How could they give that fool Michael top billing?" He snarled the words aloud, truly annoyed. Suddenly, a wonderfully twisted thought spiraled its way through his brain. "So he freed himself and now most likely intends to go home. Good old Duanesburg. I haven't been there in a while. Perhaps it's time I paid it a visit."

The skyline was just becoming visible as the sun peeked over the horizon. Dar hated the sun. He didn't like the fact that he had to be more careful about his movements when the sun was out. Although most of his attacks had been during the day, he still had to be cautious about them. It was like an art form to him. Pride was at stake with every venture. Getting caught in the act would be an insult. Stewing on the idea a bit, he remembered how Sharon had stumbled upon him at the Blunt residence. That incident had particularly annoyed him, even if it was by accident. Then he thought back to Kuchinsky's apartment. He pounded his fist against a nearby brick fixture. Thinking about the swarming cops destroying his new hideout made him angry. Those bastards had cost him a lobster dinner.

Dar shoved the paper inside his duffel bag and walked over to the ledge of the building. He peered down for a while toward the street until his saw a bus. It was too far away to jump. The he began to walk along the ledge until he came to the top of a fire escape. He climbed down and started sprinting up the block. The bus had traveled quite a distance down the street. It was a brisk run, but Dar caught up to the bus and jumped on top of it. The passengers inside heard a thud on the roof of the bus, but after a minute they all returned to what they had been doing.

Dar stretched out on the roof with a smile. He knew that this bus would start him on his journey. About fifteen minutes later, he got a lucky break. The bus stopped and the driver decided he wanted to check out the noise he'd heard earlier. After letting out all the passengers, Paul Stern walked into the bus toward the center and popped the hatch that led to the roof. Popping his head up, the driver peered around on the top but saw nothing. As he began to climb back down, he felt an impact on his stomach that caused him to squeal like a rodent. Dar had hit him so hard that it left an indent. Paul's eyes began to tear uncontrollably as Dar leaned over him.

After a moment of looking intensely into Dar's eyes, Paul stood up as if nothing had happened at all. Then he sat back in the driver's seat and pulled away from the curb. Dar took a seat and stretched out. He thought to himself that the world was his playground, and he relished in the fun he was having.

As Paul continued to head toward Duanesburg, Dar nodded off. He didn't notice that a police car had driven by them. Behind the steering wheel was a very anxious Joseph Warren. Sitting beside him, asleep, was his new partner Sharon. The two of them were heading toward the airport for a flight to New York. The flight, however, was a few hours off.

"Joe, can we stop and get something to eat? I'm hungry." Sharon lifted her head and turned toward him with a smile.

Joe responded, a little edgy, "Can you wait until we get to the airport? I want to get there and not have to worry about time."

Sharon sat up all the way. "You've got to be kidding. I'm not eating airport food. Trust me, Joe, you don't want me to eat that stuff either. Not unless you want a sick Sharon next to you on the flight." He sighed but knew she was right about the food. About a mile later, they pulled into a rest stop on the highway and entered a diner. Sharon made a comment about how pit-stop food wasn't much better than airline food. Joe gave her a look and they strolled into the trucker stop.

After a few minutes, they were seated and looked at their menus. Joe began to get a funny feeling inside. Since the funeral, they hadn't talked about what had happened to Father Bartholomew. Sharon looked at him from across the table and asked, "What's wrong?"

Joe looked up at her and responded, "Sharon I still feel like everything is out of my control. We are no closer to finding the killer and now we have the bomber on the loose. I keep trying to get a handle on things, but then some other incomprehensible thing happens. First it was Eileen Keller in the hospital, and just the other day Father Bartholomew at the funeral. Both of them are dead now, and I have no idea how it happened at all."

Sharon had been wondering what exactly had happened in the hospital. She finally got up the courage to ask again. "Joe, what really happened in that room with Keller?" Joe looked out the window and said, "You'll think I'm crazy." Sharon just looked at him, waiting for the answer this time. Joe started to talk again. "Keller had everyone else leave the room, and then she touched my forehead. When she did, I felt dizzy at first, but then I saw kind of like a vision. There was a busy street filled with people who all seemed colorless and gray. Then I saw a woman standing in the middle of them, except she had this brilliant light coming from her. It was like an angel's light. As I moved closer, I realized I wasn't looking through my own eyes. A hand reached out and grabbed the neck of the woman and sucked the light from her body. When the vision ended she was dead, Sharon."

Sharon sat there quietly. Joe was reflecting, when suddenly there was a smack on the window. Smeared across the cracked glass were the remains of a rotten pumpkin. Joe stood up and looked out. He couldn't believe his eyes. Standing there pointing and laughing was Dar. Joe mistook him for Michael Magnus. Immediately, he grabbed his gun and ran outside. At first, he didn't see the culprit, but he heard the word "Tootles" coming from a bus driving off and saw a hand waving goodbye to him. The bus was too far away to shoot, but Joe thought about it for few seconds anyway. Instead, he ran over to his car to jump in and follow when he realized the tires were flat and the radio wires had been cut. Joe kicked his car but then remembered he had a cell phone. He called the station and reported the bus.

Then Joe got a great idea. He ran up to a man and showed him his badge. "Sir, please, I need to borrow your car. There is a criminal on this highway, and with your car I have a small chance of catching him." The man handed him the keys reluctantly. Joe got in and sped off. Sharon was already outside, but she didn't accompany him. Joe had grabbed the extra police light from his car and placed it on the dashboard to clear traffic. Speeding at ninety for about twelve solid minutes, he finally got a visual of the bus. He called dispatch again and read them the license plate number. He also informed them of the make and model of the car he was driving so he wouldn't be stopped. Soon he heard sirens approaching him from behind. Joe smiled, knowing he had backup. Four cop cars caught up to the bus traveling at about seventy-five miles an hour. They surrounded it and through a megaphone one of the officers ordered the vehicle to pull over.

Without warning, the bus started to drift off the road and crashed into a tree. On impact, Paul went through the windshield. Seconds later, four police vehicles encircled the bus. Joe was the first to enter the mangled transport. Anxious and cautious, he ran up the stairs and yelled "Get down on the ground!" There was no sound or reaction. The bus was empty. Joe was thorough and then stepped out. Then like a lightning bolt, a bad feeling struck him. Without a word, he leapt into a squad car and drove over the median. He yelled, "Fuck!" And then his cell phone started to ring.

On the phone Sharon's name was displayed. Joe immediately answered and the voice on the other end was terrifyingly familiar. "Once again, Joey, you've fucked up. And now I've got your little girly here. I had no idea how much fun today was going to be. I think I won't kill her yet. If you play along with my new game, maybe you'll even get her back alive. I'll be in touch. Oh, and by the way, tough guy, you better come alone to the meeting place. Otherwise, Officer Baker won't be breathing when you see her next."

Joe asked, "What meeting place?"

Dar laughed and said, "Silly, don't you know? I'm heading home to meet my brother. Why don't you come join our family reunion? I swear, though, one siren and hot pants here is toast. See you soon."

Joe heard a click, and by the time he got back to the diner there was no sign of Sharon or Dar. Joe looked down at the ground and picked up Sharon's cell phone. He clenched his fist and punched the wall. "Fuck!" he yelled out as the other officers pulled up. "How am I going to get her back? Shit! That bastard," he blurted out in frustration. Joe sat down and just punched the wall again. He opened up the cell phone and saw Dar's symbol scratched into the screen. He started shaking. One of the officers brought a pedestrian up to him. The man reported that a lunatic had stolen his car and driven off in it. Immediately, Joe got the license plate number to the precinct, but he knew they couldn't pursue the vehicle without endangering Sharon. Dreading the conversation with the chief, Joe picked up his phone and dialed the number. This was the end of not only his sanity, but probably his career. He said to himself that none of that mattered though…all that mattered was getting Sharon back. The chief answered, and Joe said, "Sir, I have some bad news…"

Chapter 23

JUDGMENTS

Over the past two weeks, the seventh precinct had become a familiar place to KM Lockhart. He stared at the building from the sidewalk. Meyers ran back to the car. His time was up; he was there for his consultation with Judge Schmitz. During the preliminary hearing, it had seemed clear that she wasn't very fond of him. For once he was actually glad Meyers had come along, although he would never admit it.

The two of them together climbed the large stone steps that led to the lobby of the building and from there proceeded to the elevator. Lockhart was unusually quiet, Bill thought, as the elevator moved its way toward the fifth floor. A little ding sounded and the two men exited without a word. The court offices were located behind the courtroom, and so they had to walk passed the benches and then the podium, until finally making their way through a narrow hallway. All the way in the back was the office of Judge Schmitz.

Through the glass window on the door, Bill noticed that the judge was on the telephone. He suggested to KM that they should wait until she was finished before knocking. KM looked down at his watch; they were already fifteen minutes late. He knocked on the door, and they both saw the woman get up, walk toward them, and open the door, placing a finger to her mouth. She quietly spoke with an annoyed tone "Mr. Lockhart, I'm surprised you decided to finally show up."

Bill Meyers spoke out of turn, saying, "It's my fault, Your Honor, I'm not used to driving through the city."

Kathryn Schmitz eyed the scrawny intern without a word and then turned around and motioned for the two of them to follow her. She walked back to her desk and sat down. Raising her hand, she stuck up her pointer finger and picked the phone back up to continue her conversation. KM and Bill were once again silent. They waited about four minutes before the judge finally terminated her call.

She wrote some information down on a piece of paper and then sat back in her chair. Then, grabbing a glass of water, she spoke again. "I have a lot on my plate today, gentlemen, so I'm going to make this brief. I shouldn't have to tell you that all eyes are on us right now. This trial has become a media circus, which is why I had wanted it to be resolved as quickly as possible. Now, however, it seems that the accused party has conveniently escaped custody." Pausing for a moment, she sipped from the glass of water. KM remained silent despite the fact that he had no idea where she was going with this conversation.

Bill was terrified of the woman—although this was not due to her physical prowess. In actuality, she was quite short and modest in stature. It was the way she carried herself. With every motion, she seemed like she could explode. Judge Schmitz possessed real legal power, and that power commanded respect. She looked over to Meyers as if expecting him to say something. Instead, he tried to avoid eye contact by looking over to KM, who was eyeing the certificates on the wall. In the back of his mind, he was thinking about the phone call he had received in the car. The conversation with Haight had left him concerned, and he didn't want to show it.

Judge Schmitz set the glass back down and turned her attention to KM. "I've been reading the paper a bit, Mr. Lockhart. I don't have to tell you how I feel about the statement you made about our legal community. Your actions are highly reckless and irresponsible. You are actually bringing more attention to this whole situation than it merits. The gallivanting with reporters and young women has made us all tabloid fodder. I may not have any say over your actions, but I do have say as to who is appointed defense attorney on this trial. Do you get my meaning?"

KM let out a big sigh and finally opened his mouth. "Your Honor... ma'am...I realize that this all turned into a big mess, but I intend to make sure that it doesn't happen again. I may be a bit of a rascal, but I am a man of principle. That's why I became part of this great judicial system." KM ended his comment with a big Texas smile.

"Spare me the 'man of principle' speech," she replied. "One way or the other, we are not having this conversation again." KM wanted to blast back at her the first derisive words that came into his head, but he thought the better of it. Deep down, he knew that the accusations were true. His face twisted as he nodded, conceding to the judge's demand.

Bill's stomach began to stir. He felt terrible inside. To him, KM was a strong figure, and to see him torn down by the judge irked him. "Your Honor," he began. The judge looked at him sternly as if it wasn't the time or place for him to speak, but Bill continued just the same. "Your Honor, if not for the diligence of Mr. Lockhart, Michael Magnus would probably be sentenced to life in prison or worse. Any other appointed attorney would have turned their back on a guy who seemed hopelessly guilty, but not Mr. Lockhart. He heard him out, and here we are on the threshold of proving his innocence. I know that this trial has become a public spectacle, but maybe it is better that way. Every man deserves a fair judgment, not just a quick one to satisfy the mob."

KM looked at his intern, amazed at the defense the young man had uttered. He turned toward him and said, "Son, those were mighty fine words, but the judge here knows all that. And as nice as those words are, it doesn't excuse the fact that I botched things up a bit." KM paused a moment and then turned toward the judge. "Ma'am, I swear to abide by the standards of the judicial system. I will try my hardest to get to the bottom of things and end this trial proper."

The judge's face remained stern. "You better, Mr. Lockhart! Now, both of you, please leave my presence immediately! I have important matters to attend to."

After they exited the room, Judge Schmitz picked up her phone and said one word, "Now." About a block away, five men in business suits wearing sunglasses started to get ready. KM and Bill were outside the building walking toward their car when they heard a car engine. Suddenly, there was a screech and a black Mercedes pulled up beside them. Three of the men quickly jumped out, guns in hand, and ushered them into it. "What the Sam Hill?" KM began, before his mouth was covered by a chloroform-soaked cloth. Another man placed a cloth over Bill's mouth, knocking him out as well. The last thing they heard was laughter and a second screech as the car pulled away.

Chapter 24
SECLUSION

A slight shiver caused Magnus to open a single eye and peer at his surroundings. It was, after all, his first morning of freedom in quite some time. He had half expected to hear a nightstick bang against the bars as a wakeup call. Remembering that there was no cell and no Denton was the most pleasing thought in the world. For a few moments, he lay on the rickety bed without a care. Rolling on his back, he placed his arms behind his head and sighed.

After a quiet ten minutes, he drifted back to sleep and once more was thrust into a dream state. Immediately he recognized his surroundings. He was home. The family barn and the house stood in front of him. Magnus looked around and saw that he was in the vegetable patch, plow in hand. It seemed like years had passed since he'd worked on the family farm. That was the life he had grown accustomed to. In his dream, it all seemed so real.

After laying the plow down he approached the main house. Magnus got to the door, and an eerie feeling came over him unexpectedly. Something wasn't right. He placed his hand on the doorknob and it burned him. Instinctually, he kicked the door in. To his horror, he beheld his parents hanging from the rafters, surrounded by fire. Frantically, he searched for a hose to put the fire out. But then he was pushed from behind and the door was closed on him. Then he heard that familiar laughter he had come to know as Dar's. Over and over again, it plagued him in his dreams, but this time Magnus wasn't afraid. He turned around and pulled the door so hard it ripped off its hinges. Just beyond the door was an endless pit, and standing on the other side of the precipice was Dar. His image was nearly a mirror reflection of Magnus—with one major difference: he was not a man. Michael Magnus was almost certain he was a demon.

Dar said, "You've got a lot of nerve. Do you really think you're ready for me?" He raised his hand and once more a door appeared between them. It slammed abruptly and extremely hard. So hard, in fact, that Magnus was knocked to the ground and jolted from the dream. He felt a pain in his shoulder. His muscles had tensed during the psychic encounter.

Magnus sat up and stretched his arms. As he did, he counted eight beds in the room. Five were occupied with homeless men, none of whom smelled very pleasant. He looked at his roommates, the impoverished of society, and thought about the gravity of his situation. He pondered how long he could stay among them. Truly, he had nowhere else to go. He thought back to the dream. It hurt him to think that his parents were gone.

Magnus stood up and walked toward the window. Placing his hand on the glass, he felt the cold from the outside. A light rain was falling. As he watched the peaceful rainfall, it dawned on him that he could use it as cover. He knew that traveling at all was risky, but the shelter could only be a temporary stop. Sooner or later, someone would recognize him, and if that happened he would have to contend with Denton.

He tried to collect his thoughts. He knew he needed to figure out what his next step should be. A scratching noise startled him and disrupted his train of thought. He was concerned at first but then realized it was just an old man making his way to the bathroom. He turned and sat on the edge of his bed. A pleasing aroma filled his nostrils. He recognized the smell: it was bacon.

The sheer delight of eating something that tasty almost instinctively guided him down the stairs to the first floor. The first floor was filled with people, and a line had formed in front of the breakfast counter. He grabbed a tray and made his way to the back of the line.

"Hey there, Michael, how are you this morning?" The voice came from a short man standing behind him in line. Magnus looked down and recognized the homeless man who had brought him to the shelter.

"I'm doing OK. And you, Rubins?"

"Why, I'm doing just dandy. I'm having a terrific day."

"Shut up, Rubins," a voice sprang out from the crowd. Magnus looked confused, so Rubins decided to fill him in about some of the regulars at the shelter. He started with a Middle-Eastern man, whose name was Khalid; then Jacob, whom they called Jake the Rocket Man; and finally the man who had yelled at Rubins. His name was Brian. Brian especially disliked Rubins. He also didn't mind letting everyone know it. Magnus just shrugged his shoulders and turned to face forward. He was happy the line had moved a bit.

Rubins tapped Magnus on the shoulder again. "Hey, you came on a good day. They don't normally have bacon and eggs. Typically it's the gruel, but once every two weeks we get some real good eats." Magnus nodded, trying to end the conversation, but it proved to be impossible. "So, where you from, where have you traveled, and where are you heading?"

Magnus sighed. He really did not want to answer. Rubins was almost bouncing with anticipation.

The others at the shelter had blacklisted him because he was a little creepy and definitely annoying. Magnus, however, was grateful to him for his help, so he answered with an obscure response and turned the question around.

That was a big mistake. Rubins began to banter on and on about his life. Magnus received a full education as to why the others didn't talk to him. Rubins went on and on. He told Magnus about his family from Utah during breakfast. He followed him around and talked about his troubles during lunch. There was just no stopping him. The topic of his family came up for the third time when Magnus finally interrupted him, saying, "Will you excuse me? I need to go to the men's room." With the opportunity to escape, Michael Magnus looked for a bathroom that was as far away from the dining room as possible. When he found it, he locked the door. The stench was putrid, but anything was better than Rubins's banter.

After about five minutes, Magnus cracked open the door and looked out. The coast seemed clear, so he exited. His frame of mind changed when he got a sudden chill in his spine. He heard a voice down the hall that reminded him of Denton. His heart raced as he moved toward the voice. Standing with his back against the wall, he knew the man was right around the corner. He peered around the corner with one eye. What he discovered was a tall man talking to Rubins. Rubins turned and saw Magnus. He was very excited to see him again, and he introduced him to Christopher Preston, the tall man. Magnus couldn't place it, but there was something familiar about Chris. It was like he had known him for a long time but couldn't remember from where.

The two of them began to talk, and somewhere in the conversation Chris decided to show Magnus the rest of the building. First they walked to the basement. Magnus took careful note of every exit. There was an oil furnace and a lot of old furniture. Chris seemed to relish the role of tour guide. It annoyed Rubins, because he no longer had the complete attention of Magnus. Rubins eventually left mumbling to himself about rude interruptions.

Once they were alone, Chris whispered something that scared Magnus: "I know who you are." Their eyes locked, and Magnus was sure he would have to flee. Before he could move, Chris spoke again. "It's not safe here. There are many people who would rat you out in an instant if they knew who you were. Especially George Rubins back there. He is known for telling everybody everything. You have to be really careful."

Magnus was cautious about the next words that came out of his mouth. "Why would you want to help me?"

Chris explained that he had been watching Magnus ever since he arrived. Then he said, "Let's just say I don't think you're the bomber type."

Magnus smirked and whispered, "Well I need to find out who framed me and why. Plus, there's a woman's life at stake, not to mention my life as well. I'm sure to get the chair or something if they ever catch me again."

Chris nodded and said, "Yeah, especially if Denton catches you."

Magnus's eyes widened. His trust in Chris wavered again. He wondered if he was an undercover cop. The most logical question followed. He asked, "How do you know Denton?"

Chris paused, but then apologized and shared with Magnus the gift he possessed. "You see," he started, "When people have intense thoughts, I tend to hear them in my head. Most people have very few thoughts that are actually strong enough, but not you. Since you walked in here, it has been nonstop.

Actually, it's kind of scary, because your thoughts are so strong I can see images of whatever you are thinking. Let me tell you, that Darius fellow freaks me out."

Magnus didn't speak a word. He simply reflected of the validity of Chris's statement. It was definitely weird how this random guy knew everything about him. He had to sit down. It was too much to handle. First the crazy intense encounter with a possible psycho brother, and now the psychic shelter man was offering to help him. Chris just smiled, "Psychic shelter man, eh? That's the first time anyone put it that way. Anyway, come on, it's time to continue with your tour. You should know this place well in case you need to hide or escape quickly."

The remainder of their walk included nooks and crevices that made excellent hiding spots. Magnus was actually starting to feel a bit better. He wondered again if Chris was truly a guardian angel. It hadn't been easy for him to keep his secrets locked up. As the day progressed, he felt more and more comfortable confiding in Chris. He eventually shared his pain and what he could remember about Arie. It seemed as though he had a partner to help him on his journey, and with everything that had happened to him, he was grateful for one positive development.

Chapter 25
DUSK'S SHADOW

It was a gloomy morning to say the least. The overcast sky made the day seem like night, and the light rain had changed to snow falling relentlessly against the roof. The dismal weather only added to the already bad feeling that Detective Joseph Warren was having about the day to come. In room 418 of the Grand Hotel, there was a mini-stove. A pot of tea quietly brewed on one of the jets. Joe was perched on the edge of a tacky plaid couch, which served as a centerpiece to the room. In his hand he held a stiff drink. Under normal circumstances Joe wasn't a heavy drinker, but he there was no hesitation that morning to make his tea ninety-proof. His nerves were shot, and who could blame him? That thing, that horrible thing that had killed so many times before, had Sharon. Joe was a wreck. Sweat dripped down his brow as he kept thinking about all the other people who had been crushed by Dar's endless rampage.

The kettle started whistling loudly, so Joe put his drink down and stood up. When he did, he had motionless so long that the indent from where he was sitting didn't fill back in. He hadn't slept since his arrival in the cold and fierce upstate region of New York. He had just started to fill his cup with tea when his phone rang. Joe nerves were so frazzled that he nearly threw the mug at the phone. He took a deep breath and calmly picked up the phone. "Hello, this is Joe Warren."

On the other end of the line was the chief. "Joe, its Chief Frank. Are you ready to go?" Joe didn't reply immediately; he was gearing up on caffeine. Just two nights before, the chief had reamed him nearly all the way to the airport.

After letting out a heavy breath, Joe responded, "Well, the plan is to drive into town and meet up with the local authorities. We've already explained the situation, and I'll have them on standby waiting for my call."

The chief agreed that it was the best course of action but his tone reflected that he was still annoyed at the situation. "Joe, no more rookie shit. Stop letting this punk get under your skin. Take command of the situation and do whatever it takes to get your partner out of there. Play it cool, but watch your step and don't put yourself into a compromising situation."

Joe listened to the chief go on and on about procedure, and after a while he started to drift off. It was extremely hard for him to concentrate on anything except Sharon's face. As his eyes closed, it wasn't before long that he started to see images of a man on the edge of a high cliff. Joe approached the man, and as he got closer he realized it was Dar. He ran with intensity to grab him, but Dar vanished, causing Joe to fall off the cliff. As with most dreams, Joe awoke before hitting the ground. The chief, of course, was still chattering on. Joe decided it was time to get going.

Cutting into the chief's rant, Joe uttered, "Chief, I have to get going now. I need to get out of here and rescue Sharon." Joe tried to make light of the situation by jokingly stating it was all in a day's work, but the chief didn't laugh. Instead the chief snarled at him to get the job done right this time. With that, the chief disconnected the call abruptly. Joe was happy to be off the phone. He called the front desk and scheduled a car for 8:30, which gave him about thirty minutes to get ready. He jumped in the shower to wake himself up and then ran out to the waiting car.

The drive was silent. The sides of the road were covered in snow. Joe peered out the window as they headed toward the center of town. It was definitely a very rustic place. Even the people seemed to move in a rustic fashion. They all took notice as the taxi pulled up to the small Duanesburg police station. It was slightly unnerving, but there were more important things for him to be concerned about.

Joe got out of the car and entered the station, where the local sergeant was waiting for him. Sheriff Marc Cramer was a stout African American man who had let his gut grow a bit too far, and his hair was thinning. He walked up to one of Chicago's finest and shook his hand. "Welcome to New York, Detective Warren. I wish it was under better circumstances."

Joe shrugged his shoulders and thanked the sheriff. Then, Joe asked the sheriff if he could tell him anything about the Magnus family. Marc nodded and motioned for Joe to follow him. They proceeded into a room and Marc closed the door. He sat down behind the desk and motioned for Joe to have a seat. "Honestly, Detective—"

Joe interrupted. "Just call me Joe."

"Honestly, Joe, I was a little confused. I knew the Magnuses for years, and there was never anyone in the family named Darius. Donald and Michelle were the parents, and Michael was their only child. So when you called and said that this Darius fellow was heading here, I wasn't even sure who that was."

Joe wrote that down and then asked Marc another question: "You said 'were the parents.' So Magnus's parents are deceased?"

Marc frowned and responded, "Joe there was hardly anything left of them. About three weeks ago there was a fire in their barn, and we found ropes strung from the rafters. Both of them were tortured, hanged, and burned alive."

Marc took out a cigarette and lit it. "You smoke?" He held the pack out to Joe.

Joe took one and leaned in for a light. "That's fucked up," Joe said after releasing a puff.

Marc responded, "Quite." Reaching into the file cabinet, the sheriff pulled out a file and handed it to Joe. As he flipped through, Joe noticed the symbol in one of the pictures. He had completely forgotten to ask about it. This instance of the symbol was by far the biggest one he had ever seen. It was carved into the ceiling and had to be at least five feet square.

"Has anything else out of the ordinary occurred around here since this happened?" Joe asked, still flipping through the file.

"Not that I can think of," responded Marc. Then Joe asked if there was a criminal record on Magnus. Marc replied, "Nope, he's clean as a whistle. In fact, he's probably the last person who would ever bomb anything. Have you considered that maybe this Darius fellow did it, since they look alike?"

Joe stood up to make a copy of the file and responded that they had considered it, especially since they knew that Darius was at the bomb site on the day in question. Then Joe said, "Has there been any recent activity at the Magnus estate?"

Marc shook his head and said, "None. Our guys have been making rounds but haven't seen a thing. If Dar is going to show, we won't know 'til we get there."

Joe looked up and said, "I appreciate the backup, Sheriff Cramer, but I have to go it alone."

Marc replied, "OK, Detective, you're calling the shots, but I'll be a few blocks away backing you up." Joe felt a little better. That is, until his cell phone rang.

The number was private, but Joe answered anyway. As he picked up, he heard a voice he had come to recognize and despise. "Hello, old bean. Are you ready for our meeting? I hope that you are only hanging out at the precinct with Sheriff Big Gut for moral support. Remember, I'll be watching, and if you have them hiding around the corner, believe me, I'll know, and she'll get it."

Joe responded, "If you hurt her—"

Dar's laughter was cold and uncaring. "Listen, Joey, you'll do nothing but shut up." Joe was quiet. Dar continued, "Good, that's better. Now meet me there at dusk. No guns, no pigs, and by the way, walk. That's right, you heard me. No taxi. Walk from the station all the way to the house, and shut the door behind you. I'll be waiting. Oh and Joe, try to smile would you? You look like hell. See ya!" There were a few more seconds of laughter and then a click.

Sheriff Cramer sat there waiting. Joe looked up and said, "He has to be close by; he's been watching me the whole time. He knows I'm here. We'll have to try something different. He knows the plan. This guy is still one step ahead. How did he know? How the fuck could he know? Goddamn it!"

Marc was stunned. "Maybe he's on the force?"

"Doubtful," Joe responded. "He told me specifically no guns and no cops. I'm walking into a trap, and I know it. What do I do?" The sheriff didn't have a response to that question. Joe stood up and said, "Marc, thank you, but I have to handle this alone." With that, Joe walked out of the precinct and off in the direction of the Magnus farm. If he started walking now, he would just make it by dusk. With the future uncertain, Joe set forth for Sharon.

Chapter 26
THE UNKNOWN

There was a barely audible sound in the distance—the echo of water droplets hitting the inside of the basin that sat in the back corner on a dingy linoleum floor. It was daytime, although one could barely tell because there were no windows. The ceiling was rotting and had cracks. Tiny holes allowed small amounts of light to pass through. The air had a musty smell, and the scent tickled the nose of the woman seated in the center of the room. Her arms were red and worn from being tied up, and her neck was bruised from a tumble she had taken the night before.

The water continued to drip until finally the sound reached her on a subconscious level. Upon close inspection, one could see the movements behind her eyelids were growing more and more intense. She was dreaming. It had been at least a few days since she had slept, because her mind wouldn't allow her to settle down. At the moment, however, things were still, so she couldn't help but drift off. Her dream was peaceful. She found herself on the shore of a lake. A cool breeze blew the lightly colored thin hair on her arm as she looked at her surroundings. She recognized this beach. It was one she had visited a few months back in Delaware. The sand was slightly damp, and she felt certain that it would blow into her eyes, so she reached for her sunglasses. Then she noticed that a boat was coming toward the shore.

She was compelled to get up and walk toward the shoreline to get a closer look. It was a small, single man craft with a green sail. A wave of relief washed over her. Somehow this boat and the man in it were very familiar to her. She called out, "Hello!" She smiled and closed her eyes to relish in the moment.

The voice called back, "Ahoy there." The smile on his face delighted her as the boat slid onto the sand and stopped. He hopped down and embraced her. In that instant, existence seemed perfect. She woke from the dream with smile that lasted for about a minute before she remembered where she was—hell.

Reality set in. The pain from the bruises on her neck and leg were throbbing. Bending down, she lifted her torn pant leg by the cuff, revealing the black and blue mark on her calf. She touched it and cried out from the pain. Then she looked back at the basin, still catching the water from the leaky ceiling. Hopelessness staggered back into her mind. She wished that she had never woken up. Leaning back, she propped herself up against a chair. There was a noise from the other side of the door. "Get your damned hands off me!" an unfamiliar voice rang out loudly. She hopped across the room to sneak a peek at the commotion from the hall.

When she peered through a hole, she saw two men. One was skinny and the other was a bit round. The round one was doing the yelling. He had a distinct southern drawl and wore a big cowboy hat. Once they left her sight, she limped over to the far wall and pressed her ear against it. Fortunately, the two men were placed in the room next to hers, and when they began to speak she could still hear them. The Texan-accented yelling continued. "You Goddamn bastards, do you know who I am? I'm Kenneth Michael Lockhart. When I get out of here, you'll get yours."

One of the men in dark shades responded, "Would you shut up? I hope the boss tells me I can waste you just so I can get some fucking quiet around here!" She heard the door slam and then the heavy footsteps of the men walking away.

After she was sure they had gone, she mustered up the courage to knock on the wall. At first, she spoke in a mousey voice: "Can you hear me over there?" There was no response, so after looking around for a minute she decided to try again slightly louder. "Mr. Lockhart, can you hear me? If you can, please respond."

She heard some movement, and then with a much quieter version of the southern accent, he responded, "Are you stuck in here too, little darling?" The heart of the young woman pounded at the prospect of someone to talk to. She nearly cried, but then she remembered that she had to be quiet.

After settling herself down she responded. "Yes. Do you know where we are?"

Both Lockhart and his assistant were pressed against the wall, trying their best to hear the sweet voice on the other side. "We were tied up and blindfolded before we were brought here," Bill answered.

She sighed and asked her second question. "Do you know what day it is?"

This time KM replied, "Why, I believe its Monday, November sixteenth." Then in turn, he questioned her, "How long have these bastards been holding you?"

Some tears rolled down her face as she thought back over recent events. Her silence worried KM a bit, so he started to talk some more. "It's OK. I promise it will be OK. You won't have to be here much longer." Even though he made the claim, he wasn't sure if he could really back it up.

There was a long pause. No one on either side of the wall said anything. Then Bill spoke. "Miss? Miss, are you all right over there?"

She responded, "Yes. I don't know how long I've been here. Much time has passed and I've lost track." Even through the wall, her pain was felt by the two men. KM sat down and leaned against the wall. Bill followed suit and sat down also. The three of them sort of formed a triangle, with the wall between them.

"Do you know why you are here?" Bill asked. The next few words that came out of her mouth were such a revelation that their sheer magnitude could have stopped a train.

She was afraid to tell them because even she couldn't believe the events that had transpired. Eventually, the young woman decided that if she didn't tell them, who would she tell?

"I was there," she said.

KM asked, "where were you, darlin'?"

She didn't directly answer his question. "At first, one of those guys just tossed his match, then the fire began to spread, and soon after that, the ground started to quake. The fire seemed almost alive and started to fly out in all directions with explosions. They brought me there, and after everything was ablaze they brought me back here. All those people died. I could hear their screams. It was terrible."

Bill looked at KM and KM looked back at him. Suddenly, one thing was clear to both of them: whoever was on the other side of that wall knew the identity of the Chicago bomber. She was the missing link.

Bill couldn't hold back his curiosity. "Was it him?" he blurted. "Was it Michael Magnus who started the fire?"

"No," she answered. "It was the leader of the guys who brought us here."

The three of them were still again. KM was not surprised. He had suspected this from his dealings with Haight. But now what he didn't know was who the girl was. He decided it was time to ask the question. "Hun, what's your name?" In the silence before the answer, a pin-drop could have be heard.

"It's Arianna. Arianna Shoomer."

Over the next few minutes, KM sat and thought. Even though so much had come to pass, there were still so many questions. Bill sat quietly against the wall, annoyed. He was beginning to feel the severity of the situation. Part of him blamed KM for everything, and part of him was just getting disconcerted. His emotions were slipping. He looked at KM and said, "I don't know about you, but I'm getting fed up with this shit! I never asked to be in this kind of mess! It's all bullshit!"

Arie was startled.

Bill continued, "This is all a load of fucking shit! I want out of this hole in the ground. Let me out, Goddamn it! Let me out! Now! Now! Now, I said!"

KM was also stunned by what was happening. Bill had always been a shy and quiet intern. Now he sounded more like a seven-year-old throwing a tantrum. He was so loud that none of them heard the door down the hall open. Arie had buried her face in her hands and feared for the worst. Bill stood up and started kicking the door to their prison. Suddenly, it opened. He dashed at his captors. Before anyone could do anything to stop him, it was too late. The gunshot that ensued caused Arie to scream, and KM's heart sank into his stomach as Bill's lifeless body collapsed to the floor. There was a .22-caliber hole right in the temple of his forehead. The blood oozed from the back of his head where the bullet had exited.

Then the shooter walked over to the blood-splattered KM and pushed the gun under his chin. "Now I hope this place will quiet the fuck down!" And with that, one of the five men dragged the body out and the rest of the men exited and slammed the door behind them. KM doubled over and grasped his hands around his arms. His cool and calm composure was shattered. His strength and fortitude were broken. He was helpless and he knew it. He began to rock back and forth, holding himself as if he had been punched in the stomach. There was nothing he could do to stop the water pouring from his eyes. Responsibility had to be placed somewhere, and he could only blame himself. Terror and utter disgust had set in. In the darkness they sat, truly alone.

Chapter 27

MIDNIGHT RUN

Time had flown by quickly as they toured the shelter. Although he hadn't realized it, 11:00 p.m. had come and gone for Michael Magnus. After finally coming to the decision that he would stay one more night, he retired to his room. Chris had convinced him that he needed a strategy in order to move around and leave the city without being noticed. They had discussed catching a train and stowing away as cargo, hobo-style. That plan was dismissed, however, because of the high probability of being caught. Eventually, they had both agreed to discuss the issue further in the morning.

Magnus crawled into his bed, barely able to keep his eyes open. He closed them and was fast asleep before realizing it. The other men at the shelter had taken to their beds as well and were fast asleep. All of them, that is, except for Rubins. He had been thinking really hard about how to win Magnus's attention back from Chris. Rubins, at least in his mind, had claimed Magnus to be *his* best friend and his friend only. He sat in a beat-up chair just outside the mess hall flipping through a newspaper he had picked up on the street. He thought that if he read the paper he might find something to discuss that would grab Magnus's attention…at least for a while.

As he flipped through the paper, Rubins happen to see an article with the headline Chicago Bomber Still at Large. There was a reward mentioned in the first paragraph for any information leading to the bomber's capture. Rubins continued to read and almost missed the picture that was shown with the article—it was his new best friend! Beneath the mug-shot the caption read "Michael J. Magnus is on the loose. Chicago bomber escapes and police are baffled." Rubins may have been annoying and possessive, but he wasn't a complete fool. He put two and two together and realized that his new best friend Michael Lockhart was really Michael Magnus. Immediately, he forgot about trying to be anyone's friend and left the shelter to head to a nearby pay phone.

Magnus, sound asleep in the dorm-like room, had no idea that Rubins had betrayed him. Instead, he was traveling once more in the subconscious world of his own mind. This time it led him to a beach. He stood along the shore as the water rolled in and out, splashing up against some rocks. He peered into the water and a face appeared. Once again he saw her—the gorgeous green eyes and those rose lips that made his heart melt. The face was smiling at him. He spoke to the image and asked, "Where are you? I cannot find you. How do I find you?" There was a cool breeze; it was night in his dream. The moon reflected in the water along with her face. Then her face faded, and KM Lockhart's appeared. The words echoed at him. "Look for Lockhart. He is the key to finding me and the future."

A baffled look came across his face, and Magnus was about to reply, when suddenly he felt someone grab him and pull him up out of the bed. He was about to swing at the person when he opened one eye and saw that it was Christopher Preston. Chris whispered, "We need to go...now!" Despite the fact that he was whispering, his tone was strong and his eyes were dead serious. Without questioning him further, Magnus got up and followed Chris down toward the old cellar, which was never used. It had a rear exit. They heard sirens coming down the road toward the front of the shelter. They were fortunate the weather had let up; they began on foot toward the river. Chris said he knew of a place near the bridge that was safe.

Back at the shelter, there was a clamor of noise as Denton himself entered the building. As he burst into the room and saw that his prey was gone, he ran to the window and yelled into the night, "I'll get you before this night is over, freak!" The squadron of soldier-like officers tore the shelter top to bottom but found no trace of Michael Magnus. Denton was not pleased, to say the least. He was sure that he'd be victorious that evening and that Magnus was going to be his prisoner once more.

144

"Mr. Rubins, why isn't he here?" Denton nearly took the head off the little fellow as he yelled at him. Rubins was baffled. He could not believe that his betrayal had been anticipated.

Inside, Rubins was nearly as angry as Denton. Spite and revenge were the only pleasures he got out of life. In response to Denton's question, he said, "Check the log book. I know he was going under the cover name of Michael Lockhart." When they checked it, they did indeed find the signature.

Denton growled as he looked at the signature. He was pissed that he had gotten out of bed for a fucking signature. He yelled once again at Rubins for wasting his time. Denton decided he was not going to give up. Rubins had informed him that Magnus had left a car behind the previous night. With that information, Denton ordered his men to fan out and cover the neighboring blocks.

"That freak couldn't have gotten that far on foot," he exclaimed. The two patrols exited the building and spread out to continue the hunt. Denton was about to leave and join them when Rubins stopped him to tell him one last thing.

"You ought to know, Officer McKay, that there is another man with him. He goes by the name Chris Preston. He must have tipped him off; I'm almost certain of it. Either way, he's an accomplice because he is aiding and abetting the bomber."

Denton scowled a frightful look at Rubins and said, "You had better not be wasting my time."

Rubins gulped a pocket of air, very intimidated by Denton, and then walked off. For a moment, he stood there wondering if he had done the right thing, but then he saw someone else in the hall he wanted as a friend. He ran over to that man and started a conversation with him. Of course, he walked away while Rubins was chattering, and Rubins followed like a lost puppy.

Denton was steamed. As he exited the building, he looked back one more time as if trying to sense the intention of the criminal mind. He walked back to his car, picked up his CB, and radioed into headquarters that all shelters were to be searched. He also requested information for a Christopher Preston. He punched his steering wheel and sped off in a northern direction. The night was young, and he wasn't giving up quite yet.

Magnus and Preston had found their way to a nearby fast food restaurant. Chris suggested that they use the restroom there to clean up a bit. As they were standing in the men's room washing up in the sink, an employee walked in and said, "You two guys can't stay in here unless you're going to buy something."

Chris reached into his pocket and pulled out a five-dollar bill. He flashed it in front of the boy and said, "See, young man, we plan on buying something; we just need a minute." After the display of money, the boy left, and Chris continued to talk to Magnus.

"It seems we have a minute or two to catch our breath before we have to move on." Magnus nodded and asked what had happened back there. Chris explained, "Our great ally and friend Rubins recognized you and called the police."

"Why that rat bastard!" Magnus cried out.

Chris just shook his head and said, "Some people are just assholes, and well, we just learned of a new one. But forget that now. We need to press on and figure out what to do going forward."

Magnus looked at his new friend and said, "Thanks...I would have been screwed back there if not for you." He reached out his hand in friendship.

Chris accepted the gesture and responded, "We aren't out of the woods yet. We need to get out of plain sight, and I think I know where to go. I didn't really want to go there, but it seems like we have no choice."

Magnus looked puzzled, but before he could ask a question Chris walked out of the restroom and motioned for him to follow. Quickly they exited the restaurant and crossed the parking lot, ducking behind some bushes. They saw a very tall bulky man exit a police vehicle and walk into the restaurant. He approached the counter and ordered three quarter-pound sized burgers and an extra-large fries and shake."

The man was no stranger to Magnus's eyes. A flash of rage came over him, but Chris put his hand up and motioned for him to settle down. Magnus kept his fist clenched but didn't move. They watched the behemoth munch down an entire burger right at the counter and then walk out with a bulging bag of greasy food. He gobbled a second burger and then drove off, stuffing fries in his mouth as he went. Chris let out sigh.

After Denton drove off, the two men went back in and ordered some fries. There was a pay phone in back of the fast food restaurant. Chris made a collect call to the only place he could think of that might provide shelter that night. His father picked up the phone and within an hour they had been picked up and were on their way to a villa just outside the city limits. As they drove, Magnus began to realize that Chris came from a family with a lot of money. He was a bit puzzled as to why he was at the homeless shelter, and he wondered if perhaps they had had the kind of falling out where the family money was rejected. It didn't matter now. For the moment, he was just glad to have escaped his nemesis.

Magnus knew that Denton would be scouring the city all night, but for once he could get a decent night's sleep. Mr. Preston was quiet. He wondered who Michael was and why Chris said it was necessary for him to accompany them back. He figured that it meant his son would not be staying long. He wondered if they were in some kind of trouble.

When they arrived, Magnus's face lit up for the first time in a long time. Not only was the home beautiful, but he was given clean clothes and was able to have a real shower. He'd felt like an animal for what seemed like eons. After they both cleaned up, they ate and retired to a room with some privacy. It was here that Chris said, "We shouldn't stay too long. We need to formulate a plan and be on our way. There are three things we have to be concerned about: finding Arie, proving your innocence, and stopping Dar. It seems to me that they all tie together somehow. I just haven't figured out how yet."

Magnus nodded and said, "That sounds like the start of good plan, but can I please take a nap first?" Chris smiled and then showed Magnus where he could rest. Later, he went downstairs to have a long discussion with his parents. He thought it was important to give them some information to ease their minds.

The conversation was long and included a lot of emotions. Finally, it was decided that Chris and Magnus would leave in the morning. His parents would allow them to take supplies and drive the second family car. Chris's mother, Judy, had spoken up and taken control of the situation. Frank was full of anger, but in the end he gave in to the demands. They all knew at some point the police would be stopping there to check for the two men.

"You have brought hell to this house by bringing you and your friend's problems here. How could you do this after abandoning us for so long?" Frank shouted.

Judy interrupted by saying, "He had to come to us, and we will always be here for him."

Frank roared, "Judy, you baby him; that's why he's amounted to nothing. Stop your coddling! Let him take responsibility for his own actions." Eventually, things went from loud and crazy to quiet and sane. The night rolled on, and for once, there was a hint of hope in the air.

Chapter 28

WHIMS OF DESPERATION

It was a long distance to travel on foot, even for a veteran policeman who was in good shape. As he neared the end of his journey, Joe wondered if he would survive the encounter. After everything he had seen, he was beginning to believe that the creature he was about to face was unstoppable. He remembered Chuck and his sons. Then he thought back to the Teague family, Susie Blunt, Mrs. Keller, Stanley Kuchinsky, and Father Bartholomew. So many had died needlessly, and so many had suffered the loss of their loved ones because of Dar.

Trying to shake off the fear, he thought of Sharon again. She needed him, and he loved her, but what could he really do? He knew he was walking into a trap. The sky was starting to darken. Clouds were rolling their way across the horizon, and Joe had that sinking feeling. He looked down and checked the address he had written on a sheet of paper. A drop of sweat streamed down his cheek. He was only two blocks away. What would he do when he got there? Would he be attacked? Would Dar be there at all? An endless array of questions started cycling through his mind.

Joe noticed it was getting close to sundown. For some reason, there was no one in the street. Joe considered that and wondered if Dar had gone on a rampage. Then he remembered that Marc had evacuated the area quietly before he arrived. As he continued on, he felt like a character in an old Western on the way to a shootout. Only he didn't have a gun for the battle. Another bead of sweat slid down his face. Why did it have to come to this? Why did he make such bad choices? How did he let things get this bad? He started to blame himself for everything. All he wanted was for Sharon to be all right.

Peering up at the sky again, he noticed the clouds started to dissipate. For a moment, it actually made him feel better. He could see the house now. There was something moving on the porch. At first he thought it was an animal, but as he got closer he realized it was a rocking chair. Taking a deep breath, he moved in very slowly. After a minute, he began to see an outline. His heart began to race. Then he noticed long hair. It wasn't Dar at all; it was a woman. He wanted to run up to the chair, but that reaction was suppressed by the overwhelming feeling of impending doom.

Carefully, Joe approached the chair. It was rocking, but the person in it wasn't moving. The face and body were covered by a blanket. Dread entered his heart as he slowly stepped onto the porch. He was about five feet away when he heard a noise. Joe looked around in all directions but saw nothing. Facing the chair again, he cautiously pulled the blanket down. What he saw next nearly made him vomit. He placed his hand to his mouth and held his stomach. He just couldn't believe it. There she was—yet another victim in the wake of terror. Sonya McPherson sat there motionless. Her eyes had fallen in, and rigor mortis had settled into her body. Joe was absolutely disgusted. Literally, he had last seen her, alive and beautiful, not even a week earlier.

Suddenly, as if it had been there all along, he heard a voice. "How do you like my latest masterpiece?" The voice was strong, and when Joe heard it, a pain shot up his spine. He was frozen, as Dar continued from directly behind him: "So you don't like it. Well, I'm offended. This one was just for you."

Joe opened his mouth but nothing came out. He was flabbergasted. He looked at her and thought about how she had been mad at him and now he would never be able to settle that. Fear raged through his body, but he decided to turn around nonetheless. When he turned, he was stunned to see what stood before him. The monster appeared to be a regular young man in his late twenties—and looked identical to Michael Magnus.

On closer inspection, Joe could see that there was a slight difference. Darius's face was slightly darker in complexion. It was like Magnus had gotten a tan. There was a calm look about Dar. It was not at all what Joe had expected. In fact, looking at Dar, one would not have expected him to have done anything terrible at all. In any case, Joe finally mustered the courage to ask the only question in his mind. "Where is Sharon?"

Dar smiled a wicked smile. "You're a man who gets straight to the point, eh?" Joe's face was motionless, he didn't want to react. Dar spoke again. "Well, I suppose we should get down to business then. You see, there's something I have that you want, and there's something I want that I don't have. So I was thinking we could come to an arrangement that both of us could agree to."

Joe's face finally showed emotion. "How can you expect me to trust you? You killed Sonya and all those others."

Before Joe could continue, Dar held up a finger; his body started to shake, and his face began to change. The calm, pure look was replaced with a frightful expression. His skin seemed to become inflamed, and his eyes began to glow with a red hue. The change was so terrifying that it nearly caused Joe to wet himself. Once more, Dar looked up and this time he thundered. "I could just kill her now and let you watch until I kill you as well, but..." He paused for a second and returned to his former state. "I'm trying to be civilized and do you a favor. You see, Detective, I like this game we are playing too much to give it up just yet. So either choose to play or you're dead!"

Realizing he had no choice, Joe nodded and replied, "What do you want?"

Dar smiled and looked around. "I want you to do what you do best, Joey, and that is to gather intelligence." Joe was annoyed at being called Joey, but he continued listening to Dar. "I have heard about a special project—I believe it's called the Emancerian Project. Despite my obvious talents for getting information, this seems to have eluded me. So what I need is for someone such as yourself to bring me every bit of information you can about it. In exchange, I will be generous to you and extend a reprieve."

There was a moment of silence. Joe thought about everything again. It occurred to him that he should have simply brought a gun and tried to end this game. Dar spoke again. "Be careful what you think, Detective! If someone is close enough to me, I can read his thoughts—how else do you think I knew of your little plan? You can't hide anything from me."

Joe spoke back. "I want to see Sharon."

Dar replied, "All in good time, my friend."

"I'm not your friend!" Joe yelled without even thinking first.

Dar remained calm, but it obviously required effort. "Joseph," Dar continued in a contemptuous tone. "I'm hoping that we can be friends until we both get what we want. Then we shall go our separate ways, provided you keep up your side of the bargain."

Joe thought that he would do just about anything as long as he knew Sharon was all right. Dar yelled, "Fine! Come with me!" Dar walked right across Joe's path and kicked the front door open. Joe followed apprehensively. Once they were inside, Joe saw Sharon across the room. She was in a chair just like Sonya. When they entered, she looked up. Joe's eyes remained focused on her.

"Let her go." The words just trickled out of his mouth. Had he known what was about to happen, he would have kept those words to himself.

Dar's face changed once again. Joe was so focused on Sharon that he didn't notice Dar's shaking and the freakish expression. It kept going, and Dar's face turned red. Then he moved so quickly that Sharon couldn't follow the movement. He grabbed Joe's shoulder and punched him extremely hard in the stomach. Joe had never felt pain like that in his entire life. Sharon just watched as he fell to the ground and doubled over in agony. Finally, after letting out a cry of tremendous pain, Joe lay flat on his back. Dar stood over him and smiled. Then he said, "Remember, the Emancerian Project. Don't fuck this up, Joey. You know what's at stake. I'll be in touch in a few days." Dar peered at Sharon and smiled as his eyes went bloodshot. The look caused her to pass out from fear. Then he looked down at Joe.

Joe felt a paralyzing sensation throughout his whole body. Everything went dark and he felt a cool breeze blow against his face.

Chapter 29

TRUTH BE TOLD

The night had finally ended. KM was glad to have some light peeking into the room. For the better part of the night, he had sat up thinking about the last few days. His eyes were bloodshot, but he felt certain that he should keep himself focused. The room had the odor of dried blood, and every time he smelled it he relived Bill's death. He tried to shake it off, but it was the first time he'd ever seen someone shot down right in front of him. Part of him wanted to scream; part of him wanted to cry; but mostly he just wanted to get the hell out of wherever he was.

Things had been quiet ever since the incident. After toying with the idea for a while KM decided it was probably OK to communicate with the woman on the other side of the wall. "Darlin', hello, Ms. Arie, are you there? Is everything all right over there this morning?" The walls were still, along with everything else.

After about three minutes, Arie responded in a raspy voice. Her voice was so low that he had to listen very carefully to hear. "Hello…" Arie sat up and leaned her back against the wall. "Mr. Lockhart, why are you here? I know why I'm here, but why are you here and why did they shoot the other man?"

As his heart sank, KM sighed and started a long story. "Well, you see, I'm a lawyer from Texas, and one day they offered me a chance to be in this important case. They said the Chicago Bomber had been captured. I said to myself, *I'd be a fool not to take them up on that offer.* And it came with the bonus of a little fame. So I made my way here. I was assigned to defend Michael Magnus, who by the way, I later found out was innocent. He escaped though, and sometime after that, those five bastards out there started harping on me. For some reason, they wanted him to take the fall and they made it clear I was not to do a decent job as his defense attorney in the trial."

While KM continued talking, Arie was thinking back to that day. She could remember the flames of the surrounding building and the people screaming so vividly, but she was having trouble remembering who exactly started it. She remembered the five men standing in a room, and then there was a big explosion. Suddenly, it was as clear as day. Before, she had blocked it out because of the traumatic situation. "They forced him to do it as we all stood there and watched." The words echoed out of her mouth. KM stopped talking and started listening. She continued, "We were in that building, and he was there in another room and we could see him. They told him to do it or they would kill me. He had no choice but to start the reaction. I thought he had died, but I'm glad he didn't. I'll probably never get to see him again though."

"Don't you worry, little darling. You'll see him again. Fate has a way of bringing people together when they least expect it, and I'm sure there's a reason we all have come this far." The words helped somewhat, but Arie was reluctant to believe him. She thanked KM and asked him to continue his story. KM could talk the time away in any situation, and he knew it. So he babbled on about various people and events leading up to his kidnapping.

A lot of time passed—more than either of them could keep track of. KM had to use the bathroom. So he decided to ask Arie if they would let him go or should he just shut up about it. Arie told him that they usually come around and walk her to one. No sooner had she said it, a door opened somewhere down the hall. One of the five men opened the door to KM's room. He spoke briefly, "Come with me now." KM didn't waste a second. He jumped up and said, "It's about time. I was about to pee my damned self." The man, whose features were mostly hidden behind sunglasses, motioned for KM to go into the bathroom. KM took his sweet time. While he was in the stall, he heard another flush. He got up and went to the sink to wash his hands, where he saw a face that was all too familiar to him.

"Why William Haight, what are you doing here in this fine establishment?"

The bulbous man turned in an annoyed manner and said, "Well, let's just say I've got a better room than you."

KM was angry but realized the situation needed a little finesse. "Haight, I know this may be hard for you to understand, but being held like this isn't good for a man such as myself. If you have the better room, why don't we go there and discuss it."

Haight smiled. For once he had the upper hand on KM. He stated proudly, "If you want to talk, let's talk at the place best suited for you: right here amid the shit."

"OK, Haight, we'll play it your way. What is this place, and why am I here?"

William Haight was not a fool. He smelled that KM was desperate for information, and he loved that he was the only one who could supply it to him. He gave a two-word answer: "Let's go."

With that he walked out of the men's room. KM was hesitant but skirted after him. He followed Haight outside to his car, where they got in the back and a man unknown to KM got in the front and started driving.

Suddenly, KM started thinking about mafia movies he had seen. The next logical question came out his mouth: "Where are we going?"

Haight decided to let Lockhart sweat a bit. "Don't worry about it." he replied. "We need a favor from you. We want you to find Michael Magnus and contact us. Can you handle that?"

KM didn't like it, but he knew he had no choice if he wanted to get control over his situation. "Fine, Haight, you win. I'll look for him." KM's face revealed that he wasn't happy about it. He didn't want to do anything to help these people, especially now that he knew Haight was a member. "I always suspected you weren't man enough to stand up to these guys." KM used those words fearlessly.

"You don't get it do you?" Haight shot back. "Why should I fear them, when I'm the one calling the shots around here? You fool! I've been playing you all along. That little act in my office was for your benefit only. Just do what you're told and you'll be fine. Now get out."

KM hadn't noticed, but the car had stopped right in front of his hotel. The door locks were promptly opened, and Haight pointed to the handle. KM opened it and stuck up his middle finger as he left. "You may force me to help you, but I don't have to like it, tubby."

As KM walked away, Haight motioned to the driver and picked up his cell phone. "Yes, sir," he said to the person on the other end. "The plan has been set in motion."

The voice on the other end responded, "Excellent."

Chapter 30

COMMANDER ON THE PROWL

For a long time, there was complete silence at the Preston estate. The cars were cold and frosted over from the temperature drop during the night. Nothing seemed to be moving at all. Even the gray and white tabby sat still in its corner of the Prestons' living room. Magnus noticed it when he went in search of a glass of water. After getting lost for a few minutes, Magnus stumbled his way to the kitchen and accidentally bumped into a table before finding a glass to use. He was so thirsty he didn't give a second thought to drinking straight from the tap.

Magnus let out a sigh as he gulped down four full glasses of water. Then, finally feeling tired, he began his search for the bedroom he was staying in. As he walked by the front door, he saw a light coming through the window. The light came shooting in and traveled across the ceiling. Quickly, as if he had been spotted by a searchlight, Magnus froze. He didn't dare go near that window. In fact, he didn't want to budge a single inch. The few seconds that the room was lit felt like an eternity, but before long Magnus realized that he had to move. Noticing that the stairs were nearby, he scooted over to them and ducked underneath into a small, cave-like crevice. Seconds later, Magnus heard the doorbell ring. He swallowed a gulp of air and made sure he was completely concealed.

Seconds seemed like minutes. The ringing stopped, and then incessant ringing turned into knocking. Whoever was at the door was seriously persistent. Magnus kept thinking, *Nobody's home, nobody's home*, but the banging continued. The Prestons were slow to answer, but realizing they had no choice, the two finally walked down the stairs in their robes. Mr. Preston peered through the peephole and saw a tall, broad man on the other side of the door. Frank was hesitant to answer, but the policeman's uniform brought him slight comfort. If not for that, no one in their right mind would have opened the door for a man who looked as menacing as Denton.

Frank Preston saw the badge and knew that this was his test of courage. He cracked opened the door cautiously, leaving the chain connected. Denton began speaking immediately, "Excuse me. Is this the home of Frank and Elizabeth Preston?"

With reluctance, Frank Preston responded, "Yes, officer." He yawned as he examined the intimidating figure more clearly. Denton was not a polite man, but he attempted to have some tact in this situation.

"I'm Commander McKay of the Chicago Security Enforcement. Denton loved to change his title, and on that night he had changed it four times. At the last house he was a chief, and at the house before that he was captain.

Frank Preston was intent on not inviting the lummox in, but Denton wasn't going to leave until he got a look around. "Sir, I know it's late, but this is of the utmost importance. May I come in and have a few moments of your time?" Even with his polite words, Frank could tell Denton wanted to barge right though. The behemoth towered over the two people, who seemed feeble to him. Frank looked at his wife and then took off the chain and opened the door the rest of the way. He then motioned for the officer to sit on a chair not far from the front door. Denton quickly entered and looked around. This was the tenth house he had disturbed that evening. Christopher Preston, fortunately for Michael Magnus, was a common name in the area.

After scanning the room, Denton reluctantly sat down and focused his attention on the couple. He was disgusted with them and their home. If the truth be told, the idea of aging and becoming withered disturbed him. The Prestons were only in their late fifties, but in Denton's eyes they were a complete waste of existence. He talked again. "I am sure you folks are aware that right now we are searching for the Chicago Bomber. Don't be alarmed, but we have reason to believe that he has made contact with a man by the name of Christopher Preston. Our records show that you have a son by that name, so we are in need of your help. Is your son here? Elizabeth looked terrified, and Denton reacted to this with scrutiny.

Frank quickly covered. "Commander McKay, you have to forgive my wife. We have not seen our son in five years. So this news is extremely disheartening. You cannot imagine the worry that has gone through our minds since he left and we lost contact with him."

McKay nodded, and then he stood up. "I apologize for disturbing you folks, but we have to check all leads. I must ask that if your son does contact you can you please call us so that we may question him. We aren't sure that he's the right Preston, but just in case, here's the number where you can reach me." Denton handed them his card, which contained his cell phone number along with a few fast food grease stains. As he started toward the door, Denton warned, "Oh, and folks, make no mistake: this man Michael Magnus is extremely dangerous. Should you encounter him, do not hesitate to contact us." Denton looked around one more time and then placed his hand on the doorknob to exit. He was about to leave when there was a creak from upstairs.

Magnus's heart began to race. He had been expecting the door to close, and when it didn't, a bead of sweat rolled down his face. The sound of large footsteps could have made him scream, and they were getting louder and closer to him.

Frank quickly asked, "Was there something else, Commander?" Denton's expression changed quickly as he glanced up the stairs.

He answered as he moved toward the stairs: "I thought I just heard a footstep. Maybe I ought to check that out for you folks."

Frank only got part of his next sentence out, "That won't be—"

It was too late. Denton was on his way up the stairs, and there was no stopping him. He snapped on the hall light and proceeded to check the first room. Frank motioned for Elizabeth to stay where she was, and then he walked up the stairs to follow Denton.

Frank walked up right behind Denton and spoke loudly: "Do you really think someone is in here?"

Denton looked back sharply, placing his finger to his lips and widening his eyes. "Shhh!" Magnus heard the heavy footsteps continue as Denton entered one of the bedrooms.

Then all sound ceased as Frank watched the brute bend down toward the bed that sat against the back wall. He pulled out his nightstick, raising the tension. Frank began to sweat profusely. Denton snatched the blanket that was lying on the floor and then thrust his nightstick under the bed. There was a scream and a hiss, and then like lightning bolts, not one but two cats darted out across the floor and out the door. Frank smiled a sigh of relief.

Denton turned around, an annoyed expression on his face. He retracted his weapon and returned downstairs. Then he continued out the door and left without saying another word. Frank let out a heavy sigh and locked the front door. He walked over to his wife and held her hand. "We're lucky it was just the cats running around up there." Frank continued to speak about general things but winked at his wife, suspecting that their house might be bugged.

Denton got in his car, and the Prestons watched as the police cars finally left their property. Frank pulled out a piece of paper and wrote a note on it. Then he walked behind the stairs and handed it to Magnus. The note read:

I think you should get Chris and the two of you should wait about ninety minutes and then leave. It's likely they will be listening for the next hour or so if they suspect something. After that, they will return to home base and send a car tomorrow to check things out a second time. Take this money. Remember, wait a good ninety minutes, no sooner, and be on your way. Please be cautious, both of you, and contact us only via pay phone to my cell phone. Also don't make a sound, we are probably bugged. Within the note were seven crisp one-hundred-dollar bills.

Magnus was impressed with Frank Preston's knowledge of police procedure. As it turned out, his predictions were correct. Denton had deviously slid a listening device in the chair he had been sitting in. Two officers in a car down the street had been listening ever since Denton left. Denton himself had proceeded to the next house on his list, but he couldn't shake the feeling he had about the Preston house. Part of him had wanted to stay and explore the house further. However, there was a stronger feeling calling to him—his growling stomach.

He left a few officers behind and decided to hit the next house after stopping at the closest twenty-four-hour fast food restaurant.

Magnus left his hiding spot cautiously and made his way upstairs. Eventually, he found Chris, who had been hiding in a closet. If Denton had checked the closet instead of under the bed, he would have found him. The cats had saved him from being discovered. Magnus placed a finger to his mouth and handed Chris the note. Chris nodded after he read it. While the two of them were preparing to leave, Frank had a fake conversation with his wife for the benefit of those listening. "Let's go to bed, Elizabeth. I'm tired, and don't worry, someday our son will come home when he is ready. I know he's not mixed up in that stuff the policeman said."

Elizabeth agreed and the two of them proceeded upstairs together. When they got to the room she whispered in his ear. "Are we doing the right thing?" A tear rolled down her face, and he wiped it with his thumb.

Then he leaned in and whispered in her ear. "I think Chris is doing right here. He's made some mistakes, but I think he's got his head screwed on right this time. For some reason, I get the feeling that it's really important for us to help this Magnus fellow. I think he's doing the right thing. I just hope he comes back to us safely."

As they lay there in the bed, neither fell asleep, but neither dared speak any more words. There was silence, and then an hour and a half, they heard the car engine start and the garage door open. The motor vibrated their hearts, and as it faded their night turned cold with worry and doubt. Again their son was gone. Again they were alone.

Chapter 31

CALL OF DUTY

Many people had crossed the sidewalk in front of the municipal building on Court Street. However, for Christian Warren it was the first time. He had traveled quite a distance to be there. He took in the scenery for a moment. He was happy to be in a peaceful place. Over the last two years, he had been in and out of combat in a multitude of Middle Eastern countries. Compared to that, Chicago seemed to be standing still. Christian stood approximately six foot two and was a proud man to say the least. As a sergeant in the US Marine Corps, he had done and seen many things. At one point, he had even been a Secret Service officer who guarded the current president. With that position, he had traveled the world. However, now here he was at the seventh precinct. Christian had come to get some things from Joe's office. After his encounter with Dar, not only was Joe hurt physically, but his pride was hurt as well. So as a favor he asked Christian to go to his office and get some important materials.

Joe, back at his apartment, was stewing about the situation. He knew that he was the only one who could save Sharon. Dar was playing a game with him and no one else. When he made his official report, Joe had elected to leave out certain details. He was afraid someone else might endanger Sharon's life. He didn't mention that Dar wanted him to get information in exchange for Sharon. He wrote in the report that Sharon wasn't present at the location specified and that Darius Magnus had given instructions that he would be in contact at a later time with full demands.

Right after he submitted his report, Joe called Christian and started to formulate a plan to get Sharon back. He assumed Christian would be able to get clearance to certain sensitive information that Joe could never see. It was his hope that with a little help from him, the two of them could uncover the mysterious Emancerian Project.

After viewing the report that Joe submitted, Chief Frank was livid. In fact, he was up in arms that Joe had once again played into the hands of Dar. The image of Sonya McPherson's body, which he had personally viewed, had infuriated him. It was, after all, the chief's sad duty to inform her family. In his mind, he was haunted by the memories of all the injuries Dar had inflicted upon her. The monster had carved his trademark symbol into Sonya's body, starting from her back and across her entire body. The worst part was that according to forensics this was done while she was conscious. She must have felt every incision. On the day that the Chief had to make the dreadful call, he decided that he'd had it with Joe's performance and suspended him.

Chief Frank worded it to Joe in a way that he felt the detective would understand, saying, "Joe, we all want Sharon back alive and safe, you probably most of all. But the way things are going, I don't think you can do it. Your objectivity is obviously compromised, and on top of that you got yourself hurt. Consider yourself on leave until this case is done. You'll need the time to heal anyway." Joe took the news with grim acceptance. He felt that he was being held back by the department anyway.

He thought to himself, *Fuck the chief and anyone else who won't back me.* He didn't have time to waste on the needs of anyone but Sharon.

Christian was more than willing to help his brother. They had always had a tight bond. And even though it had been quite some time since the brothers had seen each other, it didn't matter. Joe had contacted Christian, and he had immediately gassed up his car and driven all the way from Jacksonville, North Carolina, to help his brother. When he arrived, the catching-up part of their reunion was unfortunately short-lived. The first thing Joe told him about was the murder of Chuck Rivera. Christian was outraged, and as he heard the rest of the story he became more and more determined to help Joe. This was, in a way, something Christian needed. He had been recently divorced, and Joe's call for help was just the motivation Christian needed to get his life back on track.

When Christian entered the lobby of the precinct, he walked straight up to the front desk and asked an officer where he would find the office of Chief Robert Frank. When he arrived on the eighth floor he was greeted by a very attractive officer. New at her Chicago posting, Officer Audrey Gaynor was top of her class. Her green eyes and dark hair caught Christian's attention right away, but he was determined to stay focused on the job at hand.

She spoke softly, "I've been asked to escort you to your brother's office." Christian nodded and they walked for about a minute before arriving at the door with Joe's name on it.

Christian noticed a few heads looking up from various cubicles as they were walking by. The looks were followed by whispering and other quiet conversations. Joe and Sharon were office gossip, and ever since the chief had found out about Duanesburg, he'd had the whole precinct on edge. Everyone was wondering how Joe was taking his suspension. Many were tempted to ask Christian, but none had the guts except Audrey, who casually said that they hoped Joe was doing all right. Christian simply nodded, but he really would have rather turned her question into an excuse for a date.

Christian wanted to make his visit as short and painless as possible. He went in and began to collect some of Joe's personal belongings, throwing them all into a bag that Audrey provided for him. While he was collecting things, he saw the picture of himself, Joe, and Chuck at the family barbeque two summers ago and paused a moment. *Those were good times*, he thought to himself. He shook his head and thought about how much stress Joe must have been going through. Joe had been powerless to save Chuck. And after all that stress and being beaten down, Sharon was still in danger.

Christian shook his head trying to banish the thought and had almost finished up when he noticed some mail sitting in a neat pile. He picked it up and started flipping through it. Joe had told him to keep his eyes open for anything they might need. Specifically, he was expecting some kind of communication from Dar. One letter was addressed to Joseph Warren but had no return address. Christian looked it over. On the front was a strange symbol. Anyone who had seen any of Dar's victims would have instantly recognized the symbol as Dar's calling card. To Christian pondered if it was important. Joe had mentioned a weird symbol earlier. Luckily, it hadn't been discovered by the chief or any of the staff. Audrey, still standing in the doorway, hadn't noticed his discovery. Christian quickly stuffed it in his pocket and headed out.

He threw a few other random things into the bag as he walked toward Audrey. Without warning, a man walked up to him with an unlit cigar in his mouth and a scowl on his face. He looked Christian up and down before speaking. "You don't look much like his brother. Can I see some identification?" Christian gave the man a look and then pulled out his wallet, displaying his military ID. Chief Frank continued to speak. The chief had actually recognized Christian from the picture in Joe's office, but wanted a closer look at what he was doing. "So you're a military guy, eh? Why did Joe really send you here?"

Christian had to think quickly. "Sir," Christian lowered his voice as if he didn't want Audrey to hear. "He was embarrassed to come here after being taken off duty." The chief snarled back, "Well, he ought to be! His performance of late was not befitting an officer and certainly not a detective."

The chief's loud rant annoyed Christian. He was obviously being intentionally loud so that all the others would hear. The chief continued, "You tell Joe to come down from that cloud he's been hanging out in! I'm sick of the cowboy shit he's been pulling! Furthermore! You tell him I've decided this leave is going to be at least two months. No, make it three, and subject to multiple psych evaluations before he can return to duty!"

Up to this point in the conversation, Christian had tried to keep his mouth shut, but he could no longer take the verbal abuse from the chief. "Fuck you, old man!" The words were so strong that the entire office went quiet. "Joe works hard and deals with a lot of shit! He doesn't need your shit on top of him too. Get over yourself and find another punching bag!" With that Christian smiled and said, "And oh, by the way, thumb dick, I don't work for you. Find some other chump to bitch to!" Christian was about to leave when Chief Frank grabbed the bag and rummaged through it. His efforts were to no avail. Annoyed at not seeing anything worth detaining Christian over, he tossed the bag back at him. Christian took the bag and started to walk way.

The chief was stunned and embarrassed, so he built up for his final rant. He looked at Christian so hard that it could have burned right through him if he had laser vision. Shouting at the very top of his lungs, he yelled, "You tell him to stay out of this, or he'll be history—permanently!"

Christian was reminded of his drill sergeant, and responded mockingly, "Yes, sir." And with a flick of his wrist, he saluted the chief the middle finger. Then he walked over to Audrey and asked her to escort him out.

Christian and Audrey entered the elevator together. As they did, Christian wiped his forehead and asked, "Is he always like that?" Audrey decided it was better to hold her tongue. She had learned during her first few days at the precinct that the chief *was* always that bad. Christian considered asking her out. She was pretty. But before he got the chance, the elevator came and he decided to walk out, thanking her for the escort. Audrey smiled and pushed the close-door button. Christian smiled back but kept on walking. As he exited the building, he kicked himself for not asking her out. But then he thought to himself that he wasn't ready. The wound from his ex-wife was still fresh.

Chapter 32

SHARON'S LETTER AND DAR'S POSTCARD

Christian's attention returned to the envelope. Now that he had gotten away without it being seen, he began to wonder about the contents. He thought of it like an assignment. Wherever it led, he would go. When he arrived at the apartment, Joe was waiting for him. Christian was glad to see Joe up and about. He winced when he saw his brother—even though he had already seen the welt Dar had given him, it was still painful to see. Joe was holding his stomach as he crossed the room. Christian plopped down in a chair and made a crack about the crazy people Joe worked with. Then suddenly, he fell silent. Joe's attention focused on his brother.

Joe watched as Christian reached into his pocket and removed the letter. He handed it to Joe, still sealed. As he took the letter, he noticed that it had been sent same day mail and that it bore what he had come to believe was the symbol of death. Joe opened it and found two objects inside. One was a letter, the other was a card. He read the letter:

> My dearest Joseph, I feel fortunate that I am able to write this letter. I would be lying if I said there was really a chance of me getting out of this alive. I am thankful that Dar found it humorous to honor my request and allow me to write you. Regardless, there are a few things

I want to tell you in case this is indeed the last time I have a chance to contact you. Firstly and most importantly, I love you and I have enjoyed every moment of being with you. Without knowing it, you have always been there for me when I needed you, and that's why I will always love you the way I do. I'll never forget the first time you kissed me. I can't tell you how much it meant and still means to me.

Secondly, don't blame yourself for this situation. I'm not sure how things got this bad, but eventually all things work themselves out. I have faith and believe adamantly that even if I do not survive, this despicable creature will meet his downfall. Thirdly, I want you to know that I have no regrets except for one, and that is that I wish we could have gotten married. I prayed for that long before you noticed how I felt. Despite this wish, I think you should forget about coming after me. It's too dangerous, and I'm afraid for your life, Joe. This thing isn't normal, not in the least. When he punched you, it felt like he punched me inside too. You passed out from one blow. I pray it hasn't permanently hurt you.

Joe, I have to hurry, so there's just one more thing I need to tell you. If I don't get out of this, I want you, not the chief, to talk to my parents. I don't think I need to explain why, and I thank you in advance for that. Before I close this message, I have to tell you that there's something special I left for you. I hid it in your apartment closet a few days ago. I figured you wouldn't find it for a while in all that mess you have. That thought made me smile just now, Joe.

Joe smiled for a moment after reading that part of the message. Sharon's final words in the letter were, "Please remember me, Joe. Please remember the way I lived and the way I loved you. Keep that in your heart long after I'm gone. That way I'll live on in you. Forever yours, Sharon."

Joe's vision was blurred from the tears he could no longer hold back. He placed his hand over his eyes and tried to maintain some dignity in front of his brother. Joe stood up and went to the box of tissues in the kitchen, blew his nose very hard, and composed himself. Christian was quiet. He thought it better to give Joe a few minutes to pull himself together. Trying not to stare at his teary-eyed sibling, he looked down at the coffee table and noticed the card that was still sitting there. Christian reached down and picked it up. It was from a gas station in Duanesburg. On the back was written another note. It read:

> As much as I love our games, Joey, you have three days until I lose patience with all this fun and Sharon dies. So you best get cracking on that information I want. In case you've forgotten, it's called the Emancerian Project. Don't try any funny business either...or that present I gave to your stomach I'll lay on her head tenfold. Let's just say there's a slim chance she'd survive it. And, oh what excruciating pain she'd experience. Mmm...just thinking about the fun—wow! You know I'll enjoy every minute. By the way, this isn't exactly fair, but I'm counting today as day one. I'll be in contact with you periodically to check your progress. Tell anyone else of this and she's dead. Play any tricks and she's dead. Tootles.

Christian walked up to Joe, who was still cleaning himself up in the kitchen. He told him about the card and said, "Listen bro, whatever it takes to get her back, I'm in. Let's get the information on that project thing and work on a plan to save her."

Joe looked up at his brother and nodded with confidence. Then he walked over to his closet, opened the door, and rummaged through it. Eventually he came upon a box he didn't recognize and opened it. It was filled with Christmas ornaments. That wasn't it. He began his search again and this time he discovered a small book-shaped object that was wrapped. Joe was about to unwrap it when he decided to wait until she was there with him. He placed it on the coffee table and then got up and said, "Let's go, Christian!" With that they were off, neither of them was sure of what they would find out, but both knew what they had to do—save Sharon.

Chapter 33

RED NIGHT

Deep in a forested area of upstate New York, tucked behind a golf course, stood a wooden cabin. The cabin itself wasn't very much to look at. It was old, rotted, and had no electricity or comforts. It was ideally suited for someone trying to hide out. It had only two rooms, furniture was sparse, and there was no heat. In one room there was a broken chair with three legs resting in a corner, and on the hard wood floor there was a woman sleeping. Her breathing was heavy, mostly due to the dust that filled the air. It made her cough several times, interrupting the silence. Partially awake, she felt a cold coming on and would have given anything for a blanket, coat, or any heavy clothing to ease her frigid captivity. Alas, she had none of these, and so the night chill continued to embrace her.

The moonlight slowly crawled in and crept its way through small cracks in the non-insulated wall. It created a star-like effect that filled the room with enough light for Sharon Baker to see. She fully opened her eyes, and the twilight danced in her pupils. Sharon kept her thoughts blank. She knew that thoughts were dangerous. Anything in her mind could aid him in hurting the people she cared about. But more self-interestedly, Sharon feared drawing his attention. He was near, and she could feel it.

From the first night Sharon had been brought to the abandoned cabin, she had been scared for her life. Dar was ruthless, unpredictable, and worst of all powerful. He created a fear in her like nothing she had experienced in her whole life. It was enough to keep her awake for nearly three days. Three long days passed, and he watched in the darkness, in the shadows, every move that she made. Without a word, without a sound, she knew he was there waiting; just waiting for something. On the third day, she began to wear out. The combination of hunger and exhaustion had finally taken its toll. She slept. And when she awoke, the moonlight briefly calmed her. Sharon gulped down some air and then called upon her training as an officer. She sat up, composed herself, and began to look around. Then the quiet was interrupt by a loud crash.

The crash came from the adjacent room. Then Sharon heard loud footsteps. It was the most sound she had heard from Dar in a while. He had been aloof since she begged him through the door to let her write a letter. For once he had paid attention to her and must have liked the idea, because shortly after her outburst the door cracked and his hand appeared holding a pencil and paper. She wanted to step on his hand, but in a blink it was gone—faster than it had emerged. Even though Dar's hand looked normal, Sharon knew it was the hand of a monster. Still, she had been grateful to be able to send Joe a letter.

At times, the situation was too much for her. It was maddening being alone and in constant fear. She would occasionally hear him tromping through the cabin. And when she would flinch from shock, a malicious cackling would follow. He enjoyed tormenting her. There were often random loud noises as if he was destroying the place, but no matter how many times he did it, it still shocked her. Dar continued to act wild and completely reckless. He indulged her fear of him. It made him stronger.

Sharon dreaded a confrontation with the beast but had no choice. She was extremely hungry, thirsty and in desperate need to use the bathroom. Standing up, she mustered all the courage she could and walked toward the door. She tried the doorknob. It was locked from the outside. Sharon hesitated but proceeded on. Raising her right arm, she was about to bang on the door when out of the quiet came his voice, deep and in a tone of great disdain.

"So…you're hungry and you want to use the bathroom. Whatever shall we do?"

Sharon paused, but Dar spoke again. "Well, dear lady, the door is now open and the bathroom…well, what one could call a bathroom…is to the right." Her hand shakily clenched the doorknob, when his voice roared: "Don't think, for a moment, that you would have even the slightest chance of escape while relieving yourself!" He chuckled and slowly backed away from the door into the shadow.

With grave uncertainty, she opened the door and moved forward. Temptation nagged at Sharon to look left where she knew he was standing, but instead she scurried to the right and straight for the bathroom. The light switch didn't work, but luckily there was enough moonlight to allow her to find the sink and toilet. The smell of the bathroom was offensive, but she had to make do. After a few moments, Sharon reluctantly exited. On her return, the hall was barely lit and she could hardly see anything. She bumped into the wall and then her stomach started to growl. Dar continued to watch silently.

This was a new experience for Dar. Never before had he spent time with victim. It was giving him an odd feeling inside. He wondered for a moment and asked himself if he was experiencing pity. Somewhat brashly he addressed her, "What do you want to eat?"

She paused and stood still, thinking, *Is he really offering me a choice?*

Dar was close enough to hear this thought and responded to it as if she had spoken aloud. "Yes, although your mind chatter is bothering me, so make it quick."

Again, without control in her mind, she thought she would just about eat anything, maybe chicken. Dar wasn't one to waste time. He moved up to her with lightning speed and stopped right in front of her. Their eyes met and she passed out, completely unaware. Dar placed her back in the room, in a somewhat more gentle way than when he'd first brought her there. Then he walked outside the shack and looked, around making sure no one was nearby.

Walking some distance from the hideout, he decided it was time to continue his survey of the area. He traveled for bit along a road, unnoticed, and passed a sign for a town called Gifford. Gifford was only about fifteen miles from Duanesburg. He had scouted it out before his encounter with Joe. Dar continued his walk and had what seemed to be a genuine smile on his face. For some reason, the quiet of the night appealed to him. He thought back to when he had found the shack, in a spot far in the back of a golf course. It was perfect; as if it had been waiting for him. He knew it would serve as a perfect spot to wait for Joe and not be bothered.

Eventually, Dar came to a part of town that had some buildings, most of which were closed. Finally, he stumbled upon a small convenience store that was still open. So he entered, grabbed a basket, and started to look around. To most people, this was quite a normal thing to do, but for Dar, shopping was fun in an odd way. He looked at the people and pretended to be one of them. He searched his pocket, fishing around for some money, and found a wad of cash. Then he remembered he had taken about sixty dollars from Sonya and thirty from Sharon. Dar thought of his victims as his own personal ATMs. Ironically, the smile stayed on his face as he realized he was about to buy Sharon food with her own money.

Dar picked up some veggies and other produce. Then he got some rotisserie chicken and a frozen pizza. As he went up front to pay, there was only one register open. He stood there waiting. Despite the time of day, there was a long line. Several annoying people were in front of him: a college student, a mother with a child who was crying annoyingly for candy, and if that wasn't enough, there was an elderly woman trying to write out a check and use coupons. Time seemed to slow, and Dar's patience thinned rapidly. He somehow managed to make it to the cashier, but the teenager crossed the line when she seemed to take forever to ring up his few items and then of course she just had to ask if he had a store card. Whether it was the store card or the total disregard for his time, it was the last straw.

Dar's thoughts warped, and his body began to feel really hot. At first, he just considered leaving without paying, but quickly it changed into the less merciful idea of destroying the young girl. And then, his thoughts ended abruptly, as Dar began to speak his mind. "Listen, you snot-nosed little puke rag—" Before Dar could continue his rant, he noticed the people behind him in line had started to stare. For the first time, Dar realized that perhaps he had acted rashly. The young girl stood paralyzed, waiting for Dar's next move. Dar felt the need to flee. He said firmly but without raising his voice, "Finish ringing me out now!"

The girl started to quickly ring up the items, and Dar reached in his pocket to pay, when suddenly he noticed the manager approaching them. The girl was frightened, which had distracted her from doing the job properly. She had started packing items without ringing them up. Once the manager got close,

Dar knew he needed to make a move. What the manager was thinking became absolutely clear. He had called the police after recognizing Dar's face and was now coming over to stall him.

Dar was furious, but at the same time he became frantic. He didn't want to risk an all-out confrontation with the police. So he focused harder on making the girl do exactly what he wanted. Without control, she started flinging the groceries into bags, and just when the manager reached them, Dar heard sirens. The cashier stopped. All the items were finally packed, and Dar slapped down two twenties and a ten. He started to push his cart out when the manager said, "Excuse me, sir! Excuse me, sir! Wait a minute!" Dar became more frantic and was about to run, but before he could exit the store, three police vehicles entered the parking lot. There were sirens blaring as they screeched to a stop near the front window of the store. Dar immediately froze. Every part of him thumped along with his heartbeat, and that hot feeling covered his entire body.

Time stood dead still. The flashing lights were glaring through the windows of the store. Five policemen got out of their vehicles and pointed their weapons at Dar from outside. A sixth officer spoke through a loudspeaker. "Put your hands up! You are surrounded!" The moment was incredibly intense. Every eye in the store was on Dar. Every mind was simultaneously out of control and in a state of frenzy. The amount of mind traffic became too much for Dar to handle. He was sweating buckets and breathing heavily. Part of him wanted to yell, but his chest was pounding.

Suddenly, like a defense mechanism, Dar's mind went blank, clearing out all thoughts from his mind except one. He concentrated on being far away. He concentrated, and in his third eye he could see a different place. The thought was so strong that it broadcast into the minds of four people standing near him. Dar's eyes went blank, and he could no longer see anything around him. Then there was a bright flash, and when his vision returned, Dar was no longer in the store. He had vanished into thin air right before their eyes. Knowing he was far enough away, he took a deep breath and headed back to the shack.

The smile that Dar had earlier was gone—his peace of mind was destroyed. For the first time, he had publicly revealed his trump card and mind-traveled. Actually, in reality he had covered more than a mile. Never before had he teleported this far. In the past, he had only been able to move short distances, but this time the intensity of the moment propelled him much farther.

Dar's breathing returned to normal. He was glad to be far away from the situation, but it worried him that so many people had seen him disappear. He continued on foot for about thirty minutes, and as he did he thought back to when he'd lost the lobsters because of the police. This was now the second time he'd had to use his ability to escape a bad situation. It seemed to him that more and more his abilities were being revealed before he wanted them to be. He walked across the green of the golf course and entered the forested area where the shack was concealed.

When he was sure the coast was clear, Dar started a fire behind the cabin where it wouldn't be noticed. He started to unpack the groceries and suddenly smelled something putrid. He picked up the milk and realized he had forgotten to check the expiration date. In a fever of anger, he threw it against a tree and it exploded everywhere. The anger made him think that he didn't need a prisoner and that perhaps it was causing too much trouble for him. He scowled a look that could have killed a man on the spot, but then he paused, remembering his cooking game, and went back to playing the chef.

Sharon eventually awoke and ate well that night. Dar even provided a napkin and some plastic utensils. Having been literally starved, she ate everything he provided. It puzzled her why he was so generous, but she let it go. After she ate, the night ended with her being locked up again and Dar slamming objects, making noise, and finally retreating to the rooftop. There he stood, poised, contemplating what his next move should be.

From this point on two things were certain. His patience was wearing thin and he needed the information about the Emancerian Project soon, and Sharon wasn't going to get that kind of hospitality anymore. The game was over. He no longer wanted to play chef, and he was quickly forgetting why he needed her alive. Sharon crouched up against the corner of her room peering out through the holes. It was cold, and she desperately missed Joe. She cried herself to sleep. The night fell silent and the moon was blood red.

Chapter 34

WHERE TO TURN NEXT

The night had come and gone, and the dreams that spun in his head had kept KM Lockhart from sleeping restfully. The hotel bed was hard, but it was far superior to the accommodations of the night before. KM needed to figure out what to do next. He had been threatened, kidnapped, and beaten up, and the situation was not getting better. In fact, it was getting worse. Somehow he had ended at the mercy of his biggest rival. Haight had tricked him into thinking that he was being threatened as well, when all along he was conspiring with the mysterious five.

KM sat up in his bed and turned toward the window. The next step to take was unclear. His mind had gone numb. He let out a deep breath and then the thought of Bill returned to him. *Poor Bill,* he thought to himself. All he had wanted to do was be good at his job, and Haight, along with those murderers, had taken that away. He thought about how he'd treated Bill during their interactions. Realizing that he could have shown him a bit more courtesy, KM regretted his actions. He felt that maybe there was something more he could have said or done that would have saved Bill, but it was too late now. Alone and out of sorts, KM broke down. No jokes or flippant words would allow him to escape his guilt.

The phone rang, and he was startled. At first he let it ring, but eventually he stood up and walked over to the table it was resting on. He paused but then picked it up. It was the front desk asking if he would accept a call from his wife;

he agreed. Madeline spoke first, "Where have you been? You haven't called! What's been going on out there? Well? Well?"

KM didn't even know where to begin. He felt like hiding from the world. "Maddy darling, I'm sorry I've been a wretch. I've been playing around out here and now things have gone out of control. I'm not sure what to do now."

She waited to hear more, but KM had stopped speaking. His breathing was heavy and for once he was at a loss for words with her. She thought for a moment and then made a choice. "Ken, Ken…listen to me. I'm coming there. We need to talk in person, and I'm not waiting for you to come back here. I'm buying the ticket online right now. I should be there in two days." KM started to tell her not to come, but then he realized he wanted her there. He needed some stability, even if he had to admit to everything. Part of him wanted to tell her everything right then on the phone, but he knew better.

"OK, Maddy, I want you to come. I'll pick you up when you arrive. There's just one thing I want to say…hurry up, I'm lost without you."

Madeline Lockhart cried a bit, then she said her goodbyes. KM put the phone back down and sat in the chair by the window. After sulking awhile, he pulled himself together and went to the bathroom, showered, and got dressed. His thoughts were a little less clouded after talking to his wife. Earlier he had seen a man in a black business suit walk into the hotel. It worried him that maybe they were coming for him, but then he realized he was just being paranoid. He was definitely feeling on edge, though, and he hated it. Internally, he thought that this was not the kind of man he wanted to be. He shut his eyes and tried to focus on what to do. He needed to report what had happened to Bill. It was the least he could do for him. He just didn't know how to do it. He had to seek out help, and he had to do it without letting the mysterious five catch on.

He tried to think of the people he could trust. For a minute, he thought of contacting Joe Warren, but he really wasn't that sure about him. Then he remembered someone he had absolutely forgotten about—Warden Peter Cahill. With all the craziness that had gone on, it had completely slipped his mind that he had had that talk with Cahill and was given the pin to signal for help. Too many things had happened so quickly. Bill had died so senselessly. However, as he thought about the situation more, he realized that perhaps Cahill was just the man to get him out of this situation. Walking over to his suitcase, he pulled out the pin and examined it. It looked simple enough. If only he had brought it with him when he was first captured. "Well," he said out loud, "I won't make that mistake twice."

KM attached the pin to the lapel of his jacket and walked over to the phone. He pulled out Cahill's card and dialed the number. The secretary answered. After scheduling an appointment for later that day, he called the seventh precinct and asked to speak with Chief Robert Frank. When he finally got through, he made the conversation fairly general. He asked if there had been were any updates on the fugitives. Robert Frank didn't seem very happy to be discussing the issue, so KM pressed a bit harder. Eventually, the chief mentioned that Sonya McPherson had been killed and found in Duanesburg.

This news floored KM. He felt completely and utterly sick again. After having just asked her out not two days ago, he now found out she had been murdered. It was too much to bear. "What a terrible waste," he repeated the phrase three times in a raspy voice. The chief concurred. KM was tempted to report Bill's death and his kidnapping, but he knew the lines weren't secure. He needed to hold that information back until the right time. The chief spoke again, inviting KM to lunch that day, but KM had to push it to the evening because of his meeting with Cahill.

After talking to Michael Frank, KM called the front desk and asked them to have a car sent for him. He advised them that he needed to be transported to the DEDC. He gathered some of his paperwork and walked cautiously down the hall to the elevator. Everything seemed OK, but throughout his career he had repeatedly learned that things were very rarely as they seemed. When he arrived on the ground floor, he approached the desk clerk and inquired about the car he had requested. The clerk walked away and returned after about three minutes. "Mr. Lockhart, we apologize for the inconvenience, but a car will not be available for another five minutes. The hotel invites you to wait in the lobby right over there, and we will come get you as soon as it arrives." KM nodded and walked away. This really annoyed him. He wanted to shout and holler about it, but instead he simply nodded and walked toward the waiting area.

The clerk was surprised and confused. For one thing, KM had a personal car; the hotel normally didn't have to provide him with transportation. But even more peculiar was the fact that he was so quiet. It wasn't like him to bite his tongue, and all the staff knew it. He was by far the loudest guest they ever had.

After about fifteen minutes, a female employee ran over to KM, apologized again for the long wait, and offered to escort him to the car. As they walked, KM again remained completely silent. The girl asked him where he was traveling to, and he didn't even acknowledge the question. She assumed he was simply being snobby and did her job. KM waited in silence on the steps in front of the building.

After a few minutes, a car pulled up, and as he got in, the driver addressed him, saying, "Good morning, sir." KM looked him in the eyes, nodded, and with that they were off. The driver turned on some strange foreign music. KM sat immersed in his own thoughts. He kept wondering about how he was going to get out of this situation. For a second time, he thought to himself, if only he'd had the pin with him when he was captured he could have activated it and at the very least Cahill would have known where Haight's hideout was.

Just then, his cell phone rang. He looked down at the screen and didn't recognize the number. He answered. "Lockhart, we are watching you. Don't get any bright ideas about volunteering any information to the authorities. I'm sure you can imagine what will happen if you do. You have one mission, and that is to give us the location of Magnus."

Lockhart paused but decided not to show any frustration. "Well, if you bastards want that information, then you better give me some gosh darned space."

Silence followed and the voice responded, "Remember who's pulling the strings here, Mr. Lockhart. We know that your wife is coming to Chicago. Don't think for a second she's safe. Every step you make will determine our reaction. Don't get too bold. Otherwise you'll find yourself truly alone in this world."

The caller disconnected, and KM held the phone for a minute before shoving it in his pocket. He didn't know what to say or do. He was caught in a bind, and he couldn't see a way out. Fog rolled in and he watched blankly as his ride seemed to be endless. Placing his hands over his eyes he said, "What a load of horse shit."

Chapter 35

TRAPPED

On each wall was an elegant wallpaper trim and a portrait of a woman. The floor was carpeted and the décor was vintage. *This is a nice room*, thought Arianna Shoomer. At least it was much better than the last place she had been held captive. In the corner, she spied an armchair, and she made her way to it quickly. To her sitting in it was like a cloud. It had been quite some time since she had had a soft place to rest. Once seated, she gazed out a nearby window. She noticed clouds in the sky and that it was starting to rain. She walked over and tried to open the window. It was sealed shut. She also tried the main door to the room, to no avail. Then she noticed there was bathroom, and the idea of a hot shower took her mind off escaping.

Arianna walked into the small room, which had a tub and a shower. She glanced at a mirror that showed just how badly she needed both. She sighed and began washing her face. Then she looked herself up and down. Arie was thin and attractive, about five feet five with shoes, and she had light-brown hair. Her disposition was sweet, but she looked tired and worn out from her situation. For two months, she had been moved to from place to place about six times. Her captives were absent most of the time, and she was always kept in a room under lock and key.

The previous night had left Arie feeling uneasy. Her captors had herded her into a stretch limo at gunpoint, and a bag had been placed over her head. She had been worried that she had become a loose end, but here she was, yet again, confined in a room. Arie had given up hope of rescue, so she bided her time waiting for a chance to escape. When she had encountered KM, her spirit had been lifted a bit because of the knowledge that Michael meant more to her than freedom. Arie pictured him as she locked the bathroom door and took her shower.

While Arianna was away at school, she had missed her home a lot. St. Louis was a nice place, but it was very different from Duanesburg. Without her family around, she had begun to feel depressed. There was regret in her heart for the way things had ended between her and Michael.

After her shower, Arie dried off, got dressed, and sat back down in the chair. She wanted to think a happy thought, so she tried to remember back to the day when she and Michael had reconnected. It was bright that day, and the sun was shining magnificently. Her phone rang unexpectedly, and she picked it up, thinking it was someone from school. To her delight, it was Michael Magnus. His voice was warm and apologetic, instantly making her relive old feelings. She felt a relief that day that she would never forget. The conversation was pleasant, and they spoke about meeting again and starting over. It had made her so happy. She was certain that things in her life would turn around again. Unfortunately, that chance never came. Before she could meet him she was stolen away—kidnapped by the mysterious five. Arie lost control of her emotions and started tearing up. They had used her as bait to lure him into a trap.

Arie tried to calm herself down, but her thoughts got the better of her. The tears streamed from her eyes, soaking her face. The memory of the fire, the explosions, the screaming, and the chaos were so vivid. All the while she was forced to watch at a safe distance. She had wanted to turn away, but they forced her to watch as they laughed and snickered about Michael. Arie hated them... she hated them all. She vowed that if she ever got free they would pay for her loss. "Christ!" she exclaimed as she heard footsteps approaching. Running into the bathroom, she quickly started rewashing her eyes and face. The last thing she wanted was to show any weakness. The door to the room opened, and when the man didn't see her he pulled out his gun.

Claude spoke harshly. "You better show yourself or I'm shooting!"

Arie responded brazenly, "Can't a girl use the bathroom?" Claude tucked his gun away and walked toward the bathroom door. Then he spoke again.

"You know you're pretty gutsy talking to me like that when I'm the one with the gun." He was tempted to kick in the door but changed his mind, thinking that he might possibly get a whiff of a nasty smell. "Hurry up in there," he snarled.

Arie finished cleaning up her face and exited the bathroom. Claude looked her up and down with a venomous smile on his face. He figured it was about time he had his way with the prisoner. The others had been teasing him about how he didn't have the guts to be forceful with women. Arie was on guard. She had no intention of being raped. After holding them at bay for two months, she wasn't going to concede now.

After a moment of silence, Claude took out his gun again. He pointed it at her and said, "You are going to do exactly what I tell you, or else."

Arie was frightened, but she was also crafty. She responded as if she was absolutely terrified. "I'm not doing anything with a gun pointed at me."

Claude looked at the young woman and thought about how to command this situation and get his way. However, his lust got the better of him. He responded, "OK, then, I'll play it your way, but no funny business or you're dead." He didn't want her to get a hold of the gun, so he carried it across the room and placed it on the windowsill. Then he pointed to the knife strapped to his ankle and warned that he would use it if he had to. Claude made an abrupt movement toward her that made Arie jump back. He laughed as if he wasn't scared, but he was. After all, he had never been with a woman. He approached her again, grabbing her arm, and then he started stroking her hair. She was disgusted, but she resisted the temptation to pull away. She needed to wait until the exact right moment to strike. He pressed his nose against her face and licked her cheek, which made him feel confident. Arie turned her head, unable to bear her disgust.

Claude spoke again. "What's a matter? You don't like me, babe? I'm a real stud, and you know it."

Arie didn't speak. She was tensing up. Claude spoke again, "Aw baby, don't tense up; you need to relax and enjoy this." Arie swallowed some air and braced herself to attack. Claude took an aggressive posture and then grabbed her left breast. She immediately turned and flawlessly kicked him in the crotch. Claude was stunned. She decked him in the face and grabbed the knife from his leg. Then she bolted toward the gun, but an unexpected voice made her stop.

"Don't take another step toward that window or you're dead, Miss Shoomer." She froze. "That's good. Now drop the knife." Struck with fear, Arie knew she had to do it.

It was Sean, another member of the mysterious five. She released the knife, and it fell to the floor. A very pained Claude limped over, picked it up, and then cut her leg. Arie screamed and bent down to hold the wound. Claude limped to the window and turned his gun on her. "You know we need her alive, Claude," said Sean. "Let's go! Leave her to bleed a bit." Arie eyes swelled from the pain.

Claude was pissed. He was still standing there holding the gun on her. His hand shook as he tensed his grip on the trigger. He screamed in a high-pitched voice, "Fucking bitch, I'll kill you!" Arie had made contact with just the right spot. Janak walked in to see what the commotion was, and when he saw Claude shaking, he responded by pulling out his gun and pointing it at him.

Of the mysterious five, Janak was the most experienced. To the untrained eye, he looked like an ordinary Frenchman, but the best words to describe him at the moment he pulled his gun were intense, composed, and deadly. Janak was no fool. He spoke. "Claude, do you wish to die for this girl, eh?" Claude did not reply. Janak spoke again, louder and with more authority. "Listen, we are associates, but we are not friends. If you do not lower that gun, I will terminate our association!" Sean looked over at his younger brother and then at Janak. Sean knew just how serious Janak was. Claude suddenly felt it as well. He slowly turned his head and faced Janak. He spoke boldly, despite his sheer terror. "Who cares about this dumb bitch anyway?"

Janak was stiff and focused until finally Claude lowered his gun and walked out of the room. Sean let out a massive breath and was about to leave when Janak grabbed him by the shirt and slammed him into the wall with both hands. "That jackass brother of yours is not going to get me killed. If he fucks up again, he's dead. You know the stakes here, and you should watch yourself too. When he screws up, you look bad for bringing him in on this job. Sean, we may be friends and associates, but I cannot protect you from the syndicate." Janak released Sean and told him to give the girl a first aid kit. Then he ordered that no one was to harm her or even enter the room without his consent. Sean nodded and got a towel.

Arie had been quietly bleeding during the whole ordeal. Sean walked over with a towel and started adding pressure to the cut. Taking a wet rag, he wiped it down and then disinfected it. While Sean was working on Arie's cut, the fourth member of the mysterious five walked in the room.

Pierre entered and asked, "What the hell's going on in here?"

Sean replied, "Don't bother concerning yourself; it's nothing." Then he asked Pierre to help him lift her up on the chair. After that, he slid over a stool for her to rest her leg on. "Miss Shoomer, I suggest you don't move that kicking leg of yours. I would consider yourself lucky that it wasn't your throat. My brother has a nasty temper." Sean stood up and motioned the others to leave.

The two started to exit the room. Sean looked back and locked eyes with Arie before locking the door. Pierre was assigned to guard the door. Sean's exact words were, "Keep Miss Shoomer from getting out and Claude from getting in." Sean then went in search of Claude. He found him drinking a beer in the common area of the suite. Sean made sure no one else was around, and then he walked up to Claude and punched him right in the face, yelling, "You fucking ass!" Then he kicked Claude really hard twice in the stomach. "Why are you so fucking stupid, Claude?" Claude was about to answer when he received a third blow to his rib cage. "You fucking imbecile! You are going to get us both fucking dead. I've told you that things are run a certain way here for a reason. We don't question why, we just do it! Got it, stupid?"

Sean grabbed his coat and walked toward the door. "If you want some girl action, get it on the fucking street or in a bar. Stay the fuck away from that girl! If you don't, you're dead, and there's nothing I can do to stop it." Sean left, and Claude coughed a few times before picking himself up. Fortunately for him, his pride was more hurt than his body. The blows from his elder brother would bruise, but nothing was broken. His temper, however, was climbing. He kicked the wall three times before exiting the hideout. In the back, after all the commotion had finally died down, Arie broke down and started crying. She sobbed and sobbed until finally she passed out from the anxiety.

Chapter 36

A PLAN IN MOTION

The drive was long and tedious, but after crossing a second state line Michael Magnus had started to feel a little more relaxed. He had been laying low in the passenger seat while Christopher Preston drove. The two of them had agreed it would be safest that way. They had made their way through Indiana without incident and were now entering Ohio. Throughout their journey, Magnus would fall asleep and have tremendously vivid dream experiences. As he slept, the thoughts that plagued him took shape in his mind. When he awoke, he wondered if they were dreams at all. He could no longer consider them to be so simplistic. It was like traveling to another place, and at times it felt just as real as physically being there. While Magnus slept, Chris would try to stay focused on the road, but it was difficult. As a result of being around Magnus so much, his ability to hear thoughts had increased to the point where he could now see the images in Magnus's dreams.

As Magnus drifted off again, Chris experienced the strength of the imagery. At first it was pitch black, but then the darkness gave way to a flash of light. A ring of fire formed in front of him. Then the shape of a woman formed in the center. She was beautiful. Chris had never seen her before, but he knew that it must be the love of his friend. In the dream, Magnus approached, but the flames rose and started to overtake her. He could see her clutching her leg in pain. Pure instinct made him react in the dream by jumping forward in an effort to save her. As he crossed the fiery barrier, expecting burns, it vanished.

With the barrier gone, he gazed longingly into her eyes. It was a still moment as he watched the tears roll down her face. Then something made him look down and he noticed a pool of blood at her feet.

Magnus scrambled to reach for her, but she vanished before his eyes. Taking her place was another woman. The face was familiar, but no name came to his mind as he looked at her. After a moment, he remembered her face. He had seen her on the steps of the Chicago police department right before his preliminary hearing. What he didn't understand was why he was seeing her now. He tried to speak to her, but she did not respond. Magnus was puzzled. Then he got a tingly feeling on the back of his neck. It crawled upward until it reached the back of his head and started burning. Someone was behind him. Slowly, he turned around, and there was his supposed brother. Dar's eyes burned with malicious intent. Normally, Magnus would wait for Dar to speak, but this time he was fed up with the deceptions.

"What do you want, Dar?" Dar pointed his finger at Sharon and she collapsed to the floor. Then he walked over to her and pressed his foot to her head. She screamed and then vanished.

"Well, dear brother, this is a challenge. Can you find her before I obliterate her existence? If this one dies it will be your fault!"

Magnus locked eyes with Dar and then Dar spoke again, "Where are you? I've been waiting and I'm getting bored." Dar held out his left hand and red flame emerged. Magnus was silent and tried to concentrate. A small blue flame began to rise from his hand. Darius laughed with contempt. "You'll have to do better than that if you want to save Sharon."

Suddenly, there was a screeching sound. Magnus awoke abruptly. Chris was attempting to regain control of the car. The dream had been so intense that Chris lost focus on what he was doing. Luckily, he regained control and they were able to proceed.

They passed a sign that advised that a gas station was coming up soon. Chris decided he wanted to stop there and rest a minute. Magnus agreed. As they were pulling into the gas station, Chris suggested that Magnus wait until they were sure the coast was clear. Chris turned the car off, exited, and walked over to the pumps. Magnus stretched a bit and rotated his neck around. Then he decided that he wanted to stand up outside the car for a minute. After looking around and seeing no one nearby, he opened his door cautiously and stepped out.

An odd sensation came over Magnus as his feet touched the ground. He lost his footing when he took a step, like a child learning how to walk. It was very unsettling to him. He decided to walk around the car. As he did, his footsteps seemed very light, and then when he tried to step hard on the ground he was thrown upward about three feet. When he landed, he held onto the car, mystified. Magnus looked around. Chris had gone inside to pay for the gas, and no one had seen what had happened. He needed to try this again. He carefully walked around the side of the gas station and then behind it. With a great lunge, he bent down and jumped. He jumped roughly seven feet on his first try, and when he landed it was soft not heavy. He decided to try again. On his second attempt, he was able to land on the roof more than twelve feet up.

Magnus looked down at the ground, astonished at what he was able to do. He walked across the roof and surveyed the landscape. For some reason everything looked small to him. It was like a new awareness. And then, he noticed his left hand. On his palm was something he'd never seen before. The symbol that all those following Dar's murders had seen and feared was there. He didn't know what to think of it, but he needed to get back to the car.

Michael Magnus jumped back down and landed somewhat ninja-like... not even disturbing the dirt. *Like a feather*, he thought to himself. He decided to test his running speed. The car was about two hundred feet away. He concentrated and pushed off the ground, running toward it, but ended up tripping and falling face-first onto the ground. Chris returned with some sandwiches as Magnus stood up. Chris didn't ask; he had had enough knowing what was going on inside Magnus's head for a few minutes.

Magnus sat quietly as they ate. After a while, Chris had to say something. He asked, "Do you know that girl, Sharon?" Magnus shook his head while he continued eating. So Chris asked another question. "Do you know where Dar is?" Magnus shrugged his shoulders. He really wasn't sure. Chris took a bite of his sandwich. "How can he expect you to find him if he didn't tell you where he is?" Magnus didn't respond or think. He didn't have any answers. Chris closed his eyes and took a bite of his sandwich.

Magnus finally spoke. "Well, let's keep heading toward Duanesburg. I think that's where he'd expect me to go. Hopefully, that woman Sharon is there. I've seen her once before in Chicago, but I don't think he'd keep her there."

Chris stewed on Magnus's points. "I think you're right," he concluded. Magnus nodded, but inside he was struck with guilt. He wondered if Dar captured Sharon just to lure him into a trap. He felt terrible that someone would undergo harsh treatment because of him. He clenched his fist in frustration. Dar was in complete control of every situation, and even though Magnus was learning these new abilities, he didn't really have control over them. Would he even stand a chance in a real encounter with this enemy? He asked himself this question over and over until finally Chris spoke again.

"We cannot let self-doubt get the better of us, Michael. There are people depending on you. Both Arie and Sharon seem to be in danger."

Magnus interrupted. "I don't think he has Arie."

"Why's that?" Chris asked.

"Well, why grab Sharon and show her to me? If he had Arie, he would have just threatened her instead. She means a lot more to me."

Chris asked Magnus to grab the map, but when he went to hand it over, Chris didn't take it. Instead, he stared at Magnus's hand. Magnus had forgotten about the symbol that had appeared on his palm. He spoke, slightly embarrassed. "Yeah. That appeared when you went into the store." Chris examined it closely with a very worried look on his face.

He stated plainly, "That doesn't exactly look natural. If you know what I mean." Magnus just shrugged his shoulders. It was just as big a mystery to him as it was to Chris.

It frightened Chris a bit that Magnus was evolving. He wondered if Magnus would end up like Dar before long. Magnus sensed Chris's concern and began to talk about his feelings. "Listen, all this is just as big a mystery to me as it is to you. This thing appears on my hand, I get these crazy dreams that feel real, and I was imprisoned for shit I didn't do. I have no idea what's going to happen next, but truthfully I don't feel like I've lost control of my senses. I'm not about to go rampaging through the streets blowing stuff up and hurting people. I just know that I have to stop Dar, no matter the cost. I may be the only person who can do it. And I know one other thing: I need your help."

Magnus's words reassured his friend. Chris nodded and picked up the map. "Duanesburg, here we come," he said with a smile. As they started up again, Chris felt it necessary to tell Magnus the truth about his psychic premonitions. He could sense that Magnus was getting stronger, but Dar still possessed more strength. "You need to increase your power somehow. As it stands, I don't think that even you can stop Dar."

Magnus grimaced and nodded. He already knew, but he was trying to keep a positive outlook. "We'll figure out a way, no matter the cost."

Chapter 37

PRECIOUS TIME

"Joe. Hey Joe, wake up!" Joseph Warren had fallen asleep in his brother's pickup truck. The two of them had been traveling for a while, until finally Christian reached the recruiting center where he had first enlisted with the marines. It was his hope that he would find a contact there who could help him gather more intelligence regarding the Emancerian Project. Joe had decided he would wait in the car. Christian promised he would be back in five minutes, but five minutes had turned into three hours.

There was a bang on the passenger window. Joe opened one eye and saw his brother standing next to the car. Joe sat up with some difficulty; he still felt a terrible pain in his stomach whenever he moved. The doctor he had seen briefly had told him that it would take a few weeks to heal. Dar's demonstration of strength stayed fresh in Joe's memory every time he moved. Joe rolled down the window, still partially leaning back. "So what's the word?" he asked, while holding his stomach. Christian told him that he had to call in some major favors just to speak to the commanding officer on the base. "Well?" Joe urged.

Christian finally spilled his guts, telling Joe that a lieutenant by the name of Steven F. Sekar had agreed to meet with him, but at first he wouldn't give him any information. Apparently, though, after babbling on about protocol, Christian was able to convince the lieutenant that their situation was dire.

Joe tapped his fingers on the car door. "So...what did he tell you?"

Christian responded, "Fine, he gave me the name of this professor—Marcus R. Caputo. All I could find out is that he used to teach at Stonybrook University, but about a year ago he relocated to San Francisco. Joe sat up painfully and asked if he had gotten a full address. Christian responded, "Yes I did, but he's not in California right now."

Joe was puzzled. "Oh, really? So where is he then?"

"Actually, it seems that for the last month or so the good doctor has been traveling back and forth between St Louis and Chicago. Supposedly, right now he's somewhere in Missouri." Joe was kind of confused about all the information, but he figured that they had to follow any possible leads. Christian continued by saying, "The flight to St Louis is only an hour. Let's go. I've already booked us on the next flight out of here." Joe asked how much it was going to cost, and Christian said, "It's all about the military discount." Joe smiled.

Christian climbed in the car and the two of them had a quick chuckle as they left. However, unbeknownst to them, they were not alone. Luke, the fifth member of the mysterious five, was hiding out in a white sedan listening in on their conversation. He had been tailing them from Joe's apartment, and while Joe was sleeping he had planted a listening device in their car. As soon as he heard their plan to fly to St Louis, he called Janak and told him they had learned about Professor Caputo. Without Janak even telling him, Luke knew exactly what his next order would be. He was ordered to fly to Missouri and eliminate the professor and any and all files he might have in his possession. Janak's words were absolutely clear, "Kill the doctor and burn the files! We have come too far to stop now! Get rid of the Warren brothers if they get in your way."

Military connections were helpful, but the kind of connection Luke used in order to board a fully booked plane was nothing short of amazing. He raced ahead of Joe and Christian and made it to the airport first. He figured out which gate the next flight for St. Louis was leaving from, and then he waited near the gate entrance for anyone who left the area. It just so happened that a male passenger who was traveling alone had forgotten his glasses in his car and ran back to get them. Luke followed him into the men's room and used chloroform to subdue him without a struggle. He tied up the man and inherited his ticket and identification. A master of disguise, Luke adapted his appearance to look like the driver's license picture. The process was so efficient that he was in the air before Joe and Christian had finished parking at the airport.

The Warren brothers entered the airport and found their gate easily enough. Their wait felt unbearable. Joe was feeling very frustrated. After all, Sharon's life was on the line. Dar had made that clear enough. He wanted that information, and he knew that he meant business. A sick feeling came over Joe's stomach just thinking about what Dar might do to her. In an effort to focus, he asked Christian if there was anything more Lieutenant Sekar had told him. Christian said that Dr. Caputo had worked with the US government for five years on various military projects. The lieutenant was unaware of the specific nature of the projects, but he knew that Caputo had broken his contract with the government and had supposedly returned to his normal life. Sekar also told Christian that after he left, the government had kept tabs on his Caputo's movements.

Dr. Caputo had fallen out of sight, but Christian had successfully obtained his last known address. Joe declared, "Well, that's a great starting point." Joe hoped that Sharon could hold out while they tracked this lead. Christian nodded and wondered what they would do if they got the information and confronted Dar. He doubted that such a vile person would even hold up his side of the bargain. As they flew toward St. Louis, every minute counted. The Warren brothers had no idea they were in a race to find Dr. Caputo and that they were losing.

Chapter 38
CONTEMPT AND REGRET

By the end of the drive, the heavy fog was starting to clear. This was a contrast with KM's mind, which was very convoluted with thoughts of recent events. He was suffering through a wide array of emotions—but mostly anger and betrayal gripped his consciousness. To KM, there was nothing worse than being someone else's puppet. And being a puppet, with G. W. Haight pulling the strings, using his vernacular, *really fried his wits*.

The taxi he was riding in stopped, and KM reached in his pocket for a tip. Unfortunately, he had left his wallet back at the hotel in the room safe. KM always knew what to do in this situation, so he said, "Son, here's a tip for ya. Never trust anyone further than you can throw 'em." He envisioned himself picking up Haight's massive body and hurling it across a room. The thought of chucking anyone, especially Haight, tickled his mind, and he let out a half-forced Texan laugh.

After he exited the car, KM walked up to the front gate of the DEDC. There he was greeted by Thomas Rutger. Procedure required that he present identification. KM told Rutger that he had forgotten his wallet. Rutger's face was stern. He contacted the warden to see if he could make an exception. To his surprise, he was advised to escort KM into the facility. As they walked, the two of them headed to a part of the compound KM had never seen before. When he tried to engage Rutger in conversation about it, Rutger put his finger to his lips to indicate that KM should be quiet. KM turned his attention to the guards at various positions covering the grounds securely. He noticed that security seemed to have doubled since Magnus's escape.

KM thought to himself that Rutger was taking him for quite a stroll. After about five minutes, they came to a slope that led underground. Once they reached the bottom, they came to yet another gate. This one was guarded by an unfamiliar officer. When KM looked at him, Fishberg also remained stern. KM was a bit intimidated. Alan Fishberg was referred to as the Condor by the other guards. He was built like a tank and in a pinch would clean house whenever there was an uprising in the prison. Fishberg questioned Rutger, "Why are you bringing this *suit* down to the lower level?" Rutger explained that Warden Cahill had given explicit instructions that Mr. Lockhart was to be escorted. Fishberg scowled and picked up the phone. After a few minutes he received confirmation. He stood aside, allowing Rutger and KM to proceed.

From there, the two walked farther down the slope until they came to yet another gate. It was made of solid steel and had two cameras directly above it. Rutger swiped his badge in the scanner three times before the gate opened. They entered, and it forcefully shut behind them. The lighting was dim. To KM It looked like a cave. KM asked Rutger if this was the place where all the bodies were kept. The joke nearly flew over Rutger's head, but after a few seconds he got it. Rutger laughed and momentarily lost his serious disposition.

Tom Rutger was a pretty decent corrections officer. Ever since Denton had requested temporary reassignment in order to track Michael Magnus, Tom and Julius had split the command responsibilities. He enjoyed the power of a leadership role, although he really wasn't cut out for it. He fancied himself the authoritative type, but after KM joked he started making a few jokes of his own in an attempt to get KM to laugh. "How is it in the outside world?" He asked in a humorous tone.

KM was hankering to vent, so he did so with a Texan yell. "Woo-ee!" he whaled. "It's crazy out there! One headache after the next. But I suppose you folks round here don't know anything about headaches, do you?"

The question was obviously meant to be sarcastic, and Rutger played right along. "Oh, no," he responded, "I never heard of anyone getting a headache round these parts." They both laughed, and then Rutger asked, "By the way, what's a headache?" The two men broke out laughing hysterically. It was silly and lasted until they spotted two figures approaching them.

Tom was the first to stop laughing, and KM followed shortly after. Julius walked up and looked at Tom sternly. Then Cahill walked up. He got straight to the point. "Gentlemen, follow me." They all continued to walk down the long hall until they came to a door labeled Quiet Room. KM thought it was somewhat humorous to actually call a room the quiet room, but he kept that to himself.

KM actually remained silent until they were all seated and the door promptly locked. Cahill spoke first. "I just want to make this clear. If you are in this room, then I trust you. Therefore, you should also trust anyone who is in this room. He paused and greeted each man with a firm handshake and a deep stare in the eyes, except Julius, who had already been there with him. Rutger was surprised to be included. He really hadn't spoken very much with Cahill during his time there, but he figured this must be very important.

Rutger spoke next. "Sir, May I ask why we are all here?"

Cahill nodded, taking a seat. He then motioned for the rest of them to have a seat as well. KM was itching to speak. Before he sat down he blurted out "Conspiracy! There's a conspiracy brewing isn't there?"

Cahill took over speaking. "For some time now we have suspected the existence of a secret underground syndicate. This group has been quietly manipulating certain events to gain power and influence—"

KM interrupted. "If it's the same group that kidnapped me, they're a bunch of cold-blooded killers! My assistant Bill Meyers is dead! He was gunned down right before my eyes!" KM continued blurting out what he knew. "They're also a bunch of no-good kidnappers. They have that girl Arianna Shoomer—the one my client was looking for—all locked up!" Cahill tried to get a word in, but KM couldn't hold his tongue. "They have beaten and threatened me to *not* do my job and to be their fuckin' patsy! They want Michael Magnus real bad for some reason. And worst of all, William Haight is one of them."

Cahill nodded and clenched his fist; he finally got a few words in: "This may come as a shock to some of you, but I believe that Denton McKay is part of this organization as well." Tom and Julius were taken aback, but not completely surprised by the possibility of Denton being a traitor.

KM took it all in and then shouted, "Those bastards have got to be stopped. Poor Bill never had a chance! He freaked out and they shot him right in the head and dragged his body off.!" KM's eyes welled up, but he held back the tears.

Julius spoke. "Isn't Denton still under your command, sir?"

Cahill responded, "I haven't been able to confirm my suspicions yet, but I'm having Denton watched. I'm hoping that he will slip up and we'll get a location of this group's center of operations. Right now, we're stuck. They blindfolded KM here and he didn't have the pin to activate his homing beacon. However, I've been in contact with Robert Frank, chief at the Seventh precinct, and I believe that with his help we'll get the evidence we need. Since we are currently in a joint effort to recapture Michael Magnus, I know that his men will be all over Denton if anything suspicious goes down. When and if it does, we'll have a basis to act on."

KM interrupted. "They asked me to be a damned stoolie." The others focused their attention on him. "Yeah, that porpoise Haight threatened my family. He told me if I didn't cooperate they would be in danger. And he said he would be watching me."

Cahill jumped back in, handing KM a cell phone. "For now, play it dumb. Do whatever they say. Keep this meeting secret of course, but tell them whatever you think will satisfy them. If you need to contact me, use that cell phone. Keep up a good act until we can close in on them.

"As for the rest of you," he continued, "everything spoken here stays here. It has to remain absolutely confidential. This is the first step in formulating a strategy for this war against something much larger than I think we even know. Effective immediately, Julius, you and Tom are reassigned. I want you to head to Duanesburg. I think we will need you out there. Keep your eyes open and report directly to me." He handed Julius and Tom two-way radio cell phones. "These phones cannot be traced. OK, that's it. This meeting is adjourned."

Each man left the room with a knot in his stomach. Before he left, Julius asked one more question: "What about Magnus, sir? Are we going to try to help him?"

Cahill responded, "As things unfold, we will do what we can, but remember, we have hostages and a lot of dangerous people out there. We have to choose our steps carefully." He handed Julius a small paper with phone numbers on it. Julius thanked him and left. They both knew trouble was around the corner. The pot was full and about to boil over. The only question was when would it happen?

When would this all be over, and how would it end? And at what cost?

Chapter 39
CALL OF THE WILD

During the night, Sharon could hear footsteps moving around on the roof. Dar was pacing about impatiently, and when he stood still he would bellow a piercing howl. Dar had a way about him that induced absolute terror. When he howled, Sharon thought even the shack seemed to quiver in fear. Dar was incomprehensibly disturbing to her, and with each bellow Sharon's heart seem to stop altogether. She wondered how long it would be before Dar grew tired of keeping her alive.

The next morning, the taste of real food lingered in her mouth as Sharon awoke. To the unsuspecting eye, it seemed like a peaceful day. The birds chirped and life seemed to be renewed. Though a hole in the wall, Sharon peered out and could see the green of the forest. She coughed a few times from the dew that had settled in her lungs. And after taking a deep breath, she focused her mind on her current situation.

For Sharon, events were standing still. She was a captive with nowhere to run and no means of escape. She was still puzzled as to why Dar had cooked all that food for her. It wasn't his normal pattern of behavior. However, her contemplation would have to wait because she needed to use the bathroom again. This time she felt a little more comfortable knocking on the door. She stated firmly, "I need to use the bathroom!" One of Dar's eyes opened, but he remained perched on the rooftop. He had been in deep meditation. When he didn't open the door immediately, Sharon began to bang louder. Dar's other eye opened. It annoyed him that he needed to be at her beck and call. He tried to remain vigilant and return to his mind training, when once again the banging disturbed him. She had lunged her body at the door, making a thunderous whap.

Sharon was beginning to lose patience. She felt the anger build in her. So she took a deep breath and let out a screech that could have awakened the dead. Unfortunately, there was no one around to hear her. Frustrated, Sharon decided to try to bust the door down again. She backed up and took a running start. She barreled toward the door, and when she connected, the hinges snapped, causing the door and herself to fly forward and hit the floor.

The thud was very loud. Dar sprang up, bolting down into the shack. From a distance, he noticed that his prisoner had somehow managed to force the door open. Sharon raised her head and was about to get up when she noticed his shoes directly in front of her. She uttered, "I have to pee, damn it!"

Looking down at her, Dar laughed and said, "Well, all you had to do was ask."

His laughter caused Sharon's anger to boil. In her mind, she cursed him and his existence. Dar responded to it, "Temper, temper, my dear Ms. Baker. You want to survive long enough to see your hero again, don't you?" The way Dar had threatened and sneered deserved a smack, but Sharon knew she shouldn't try. Then he mentioned the letter she had written. "Your little letter to Joey was so touching. If I hadn't puked, I would've have cried." He let out another laugh. This time she scowled at him with contempt and picked herself up from the floor.

Dar moved aside, smirking, and then pointed to the bathroom. "Don't take too long now. A great many things must be done today." Sharon closed the bathroom door and for a few moments she had peace of mind. She was fearful of what Dar meant. It was obvious to her that Dar was being way too friendly. She thought it was possible that she might not have outlived her usefulness yet.

As he waited, Dar pondered how to handle what was coming. He needed to be mobile, and Sharon would only slow him down. His senses were clear, and Michael Magnus was on the way. He had been waiting for what seemed like forever. The excitement was more than he could handle. At last, he would get to complete his goal. Dar sneered a vicious smile. The life energy he had stolen from his victims would finally serve its true purpose. He relished the thought so much he nearly forgot all about Sharon.

When she emerged from the bathroom, Sharon noticed Dar leaning against a wall. He looked up at her and started twirling her handcuffs around his finger in a taunting fashion. Then he motioned for her to approach him and told her to have a seat. Sharon was very apprehensive but followed his directions. As she approached him, she noticed his eyes looked different. They weren't as menacing as they had been during their first encounter. It was the second time she had been able to look at him without passing out. It puzzled her.

Dar, sensing her thoughts, turned his head and gritted his teeth. Taking a more aggressive stance, he pointed to a nearby chair. As she sat, he started to make small talk. "Do you know my brother?" He asked the question very callously.

Sharon thought about her answer but realized that Dar could read her mind anyway. She answered, "No."

Dar smiled. "Well, he's on his way to try to rescue you. It's rather annoying. He hasn't the slightest inkling about my little game with Joseph."

Sharon thought to herself, *what do I care? I'm glad he's interfering.*

Dar became angered and said, "That wasn't very nice." As swift as lightning, his hand crashed into Sharon's cheek. She tumbled to the ground. Dar started to pace the floor. "I'm going to kill Joe, you know.

Sharon screamed at him, "You're a monster!" Dar smiled. He enjoyed the fact that he was getting to her.

A cold chill came over Sharon as Dar spoke again. "My dear, I haven't shown you my true face yet. That's the real monster." As he spoke, Dar turned his face toward her and summoned all the energy in his body. No words could describe Sharon's horror. Sheer terror shot through her entire body. Her heart raced, and tears streamed from her eyes.

This is the end, she thought. She believed Dar was showing her this for only one purpose—an end to his means. She would see no more sunrises, no more sunsets, and no more of the one man she loved with all her heart. A dark cloud sprang forth from his body and engulfed her. She called out for Joe with the last of her spirit, and then she collapsed. Dar stood over her body and looked down, wondering why he had been so kind to this pathetic creature.

The moment of reflection ended. Dar left his hiding spot to make preparations. He knew that it was going to be the most glorious fight ever. It would be a onetime treat. Never again would he be able to kill Michael Magnus, and he wanted to savor every moment of it. He licked his lips and headed toward Duanesburg. Today was the day—the day of his ultimate glory and triumph. And by nightfall he would put an end to his only true adversary.

Chapter 40

TRIUMPH OVER ADVERSITY

The previous night in Chicago, around the same time as Dar's night pacing, the sound of loud, thumping music could be heard coming from a dance club called Jazz. Sean, one of the mysterious five and Claude's elder brother, was walking through the park not far from the club scene. He was trying to clear his head after having a few beers. Boredom from drinking alone had led him to take a walk. And that walk had led him to this club.

Sean stood in the street under a large neon sign with purple letters that spelled out *JAZZ*. In front of the building, lined up against the wall, were lots of people dressed in club gear waiting to get their drink on. Sean didn't feel like waiting. Instead, he approached the bouncer and made eye contact. To the average person, Sean appeared to be a typical guy, but this particular security guard knew immediately. Word on the street was that members of the crime syndicate known as FENCE were in town. Everyone knew that to mess with FENCE was like a death sentence. The guard stepped aside quickly, and Sean entered. As he did, one man complained about having to wait in line for twenty minutes. The bouncer picked him up and threw him to the ground and barked, "If you have a problem, leave!"

Sean barely noticed the skirmish as he entered. He was far too busy noticing the legs of various women walking around in very short skirts. A smile accompanied his face all the way to a tall table leaning against the wall with two stools permanently mounted to the floor. The floor itself was covered with liquor, but again Sean was far too interested in the women dancing to be concerned about that. A waitress walked up to him in a black miniskirt paired with black stockings, and with a sweet voice she asked him what she could get him. He asked for three things from her—a Long Island iced tea, a rum with Coke, and her phone number. The young girl was flattered and winked at him as she went on her merry way to get his order.

When she returned, she placed the drinks on his table and asked for payment with a big smile. He paid her and asked her to join him. She explained that she had to work but said she might save him a dance later if he stuck around. It was a cheap trick to keep him buying alcohol, but he was too intoxicated to notice. He yelled, "You got it baby!" as she walked away. He took a big gulp of his LI iced tea and then went for the rum and Coke, but it tipped over and spilled out across the table, running down his pant leg. He jumped up, yelling, "Shit!" The waitress noticed and came back over to ask if he wanted another drink. He shook his head drunkenly, thinking that she was a dumb bitch.

As the waitress cleaned the table, Sean calmed back down. He noticed a big group of people in the center of the dance floor, and as he watched them, one girl flashed her breasts. This brought back his smile. Lighting a cigarette, he took a puff and another sip of his drink, enjoying the delightful sensation of the alcohol working its magic on him. He chuckled to himself and took a few more drags. Suddenly, he threw the cigarette to the floor and stood up. A girl was shaking her booty to a reggae song right in the middle of a large neon purple letter *J* that was part of the floor. It illuminated her legs and made him desire her even more. He staggered his way up to her and made eye contact only for a second before latching his hands around her waist. At first she pulled away, but he was persistent, shouting in her ear that she was the sexiest thing he had ever seen. The mindless flirtation was enough for her to give in to his advances, and she stopped pulling away.

Sean was a lousy dancer, and she could tell instantly. However, he was very aroused by her, and she could tell that as well. This kind of scene was nothing new to Sean. He was very aware of what he needed to do to bed a full-figured woman in the same night as meeting her. Whispering in her ear, he would ask her to buy him a drink. She would typically ask why, and he would respond, "Then why should I buy you one?" The young girl would generally ponder over this for a minute before he would say, "Listen, baby, I'll buy you drinks all night if you give me a good enough reason to."

Like so many others, this young girl had fallen prey to his wit, sarcasm, and confidence. She liked his brown hair and good physique from working out. She turned around and they continued to dance, facing each other. Their legs intertwined and their faces grazed each other, causing glitter from her face to end up on his cheek. Sean could feel her sweating, which aroused him even more. He was about to slide in for a kiss when suddenly he spied Claude and Pierre across the room dancing with two girls. One of them looked sexier than the one he was dancing with. Sean looked down at the girl he was with and said, "Shit! I gotta bounce, baby." Then he grabbed her butt and pulled her in for an extremely drunken kiss.

When Sean tried to walk away, the girl held onto him. He gave a cheesy line about being right back with some drinks. Of course, he had no intention of buying her anything or returning. Sean considered himself to be quite the playboy, and he didn't care if one female got away as long as another was there to take her place.

As soon as he got away, his attention was focused across the room, where Pierre was standing. Pierre was scratching his head while a young girl tickled his beard. She leaned in and kissed his nose playfully. Claude was directly in front of them, dancing with his own girl. His partner had really sexy dance moves. This was, in fact, what had first caught Sean's attention. Claude could be described as a thinner, less muscular version of his older brother. Brown-haired with a mustache, Claude tried his best to hold onto the young girl, who was outdoing him with her dance moves.

As Sean approached, he noticed the bruises on Claude's face, for which he was responsible. For a second, he felt bad about having done that to him. But he knew that if he hadn't done it, Claude would have probably ended up dead by Janak's hands. There was a chain of command within FENCE. To disobey a direct order from someone higher up was the worst thing to do. Sean shook it off and continued to stumble his way through the crowd. Sean thought to himself that he had let himself go too far. He was drunk. No…he was very drunk.

Sean's initial reaction to seeing the other two guys at Jazz was that it was comical. He decided to slip in and steal the pretty Spanish girl away from his brother. Evelyn Torres was extremely attractive, with long wavy black hair and a body with all the right curves. When Sean got a close look at her, he was wowed. He thought that she seemed way too hot for his kid brother.

Sean continued to dance his way through the crowd. It was extremely crowded. People were shoving and pushing to make room to dance. One heavy-set guy bumped Sean pretty hard, and it nearly caused him to get crazy, but he chose to ignore it when he made eye contact with Eve. She was feeling his lustful gaze even from a distance. It irked her a bit.

Sean made his approach by swooping in and dancing in front of Eve. He grabbed her waist while Claude continued dancing with her from behind. A silent battle occurred between the two brothers; neither was willing to let go of Eve. Inevitably, the situation turned ugly. Claude attempted to remove his brother's hands from Eve, but Sean just shifted his hands to her butt. Claude didn't like that at all. He scowled at his brother to buzz off. However, Sean was too drunk and high to care. Sean laughed and pulled Eve off his brother. Eve wasn't too pleased by this, but she figured it was all part of the fun.

Claude's pride was bruised for second time, and he started to get very angry. Pierre was concerned. He knew just how mad Claude was at Sean. In fact, he had offered to take him out to blow off some steam. Sean continued with Eve, dancing as if his brother wasn't even there. Claude's fist began to tighten. And then, as if time froze, the bottle in Claude's hand flew across the room and slammed into Sean's head. Shards of glass hit the ground.

After the impact, Sean changed. He went from jovial drunk to completely out of control. Sean dashed away from Eve and lunged hard at Claude. The music stopped, and a crowd formed around them. Sean was the stronger of the two, but Claude wasn't going to back down without a fight. Pierre stood back, considering whether he should break them up. He decided that a family disagreement should remain just that. The club bouncers, however, did not share his opinion. They forced their way through the crowd, finally separating the brothers and dragging them outside. Eve was ejected as well. She began yelling and screaming at the bouncers for being rough with her.

Once outside, Sean locked eyes with Claude. He was about to continue the fight when it suddenly dawned on him that Janak had left to meet with Haight. This left the three of them to watch Shoomer. He screamed, "Shit!" Claude was startled by Sean's outburst. Pierre had made his way through the crowd and walked outside. Sean addressed him. "You fucking idiot! You were supposed to watch the girl. What were you thinking coming out here?" Pierre was silent. There was nothing he could say in response. He had been thinking about Claude and forgot the girl.

Sean was about to run to his car when Claude spoke. "You're no brother of mine. Fuck you, Sean!" Sean looked at his brother, who was filled with contempt. Claude had pulled out his gun, which he'd kept hidden inside the club.

Sean said, "Listen, Claude. Don't be stupid. We are all dead if that girl escapes."

Claude responded, "I don't fucking care."

Pierre pulled out his gun and pointed it at Claude. "Enough, Claude. This has gone too far. It has to stop." Claude's face turned red with anger.

"Stay the fuck out of this Pierre," Sean yelled, despite still having the gun pointed at him. "The girl is going to escape! You fools left her alone! Janak left; he had some important things to take care of, which means that bitch is all alone." Just as Sean was yelling, Pierre became distracted by a cab speeding down the road. He could just make out the passenger in the back seat: Arie. Although injured, she had seized the opportunity and broken free.

Pierre turned and stood between the two brothers. He was about to say something when he was shot in the chest. Claude, in his drunken anger, shot him point blank. He refused to let go of his conflict with Sean. Pierre fell to the ground in agony. The people around them started panicking. One woman screamed. Amid all the chaos, Claude, still holding the gun on Sean, was shot by Pierre, who managed to pull the trigger of his gun twice. One bullet hit Claude in the arm, and the second bullet grazed his back. Claude couldn't move at all. He pounded the ground as Sean ran off. There he stayed until the police and paramedics came. Pierre wasn't so lucky; he was dead before they arrived.

Arie was on her way to the hospital. She hoped after calling the police everything would work out. Limping her way into the emergency room entrance, she was met by a nurse and taken into emergency care for her knife injury. When they rolled her into the ER, Arie had a half smile on her face. She thought to herself, *I got away.* There was now a chance that she would get to see Michael again. With that hope in mind, she closed her eyes and endured.

Chapter 41

A TOUGH CHOICE

The drive was long and boring. Both Chris and Magnus were tired of being stuck in the car. It wasn't a very luxurious ride. The cramped white Honda Civic sputtered a bit as they worked their way down the interstate. It had a dark gray interior and its pleather seats felt stiff. Worst of all, the pungent smell of smoke lingered despite the fact that they kept the windows open. Chris's father had quit smoking some time ago, but the smell was a permanent addition to the automobile. About midday, the temperature inside felt like ninety degrees, and with no air conditioning, Chris felt like a cigarette lit inside a box.

As they traveled along route 80, they both noticed a bright red Mustang convertible heading in the opposite direction. Magnus played with the idea of being in that car, racing down the road with a nice cool breeze rushing by his face. However, his daydream was ended when the reality of a how conspicuous a red Mustang would be. He snapped on the radio. A song from the nineties took him back to a simpler time. His childhood seemed more distant than ever; so much had changed since back then. The life he'd expected to have had definitely taken a few unexpected turns. He thought about all the new abilities he was apparently developing and realized that things were definitely about as different as they could be.

Magnus felt a warm tingling sensation that stretched from his pinky toe all the way though the hair follicles on the top of his head. It felt like standing in the cold during a bitter winter night and then finally coming inside and defrosting by a fire. And as time passed, the sensation intensified more and more. Physically, Magnus had started to look more defined. Chris had noticed but didn't say anything. He focused more on Magnus's thoughts.

Chris was concerned about the mental state of a man who was undergoing a drastic metabolic change. *What would a normal person do?* He thought. *And what will Michael do when his evolution was completed? Can he ever live a normal life again?* Chris could sense how badly Magnus longed for normality. He sensed his desire to be with Arie and the frustration of time lost in prison.

In the midst of all his heavy thinking, Christopher Preston began to ponder his own life. He, too, had gone through an extraordinary change. Once upon a time, five years earlier, he had left home to start a new life. At that time, school was his focus. He had studied astronomy, wanting to gaze at the stars. However, that dream had long since left him. He was still tormented by the incident, buried in his memory that had happened at Stonybrook University.

Just as his life had started to come together, a chance for popularity led him down a bad path. Chris made the mistake of participating in a frat house hazing event that caused a freshman to die. Mitch MacDonald was flogged and forced to consume large quantities of alcohol. His body went into shock, and the rest was history. The fraternity was closed down, and all parties involved were expelled.

Disappointed, Chris left everything. He wasn't able to face his parents. Looking back, he knew it wasn't the best of choices, but there was no going back at that point. And as one might imagine, being homeless for years, even harder times fell on him. Moving from shelter to shelter, he fought hard just to survive.

On the streets begging for money, one day something changed. On a crowded city morning, he reached out for help from a woman with a small child. She sneered at him and yanked the child up into her arms. The loathing she felt was so intense, it affected him in a way he'd never felt before. Something in him snapped, and he was able to *feel* the woman's thoughts. Despite their distance, he heard and felt her utter disgust. She cursed his kind and scolded her child for paying attention to him. Her thoughts were cruel, but it marked a turning point in Chris's life. His focus turned to developing that ability. Over time, he was able to hear more inner voices. At times it felt like seeing people with their clothes off. The true nature of a person, he found, was often quite different from what was on the surface.

When Chris encountered Michael Magnus, it was the first time he'd experienced imagery with thoughts. It was intense, but also quite addictive. Deep down, he thought there must be a purpose for his gift. However, he never imagined he would end up on a quest to stop a monster. Just as he was pondering the situation, a sign became visible on the right that read Welcome to the State of New York. Their destination was getting closer, which filled both of them with anticipation.

As Magnus returned to the borders of his home state, he could sense Dar was near and that their conflict was imminent. Shutting his eyes, he tried to focus. He felt pain in the center of his chest, but he tried to shake the anxiety.

Chris shared his fear. Part of him wished he had a gun or a least a bat to defend himself. He feared Dar's apparently superhuman strength. Being a hero wasn't as easy as he thought it would be, but he continued on.

They were roughly four hours west of Duanesburg. Chris started to feel fatigued from driving. Magnus felt it as well and broke the silence. "Why don't we just pull over at the next rest stop?"

Chris quickly responded, "Sounds good to me." The two of them stopped and Magnus exited the vehicle first. He took in a deep breath and let it out before addressing Chris. He looked as if he was going to be sick, but then he began to speak.

"I want to thank you for your help and concern, Christopher Preston." His tone was eloquent. Chris was surprised by it. Magnus continued, "The air is clean, and it fills me with strength." Chris twisted his face, sensing that he wasn't going to like whatever Magnus was about to say. "However, I think it is time that we part ways."

Chris shook his head in disagreement. Then he responded in a somewhat offended manner. "I've come this far with you. Why stop now?" Magnus sighed and looked at his companion.

"For your safety, Chris. I cannot endanger anyone else! Dar is ruthless! He's killed my parents and a lot of other people! I can't bear to think what he would do to you now that I consider you a friend!"

Magnus really didn't want to go it alone, but he felt responsible—especially after Denton had shown up at Chris's parents' house. A breeze passed by their faces before Magnus spoke again. "I sensed your apprehension, Chris." Chris's face contorted; he was stunned by Magnus's statement. "I think by being around you I picked up some of your ability to read minds. Listen, Chris, you don't have to do this! I do—you don't. You and I both know that if I don't stop him, nothing will. Like me, he's getting faster, stronger, and—"

"You're not strong enough alone, Michael," Chris interrupted. "You could die. And then what? What chance would we have then? I hate to sound cliché, but the world needs you. We all do! Running off half-cocked isn't the way to go. We have to do this together!"

Magnus leaned on the car and thought carefully about Chris's words. Some of them had sunk in. And then something else happened—their conversation continued silently via the thought waves transmitted between them. A conversation of thoughts is quite different from typical spoken communication. Like waves in the ocean, thoughts and images were shared between the two men. In the end, Chris was able to persuade his comrade to let him continue on the quest.

Tired, they decided to eat and rest for about thirty minutes before traveling again. During the debate, they made a plan to wait until Dar was distracted by Magnus. Chris's role would be to save Sharon. Chris agreed to this, thinking it was a sensible plan. As they pulled back onto the road, one thing was certain: before the day was over, they would be engaged in a titanic battle. The fates of many people were in their hands. They had to be strong; they had to be wise; and they had to *stop Dar!*

Chapter 42

THE CHASE IS ON

The clock was ticking. Joe and Christian Warren hustled out of the airport. They rented a car on the department's dime. Joe, still suspended, flashed a badge and lucked out that the billing codes hadn't changed. (The chief had, of course, taken Joe's detective badge, but Joe and his father had the same name, and he always carried his father's badge for good luck.) Once they had some wheels, they were off to the last known address of Dr. Caputo. When they entered the highway, Joe started stewing abo0ut how the chief had suspended him. It bothered him a lot that the chief couldn't see past jurisdiction to allow him to go help Sharon. *Fuck that!* He thought to himself. *Even if I'm never a cop again, I'm going to save Sharon!*

Christian, seated in the passenger seat, had completely different thoughts on his mind. He was wondering what to do if the address turned out to be a dead lead. It seemed to be a bit of a wild goose chase. After all, the military was having trouble keeping tabs on the doctor. The two brothers drove past the Saint Louis Arch and a few other landmarks, until they came to a residential area. The address was 1019 Providence Street, Apartment 9C. And fortunately, they had an onboard GPS that guided them directly to it.

"This is it," Joe said as they drove up to a brick building. They surveyed the area, then they exited the car. The doorway had buzzers for each apartment in the building. Chris pushed the buzzer for the superintendent. A deep, masculine voice responded through the intercom system.

"Yeah," Joe responded, "This is Detective Warren of the police department."

"I'll be right there," the voice replied. A heavy-set man of about fifty walked up to the door dressed in a tank top and shorts. Joe thought it was crazy that he was dressed like that in November, but ignored it and returned his focused on the task. He opened it and introduced himself as Wayne Jensen. Joe showed him the badge.

Jensen was a little annoyed at being interrupted. "You policemen sure are lucky I have today off."

Chris responded, "Oh? And why's that?"

"Well," Jensen retorted, this is the second time today you guys have been by, and I was here to let you in. Let me guess: you two want to see 9C, that Ron Caputo guy's place, right? He hasn't been here in months."

The brothers glanced at each other before Joe responded, "You guessed it."

Jensen huffed, "Well, I hope you two aren't in such a rush like that last officer."

Joe nodded but was swift to take advantage of an open-ended statement.

"Say, Mr. Jensen, we aren't sure which officer they assigned to come down here from the bureau. Can you describe him?"

Jensen described a tall, red-haired man with glasses, and he added that he looked he had a bad attitude.

As Jensen continued talking, the Warrens sensed that they were on the right track. It seemed as though another party had tried to reach their target first. As they walked up the stairs, both wondered if the previous visitor really was a policeman. When they entered the apartment, they were surprised by the mess. The apartment had been turned upside down. Jensen was upset and had opened his mouth to complain when Christian abruptly asked him to leave them alone for a moment. He said they needed to call this in and would come down to see him in a few minutes. Jensen left begrudgingly. Joe asked Christian to check the street from the window and to avoid being seen.

As he peered up and down the block, he saw exactly what Joe was hoping he would see: about half a block away was a mean-looking, red-haired man peering up toward the window. Christian didn't need his four years of military training to tell him this was the guy. He blurted out to Joe, "He's down there!" Joe nodded, realizing they would get far more info from that guy than from anything in the apartment. He asked Christian to wait and continue the search for anything the red-haired man might have missed.

Joe ran down the stairwell and came out the back entrance of the building. He hopped two fences and made his way halfway down the block. Then he walked casually onto the sidewalk, looking like a random pedestrian. He crossed the street and snuck up on Luke, who was still focused on the window of apartment 9C. Joe pulled his gun on him. "Don't make a move."

Luke was stunned. *Shit,* he thought to himself.

"You're going to answer some questions, buddy, but not here." Luke complied. He felt like an amateur, being caught so easily.

Joe searched him and made sure he was unarmed. Then the two of them entered the building and joined Christian. "Well, look what you found!" Christian blurted out as the two arrived. Luke spied the window as they walked in. Joe motioned for Luke to sit down on the couch. Suddenly, he ran for the window to jump. Christian instantly responded by tackling him to the floor. Luke's attempted suicide was thwarted just inches from the window.

As soon as he was pinned, Luke started screaming, "Get the fuck off me! I ain't telling you pigs nothing!" Christian placed his elbow in the side of Luke's neck. Then Joe ran up and kicked Luke right in his scrotum from behind. Tears streamed out of Luke's eyes. Joe kicked him three more times before stopping. Luke screamed out in pain.

Joe screamed at him in anger: "You ready to talk yet, shit-face? You're not going anywhere until we get some fucking answers!"

Joe was desperate for a way to help Sharon, and his frustration came out through his foot and into Luke three more times. Luke gasped for air as Christian's elbow dug deeper into his neck. "Fuck you, pigs!" Luke yelled again.

"Why are you looking for Dr. Caputo?" asked Joe.

Luke huffed and gasped. "To fucking kill him, just like I'm going to kill you two fuckers for nosing around where you don't belong. Now, fucking leave me alone!"

Joe was about to ask him another question when the door opened and in walked Dr. Caputo. Luke used the distraction to spin and elbow Christian in the head. Then Luke grabbed the knife on the side of Christian's leg and lunged at the doctor. Joe shot his gun, hitting Luke in the chest. Both Luke and Caputo fell to the floor, blood spilling everywhere. Joe looked over at Christian in concern, and Christian nodded back to indicate that he was not hurt.

Joe ran to the doctor and shook him, yelling, "Doctor, doctor! The Emancerian Project—what is it?" Doctor Caputo tried to speak but just coughed up blood.

As he lay on the floor, Dr. Ronald Caputo slipped from this world. Joe shook his head. The knife had been perfectly wedged in the doctor's neck. Joe was beside himself. He released the doctor and looked at the blood smeared on his shirt. He was about to give up hope when he noticed a piece of paper grasped in the doctor's dead hand. It read, "Doctor, your talents are needed to correct the failure of the E. Project. Gather your things and meet me at the Falcon Plaza tomorrow at two o'clock."

Joe searched Caputo's pockets and found a plane ticket to Chicago. "What now?" Christian asked. "The local PD are probably on the way here. That gunshot wasn't exactly quiet."

Joe responded, "I highly doubt they'll let us just leave without a shitload of questions. We need to leave now." Joe kept the plane ticket so there would be no evidence left behind. If they hurried, they could drive the rental car to Chicago and try to catch whoever the doctor was going to meet. The note was signed Janak. Joe hoped it would be enough to get them what they needed. They charged out of the room and back to the car, still racing to save Sharon's life.

Chapter 43

A MAN'S PRIDE

The wait at the airport seemed to last forever. Without realizing it, his eyelids had closed shut. Muscles stiff and lips dry, KM Lockhart stood up and stretched with a giant Texan yawn. Over the last few days, he had been threatened, kidnapped, beaten, and bruised. He even had to endure watching a friend die. However, none of this scared him as much as dealing with the woman who was about to step through gate fifteen. KM took a deep breath and sighed, fearing the worst.

Madeline Lockhart could be heard from a distance as she approached the gate. She was hollering into a cell phone. "Now, Peggy! You had better be watching the others and behaving yourself." Peggy was the eldest of KM and Madeline's three children. KM watched his wife silently as she came into the waiting area. He thought about the last few fights they'd had. Thinking about how bad this one would be made his heart begin to race. Their relationship had survived many battles, but this time it was possible he had gone too far.

KM continued watching her as if she were a woman on a movie screen. Bluntly put, he stared at her breasts and butt. She had lost some weight since the last time he had seen her. His eyes worked their way around her body. She looked just over thirty, but her age was actually forty-two. As his eyes made their way back up her body, he stopped at her lips and remembered that they were what had first attracted him to her. Madeline began to sense she was being watched. Her first reaction was fear, especially given the situation. KM stood up and continued to watch lovingly as she turned her back to him. He smiled at finally getting a good look at her round butt. He admired her tight jeans; they flattered her greatly.

Had it been a normal day, under normal circumstances, KM would have scooted right up behind her and given her a hearty slap on the backside. However, today wasn't the day for such frivolities. As he closed in, he noticed her dark brunette hair swaying as she picked up her suitcase. Madeline was some distance away, but once they finally locked eyes, there was a magic that connected them. KM hastened his pace, nearly running up to her. They embraced and he leaned in, kissing her with a passion he hadn't shown in years.

At first, his kiss was welcomed, but after a few seconds she pushed him away and just glared into his eyes. KM was no novice; he knew she was trying to read him. Every part of his body was aware of her test. He reached for her hand and she pulled back, continuing to peer intensely into his eyes. KM wanted to speak but no words came out. Madeline reached into her purse and removed a crumpled up newspaper. It was folded to the third page, where in big red letters it spelled out JUDICIAL SCANDAL! News Girl Found In Closet Abused! Madeline had read the details of how a girl heading out of his room had been beaten and raped by an unknown person. In the article, she admitted to spending part of the evening with KM Lockhart.

After glancing at the page, KM's eyes welled up. Madeline took a step back. The air between then was still, and they both were silent. KM attempted to compose himself. "Darling I—"

"Don't you 'Darling' me, Kenneth Michael Lockhart. Who the hell do you think you are, gallivanting around like a damned fool? Did you think I wouldn't know? You don't care a lick about who you hurt when you start thinking with your pants! How dare you call me all the way here? How dare you tell me you need me after you pull this shit! You're lucky I bothered to show up at all! Well? What do you have to say for yourself? Well?"

KM started to talk, but she interrupted him. "And another thing…how do you think your children will feel? When they see this shit on the Internet? What will they think of their father?" She slapped him so hard across the face that in addition to having a hand-shaped red mark on his cheek, he heard a ringing in his ear.

The yelling continued for some time before Madeline broke down and started bawling loudly. She wailed so loud that people walking through the airport stopped to look. One woman hit KM with her purse. All the makeup on Madeline's face had run. KM, in his infinite wisdom, offered her a hand-kerchief. Then he started to verbalize slowly and most timidly an apology.

"Maddy, listen to me. I'm a fool and I know it. I forgot what was truly im-portant to me." He sighed, emptying his lungs. "I'm in real trouble this time, Hun. It's not my fault, but I'm knee deep in a pile of dung."

From behind the handkerchief and through all the smeared makeup, for the first time since she had arrived, Madeline Lockhart showed a sign of com-passion. "Well, you jackass, what is it?" She uttered the words and he knew that she still cared about him. KM spilled his guts about everything. He told her about Michael Magnus and Haight's threats. Breaking into tears, he told her about Bill Meyers and his savage murder. She embraced him, and it really helped him to relieve a lot of the stress. The burden of keeping it all in had been eating at him relentlessly.

"Maddy, I love you! I know you must not think that means much coming from me, but I do. Thank you for coming." KM spoke with sincerity. The scene was touching. Madeline relished holding the man she married. She sniffled and tears fell from her eyes.

Eventually, she asked, "So what now? I feel stupid just sitting here."

KM responded, "Let's get out of here." He stood up and grabbed her arm, and together they walked outside.

As the two of them exited the airport, KM hailed a taxi and told the driver to head toward the middle of the city. The ride was quiet until Madeline said she was hungry. They stopped at a restaurant that served a southwestern-style breakfast menu.

"You know, just because I'm here doesn't mean you're forgiven," she mum-bled as KM smacked his lips at the food spread out before them.

Madeline did feel bad about his predicament. In between gulps, KM elab-orated more on what it felt like to be locked up in the room with Bill's rotting body. Also, he mentioned Arie, who was trapped on the other side of the wall. "It was the scariest moment of my life," he said, looking her in the eyes. He reached for her hand and she held his, despite the overwhelming urge to crush it with a mallet.

She started to shake her head and then she said, "There's not much I can do here for you. You've to get out of this situation by doing what they say. You don't want to endanger the lives of our children—"

KM interrupted. "You're wrong! I need all the support I can get. I can't just sit on my duff and do nothing. I am a man of principles."

Maddy just frowned as she thought, *where were his principles when he took that girl into his hotel room?* She shook her head. Deep down she began to think their marriage was probably a lost cause. She tried her hardest to keep from crying again. *Don't cry,* she told herself. *Don't cry.* Tears welled in her eyes, she put her head down on her arms, and then the words just seemed to drift out of her mouth like a canoe down a river. "It's over…" She shook her head again, tears flowing in every direction. "It's really over…" Her breathing was erratic. KM's throat became extremely dry. And then the scariest thing happened to Kenneth Michael Lockhart that he could ever imagine. Madeline picked her head up, looked him in the eyes, and said the words to his face. "Kenneth, it's over…"

Suddenly, everything else in the universe disappeared, including KM's pride, as he gasped, "Madeline. Please!" There was no response from her side of the table. He repeated, "Please, Maddy!" This was not the cool, calm, big shot from Texas talking. It was a humbled man begging for forgiveness. KM turned into a mess. He would get a word out here and there, but he couldn't stop sobbing. Deep down, he knew he deserved it, but he truly felt sorry for his actions.

KM was a man of pride, but in an instant, none of that mattered. All he could think of was life without her. He realized that he should have thought of that earlier.

Madeline was not budging. She'd had enough of his poor judgments. She removed the ring from her finger and placed it in her purse. Her face turned cold and stern. "Look! I've loved you a long time, but that wasn't good enough for you. You needed meaningless sexual episodes! Don't sit there and pretend that this was the first 'cause I know that this was just the first time you got *caught*! Madeline stood up and started gathering her things.

KM's heart sank into his stomach. Over the years, he had taken her love for granted. Every time he cheated, it got easier, and he told himself it didn't mean anything. As his daddy might've said, *regret had stuck to his chest like bird shit on a windshield*. He couldn't bring himself to laugh at his thought. She had already started to turn and walk away when he spoke. "Maddy, before you go I want you to know I never meant to hurt you, and I'm truly sorry." His face was drenched with tears. There was silence. And then just as quickly as she had come, she walked out of the restaurant and jumped into a cab. She looked back one last time and cried like a baby.

Chapter 44

BLOOD THIRTY
VENGEANCE

The afternoon came with a cool breeze. It brushed passed a very disturbed Darius Magnus, who was impatiently thinking about his upcoming confrontation. A scowl seemed to be burned into his face. Michael Magnus was getting closer, and he could feel it. Dar's blood boiled as he ate some red meat for lunch. He thought back to the prison and the wall that had been between him and Magnus. At that encounter, Dar didn't want to take the chance of being caught, but now there was no prison to stop him.

As Dar continued to devour his meal, Sharon Baker lay in a corner, bruised and unconscious. Deciding to keep her alive had been difficult for him, but behind his rage Dar realized that she might still be useful as a hostage. The Emancerian Project was still a major goal for him. All he had was a name, but he knew he was somehow tied to it. Dar wanted answers at any cost. Using Joe seemed to be the best way.

Dar stood up and made his way behind the cabin into the forest. He wondered if he'd have his answers soon. In the meantime, he needed to prepare mentally for the upcoming clash. Stretching his legs, Dar walked over to a spot for his meditation. With his ability, he etched a symbol into a large flat stone. It was the same symbol he had used on his victims. When the sun reached its zenith the symbol on the stone became illuminated. Dar sat in the middle of the stone, closed his eyes, and placed his hands in a triangle configuration. After a few deep breaths, he began to make a humming noise. The low hum slowly rose and seemed to spread out and echo from the stone. Sitting perfectly still, his body started to radiate a red aura.

As the humming got louder, it could be heard a mile away. Three locals, Curt, Jeff, and Ryan, were on their weekly hunting trip when they noticed nearby animals becoming spooked and running by them. Unfortunately for the hunters, they decided to investigate what caused the disturbance. They headed in Dar's direction, completely unaware of the danger they were walking toward. They fanned out but kept in contact on their handheld two-way radios. Dar became aware of their presence and stopped meditating. He decided to use them as practice.

Ryan was the first to approach Dar's location. Stumbling upon the cabin, he decided to investigate. Being cautious, he approached the cabin with his rifle in hand. As he approached, an ominous feeling came over him that made him grasp the rifle tightly. The scene went quiet as the humming sound stopped. And then, without warning, Ryan was dealt an intense blow to his lower back. The sound of his bones crumpling echoed in his ear as he fell backward, instantly paralyzed. Dar caught him as he was falling. He allowed his victim to meet eyes with him. For ten seconds, fear filled Ryan's soul. Mercilessly, the man's head had been severed from his shoulders.

Dar pilfered Ryan's belongings and dragged his body under a bush. The two remaining men, Curt and Jeff, had decided to meet up after losing contact with Ryan. They tried repeatedly to radio him with no success. Curt, the smarter of the two, was marking their path by carving a slash into each tree they passed. Jeff followed, keeping a watchful eye. Suddenly a gun went off, and Curt immediately turned to see Jeff breathing heavily. "What? What is it?" he blurted out.

Jeff laughed. "I saw a squirrel. I got him!" Then he ran into a thicket.

Curt watched as his friend retrieved the dead squirrel and started yelling, "Who's the man?" Curt just shook his head at Jeff, feeling a little relieved. Just then, a dark figure descended from high above, punching its way through the top of Jeff's head. Dar struck with such force that the blow busted Jeff's skull open, causing it to explode.

The blood from Jeff's head spattered onto Curt's face. Dar licked his lips and smiled at Curt. Instinct took over, causing Curt to flee. He dropped his rifle and ran for his life. Dar smiled again and laughed, yelling, "Who's the man now?" His laughter caused Curt to run even faster. His breathing became erratic; his panting was getting louder and louder. Curt looked back for a second and accidentally tripped over Ryan's head. The sight caused him to vomit violently. He had seen enough horror movies to know what was going to happen next. *And to think, I used to like those movies,* he thought to himself. Curt closed his eyes, thinking these were his last moments alive. He cried as beads of sweat poured from his forehead and nose.

Suddenly, he heard a friendly voice. "Hey you, are you OK?" The voice spoke again. "Sir, I'm District Ranger Vallone of the park rangers. Are you OK?" Curt thought for a moment. Could it be that he had been saved? Had this ranger scared off that demon? A sigh of relief came over Curt, and he started to breathe calmly again. He turned to face his savior, but the name and rank were just a cruel joke. The eyes looking back at him were those of Darius Magnus. At that moment, Curt soiled his pants. Every bodily fluid that could poor out of his body did all at once.

Dar smiled. This game had been fun, but it was time to end it and get back to his preparations. He chose the cruelest of ways to finish Curt—mind invasion. All at once, he invaded Curt's mind, building his terror higher and higher. Curt's heart began beating faster and faster, until finally it burst in his chest and he collapsed. It was a wondrous sight for Dar—a spectacular ending to his great new hunting game. Dar dragged the three dead bodies into the cabin and threw them into the corner with Sharon. Then he returned to the stone. His eyes burned red with hatred, contempt flowed all through his soul, and soon he hoped he would drink the blood of Michael Magnus.

Chapter 45

UNPLEASANT REUNION

"Get the fuck out of my way, orderly! I don't give a fuck if you have to clean that room. No one is going in there but me!"

The hulking brute was back. With fast food on his breath and ketchup stains on his teeth, Denton McKay leered down at the smaller man just trying to do his job. Eventually, he won the disagreement. He did, after all, have the law on his side, no matter how much he bent it.

As the orderly left, Denton looked over at his lieutenants and said, "You see, that's how you treat these hospital fuckers!"

The two junior officers responded, "Yes, Sir!" Officers Percy and Smithy didn't like Denton very much, but they respected his rank. So whenever he said jump, they pretty much asked "How high?" They had both been assigned to accompany him to the hospital to follow up on the manhunt for Michael Magnus. Apparently, a vital witness to the case had been admitted to the hospital.

Denton walked back into room P77. There on the bed was the person he was assigned to protect, Arianna Elizabeth Shoomer, a woman he had never expected to encounter, yet there it was, plain as day, on her paperwork. She lay unconscious. He stared at her intently. He knew what her presence meant. The hunt would be over if she testified to Magnus's innocence. *Why did this bitch have to surface?* He was so angry, he nearly uttered his thoughts aloud. Then he thought to himself that if she had to be here unconscious, maybe he could take advantage of the situation. Denton was needed to sow some oats. He noticed that she was only wearing a hospital gown. He leaned over to try to get a peek up the gown, but he was unsuccessful. He thought to himself, *Well, I can't say the freak doesn't have good taste.*

Denton licked his lips and was about to molest her when there was knock at the door. Extremely annoyed, he yanked open the door and yelled, "Didn't I tell you not to interrupt me?" But it was Arie's doctor this time. Denton was a little surprised, but he didn't apologize.

Dr. Tina Blythe walked through the door and said, "Excuse me, Officer McKay, but it's time for me to check on the patient." Dr. Blythe was very professional. She knew exactly the type of buffoon she was dealing with. The nurse accompanied her, and she promptly asked Denton to leave.

Denton begrudgingly exited the room, mumbling, "I'll be on the other side of this door, so don't try anything." Everything Denton said sounded like hogwash to the doctor. It was obvious that when it came to Arianna Shoomer, things weren't exactly on the up and up.

Once Denton was gone, Dr. Blythe spoke to Arie. "You can stop pretending to be asleep, Ms. Shoomer. I need to check your vitals. I'm a mother. I can tell when someone's faking." Arie sat up and smiled at her physician, an attractive woman in her late thirties with brown eyes and a fair complexion. She walked over to Arie and examined the stab wound on her leg. "It's healing nicely," she said reassuringly.

Arie nodded. She trusted Dr. Blythe, but just outside the door was a man who gave her the exact opposite feeling. Arie decided to voice her apprehensions. "That cop out there is a pig. And I mean that in the literal sense. He was in here staring at me, and he even started to lift up my gown. Can you do anything to keep him out of here?" Dr. Blythe smiled and said to leave it to her. When she and the nurse were done, Dr. Blythe noted in the patient's chart that Arie was in a fragile emotional state and that the patient was not to be disturbed.

Dr. Blythe showed the paper to Arie and then walked outside and started talking to Denton in a very authoritarian tone. "Officer McKay! Your presence is affecting the emotional state of this patient. She held up the chart and showed him. From this point on, I want you and your men stationed at the end of the hall. If you have a problem with that, I will contact your captain and have you removed from the building and replaced." She waited for them to move. Denton sneered at her with a bruised ego as he and his men retreated to the far end of the hall. He didn't utter a word.

After this embarrassing episode, Denton decided to get some food. The junior officers snickered behind his back after he left, as did Arie, who had heard everything from her room. She loved every single word. It made her feel somewhat safer, but she had a feeling that the men from FENCE would be looking for her. They weren't the type to give up easily. Arie shuddered at the thought of what they would do to her if they caught her again. She contemplated what her next step should be. Little did she know that two floors down in the critical care unit was Claude.

After being shot in the back, he had been rushed to the emergency room. Luckily for him, the bullet had exited without doing any permanent damage. His pain, however, was excruciating. Claude opened one eye and panted a bit. Mostly the pain was in his chest, which made it difficult to breathe. For Claude, the day had been quite traumatic. The only thought in his head was to get out of the hospital. He tried to move, but his back was also sore. His spine was in shock from the bullet that had passed close to it. He tried to move again but failed. Then the door opened, and terror set in. After his mistake, he knew FENCE would be after him. He was frantic; but then he heard the familiar voice of his brother. Sean walked up to him and looked him in the eyes. He was crying.

Sean spoke softly. "I'm sorry this happened to you. I'm so sorry, Claude." Claude looked into his brother's eyes and knew that he wasn't there to help him. He tried to scream, but before he could there was a pillow over his face. Claude's mind raced as he struggled. He swung his arms, hitting Sean repeatedly, until finally he was subdued. A single tear came from his eye as he passed out. Sean removed the pillow and looked down at his brother. He knew it had to be done this way. FENCE had deemed his brother a liability and was going to send someone else to kill him—and it would be brutal. Sean volunteered to do it instead so it would be quick and painless. He knew that there was no escaping FENCE. As Sean took one last look at his lifeless brother, he pulled out his gun, which was fitted with a silencer. He removed the safety, thought up an apology to his mother, and placed the gun in his mouth. It was the last thing Sean ever did. He pulled the trigger and joined his brother.

Janak and Denton sat in a car outside waiting for Sean's report. Suddenly, Janak punched Denton in the face. "You fucking idiot! You had a chance to end that bitch's life, but you didn't. Why?"

Denton rubbed his cheek and responded, "Sir, it wasn't the right time. There were too many people watching. If I had killed her then and there, they would've known it was me." Janak cracked his knuckles.

"I want that bitch dead. She knows way too much. She could expose FENCE. You better take care of this, McKay."

Denton nodded, knowing full well that he might be next on the hit list if he failed.

He exited the car, placing his gun back in its side holster. Then he asked Janak for an untraceable gun. Janak got out, opened the trunk, and handed him a gun. "Don't mess this up!"

Denton told Janak he would wait until things quieted down and then take care of Arie. He wanted a chance to finish what he had started earlier. He imagined the look on Magnus's face just before he was put to death. He would wait until that moment to tell him that he had raped and killed his woman. It would be Denton's biggest win ever. He laughed a wicked laugh and reentered the hospital. This was going to be one of the days he truly loved his job.

Chapter 46

ARRIVAL

"We are getting really close, Chris. I can feel him all around us."

Chris nodded and replied, "So what's the plan?"

With a sigh, Michael Magnus said, "Well, I have no plan. The element of surprise is certainly out. If I sense him, he can certainly sense me."

Chris thought for a minute before saying, "Well, he can't sense me. Maybe I could sneak up behind him."

"I don't want you fighting him, Chris; this guy is a murderer. He wouldn't hesitate to kill either of us. I need you to get that girl while I distract him."

Chris interrupted. "But what if he's still too strong for you?"

To which Magnus replied, "I'll have to take that chance."

As they exited the thruway, Magnus started to remember the area. Everything was familiar—the buildings, the people. It was all home. It had been so long that part of him felt nostalgic. They pulled up to a traffic light, and Magnus surveyed the area. To his complete amazement, sitting outside of a coffee shop were two people he would have never expected to run into in Duanesburg—Julius and Tom, the prison guards.

Julius took a sip of his coffee and said to Tom, "Now that we're here, where do you think we should start?" Tom was just about to say that maybe Magnus would come to them when a white Civic pulled up next to them. From the passenger side of the car, in quite a gutsy display, Michael Magnus called out to the two prison guards.

Tom and Julius were absolutely flabbergasted. Julius was the first to say something. "What the hell are you doing?" he asked. "Don't you realize that every cop in this town is out for your blood? You shouldn't be out in the open!" This was the first time Tom realized how far Julius's support of Michael Magnus truly went.

Magnus dropped his friendly tone and became stern. He looked at them both and said, "Listen, I need your help. Something big is going down here." Julius had a puzzled look on his face, but then he remembered that video he had seen at the DEDC. Magnus interrupted his thoughts. "I'm heading to the parking lot behind the movie theater. Bring burgers; we're hungry."

The two of them left Julius and Tom behind and drove toward the movie theater. Chris asked if they could really trust them. Magnus looked at Chris and said, "My memory has been shot this past month; all I have is my instincts. I've been living by my gut, and my gut tells me that these guys will help us. Think about it. Why didn't they just bust me right there at the coffee shop? They could have, but instead they're bringing us burgers." He smiled, and Chris nodded in agreement. Chris hadn't picked up any negative thoughts from them earlier so he decided to trust in the situation. While they waited in quiet, Chris's stomach growled. They were both famished.

Fifteen minutes later, Julius and Tom rolled up. "It's about time," Chris bellowed. The growl in his stomach had gotten even louder. Julius rolled down the window and handed Chris a bag of burgers. Chris immediately removed one and started munching. Magnus followed suit. After a few minutes, the four of them stepped out of their respective cars and started talking.

Magnus felt as if he needed to drive the conversation. "We are all here now, and a lot has to be said. For one, it was a long trip to get here with a lot of bumps along the way. I have to clear some things up with you guys. I am *not* the Chicago Bomber. I don't know the first thing about explosives. Secondly, I didn't kill that lady back at the prison. I found her in the trunk of the car I drove away in. I left her behind as a courtesy to the poor victim. Third, and lastly, Dar is here…close by. And I believe he is responsible for everything that has happened. We must work together to stop him."

Julius nodded and then spoke. "I have important information for you, Magnus. Arianna Shoomer has turned up. She should be able testify to your innocence. Presently, she is at Liberty Hospital back in Chicago."

That got Magnus's attention. He asked, "Was she hurt?"

Julius informed him that she had been stabbed in the leg but from the information he had, she was going to be fine.

"Who stabbed her?" he asked angrily.

Julius responded, "My connections believe it was someone in an underground syndicate known as FENCE. We're hoping that she will shed some light on them for us."

Magnus asked again, "She's OK though, right?" Julius nodded. Magnus let out a sigh of relief. He was happy that Arie was alive. Now more than ever he was determined to protect her from the monster.

Julius hated to spoil the moment, but he had more to tell. "There's one problem. Because he was assigned to find you, you-know-who was sent there to watch over and then question her."

Magnus's face turned to horror. "No! Not him..."

Julius was equally distressed about it. "Yeah...Denton."

Magnus erupted. "We need to get back there now! There's no telling what that brute will do to her."

Julius agreed. Both he and Tom knew that Denton could not be trusted.

Then Magnus said, "But first things first—we have to save Sharon. Dar has her in his possession. I've seen her." said Magnus.

Julius had been briefed about her and described the encounters she and Joe Warren had had with Dar. Magnus responded, "Well he's nearby, so she's here too. He's planning to kill her soon. We're running out of time, and we need to get her and then get back to Chicago to help Arie."

Tom had been silent, but he finally spoke. "Can you sense exactly where he is?"

Just as he was about to respond, Magnus froze, focusing his eyes behind where Julius and Tom were standing. Julius felt the hairs on the back of his neck stand up, and when he looked into the eyes of Michael Magnus, he saw a demon in their reflection. Right there, standing among them, was Dar.

They all turned, facing the murderer. It was like seeing Michael Magnus's mirror reflection standing just ten feet away. Dar spoke in a devilish manner. "I've grown impatient waiting for you to find me, brother, but I suppose I could wait just a bit longer. Your conversation was quite informative. Sweet little Arie at the hospital, with her leg all stabbed up. That just won't do. I'll have to make a special trip out there to see your girlfriend. Mmm, I can almost taste a piece of that succulent meat in my mouth right now."

Magnus tightened his fists, and Dar noticed his anger. "Oh come now, Mikey, don't get like that. You don't have to worry, because you'll be dead. I plan to rid myself of you first, and then I'll have a little fun with her." Dar snickered and grinned in a way that sent chills up Julius's spine.

As Dar spoke, Magnus grew more and more angry. He wanted to put a stop to Dar right then and there. Dar smiled again and said, "Temper, temper. You'll have to catch me first. I think it's time I head back to Officer Baker. If you want to play some more, you'll have to come to my little cabin about ten miles that way. Dar pointed his finger and said, "If you want to save the girl, I'll be waiting for you there. Oh, and by the way, if you bring these other fools I'll kill them too." Dar laughed demonically.

Suddenly, Tom pulled out his side arm and yelled, "Freeze!"

Dar laughed even harder before saying, "You fool!" Tom was about to yell again, but before he even got a word out, Dar was already behind him. There was a loud whapping noise as Dar kicked Tom right between his legs. Then Dar jumped at Magnus, stopping his fist just an inch from Magnus's face. Julius and Chris couldn't follow Dar's movement at all. Magnus, however was stolid, and he kept his eyes fiercely focused on his foe. Dar laughed once more and said, "Not bad, Mikey, not bad." With that, just as quickly as he had appeared, Darius Magnus was gone.

The four men didn't hesitate. They got into their respective vehicles and started to drive in the direction Dar had pointed. Tom was in horrible pain, but he managed to climb into the car. The group drove for about ten minutes when the lead car signaled and pulled over. Magnus was the first to get out. The others followed him into a wooded area. He started running, following his instincts. He had told the others that he was going to distract Dar and they were to head toward the back of the cabin. It seemed like a good plan. Magnus was much faster than they were. They figured if he distracted Dar for even a few minutes, they might be able to rescue Sharon.

As he ran, Magnus could feel how much faster and stronger he had become. The wind whipped by his face. It wasn't long before he was standing in front of the cabin. He called out to Dar. "Come out here, monster! Come out here now!" The cabin was silent. Magnus yelled the words again. "Come out here, monster!" It seemed like the whole world was silent. Magnus's heart was thumping. *Thump! Thump! Thump! Thump!* A bead of sweat rolled down his cheek. *Thump! Thump! Thump! Thump!* Suddenly, he heard footsteps running through the house. He braced himself for whatever was coming through the front door. His body tensed up to the max. Magnus threw his body forward toward the cabin, ready to pounce upon Dar. There was a scream, the door opened, and it was Chris. Magnus stopped his fist just short of his friend's face.

Chris looked horrid. He told Magnus that there were three mutilated bodies in the cabin, and to his shock their blood had been smeared throughout the house. The smell made Chris sick. He fell to his knees and threw up. Julius and Tom continued to search the premises, but aside from the bodies, no one was there, no Dar or Sharon. There was, however a note. Julius handed it to Magnus. After reading it he dropped it to the ground and said, "We gotta leave right now!" Tom stayed behind to wait for the local police. He decided it was best since he was still in a lot of pain. Besides, someone had to explain what had happened here. The others immediately started back to the car. Tom limped over to the note, picked it up, and read it.

Dear Brother,

I've changed my mind. I don't think it's fair to leave Arie out of all the fun. So I've left to go pay her a visit ahead of schedule. The way I figure it, since she's so hurt, she can't come to us. Let's meet up with her there instead. I hope you like my little idea. I'm sure Arie will be surprised to see me—I mean you—alive. Oh wait, she can't tell us apart, can she? Oh well, I guess she'll figure it out eventually. By the way, I brought Sharon along too. I figured the more the merrier. You see now everyone will bear witness to your destruction. Doesn't that sound great? See you soon!

PS I hope you realize that by the time you read this, I will have already stolen that chubby officer's car. After I kicked that skinny one, I stole the spare key. You still have that other crappy car, but don't take too long. Otherwise, the two ladies will only have each other for comfort as I burn their skulls!

Chapter 47

TYING UP LOOSE ENDS

Joe and Christian were making their way down the stairs when they were confronted by Wayne Jensen, the super. He started to ask them questions about what was going on. He had heard the gunshot and wanted to know why the apartment had been ransacked. Both Christian and Joe knew that they didn't have time to answer questions. They needed to get to that meeting in Chicago. Joe tried to calm Jensen down, but when he heard sirens approaching, he knew it was time to go.

By the time they got to the front entrance, it was too late. There were three squad cars screeching up to the sidewalk. Joe was an experienced officer. He stood his ground calmly. Christian followed suit. The state police jumped out of their cars and shouted at them to place their hands on their heads. Both Warren brothers complied. Joe identified himself as Detective Joseph Warren of the Chicago Police Department. He continued by saying that he was part of the seventh precinct and that his badge number was M519SJ. Despite his words, the two were handcuffed and placed into custody.

Four hours passed while they waited. This was exactly what Joe had feared would happen. He just hoped they would let them go when it was over. An officer walked into the room. All right, gentlemen, I want to know why you were in that apartment and what was going on? Also, I want to know why there are two dead men in there. Joe responded to the question with a question. "Did you contact Chief Robert Frank at the seventh precinct of the Chicago PD?"

The officer rolled his eyes and motioned for another man to come into the room. The second officer came in with a cell phone in hand. He handed it to Joe.

"Hello?" said Joe.

The very unpleasant voice on the other end immediately started screaming. "What the fuck do you think you're doing? I suspended you! That means you don't fucking do anything! This is a Goddamn mess! You shot someone and used fucking police funds to travel to another state. I ought to let them lock your ass up!" Joe did not know what to say in response, so he figured it best to let the chief rant as always. The chief was yelling so loud that all the other men could hear it through the phone.

Eventually, the chief stopped, most likely because he was out of breath. Joe took advantage of the opening and started explaining the information he had gathered and how close he was to getting the information required to save Sharon. He finally fessed up to what Dar had told him in Duanesburg and told him about the Emancerian Project.

There was a pause in the conversation when Joe stopped speaking. Neither party said anything. Joe was beginning to wonder if the chief was even still there. He opened his mouth to keep talking, but the chief immediately jumped back down his throat. "You know, Warren, you are so lucky for two reasons: one, I need you for this case, and two, Baker is more important than all this shit. There is shit going down here too, you know. There's a witness to the Chicago Bomber up at Liberty Hospital with a knife wound to the leg. I think this whole thing is tied in with this Emancerian Project you mentioned. I know that FENCE has got its hands dipped in this shit."

Joe was no stranger to the FENCE organization. He had had a few run-ins with them in the past. The chief continued, "I have been conferring with Warden Cahill at the DEDC. He thinks something may go down soon at the hospital. So get your ass back here!"

At that moment, the chief reinstated Joe. Furthermore, both Joe and Christian were granted clearance to be airlifted via helicopter to the airport, and from there they would catch a flight back to Chicago. As they made their way to the roof, they were informed that the man they killed was Lucas Black, a known international criminal. Joe nodded as he took in that information and departed with his brother to the airport. Once they got to the terminal and were finally free of escorts, Joe let out a sigh. He'd had his doubts for a while in that situation, but now he had renewed hope that he could still help Sharon. Christian placed his hand on Joe's shoulder and said, "Don't worry…"

There was a short delay before takeoff, but once they took off it was smooth sailing all the way back to Chicago. The flight was not long, and both of them took advantage of the time to get a little rest. When they arrived, an escort was waiting for them. It was obvious the chief was going to keep tabs on them. They were immediately driven back to the station, where the chief was waiting to debrief them. Exiting the vehicle, they entered the building and rode the elevator up to the eighth floor. Joe asked Christian to wait outside the chief's office. He expected a full barrage of verbal abuse.

The walk to Chief Frank's office seemed longer than ever. When the chief saw Joe approaching, he pondered how he should deal with his insubordination. Joe knocked on the door. As the door opened, smoke poured out and Joe coughed. The chief didn't speak a word. Instead, he motioned for Joe to sit down. After he was seated, Joe remained silent. Three solid minutes passed until finally the chief was ready. "Joseph, I've reinstated you because of this case. No one else has made headway like you have. In fact, until Cahill called me, we were sitting on nothing but suspicions. Unlike you, who decided to kill the first solid connection to FENCE we ever had!"

Joe tried to get some words in: "Chief, that was because—"

The chief interrupted. "You need to shut it, Joe!"

Joe took a defensive posture and quieted back down. In the most sensitive tone possible, the chief explained that Arianna Shoomer had been a witness to the bombing. And then he told Joe about something he hadn't mentioned before: that there were two dead men in the same hospital who were also international criminals. "One," he said, "was smothered to death, and the second had a bullet in his head. Apparently, it was suicide after he smothered the first guy, who turns out to be his brother. We plan to have Ms. Shoomer identify these men to see if they were her captors, but I have an overwhelming feeling that someone else is going to try to put her out of commission before she can.

Joe was taking in all the information but was more concerned about getting Sharon back from Dar. The chief continued, "We matched the bullets from that gun with the bullet found in Patricia Zellman, William Haight's assistant. And just ten minutes ago, they matched prints from the guy you killed with prints on the car that her body was stored in—the same car that was stolen by Michael Magnus when he escaped the DEDC." The chief paused to make sure Joe was keeping up. "Listen, Joe, I'm giving you the chance to connect the dots and piece together what's going down. This meeting at two o'clock tomorrow—I want it to go smoothly. You'll have men at your disposal to back you up."

Joe told the Chief he planned to bring his brother along. He used the excuse that he had the military connections that had led them to Dr. Caputo. The chief begrudgingly accepted this.

The two of them strategized for the upcoming day. As Joe was leaving, the chief warned him that he needed to keep a clear head. He knew that Joe was charged with emotions concerning Sharon. For the moment, Dar had the upper hand. He just hoped that they could use the information they had to bargain for Sharon's life.

Joe and Christian returned to his apartment. Christian collapsed on the couch and passed out fairly quickly. Joe found the gift that Sharon had left him. He picked it up and opened it. Inside was a diary that Sharon had written for him. It contained years of poetry and thoughts about how much she loved him. As Joe read through the pages, his eyes began to get heavy. That night he fell asleep with her on his mind and with a tear in his eye.

Chapter 48

DOWN RIGHT DEPRESSED

After she left the restaurant, the time seemed endless. He was awake for the entire night, and his chest hurt like she had punched through it. No matter how much food he ate or drinks he had, KM Lockhart could not fix the emptiness he felt. The tears of pain that poured from his eyes would not dry. Feeling poetic, he thought to himself, *Maddy has fractured my soul. Now I am a mere fraction of what I used to be.* With bloodshot and crusty eyes, KM watched the sun rise. It reminded him of her. Everything reminded him of her.

He reached over from his chair and grabbed the phone on the desk. Dialing zero, he called for room service. "Hello? Hello? Yeah, this is Mr. Lockhart in room 519. I'll be needing another steak. In fact, make it two, with taters, and bring another bottle of whiskey." Normally, KM would not go beyond a few shots in one sitting, but when he called room service it was for his fourth bottle of Tennessee Bean Whiskey. It was his favorite, but even that didn't help his suffering.

Ephraim, the hotel restaurant manager, could not believe how hungry the patron in 519 was. On the eighth call, he decided to deliver it personally. And of course, he ended up having a drink with the depressed, drunk, but downright friendly lawyer. After hearing KM's sad story, the manager decided to not cut off the flow of alcohol. In fact, he advised his staff to take extra care of the patron in room 519.

KM had spilled his guts, telling Ephraim that he was a lowdown dirty scoundrel who never deserved an angel like Madeline. He shouted, "My angelic Madeline is gone!" He sobbed and tore into the whiskey. Ephraim politely listened, but after about twenty minutes he needed to get back to work. He was thankful that his cell phone rang and he was able to slip out. After politely excusing himself, he returned to the restaurant. Lockhart called back for food two more times that evening. Ephraim laughed, thinking that the man was absolutely bottomless.

Around nine fifteen, KM received a call from Warden Peter Cahill. Cahill was trying to get an update from KM. He wanted to know if he had had any further contact with the prosecuting attorney. Haight had fallen off the map. His men had been keeping tabs on Haight's office and home, but there had been no sign of him for days. KM sucked up his tears and let the Warden know that things had been quiet. He was tempted at first to speak about his issues, but despite his drunken state, he was able to hold back. Cahill could tell that something was wrong so he thought the good news that Arianna Shoomer had shown up at Liberty Hospital would cheer him up.

This news did make KM feel a little better. Cahill also told him that he had spoken with Robert Frank and that Shoomer planned to make a statement soon. At that moment, KM decided he would pay her a visit and show his support. Cahill advised him to be cautious. He knew very well that Denton was there.

KM heard the warning but paid it no mind. He realized that something big was going to happen down there, and he wanted to be in the mix. The way he figured it, he owed it not only to himself but to Bill and Arie. He said to Cahill, "That little girl was locked up with me and Bill, and I couldn't do anything to help either of them then. It's about time I grew a pair and did something." Cahill laughed and replied that he wished he could go down there with him. He suggested that KM ask Chief Robert Frank to accompany him instead, as it would probably keep the officers on their toes. KM thought about how easily they had gotten to him and was concerned for Arie's safety. Despite their conversational laughter, KM knew that FENCE was no joke. They had proven to him that they were capable of anything.

A few hours later, after a brief nap and some sobering up, KM got dressed and called for a car service. He picked up his phone and called Chief Frank to ask him to accompany him to the hospital. *Definitely a smart idea of Cahill's,* KM thought to himself. The chief would be armed, so he would be much safer. And beyond that, he trusted Chief Frank. There was a call on his room phone. The car was waiting. KM closed the door behind him and made his way down to the lobby.

As he rode the elevator down, KM felt anxious. The elevator was glass, allowing him to see out as he descended. He noticed a group of men watching him. *Shit!* He thought. KM quickly pressed the 2 button and exited on the second floor. He ran to the end of the hallway and took the stairs down to the basement level. He left through the rear entrance of the hotel. Feeling like he had outwitted the group, he walked around the building and slipped into the car that was going to take him to the police station. Just then, a man walked up with a microphone and another guy followed with a camera. They tried to get an interview with him, but the car pulled away.

The ride from the hotel was swift. When he arrived at the station, he waited for an officer to escort him up. Seven minutes passed, and finally a female officer came to get him. Normally, he would have started flirting immediately, but KM didn't even speak a word. As they arrived on the eighth floor, KM could hear yelling coming from Chief Frank's office. Through the glass, he saw Detective Joseph Warren. He decided to wait until they had finished their discussion.

While he waited, KM tried to eavesdrop on the conversation. He couldn't exactly make out what they were saying, but he heard something about Joe being lucky he had been bailed out of a bad situation and something about throwing his ass in a cell. KM wanted to laugh, but he tried to stay focused on his objective. He decided to sit and wait. It seemed like he was going to be waiting awhile. He had arrived at 1:30 a.m., and by 2:15 p.m., Joe was finally set free from the chief's office of doom.

KM watched as Joe raced out of the office. He thought to himself that he was glad he didn't work for the chief. Joe looked like he had somewhere important to be. As his attention returned to the office, KM noticed the door was finally open. A number of people bustled in and out. He overheard updates on various cases. There was one about a drug bust involving some children and another involving domestic violence where the husband lost an ear. All of it seemed fairly run of the mill compared to Michael Magnus: the Chicago Bomber. He wondered if he'd ever see that young man again. He truly hoped that he was long gone and safe from the clutches of FENCE.

Lost in thought, KM didn't notice that a stout man with a cigar in hand was standing on his left. He turned his head and was greeted by Chief Frank. "Sorry to keep you waiting KM." Lockhart stood up and followed the chief back to his office. Once inside, the chief closed the door behind them. They discussed the information relayed to both of them by Cahill. The chief agreed to ride to the hospital together. He also figured that Arianna could use some encouragement. The chief said that he would be able to go at roughly 4:30. KM had some waiting to do. KM nodded and left the office.

For once, KM wasn't hungry, so time really dragged for him. He walked around the building too many times to count. When five o'clock came around, he was more than ready. The two men departed for Liberty Hospital. The chief had a heavy look on his face. KM asked how it felt to have the world on his shoulders. The chief smiled and said, "It's fucking heavy." They laughed, and for a moment KM forgot his problems. They proceeded onward, both not knowing how the day would close, but both hopeful that things would work out.

Chapter 49

POWER AND LIMITATIONS

What a gorgeous smile I have, Dar thought as he peered into the rearview mirror of the maroon car he was driving. Sharon, stretched across the back seats, was still unconscious. Dar coughed a few times. He was tired. He had used a lot of strength to transport himself and Sharon in order to escape the encounter with Michael Magnus. It was easy for Dar to transport himself a couple of times, but transporting himself and someone else more than a few hundred feet really took its toll. The distance from the cabin to the car was a good one thousand feet. Dar had also had to time it just right so that Michael Magnus wouldn't sense that he had left.

Dar coughed some more and banged his fist on the steering wheel. He hated getting tired. He hated any restraints or limitations on his ability. "I need more energy," he said aloud. Then he asked himself the question. "Where?" As he pondered about where to find his next victim, Dar suddenly sensed Magnus gaining ground on him. "Shit," he said, "he's not that far behind me. I need more distance." He accelerated to eighty-five miles per hour, and then to ninety.

Dar pondered just how strong his counterpart had become. When he saw him he could sense that he was a lot stronger than he had been at their previous encounter. There was definitely a change, and it worried Dar just a bit. The last thing he wanted was for Magnus to get any stronger. Dar continued to speed, reassuring himself that his power was still far superior. All he had to do was make sure he sucked Magnus's energy dry, and he would have all he needed to destroy everything and anything he wanted. He knew just how to win too.

Michael's weakness is his compassion, Dar thought. *He cares about this bitch, his bitch, and all those others. He won't be able to do a thing when I hold Arie's life in my hands.*

Glancing down at the gas gauge, Dar noticed the gas was getting low. "Fucking people," he said aloud. "They didn't even fill the gas tank. Next time I'll use their blood as fuel, those assholes." The gas light come on. Dar started looking for gas stations. He was so distracted that he didn't hear the siren or see the flashing lights behind him. A few miles back Dar had sped past a highway patrolman doing ninety-five. The cop had been following him for some time. Dar finally noticed when the patrol car pulled up alongside his driver's side door. The policeman in the passenger seat yelled out the window for Dar to pull over.

This brought a smile to Dar's face. First, he gave the death stare to the policeman in the passenger seat, which caused him to pass out. Then, after putting his vehicle on cruise control, he transported himself and Sharon into the back of the police vehicle. The next move Dar pulled was so quick and smooth that it's hard to fathom how something like it could even be possible. From the back of the police car, Dar ripped opened the steel bars, slid his body through, and in one spinning motion ejected both officers through their respective windows. The bodies of both policemen were propelled out onto the highway, where they were decimated by oncoming vehicles. Causing a horrendous pileup of cars, Dar managed to escape completely unharmed, with a smile on his face the whole time.

Dar looked back. He could tell that he had backed up traffic a lot. It was a perfect way to allow him to put more distance between himself and Magnus. He smiled and laughed to himself thinking, *Damn, I'm good. I'm a God. Yes, that's it.* He started yelling, "I'm not a man. I'm a God! Bow down to me, Michael Magnus! I have nothing to fear from you." *What a joke he is. He can't even teleport. What a loser. That fool truly has no idea what he's up against.* Dar continued to speed for a while until he saw two patrol cars waiting for him up ahead. As soon as he passed by them, their sirens blazed and they gave chase. "How utterly annoying, don't you think, Sharon?" He laughed—it was so funny to talk to the incapacitated Sharon. "Oh well, so much for this patrol car. It's too much of an eyesore, really."

The trailing police vehicles watched as the patrol car Dar was driving drifted off the road and crashed into a ditch. They surrounded the patrol car but discovered it was empty. Confused, they searched the area and still found nothing. There was no trace of the madman and his hostage. Dar couldn't stop laughing and smiling. He and Sharon were on top of a bread truck, speeding down the highway. Once the police were out of sight, he lay back with his arms behind his head. "What morons. They have no chance of ever catching me."

Dar laughed again and then popped himself and Sharon into the truck. He had grown tired of driving himself, so he controlled the driver's mind and pointed them all toward Chicago...and Arie. He knew that soon, once and for all, he would have a chance to show his true might. He would humiliate Magnus in front of all the people he cared about. Then at the height of the moment, he would kill him and take his powers, ascending to his rightful place as the only true God!

Chapter 50
ORIGINS OF F.E.N.C.E.

Earlier that same day, as daybreak approached, a blue hue crept its way through the windows on the west side of Liberty Hospital. The sleeping Arianna stirred from under multiple blankets. The night was uneventful but had seemed extremely long and drawn out. Arie rolled over and tried to go back to sleep, but in her mind she kept seeing the image of an owl. It scared her. Its wings spread wide and eyes glaring yellow, the image seemed to be a warning. She also felt very much out of place; after being a captive for so long, she had forgotten what it felt like to be free.

Arie's mind began to race through what seemed like a million thoughts… Michael, Denton, her captors, and her parents…she had been through so much. She'd called her parents from the hospital earlier and left a message for them, and she wondered why they hadn't returned her call. Even if they were away, surely by now they would have seen a news report or something. She thought the worst for a moment. Maybe FENCE had gotten to them. She knew that the members of FENCE were still after her. Anything was possible at this point. It made her feel scared and alone. Arie knew just how ruthless they were. During her captivity, she had heard and seen a lot of things that she would prefer not remember. She knew that FENCE had been founded by fifteen very bad men who decided they wanted to form a crime syndicate.

Arie overheard many conversations taking place just on the other side of the door wherever she was being held. Sometimes they'd blindfold her and keep her in the same room with them. From what she could gather, the organization had about forty to sixty members. Janak, she learned, was the nephew of Pedro Castian, one of the original fifteen. Pedro had amassed great wealth through unscrupulous means. When he contacted Janak's group, it was always a big deal. They would all quiet down and wait for his instructions. Then they would all talk about how much power he had. Pedro was always referred to as Castian or the Big Boss, except by Janak, who called him Uncle. Arie had wondered what FENCE stood for, until one day Claude asked Sean. Sean responded Fifteen Enemies Now Capitalists and Entrepreneurs. Claude was too stupid to understand, so Sean clarified by explaining that the fifteen men committed themselves to making a lot of money by any means necessary.

Arianna, at the time, had just wanted to go back to a normal life, but now she knew her information could lead to their takedown. The irony was that she wasn't sure what normal was anymore. She started crying, which actually tired her out enough to slip back into slumber. There, in her mind's eye, she saw the owl again. It flew across her path, and then it slowly turned and flew toward her. It landed, and she could see it was much larger than her. She was frightened, but it seemed docile. It nudged her in a fashion that made her realize it wanted her to climb on its back. Arie mounted the bird, and together they soared over an ethereal world. It was quite a fantastical dream. Eventually, they headed toward an enormous tree. This tree was so large that if it were real it would cast a shadow over a third of the earth. As they approached, she felt the essence of good, purity, love, hope, and justice.

The owl landed on a branch wide enough to be a road. Arie dismounted and surveyed the treetops. She felt peaceful. All her fears and doubts left her, and for a time the dream was still. However, without warning, the owl flew off, screeching as it went. Arie did not understand what had spooked it until she looked down at the ground below. She saw him. At first she thought it couldn't be him, but it was. It was Michael. She couldn't believe it. It had to be a dream. There he was, just standing there smiling at her. She couldn't stand to wait any longer. Arie began the long climb down, which seemed to take an eternity. As she was climbing down, she smelled something. She inhaled deeply. The scent filled her nostrils and made her cough. It was horrible. She paused and looked down. Michael was nowhere to be seen. The tree had caught fire and the flames grew, approaching her swiftly. They seemed to be almost alive. She heard laughter and mocking coming from the fire. And then an eerie voice called out her name: "Arie…" The eerie voice paralyzed her with fear. It called out to her again and again: "Arie…Arie!"

A chill crept up Arie's spine and stopped at her neck. Remaining frozen, she could feel something behind her. Arie tried to move, but she was stuck. The sound of breathing getting closer vibrated in her ear, and then she felt someone or something behind her breathing on her ear. In the dream, the hairs on her neck stood up. She tried to scream but couldn't. Then the branch began to shake. She clung to it for dear life until finally it snapped and she tumbled with it. The ground was coming fast, and she was stunned for a moment. She stood up to brace herself. There in front of her, she saw a warped version of Michael, laughing. She asked why he was laughing. He looked at her with piercing eyes and said, "I'll find you, Arie, and then I'll kill you." She screamed in the dream and in her hospital bed. The intensity was so real it woke her up.

When Arie awoke, she felt a pain in her back. The dream seemed so real. She was breathing heavily, and her sheets were soaked with perspiration. Suddenly, the lights snapped on and Dr. Blythe entered. She had been checking in on other patients when she heard Arie scream and had run to her room.

She asked, "Is everything OK in here?" Arie was still breathing loudly as she nodded. "Well," Dr. Blythe continued, "I don't have to guess how you slept." Arie nodded again, still somewhat dazed. Dr. Blythe walked over to her and smiled. She whispered, "You know, I wouldn't sleep so well either knowing there was a Sasquatch outside my door." This comment made Arie laugh. She agreed that Denton was sort of Sasquatch-like. Dr. Blythe checked her leg and vitals and told Arie that she could be released later that day.

Arie thanked her for everything. When Dr. Blythe mentioned her being released, Arie wondered if she would be escorted by the Sasquatch to the local police station. Referring to Denton that way made her laugh, but she dreaded the idea of being stuck in a car with him. Dr. Blythe paused before exiting the room. Reaching into her pocket, she pulled out a card. She looked at it and then handed it to Arie. She whispered again, "Some time ago there was an issue here, and a very competent officer helped us. That's his card. You might want to give him a call."

With that, Dr. Blythe placed a finger to her lips to indicate that Arie should keep it a secret. Then she looked around the room and touched her ear indicating that there were ears listening everywhere. Dr. Blythe's instincts were very much on point. In true dirt bag fashion, Denton had placed a listening device in the room. He wanted to make sure that if Arie made any phone calls he would know about it immediately, especially if she contacted Michael Magnus.

Dr. Blythe exited the room, and Arie looked at the card. She read it quietly to herself thinking it would be great to find a cop she could trust. Detective Joseph Warren sounded like a trustworthy name. Arie decided it was time to act. Buzzing a nurse to her room, she asked to be escorted to someplace where she could make a private call. Denton had left, and one of the two officers didn't notice Arie leaving the room because he was too busy stuffing his face, but the other one saw her and asked where the nurse was taking her. Arie quickly responded that the bathroom in her room wasn't working and that she would be right back. The officer wasn't the brightest, and he let them go. The nurse didn't say a word as she escorted Arie to another room with a phone. Once alone, she dialed the number on the card. It rang a few times, and then a strong voice answered. "This is Joe Warren..."

Chapter 51

WHOSE WHO

The wait was unbearable. The two of them had been waiting for more than two hours. It was about three thirty. Christian had nodded off. Joe had been surveying the area when he got a call on his phone. He didn't recognize the number. He hesitated but then decided to answer it. "This is Joe Warren." There was a brief pause and Joe repeated himself. "Hello? This is Joe Warren." Still not hearing anyone on the other end, Joe was about to hang up when a sweet, soft, feminine voice spoke.

"Joe? Joe, is that you?" Joe's heart dropped. It was Sharon!

"Oh my God, Sharon, is that you?"

"Yes," she responded. "I love y—"

Before she could finish the sentence, she started crying. Then there was some rustling on her end and a familiar, maniacal voice broke in. "Hello, Joey." Dar let out a blood-curdling chuckle. "As you can hear, she's still alive—for now. Do you have the information I'm looking for? You know you only have twenty-four hours left, Joey." Dar laughed again, loving the power he had over Joe.

Joe gulped but boldly answered, "Yes, I have it. Where can we meet tomorrow? What's the time and place?"

"You know what, Joey...I'm not sure I believe you. Maybe you should say your goodbyes now."

Joe tensed up but quickly responded to Dar's threat. "If you kill her, you'll never know the true purpose behind the Emancerian Project. You'll never have your answers. I have the documentation here, and there are no other copies."

Dar thought about the detective's words. After a few seconds he said, "Fine! I'll spare your little wench, but if you're playing me, Joey, the torture she'll endure will make you want to kill yourself. You saw what I did to my last three playmates. Sharon here won't have it as easy as them. Don't fuck with me! I'll be in touch."

With that the call ended. Joe gasped for air. His heart was racing so fast he couldn't calm it down. Christian, on the other hand, had slept through the whole thing. Joe was about to wake him when suddenly the phone rang again.

Joe nearly puked as it rang. His body tensed up—it was a different unknown number. "This is Joe Warren."

The voice on the other end spoke swiftly. "Detective Warren? I got your number from Dr. Tina Blythe. I don't have much time to talk." Joe sighed and decided to let this person know he didn't have time to help anyone at the moment.

Her words came quickly out of desperation. "Please wait!" The fear in her voice persuaded Joe to give her a chance and hear her out. She continued, "My name is Arianna Shoomer. I'm calling concerning Michael Magnus and my safety."

Joe immediately sat up and took interest in what she had to say. Their conversation was brief, but a lot of information was exchanged. Joe asked her about her encounter with FENCE. He, in turn, told her about his experience with Darius Magnus. Arie was very surprised. She told him about Magnus's parents. She said that they were the nicest of people, and it hurt her deeply to learn of their deaths. In addition, Arie confirmed what Joe had suspected. She had never met a Darius Magnus. His true identity remained a mystery.

Joe pondered the situation for a moment, trying to piece facts and events together. Michael Magnus was there at the explosion, yet he didn't die. Darius was there at the same time. The five members of FENCE were there, and they were in league with Dr. Caputo, the ex–military scientist. The wheels in his head started turning. He speculated that maybe it was some kind of cloning experiment gone wrong, or perhaps Michael Magnus was the scapegoat of some failed plan. He thought it was conceivable that Darius Magnus had gotten plastic surgery to look like Michael Magnus. If that was case, then what was the reasoning behind it? He wondered if Dar was in league with FENCE. And if he was, then was he following orders or had he gone rogue?

As Joe was thinking of various possibilities, Christian woke up and asked who was on the phone. Joe held up his finger to his mouth. He was listening carefully to everything Arie had to say. Christian turned his attention to the surroundings. It was almost four o'clock, and they had just about given up hope of finding the person who was supposed to meet Dr. Caputo. Just then, Christian noticed a man some distance away step out of his car. The man immediately walked up to a building and leaned up against a wall. The whole thing seemed to be conspicuously inconspicuous. Christian's military training gave him a keen eye for noticing the unnoticeable.

Christian told Joe he would be right back. As he exited the car, Joe nodded, but he wasn't really paying attention. He had no idea Christian had spotted someone suspicious. Christian casually walked right past the man as if he hadn't seen him. Then he stopped, walked back, and asked the man if he had a light. The man was annoyed but granted Christian's request. Christian lit a cigarette and blew the smoke in the man's face. "So, how long do you intend to wait for Dr. Caputo?" The man coughed and then immediately reached for his gun, but Christian quickly took out Janak's kneecap and performed a clothesline maneuver to Janak's windpipe. The tall Frenchman fell to the ground, holding his neck and gasping for air.

From there, Christian disarmed and cuffed him. Then he proceeded to march him back to the car. Joe, who was still on the phone with Arie, was shocked when a man's head went thud on the hood of his car. Joe asked Arie to hold on for minute. He placed the phone down and opened the door. Christian exclaimed, "I got him!"

Joe asked, "How did you know?" Christian explained that it was his soldier instinct. Joe smiled and said, "Well, now we're in business." Joe opened the back door and both Christian and Janak got in the back seat. That was the best course of action, since it wasn't a traditional police vehicle. Christian pulled out a gun and held it to Janak's neck. "If you try anything, your neck is going to hurt a whole lot worse!" Janak was pissed. He couldn't believe that Christian had gotten the jump on him. He looked at Christian and thought to himself, *that fucking lucky kid. When I get free I'll kill them both.*

Joe finished his conversation outside the car. He advised Arie that he needed to get a statement from her as soon as possible. Arie made it clear that she didn't want to be transported to the station with Denton. Joe also told her that he would drive to the hospital personally to pick her up. She was very grateful. Then she said that she would take care of all the hospital paperwork so that they could leave as soon he arrived. Joe hung up the phone. Christian asked, "Was that who I think I was?" Joe told him that it was Shoomer and that they needed to make a stop at the hospital.

Christian said, "Not a problem; I can handle this chump." Unfortunately, Janak's two-way radio picked up the entire conversation. Christian had removed his gun but missed the radio.

On the other side of that radio was Denton, who had been listening while he was waiting to pick up Janak after he killed Caputo. And when he witnessed Janak's capture, he immediately contacted Pedro Castian. Castian was very angry. It was obvious that Joe had gotten in contact with Arie. The police were getting too close. Things had gotten out of hand; he ordered Denton to eliminate everyone connected to the Emancerian Project.

His exact words were, "Kill Joseph Warren, his brother, Julius Spencer, Thomas Rutger, KM Lockhart, Chief Robert Frank, and especially that bitch Arianna." He went on to say that she had turned out to be a lot more trouble than she was worth. He even said if need be Denton could eliminate Janak, his nephew.

Castian wasn't taking any chances about information being leaked. Denton was surprised he left out the two main people involved: Michael and Darius Magnus, both of whom Castian specifically ordered him not to touch. Castian alluded to the fact that FENCE's interests lied in letting those two play out their destiny. Denton was pissed. He wanted Michael Magnus dead, but he agreed to just bring him. Once the two had fought, he was to capture the survivor and bring them to him.

Joe started to pull away from the curb, and Denton realized that if he wanted a shot at killing Arie before they arrived, he would have to move fast. He knew that his life was on the line if he failed. Arie had the power to implicate FENCE in the bombing and everything else that was blamed on Michael Magnus. It was his job to keep FENCE out of the public consciousness. He decided he would take out Janak too. He had never really liked Janak anyway; he was always trying to boss him around.

The race was on, and Denton intended to win. He stopped at a red light, and a car pulled up right next to him. At first he ignored it, but something made him turn his head and look. There were two familiar faces staring right back at him: Chief Robert Frank and KM Lockhart. They too were on their way to the hospital to check the status Ms. Shoomer. The chief scowled at Denton and opened his window. "What are you doing here, McKay? Why aren't you at the hospital protecting that woman?"

Denton had to think quickly; he couldn't afford to make the chief suspicious. "I was just grabbing a quick dinner for me and the boys. You know how disgusting hospital food is!"

The chief's expression didn't change. "You idiot," he snarled. "Haven't you heard? Two officers at the hospital are down. Something's gone terribly wrong over there, and it's all because of your blundering. And there's no sign of the witness. Shoomer is missing!"

The chief put on his sirens and advised Denton to follow them immediately. Denton cursed to himself but followed the chief. He realized that he would have to find another way to kill everyone. The hospital would be swarming with cops. When they finally got close to the hospital, Denton saw three squad cars in the main parking lot, lights flashing. Joe and Christian had already arrived. Janak had been transferred to a real squad car. When the chief got out of his car, he ordered two officers to take Janak back to the station and hold him for questioning.

The chief walked into the hospital with Joe, KM, and a group of officers. Denton put gloves on and screwed a silencer on his second unmarked gun. He then walked up to the car that Janak was sitting in and tapped on the driver's window. The officer rolled the window down and asked Denton what was up. Denton's response was a bullet in the forehead. The cop's partner went for his gun, but Denton killed him before he had a chance. Janak was relieved but at the same time he was annoyed. He thanked Denton and asked him to get him out of there. Denton smiled and opened the back door as if he was going to free Janak, but instead, he pressed the gun to Janak's head. Janak was about to say something when Denton pulled the trigger. Janak's head exploded everywhere. Denton backed up and cleaned his gun. So far things were going his way. Everyone was in one place; he just needed to pick them off one at a time.

Denton closed the door and was about to go kill the rest of his hit list when he came face to face with a monster. A smile crept up the face of the demon. "Well now, there's no glass between us this time—is there, Officer McKay?" A bead of sweat rolled down Denton's left cheek. He knew there was no way he could defeat this beast. He gulped a breath of air and pointed his gun at Dar. The gesture was pointless, Dar sensed Denton's thoughts and laughed at him, asking, "Do you really think that your pitiful toy is going to make a difference?" Denton tried to fake confidence; he was about to launch into a battle for his life. Standing face to face with a true villain, who had no compassion, remorse, or mercy, all he could do was laugh.

Chapter 52

STEPPING UPON THE BRINK

Many hours had passed, but finally Magnus, Julius, and Chris entered the busy streets of Chicago. After Dar's stunt on the interstate, they had been stuck for over an hour standing still. The police kept traffic blocked off as they searched the area endlessly. Magnus was apprehensive. He was upset that Dar gotten the better of them. Not only that, but they were back in the city where he had been locked up for months. He had finally escaped, only to come right back. Once all this was done, he thought, he would never return to Chicago again.

Chris sensed Magnus's agitation. He, too, was feeling on edge, although he was more upset about dealing with Dar once they got there. Chris was trying to stay focused on what had to be done. Chris projected himself into Magnus's mind. Julius was unaware of the telepathic conversation taking place between them. Chris said, "When this is all over and Dar is destroyed, I'm buying you a drink." Magnus smiled. He hadn't indulged in so long, the idea made him laugh to himself. He figured he would really need one.

Magnus then asked Julius a question. "Hey, Julius? If we capture Dar, do you think the charges against me will be dropped?"

Julius wasn't sure. "Most likely you will have to go back into custody until things are sorted out."

Fuck that, Magnus thought. Chris laughed, having heard his reaction telepathically.

Julius shrugged his shoulders and said, "I say we sort all this out after we catch the asshole."

Magnus responded, "That's not going to be so easy. We all saw him just disappear."

Chris interrupted and said, "Well, can't you do that too?" Magnus looked at him as if he was crazy. "Well, why don't you try?" Chris plainly asked. Magnus thought for a moment and then stared out the window. Julius was quiet. Chris stopped at a red light. Magnus looked at the street corner and decided he would try to transport himself there.

The light changed, and Chris took his foot off the brake. He glanced toward the passenger seat; Magnus was no longer there. Of course, Julius noticed too. They were shocked.

"He's gone!" Julius exclaimed. Chris pulled over and stopped the car, and they both looked around for their friend. Unexpectedly, there was a knock on Chris's window. The two men looked over and saw Magnus standing there. Chris unlocked the doors and Magnus got back in.

"Well, I was able to leave but I couldn't get back."

Chris chuckled and said, "Well, that's a start. Maybe if you just try to focus on him you'll be able to follow his movements."

Magnus said, "Maybe." But he was somewhat doubtful.

Chris pulled off again. It dawned on him that both Dar and Magnus were way out of his league in terms of ability. He also realized just how dangerous someone like Dar could be if left unchecked. No prison could ever hold such a being.

Julius believed Magnus was innocent of the Chicago bombing, but just for a moment he wondered, as Chris had earlier, could any man with such power truly use it only for good? Or would that power compromise the morals of anyone who wields it? Chris and Magnus both heard Julius's thoughts and remained quiet about it. They agreed it was a fair question.

Julius wondered if, when the time came, he'd even be of any help in this battle of titans.

Some time passed, and Chris turned on the police scanner, adjusting it to the local police band. The three men heard a dispatcher attempting to check in with two officers escorting a prisoner for questioning. They also heard that two officers were killed at the hospital and learned that the woman they had been guarding, Arianna Shoomer, was missing. The two cops had the serial killer's mark etched into their foreheads. The three of them listened intently. Magnus realized that the hospital was probably crawling with officers. He was worried about being caught before he could confront Dar and save Arie. Chris tried to reassure him by telling him not to worry and that they were all in this together. Julius agreed. From that point on, there was no need for words. They were minutes away, and they all knew what had to be done. Time was running out.

Meanwhile at the hospital, Joe, Christian, and Chief Frank walked up to the crime scene. There was blood splattered in each of the corners where guards had been stationed. Joe covered his mouth in disgust. The murders were brutal, and again their foreheads bled from the symbols etched into them. Some of their body parts had been torn off altogether. When they entered Arie's room, a drop of blood fell on the chief's forehead. He and Joe looked up and saw a giant symbol painted on the ceiling in the two victims' blood. Arie was nowhere to be found. Joe speculated that either she was hiding or had been captured.

KM Lockhart was standing down the hall. His nerves were shot, and the smell of death was nauseating to him. His mind flashed back to Bill's murder. He needed air, so he looked around for the nearest exit. He noticed a door down the hall. It was slightly ajar. When he approached it, he noticed it was labeled Air Lift. KM placed his hat on his head and wandered through the door and up a few flights of stairs. When he reached the top level there was a heavy door labeled Roof. After throwing some muscle into it, he managed to get the door open. A burst of light filled the stairwell all at once. KM covered his eyes and then proceeded forth. *This is good,* he thought to himself. *The air is crisp and pure.* He took a nice, deep breath.

After a few minutes, he lit his Cuban cigar and took a drag. He was enjoying himself until he was startled by a voice. "You know, Lockhart, smoking is a nasty habit."

KM turned and stood face-to-face with Michael Magnus. Magnus had transported himself from the car. "Why, son," KM said, "I never thought I'd see you again." In his mind, he had nagging doubts: was Magnus responsible for these murders?

Magnus responded to what KM was thinking. "No, I just got here. I didn't hurt those people below."

KM was stunned. He stood there examining the man standing before him. Magnus didn't look quite the same as he did all that time ago at the jail and in the courtroom. There was a hardness about him that made him look very intense. The moon shone down on him brilliantly. Later on, when telling the story, KM would describe it as if Michael Magnus had anointed him right there on the rooftop. As if he was chosen to fulfill a destiny.

KM was about to speak again when he noticed two moving objects behind Magnus. Magnus heard his thoughts and immediately turned around. There were two garbage bags poked full of holes sitting on the roof, and two people were struggling inside them. They had been stashed out of sight, but in the attempt to free themselves they'd moved into view and caught KM's eye. Magnus ripped the bags open, releasing the captives. The first discovery was Sharon, battered, bruised, and tied up—but still alive. The second was someone Magnus felt like he had spent a lifetime trying to find. He couldn't believe she was right there in front of him. The experience was unreal. As their eyes met, an emotional wave swept over both of them. In that instant, a tear poured from his right eye, and a tear poured from her left. There was no need for words—their hearts spoke. Magnus leaned in to untie her, and their cheeks graced each other. Once her arms were free, she fastened them around him like a belt. He fell to the ground and locked his arms back around her. The embrace was so endearing that even KM shed a few tears. When they finally kissed, it was the kind of kiss where both of them ceased to be individuals. It wasn't sexual…just pure everlasting connection. The kind of connection where the world around them disappeared, leaving only their love. Forever linked, their souls had finally rejoined.

Chapter 53
PIECES FALL INTO PLAY

Christian had gone to the restroom while the chief and Joe checked the surrounding areas. Their search had revealed that there were other victims besides the two security guards. They found an orderly and a nurse in nearby rooms stuffed into closets. The orderly's clothes had been removed. They continued to search for Dar, but there was no trace of him. The chief decided to radio for an update. He learned that outside the hospital the bodies of Janak and two men of his men were found. They were dead on arrival. When they informed Chief Frank, he immediately contacted dispatch for backup and left to find someone in the hospital who could tell him what happened. He had done so much hard work to catch him.

In the bathroom stall, Christian continued to stew over the events that transpired for some time. It had been quite some time since he'd had a minute to think, and he figured he'd stay awhile and use the opportunity to his advantage. Eventually, his mind wandered and thoughts from his childhood came back to him. He and Joe used to play imaginary adventures when they were kids. He cherished those moments. Their lives had grown a bit distant after Christian joined the military and left home. Even more destructive was the divorce. That had changed him forever.

His life seemed to be flashing through his mind. He remembered getting married. He had proposed to the girl of his dreams in front of the Sears Tower. However, in the end, that adventure had ended badly, with his wife falling into the arms of another man while he was away on duty. For a while he was crushed, but eventually he healed and devoted his life to the service of his country. Joe wasn't happy about that decision, but he supported him. Christian felt he should do the same for his brother, which was why he had come as soon as Joe needed him.

Suddenly, he heard the bathroom door open and close with a slight creak. Christian's military training had given him a heightened sense of danger. He instantly lifted his legs so that he would not be visible from under the stall. All was quiet, and then the light in the bathroom went out. Christian's heart began to thump. Then he heard footsteps approaching his stall. Caught in quite the precarious position, Christian was afraid to move. The steps got closer. He reached for his gun, but it was just out of reach. Suddenly, there was a flushing sound. Christian was so scared that when he heard the flush, he nearly busted out laughing.

The smile left his face as quickly as it had come when he heard two shots hiss out of a silencer and make impact into a hard surface. He decided to yell through his cupped hands, causing a megaphone effect. "Get down on the ground! I've got a gun!" The bathroom door opened and slammed shut. Christian took a deep breath and checked himself to see if he had been hit. There were two bullets lodged in the door of the stall. Luckily for him, the bullets didn't completely penetrate the door.

For a good two minutes, Christian didn't move an inch. He was afraid if he moved the killer would make a second attempt. He had had some close calls in the army, but never that close. Eventually, he made the slightest of movements. He grasped his gun and slid his pants back up. Then he dropped to the floor and checked the floor for feet. There was no movement. He crawled along the floor underneath the stalls until he reached the light switch on the wall. Slowly he stood up and flicked the switch, poised to shoot anyone in there. The room was empty.

Christian quickly cleaned up and decided he would pursue his would-be assailant, but first he needed to inform his brother and Chief Frank of what had just happened. Liberty Hospital was especially huge, and he knew it wouldn't be easy to cover it without help. As he exited the bathroom, an unidentified officer was approaching. Christian pulled out his sidearm. He didn't know who to trust. The officer pulled his as well in response. The two were in a stand-off. Christian yelled, "Identify yourself!" The officer paused for a moment and decided that the best way to defuse the situation was to lower his weapon first.

"My name is Julius Spencer. I'm with the DEDC security force. I'm looking for Detective Joseph Warren."

Christian was a bit suspicious, but after taking a minute to look Julius over he decided that he was telling the truth. Julius nodded, acknowledging the trust. Christian identified himself as Christian Warren, brother of Detective Warren. He explained to Julius that someone had just attempted to kill him in the men's room. Then he said, "There's some crazy shit going on in this hospital. I'm not sure who the good guys are." Julius agreed and asked if he could accompany Christian as he rejoined his brother. Along the way, they met up with Chris Preston, who also joined them.

Together, they made it back to Arie's room, but when they got there, the chief and Joe were no longer there. Another officer was standing there waiting for their return. Christian asked where his brother and the chief had gone, but before the officer could reply a bullet pierced right through his skull and his blood splattered all over their faces. Chris Preston dived to the floor, and both Christian and Julius pulled their guns out.

They swept the area they suspected the shot had come from. There was no sound when the single shot had been fired, so Christian figured it was the same assailant who had attempted to get him moments earlier. After two minutes, Chris got up enough courage to run into Arie's room and push the emergency button next to her bed. Some nurses and crew members responded. One of them fainted when they saw the wounded officer and his blood everywhere. The situation was getting out of control. The crew carted off the body toward the emergency room.

Christian was shocked to discover that the staff hadn't been evacuated from that wing of the hospital with all the craziness happening. He figured Dar must have pounced on the scene so quickly that no one had been informed of the quickly escalating situation. Suddenly, it dawned on Christian that he still had his cell phone and could use it to call his brother. It rang five times before Joe finally picked up. Christian yelled, "Where the fuck are you? We're under fire down by Arie's room. Another one of your men is dead!"

Joe told his brother he would be right there. He and the chief immediately responded. They were accompanied by two more officers. As they were on their way back to the room they came under fire themselves. Caught off guard, the two officers trailing behind Joe and Chief Frank ended up as human shields against a spray of bullets that came from the rear. They both ducked into a room and turned to find there was no assailant pursuing them. Joe called for backup but got no response. After that, they had to assume that all the extra men the chief had called in were dead.

Joe told Christian his location. They agreed on a location to meet and started running toward that location. Chris followed behind Julius, still unarmed. Julius handed him a gun, saying, "You're gonna need this. This whole situation is way out of control!" They rounded a few corners and finally closed in on Joe's location. Joe and the chief were standing guard over the wounded men. The shooter had escaped unseen again. Once they were all together, Christian told them about what had happened in the men's room. It had become clear to all of them that they were being carefully and meticulously hunted.

Julius told them that he had tracked Darius Magnus to the hospital. He knew that he was lurking around somewhere. Joe wasn't shocked; he had seen the marking on the murdered cops. Julius explained that they had trailed him all the way from Duanesburg and that he was after Arianna. He also said that Dar had injured Thomas Rutger and that Michael Magnus was also with them. The most startling part of the story was Dar's ability to teleport himself. Joe finally understood how Dar was always a step ahead of him. He thought about it for a minute and said, "Wait. Dar doesn't use guns; it's not his style." They all considered this for a moment and agreed.

Julius asked, "So if it's not Dar, then who is hunting us?"

Chris Preston interrupted and said, "Wait. Just before the shots went off in the men's room, I heard a man's thoughts. At first, I didn't know who it was, but now I just remembered something Magnus told me about a rogue corrections officer by name of McKay, Denton McKay. That's who is shooting at us."

The chief made a face and said, "Who the fuck are you? Am I supposed to believe you're some kind of psychic?"

Chris Preston took a firm stand and said, "Listen, Michael told me of that man's cruelties, and I remember his thoughts from when I saw him shoving food down his throat at a fast food restaurant. Yes, I can hear thoughts. Right now, you're thinking about someone named KM Lockhart. You're wondering what happened to him."

They were all quiet for a moment as the chief confirmed Chris's statement. Julius wasn't surprised. Denton had always been his rival, and now he was a deadly one. Joe was about to say something when suddenly there was a call for backup. They were all silent as they listened to the distress call. "This is Officer McKay. I need backup. I'm under fire."

Joe radioed back after first placing a finger to his lips. "What's your position, McKay?"

McKay radioed back, "I'm at stairwell 5A. I hear more gunfire here. I'm going to check it out."

"Negative, McKay. Wait for backup."

McKay acknowledged.

Joe wasn't sure what to do. If Chris was right, they were walking into a trap. If he was wrong, then an officer was in trouble.

Denton kneeled down in the stairwell and connected some wires to a bomb. He connected the trigger mechanism to the nearby door. Then he hid the bomb as far out of sight as possible. Without realizing it, he had exposed his back. The hairs stood up on the back of his neck. Someone was there.

A dark voice spoke to him. "Are you having fun, Denton? I thought you said it would be fun if I watched you for a while, but I'm getting bored."

Denton realized that he was losing control over Dar. He said, "Just wait, Darius. This little toy is going to blow everyone up when I push the button. It will be loads of fun, just like when I planted that bomb in the warehouse district.

Dar responded with a yell. "I hate being called Darius! It was a dumb name when you gave it to me! I'm Dar!"

Denton swung around, grabbing his gun to fire. He got off a shot, but he missed the target. The next thing he knew, he felt the pressure of Dar's hand on his throat. Dar squeezed tightly, cutting off Denton's airflow. Denton's face turned red. Then Dar balled his other hand into a fist and without warning started whaling on Denton's stomach. Over and over again he pounded into his gut. The second Dar released him, Denton spat up blood. Some of it landed on Dar's cheek. Dar licked it and smiled. Then Denton dropped to the floor. Dar started dragging his body up the stairs toward the roof, leaving a trail of blood that he intended the others to follow. He had already sensed that Michael Magnus was on the roof; now all he needed were the pawns to join the king's court. All of the pawns would bear witness to his coronation—King Darius, the First.

He laughed and yelled out loud. "I like the sound of that!"

Chapter 54

SINS OF REVELATIONS

Michael Magnus was so overjoyed about being reunited with Arie that he didn't feel Dar's presence. Still holding her in his arms, all he could think about was the time he had lost not being with her. KM pulled himself together and started attending to the extremely weary Sharon. She could hardly muster a thank you as he began to lift her from the ground. Just then, the metal door to the roof flew open. At first no one emerged, but then out walked Dar, who was dragging Denton's body behind him. In a show of strength, he tossed the 285-pound behemoth at the wall near Sharon. She gasped as Denton's badly beaten body collapsed next to her. He was alive, but he looked as though he had been hit by a truck.

Denton coughed up blood. Magnus looked over at the enemy who had plagued him horribly and thought to himself, *what a fitting end for such a bad person.* Even so, part of Magnus felt pity for Denton despite their history.

Denton opened one eye and saw Magnus kneeling not far from him. He sucked in some air and spit blood at Magnus. "Fucking freak!" He coughed more blood as he spoke. "I wish it could be me that gets to beat your ass, but I'll enjoy watching him do it. And even if I die, I hope he sends you to hell with me!"

Dar laughed. "Well, dear brother, I've done what you couldn't. I've beaten the snuff out of the crooked corrections officer over there." Sharon turned her head and looked for the first time into the face of Michael Magnus. She saw the strong resemblance between him and the demon. Instinctively, she moved away from him, fearing that he was no different from the one who had imprisoned her. Arie, on the other hand, took the hand of her beloved. When she looked over at Dar, everything became clear. She understood the origin of the monster.

Dar spoke again. "So it comes down to this, Mikey. I've been waiting so long to destroy you. Not just your body but also what you represent. Your very existence pollutes the path of my greatness!"

Michael Magnus stood up, letting go of Arie's hand. He responded to Dar's challenge. "What greatness is that, Dar? All you do is terrorize and kill. You kill just about everything you touch. That's all going to end here. I'm not afraid of you!"

The rooftop door opened again. Joe, Christian, Julius, Chief Frank, and Chris came out. Dar yelled out, keeping his focus on Magnus, "Ah, Joey. Glad you made it! All you gentlemen can go over there and stand with the ladies. I have summoned you here for a purpose."

Joe responded, "It ends here, Dar! I won't allow you to hurt anymore people!"

Dar laughed. "And how do you intend to stop me, Detective, with your gun?" Joe looked down in his hand and realized it was gone. "Don't bother, Joey. I took the liberty of disposing of your weapons." The others realized their guns were gone as well. "Go on now, take your places. You all shall be the first to see my rebirth."

Cautiously, they joined Sharon, Arie, and KM. Joe looked into Sharon's eyes for the first time since she had disappeared. He moved over to her and laid his hand on her cheek. "Are you all right?" he asked.

She answered, "Now that you're here, Joe."

Dar bellowed, "Don't make me sick! All that sentimentality is revolting. Joe, you aren't out of the water yet. Where is that report on the Emancerian Project?"

Joe was about to speak, but Arie shouted, "The Emancerian Project is you, Dar! The leaders of FENCE found a way to bring out a man's true potential physically and mentally. They hired a brilliant doctor to lead the research."

Joe blurted, "That man was Dr. Caputo. They killed him to keep the project a secret."

Magnus was trying to remain focused on Dar, but the conversation was distracting him. Denton, realizing he wasn't going to survive, started to speak. "You people are all stupid. You're all so close to the idea but keep missing the big picture. I was there when they captured that little shit Magnus." Denton coughed up some more blood. "The Emancerian Project was *him*. They found his files by going through medical records. He was selected to be the test subject because of his genetic makeup. I don't know all the medical mumbo jumbo, but he had some kind of genetic abnormality that gave him the ability to evolve. *Freak!* Once you were marked as the guinea pig, it was easy enough to snatch you on your way to see your little girlfriend over there."

Magnus didn't respond to Denton's taunts. Denton continued, "Then we picked her up for insurance. If you wouldn't cooperate with us, we could threaten to kill her. But you're so weak and pathetic, you forgot all that after the experiment." He paused. Denton's voice was weak and trembled as he coughed up more and more blood. "They were trying to create the perfect weapon. Caputo invented a serum that would react with your chromosomes. He called it the Full Potential Compound...FPC. The compound was designed to augment a person's natural abilities. Bah! Whatever! The whole thing was a failure. Dr. Caputo gave him the serum and nothing happened. We used the warehouse to conduct the experiments. When it failed, we had to torch the place to make sure no evidence was left behind, but the bombs I planted went off early. That fucking bastard! Instead of being killed by the explosion, he somehow split into two people. That other freak over there was the result. A perfect fucking killing machine, but completely out of control!"

Denton started wheezing from the pain in his body. It was obvious that his internal bleeding was severe. "We left the original freak behind to take the blame for the bombing, and we took that monster to use as a weapon. Somewhere along the line we called him Darius. We thought he could be controlled, but as you can see, he's nothing but a monster. He got away, and then you escaped from jail." Denton paused for a moment and then said, "Which brings me to the present. It's my job to clean up all this mess and eliminate all parties involved."

Christian laughed and asked, "How do you intend to do that now that you've been beaten to a pulp? Are you telling us all this 'cause you know there's nothing—"

Denton lifted his hand and uttered his last words: "Fuck you, Michael Magnus!" With that, he squeezed the trigger on the detonator.

The bomb that he had planted in the stairwell a few floors below started a ten second countdown. He had waited the whole time with the detonator in hand until everyone was together. After squeezing the trigger, Denton's body slumped. He had told them everything because he intended to finish his final mission by taking everyone out at once with the bomb. He knew he wasn't going to survive. And because of what he knew, Castian would have ordered his death just as quickly as the others anyway. As the last few seconds of life left him, all he could hold onto was the hatred in his heart. Denton took one last look at his nemesis and died.

At that moment, an explosion shook the entire building. The roof began to crack, and Denton's body fell through a hole into the flames. Everyone else was knocked down except Darius and Michael. The two had locked eyes like magnets. As the fire spread throughout the floors below, they both knew what came next.

"That's the sign to begin," Dar said smugly. Then he began to shout, "I don't care who you are! There is only room for one of us!" At that moment, an exploding oxygen tank shook the rooftop a second time. Dar lunged toward his counterpart with red fury in his eyes. There was nothing stopping it now. The battle had begun, and each poised for the final conflict.

Chapter 55
THE FINAL CONFLICT

A growl surged through the air as Darius Magnus lunged toward Michael Magnus. Magnus sidestepped, catching Dar off guard. He threw a punch, catching his alter ego in the side of his body. Dar flinched. It was the first time he had ever felt pain. Magnus simultaneously also flinched, feeling pain on his right side. Dar was surprised that Magnus had been fast enough to actually hit him. Magnus was shocked that Dar somehow got a shot in without him noticing. Dar teleported and landed a blow to the right side of Magnus's head. Arie gasped as her love was struck. The others simply watched in amazement, trying hard to follow the movements.

Magnus held his face. The pain was great. Fortunately, the pain was equally as great on Dar's face. He also paused in pain. Neither was aware of the other's pain, and the fighting continued. Magnus ran at Dar and attempted to kick him. Dar teleported behind him and attempted to punch him again. Magnus also teleported, dodging that blow, and actually landed a jumping kick, hitting Dar in the ear. Dar fell to the ground and Magnus was sent flying by the force of his own move. Their moves were fast and powerful. The others could not believe the force behind each blow. They could actually feel the throwback from each punch that landed.

The two gladiators paused for a moment, both breathing heavily. Dar suddenly dashed forward, jumping up and grabbing Magnus by the shoulders. Then he pulled Magnus down and kneed his face repeatedly with both of his knees. Arie winced and cried out at each blow. It looked incredibly painful. The chief was beginning to feel useless. He watched as Magnus's face was pounded over and over. Both Chris and Christian clenched their fists in anger. Joe looked after Sharon, who was turning blue in the face. She needed to be downstairs receiving medical care. Joe walked over to the door on the roof. Smoke was pouring out and the stairs were gone.

He yelled out to the others, "There's no way we can make it down that way. The fire has destroyed the stairs."

The fire was raging intensely, burning its way through the roof. Smoke was pouring out the windows all around the building. The sounds of sirens filled the air. Julius walked over to the edge of the roof and saw three fire trucks pull up and some firemen jump out. Julius yelled, "Hey, we're up here!"

Dar turned sharply toward Julius and moved quickly in his direction. He managed to grab Julius's shirt and throw him to the ground, but Magnus caught up to him and double-fisted him in the back of the head. All three of them hit the ground simultaneously. The ground cracked beneath Dar. He didn't get up as quickly this time. Magnus felt the pain in his head as well.

"What a headache," he said. Something wasn't adding up. Every time he hit Dar, he felt pain, either in the same place or on the opposite side of where his blows made contact. Magnus halted his attack momentarily and observed Dar as he recovered. He was holding his face as if he had been kneed in it as well.

Dar realized that he wasn't making enough progress by attacking Magnus head on. He had taken far more damage than he expected, and he couldn't believe that anyone would be able to keep up with him. It was time to try a nonphysical strategy. While Dar was pondering that, Magnus was beginning to worry about the others. He wasn't making any progress defeating Dar, and the building was becoming more and more unstable. He needed to find a way to take Dar down without damaging himself. The two became locked in a stare down, both waiting for the other to act first.

KM elbowed the chief and said, "Would ya look at that, it's a stalemate. When they were throwing down I couldn't even follow half their movements. It's like we're watching some crazy sci-fi movie front row!" The chief nodded, not taking his eyes off the combatants. Joe returned to Sharon, who had thrown up. She was getting worse. She hadn't eaten in quite some time, because Dar had stopped caring about her condition. Joe thought back to the teacher named Keller who had died right before him. Sharon was heading that way. He needed to do something, anything, to stop it.

Julius took a defensive posture in front of Arie. He figured the least he could do was to help Magnus protect his woman. Christian walked over to the ledge to see what was happening below. He saw people evacuating the hospital. Dr. Blythe stood below in a crowd of people, tending to those who needed care. Blankets were being passed out to those who needed them. Chris Preston thought that if he could read Dar's mind maybe he could help, but Dar's mental power was too strong for him to penetrate.

The battle started up again. Magnus landed an uppercut to Dar's chin, causing Dar to fly upward. Magnus bit his tongue and covered his mouth in pain. Dar lost control and landed badly. This was the last straw. Dar stood up and stared right into Magnus's eyes. Then he invaded his mind. Now it was a battle of willpower.

They met in the astral plane, where the fight became much more intense than the physical. While there are boundaries in the physical realm, there are no limitations to thought. Joe watched as they both sank to their knees. From the outside, it looked like a strange kind of meditation. Chris Preston, however, had a different perception. Through Magnus's mind, he could see what was going on. At first, the intensity was too much for him, but he was soon able to describe to the others what he was seeing.

As Chris started to speak, his words were terrifying. "It's dark, but the redness is coming. The red light is surrounding his body." Then he yelled, "Watch out, Magnus!"

Arie asked, "What's happening?"

Chris' tone was so eerie that it sent chills up Arie's spine. It captured the attention of Joe and the others as well.

The fire continued to burn beneath the roof, and smoke filled the air. Everyone huddled together, waiting to be rescued. Chris continued describing what he could see. "The demon walks and the world shifts with him. No! No!" Chris saw Dar gain the upper hand. The stage they fought on looked like a Roman Coliseum. Dar had constructed it from an image in his mind. Chris could see the arena clearly, and the sky above it was pitch black.

Magnus stood in the center. It was an ethereal form of him, which looked like him with a greenish-blue aura outlining his body. Across from him stood Darius, his aura a strong red hue. They looked like two Roman Gods displaying their powers for the universe to watch. Dar had been slinging objects at Magnus, striking him a few times. Then from the ground arose vines with spines that wrapped around Magnus's body. Bound and unable to move, Magnus squirmed for freedom.

Chris could only watch as his friend was tortured by Dar's mind manipulations. Dar laughed—that is, his physical body laughed. In the Astral Plane, like before, Magnus heard the sinister cackle echo through the vastness. Floating over to Magnus, Dar said, "What now? You may share something in common with me, but I've beaten you." Dar laughed again. "And I know a way to destroy you." Dar floated away from his adversary, and the walls of the arena started to close in around them. He snickered and watched, enjoying every moment.

Chris was describing it all, and when he saw the walls closing in, he screamed, "No!" Chris fell to his knees and the others were frightened.

Without warning, Julius ran at Dar's body and attempted to kick him in the head. As he got close to Dar, he fell backward in pain. Dar had managed to catch his foot and throw him back. Joe helped him up, saying that it was a noble effort, but he needed more manpower. He looked over to Christian and Julius and then to the chief. They all sprang up and prepared themselves.

Joe yelled, "Go!" In that moment, they all ran toward Dar simultaneously. Christian, in front, clenched his fist and struck Dar in the face.

Dar did not even flinch. He opened one eye and turned it toward the younger Warren brother. Christian passed out from Dar's stare. Instantly, his mind was pulled into the astral plane along with Michael Magnus. The remaining three men attempted to free Christian, but each suffered the same fate. As they tried, they fell unconscious and were drawn into the arena. KM was the only male left conscious. He ran to the edge of the roof and called for help. The women huddled together as the roof began to heat up. They could hear it buckling. Chris was no longer talking. He was attempting to help Magnus any way he could. He kept thinking that since he could *see* what was happening, he should be able to interact with them.

While Chris was trying to help his friend, the others were feeling disoriented. Each had been yanked into the hellish nightmare Dar created. Eventually, they could all see Michael Magnus in the center of the arena, still bound by thorny vines. He was struggling in vain for his freedom. The vines had loosened just a little when Christian made contact with Dar's face. Bringing all of them into the arena had distracted Dar briefly, but his mind remained focused. His control of the astral plane was too strong to break.

The others were trapped out of Magnus's reach, each wrapped in vines created by Dar. All they could do was observe the battle, powerless to help. Dar yelled, "Now you all can watch as this fool dies!" The words echoed, and they watched as Dar's metaphysical body changed shape. He no longer looked like Michael Magnus. His form grew larger and contorted. Eventually, Dar no longer looked like a man at all. Dar took the form that Joe had once seen in the mind of the teacher, Ms. Keller: a true demon form. He had red eyes and long fangs, with a furry, slender body. He was muscular and jackal-like. Sheer terror poured into the spectators.

Dar roared a ferocious howl that shook the entire ethereal world. It was obvious what was about to happen. Dar extended his razor-sharp claws. The red glow around his body intensified, and drool leaked from his mouth. He snarled at Magnus, and the hair on his body stood up. He was about to snap at his prey when something caused him to hesitate. A yellow glow began to form on the side of the arena some distance from Magnus. Suddenly, for the first time, Magnus made a sound. He screamed, "No!" The scream was piercing as it shook the arena. The others watched as the glow began to take shape. The yellow light intensified, taking the shape of a body with wings. Finally, Chris Preston's face appeared, and he stood there like a pure celestial being. Magnus screamed again, "No, Chris, don't do this!" He knew exactly what Chris was planning, but there was no time. Dar snarled and charged Chris's ethereal form. The light was the purest he had ever seen. All he could think about was how strong it would make him. He wanted to devour Chris's soul and destroy him. There was nothing Magnus could do. He wasn't strong enough to break Dar's hold.

Chris's spirit glowed brighter and brighter until it was hard for the others to look upon it. Dar charged ahead, headstrong. A tear rolled down Magnus's face as the light grew even more brilliant. He knew what was next. He screamed, "Don't do it! We'll find another way!" However, his pleas were in vain. As Dar reached the center of the light, a massive explosion enveloped the entire arena.

Then there was silence. Magnus lay on the ground, freed from the vines. He felt disoriented and confused. Then he remembered that Chris had sacrificed his own spiritual energy to save everyone else. He had heard his thoughts before he appeared and knew what he was planning. In the real world, Chris's body collapsed. Magnus knew the most important rule about the astral plane—the physical body cannot live without its spiritual essence. He sobbed for the loss of his friend, slamming his fist into the ground. He had never thought their quest to stop Dar would end this way.

Eventually, the others, released from their vines, came up to Magnus. They didn't understand what had happened. Joe asked, "If Dar is defeated, then why are we still here?" Suddenly, the light dimmed, and from the darkness, the red aura reappeared.

There in front of them, still in his demon form, was Dar. "I am not so easily destroyed," he called out. His red eyes and aura glowed even stronger. Then his body sprouted thorns and he grew four times in size.

Magnus knelt, engulfed in his grief. The other four men stood paralyzed with fear. Dar turned his attention to them first and lunged in their direction. In a horrific display, he absorbed them all into his body. His blood red eyes glowed, and he smiled with feverish pleasure. Magnus banged the ground again and Dar laughed mockingly. "Are you supposed to be my better half? You're weak! Pathetic! History!"

Magnus stood up, facing his dark-self. He looked into the eyes of the demon and saw all his anger and fears. Yet he didn't know how to defeat that part of him. Dar's will was too strong to conquer.

Dar paused and sneered at his supposed positive side. He didn't really want to believe what Denton had said. He thought to himself, *Even if we were at one point the same being, I don't need that part. I'm strong enough on my own to conquer whatever he desired.* Dar was angry; he didn't want to be some *part of* someone else. He was so angry that he got caught in a cycle of self-pity. He yelled, I'm the one they fear! I'm the strongest! You're nothing without me!"

While Dar was distracted, Magnus realized that this was his last chance. Magnus closed his eyes and tried to summon all the strength he had. Dar watched him and laughed, yelling, "You will never defeat me!" Magnus kept pulling all the spiritual energy he had, and as he did, he unexpectedly felt warmth around him. He opened his eyes and a golden yellow glow surrounded him. It was the same pure light that comes from within all good people.

It was in that moment that everything became clear. Michael Magnus gained a new understanding and finally knew how to defeat Dar. The spirit of Chris Preston, having been completely separated from own his body, had been combined with Magnus's spiritual energy. With this new power and knowledge, he had full control of his abilities. Dar sensed the change and immediately charged at him. Magnus had turned golden, with the same wings that Chris had had before. Dar shrieked as he approached the evolved form of his counterpart.

With a thought, Magnus repelled him like magnets with the same polarity. Dar was projected away with extreme force, and he hit the ground stunned. In shock, he stood up and quickly launched another assault. Dar came at Magnus with everything he had. He unleashed a slew of punches, kicks, slashes, fireballs, and energy waves. They were all absorbed with no effect. For the first time ever, Dar was afraid. He was now the one powerless against a stronger foe.

Finally, in an awe-inspiring move, Michael Magnus floated up to Dar and locked eyes with him. In that instant, Darius Magnus returned to human form and shrank back to normal size. Michael stretched out his arm and pointed his finger to a spot on Dar's head between his eyebrows, and right in front of Michael's finger appeared Dar's third eye. When Michael pressed the eye, Dar screeched an ear-piercing wail. His body started to distort, and slowly he was absorbed into Michael's spirit. The mighty demon was falling. At first he yelled and screamed that he was a God and could never be defeated, but eventually his arrogant superiority faded and he began to beg for his freedom. Michael was stolid and didn't utter a word. He simply dealt Dar a blow to the abdomen that silenced him. Miraculously, the final conflict was over. Once Dar's essence was completely absorbed, Michael Magnus awoke in the physical world.

Chapter 56

CLEANING UP DAR'S MESS

The fire department had flooded the building with enough water to extinguish the fire. The scene was still as the embers floated away. The smell of ash and smoke filled the air. Arie, Sharon, and KM had been watching over everyone in the physical world as things played out in the astral plane, Sharon sobbing over Joe. Then they all witnessed the kneeling body of Dar fall sideways to the ground.

None of them moved, still frightened that Dar might rise again. None of their comrades and loved ones were moving. Arie had just about worked up the courage to go check on Michael when paramedics and policemen rushed onto the rooftop. They immediately got a stretcher for Sharon, and a policemen started to question them. Sharon was traumatized. She couldn't speak about what had happened to her over the last week. Arie was concerned for the others. The paramedics checked everyone at the scene and determined that everyone was still breathing. Everyone that is, except for Christopher Preston and Darius Magnus.

The creature who had held Chicago in terror for weeks was stiff. After the paramedics declared Dar dead, Arie ran over to Michael Magnus and placed her hand on his face. As she rubbed her thumb between his eyebrows, a tear rolled down her check and fell on his nose. The tear woke him up. When their eyes met, Michael smiled.

He spoke two words. "I remember."

She looked puzzled and asked him, "What do you remember?"

He responded, "Everything—I remember all the details of every moment of every life I've ever led."

Arie had a puzzled expression, but Michael Magnus had gained an insight that few could understand. He looked around; his perception of everything had changed. Arie hugged him. She didn't care what he meant; she just was happy that he was alive.

A few feet away, Sharon didn't share Arie's enthusiasm. She was refusing to get on a stretcher until she knew if Joe was all right. He was still not moving. The police were about to arrest Michael when she yelled, "Hold it! You can't take him yet!" Victim or not, she was going to have her say. She turned to Michael and said, "What's wrong with them? None of them are moving." When she looked into his eyes, they were glazed and full of strength. He spoke not a word. He moved over to Joe so quickly that none of them could follow his movement. Michael touched Joe's forehead between his eyebrows and proceeded to do the same for the others.

He looked at Sharon, and before her eyes, Joe awoke. He was groggy but happy to be greeted by a teary-eyed Sharon. She hugged him tightly. One by one, each of the men regained consciousness. Somewhere in the background, KM let out a Texas yell. "Woo-ee! They're all OK." He looked over to Michael Magnus and said, "Son you did good." Michael did not respond; he just half smiled. Christian shook his brother's hand and gave him a hug. Seconds later, the chief patted Julius on the back and shook KM's hand. There was a feeling of great joy and relief...until Michael approached the body of Chris Preston.

Everyone watched as he kneeled down next to the lifeless body. He spoke quietly. "I remember—" Michael paused briefly before placing his hands together as if in prayer and then raising them above Chris's body. The others watched, waiting for something to happen, but just then Arie saw something the others could not. There was a golden glow coming from Michael's hands. She was awestruck; she didn't say a word, just watched and smiled. After a minute, he whispered something in Chris's ear that the others couldn't hear. Then in a movement faster than any of them could follow, he was next to Arie. He smiled at her and took her hand. She smiled back noticing the now balanced yin-yang tattoo on his arm that seemed to shimmer. Then Michael Magnus stood tall and looked fondly at Joe, Sharon, Christian, KM, and Julius. Julius knew what was next. In the blink of an eye they were gone. Julius couldn't help but let out a little laugh. He knew deep down that he would never see that innocent man again.

In fact, it was a thought they all shared. In that moment, they all paused with an understanding that Michael J. Magnus had evolved into something much more than even he thought he could be…a true Emancer. Now he was a being with the ability to go beyond the normal limitations of men. It's hard for anyone to face his or her inner darkness, but for Michael, there was no choice but to look his dark side straight in the face. Dar was the embodiment of all the darkness that lurked quietly in his heart. Facing that fact gave Michael a greater insight into himself. He would never be the same again. It was a rebirth.

The chief placed his hand on Joe's shoulder and said, "I think it's time to go." Joe looked back at the chief and nodded. Together they all left.

Chapter 57
TO THE UNKNOWN FUTURE

A few days later, things returned to normal. Sharon was released with a clean bill of health, and Joe returned to the force without incident. Michael Magnus was cleared of all charges, thanks to the help of KM Lockhart. Judge Schmitz threw the case out based on the character testimonials from Julius Spencer, Sharon Baker, Joseph Warren, and a few others. The bombing and all the murders were attributed to Denton McKay and Darius Magnus. Dar, in fact, would go down in history as one of the most notorious murderers in modern times.

William G. Haight mysteriously vanished. KM testified on the record about Haight's involvement with FENCE. A few months later, his body turned up. The police figured that like others involved with FENCE, he had simply been eliminated. Judge Schmitz's involvement in the whole ordeal remained unknown. KM eventually returned to his home in Texas. When Madeline saw on the news that he had almost died, she decided to take him back and give him one more chance, and from that point on KM was a good man to her. Neither his heart nor his body ever strayed again.

After dealing with such a crazy adventure, Julius Spencer started to take interest in paranormal cases. Eventually, this led him to leave the DEDC. He became an FBI agent and in time found himself in charge of a paranormal division. A year after Julius left, Thomas Rutger also left the DEDC. He became a writer and wrote a book called *The Dark Days*. In it, he mentioned an encounter with a possessed man who took on the traits of a demon. Daniel Frost remained a security guard and led an uneventful life.

Peter Cahill remained warden for many years. He never saw the likes of Michael Magnus again, but he did hear rumors about sightings of him. In fact, rumors about the Emancerian Project and the Chicago Bombing circulated for months. The media had no solid information on any of the occurrences but had picked up tidbits here and there. A few of the hospital staff who were there may have told stories about it to their friends and family, which eventually resulted in non-provable information being leaked to the press.

About a year after the incident, Joe and Sharon got married. Chief Frank attended the wedding and gave his blessing. As a gift, he decided to expunge Joe's file of any disciplinary action. It seemed he had actually grown a soft spot for them. Anyway, he decided that he had given Joe enough grief during the whole ordeal. Also, the chief figured, he could use it to keep Joe in line. The wedding was a great celebration. Christian Warren was the best man. They had 150 guests who danced the night away. Sharon made a beautiful bride. Both of their families were happy to finally see them together.

During the wedding, Joe was very nervous. He was sweating bullets at the altar, but once he saw Sharon walk down that aisle, all his worries disappeared. They pledged their eternal love for each other. At the reception, Joe told Sharon that while he was waiting at the altar he thought he saw two familiar faces in the background for just an instant. However, no one else could recall seeing Michael Magnus or Arianna Shoomer at the wedding. Joe said to Sharon with a smile, "Well, if they were here, it was nice to have their blessing."

After the wedding, Joe decided to take a leave from the force for a year before returning to his detective work. Sharon left the police force altogether and decided to concentrate on becoming a mother. She got pregnant not long after the honeymoon. It was a joyous time. Christian was very happy for them. The whole experience had helped him grow. After the wedding, he decided he would continue his career in the army for another four years. He soon shipped back out to Iraq and received a commendation. Later on, he would be promoted to a full officer with the title of Lieutenant. Christian knew that his life would take him in many different directions, but somehow he felt that he would meet up with them all again someday, especially Chris Preston. It was strange, but he just felt certain that the story wasn't done.

Christian didn't know how right he was, for on the day of the fire, Christopher Preston awoke on that rooftop, happy but confused. He had no one to thank for his life. Michael had been his only friend, but thanks to him, he now had some new ones. Preston returned home to his family and started his life over. He went back to school but made sure to attend Joe and Sharon's wedding.

He never told the others what Michael had whispered in his ear that day on the rooftop. In fact, he pretended he hadn't heard anything. However, Michael Magnus's words echoed in his mind for years.

They were clear and direct: "You too have touched the next plateau of evolution. Like me, you will struggle to understand it, but be prepared to embark on your own journey to find your true self. When you're ready, brother...come find me. Until then, walk tall, run strong, and fly proud!"

The End?

ABOUT THE AUTHOR

Myael Christopher Simpkins discovered his creative side at a very young age. In the elementary years, he was quickly known for being extremely gifted in the art of storytelling. He excelled scholastically, but unknown to him his passion for creative writing assignments would one day furnish a skilled author. As he proceeded his way through high-school and college, literature teachers took note of his creative prowess. However, it wasn't until he was published in a few collaborative poetry books (Gardens of Youth in 2003 & Colours of the Heart in 2004) that he himself recognized that his talent had become a passion. Signs of the First Emancer, the first book of the three part Emancerian Chronicles, is the culmination of twenty years of personal expression. It is his hope that through this fiction novel the readers get a sense of his style, his presence, and most of all his passion for the creativity.

ACKNOWLEDGEMENTS

Special thanks to Nancy Simpkins and Gladys Johnson whose love and support watch over me and everything creative that I do. Additional gratitude goes to Nancy and Wayne Johnson. Without their feedback and financial support this project would not have been possible. To Trina Blythe and Elisha Johnson who played heavy roles in the storyline continuity their time and patience greatly contributed to this project's completion. Finally, an overall thanks to all readers and editors that helped to move this novel forward and to future readers and supporters whose enthusiasm helped me to finish this ten-year long process.

Made in the USA
Middletown, DE
31 March 2015